Shifter
and the Crimson Eclipse

By Robby Schlesinger

Long Creek Music & Publishing, LLC
175 Virgil Drive
Spanish Springs, Nv. 89441
www.LongCreekPeak.com

© Copyright 2008 Long Creek Music & Publishing, LLC.
All rights reserved.

No part of this book may be reproduced, stored in a retrieval system, or transmitted by any means without the written permission of the author.

First published by Long Creek Music & Publishing, LLC on 1/24/2008.

ISBN: 978-0-6151-9182-9 (sc)

Printed in the United States of America.

This book is printed on acid-free paper.

Author's Note

Writing the book was the easy part. After all, it was all in my head. The characters aren't asking for royalties…yet anyway. We'll see how things go.

There was a lot more going into this than creative thought alone. Because of that, thanks are in order.

First and foremost: my family. My dad, for his business saavy and ingenuity, and most importantly his conviction; my mom for her undying support and her persistent thumbs up signals; and my sister for inspiring conversation.

I'd like to thank Virginia Castleman for everything she taught me and everything she did for the story. I still have a lot to learn from her.

I am also thankful for the legal counsel of Patrick M. Mooney Esq. and the tax and accounting services of Chris Cochran; without their help, this book would still be a manuscript.

I always loved reading, but English itself wasn't fun until Erin Mahr, so a definite big thanks to her.

There are a lot of friends who've somehow made their way into this book as characters. These people I would also like to thank. So Charlie Glynn, Sidney Selert, Kaitlyn Schwartz-Reeves, Tim Ulibarri, Tyler Swader, the Anthonys (Pitt and Crew), and Annalynn Wileman, thanks for having my back fictionally and in the real world.

People have been writing words down for a very long time, and some of those people really did inspire me. I'd like to thank Oscar Wilde, F. Scott Fitzgerald, Jack Kerouac, Jonathan Stroud, and Douglas Adams, all of whom gave me ideas about and insights into the world.

I tried to put a message or two in here, and I think that was partly due to the fact that I listened to Rise Against a lot while writing. For their wise words and powerful music, I thank them.

For you, this might be a beginning. For me, this is *the* beginning. All stories have them. Let's read on and find out what happens next.

—Robby Schlesinger

P.S. Daniel Gugich is my biggest fan.

Chapter 1

The Eclipse—892 AD

silver mist, carrying a rank scent like rain on shale, rose from he ground, swirling into strange shapes. Beads of dew resting on the leaves of bushes and trees quickly turned to ice as the temperature dropped. A cold breeze parted the fog for a moment to reveal the hard, fallow earth while high above, stars seemed distant, cold, and unaware of the frost. The cloudless sky offered a clear view of the full moon, which painted the heath with pale light.

Slowly, out of the trees, a host of shadowy figures appeared, their breath clearly seen in the cold, night air. Like oil parting from water, they filtered out from the forest. Moonlight glinted off their armor and helmets.

The never-ending stream of bodies thudded loudly through the darkness; their clanking armor sounded like rain pounding on stones. They were not interested in a quiet approach or uniformity; their armor and tunics varied as much as the soldiers themselves. Some were tall and elegant, with pointed ears and golden hair tucked underneath their helms. Others were broad and toned. Some were short and grizzly, with long beards and sloping features. But as different as they all were, their eyes were all the same.

Wide.

Alert.

Anxious.

Finally, as the last figure left the sanctuary of the trees behind, they set off toward the mountain range on the other side of the immense heath. Exposed now, they crept more slowly, making no more noise than weasels in the dark, when suddenly, the silence of the night was shattered.

"AHHHHHH!" Bowen Montressor gripped his chest.

"You *idiot*!" seethed the captain, whipping around to face him with eyes full of rage. "What was that for? You probably just gave away our position to any minion of the Red Sovereign for two miles round!"

Bowen gave no response. He only pointed a trembling finger into the sky. The captain turned and gasped.

The moon was no longer silver.

The moon was no longer full.

Half of the moon had disappeared as though erased from time and space. The other half looked as if it had been painted with blood, and glowed with a livid scarlet that cast its eerie light all around.

The captain's face grew grim. This could mean only one thing: Ozmodion had launched the attack. He tightened his helmet, unsheathed his sword.

"Charge!" he bellowed.

The command reached the ears of every creature of every army of the Resistance. The air cracked like ice as the leaders of the other armies repeated the order. Amid the thundering masses, a drum and a flute took up a tune, signaling the battle to begin.

The enormous company ran hard with their weapons waving. A swarm of dragons, spewing flame, soared above through the inky veil of night. Elves pulled bows from their backs, placing three arrows each against the frames. Dwarves unfastened war axes and spears from their belts, sounding more war cries into the abyss. Mortal men unsheathed their swords as they prayed to the gods under their breaths.

The forest of Ÿalnz Dàr shrank away behind them, but before them, rising into the sky like a crooked, rocky backbone of the earth, were the Mountains of Midnight, the barrier of Saurindon. They, the Resistance, had been plodding their way to these dark gates for nearly three months. Now they locked on the craggy peaks of the black mountains with a mixture of awe and fear.

Far off, the slopes of the mountains suddenly exploded with light and movement. Thousands of torches cascaded at an alarming rate down the Midnights. As the two armies closed in on one another, the creatures came into focus.

They had grey skin and towered a foot taller than the tallest man in the Resistance. Their heads were as big as chariot wheels, with mouths so wide they could easily swallow a young goat whole. Two gnarled horns stuck out on both sides of their heads above their pointed, furry ears. Mats of tangled, messy black hair grew in all kinds of impossible places. They ran toward the Resistance with bent swords held aloft and round, dented, rune and symbol-bearing shields at their sides, their green eyes glistening in the dark.

"Goblins!"

The troops hesitated. As their pace slowed, the captain shouted over his shoulder, "Harden your hearts, boys! We have much Ozra blood to spill this night. Let us let Saurindon know we have come!"

Cheers erupted behind him, but were soon drowned out by the low growls and guttural roars of the goblins that were now a mere hundred yards away. Already, their thick putrid stench—a mix of blood and death—hung on the air.

The Resistance slashed at the beasts as they came in striking distance. The initial surge of monsters slew some of the soldiers—Bowen Montressor was among them—only to die by the swords of the Resistance. Relentless, the goblins continued their charge.

"Attack!" the captain ordered sharply, "Show them no mercy! Cleave their heads! Hollow their chests! Slash their limbs! *Attack!*"

A goblin then plunged his sword deep into the captain's breast. One quick intake of breath, a slow look up to his attacker, and the captain went limp. The goblin roared and pulled his sword out of the fresh corpse.

Moments later a second brigade of Ozmodion's forces raced toward the Resistance. They were not goblins but trolls. They ran, brandishing long, broad, sharp swords; their stench trailed them. They bore black armor with red, half-circles painted on the breastplate. The insignias matched the red, half-moon that towered above them.

With supreme accuracy, the Resistance's archers fired a swarm of arrows at the trolls from trees and foothills. As the first of the trolls fell, dragons descended and took hold of the monstrous creatures by their shoulders, blasting flames in their face. Goblin archers fired arrows into the sky, and many of the dragons had black arrows protruding from their legs and underside, but they continued their attack.

Elves wielded their staffs, weaving spells and curses. The night lit up with the bright colors of their magic. Wind swept through the combatants as the elves called on the powers of the earth.

Dwarves swung axes and short swords. Their height gave them great advantage over the taller goblins and trolls, stabbing their legs with cruel, cold steel.

Throughout the battle, warriors of both sides vanquished and fell. The cries of the dying and the triumphant mingled in chaotic harmony. Blood from both sides drenched and stained the rocks and trees of the valley.

And what cause had they to make such epic battle? Who was responsible for this stream of horrendous carnage?

One mile away, on the first foothill of the Mountains of Midnight, was a golden red throne. It rose from the rock like a masthead on a ship. On the throne sat Ozmodion, who wore a scarlet, hooded cloak. He always wore his hood up, leaving his face shrouded and dark.

Known to most of the world by reputation alone, Ozmodion was a sorcerer, a powerful one. The few that had ever met him rarely lived past the encounter. His story was a mystery masked in shadow and myth.

Ozmodion stared down on the ensuing battle. He wrestled with his memory, attempting to recall the curse that would shake the very core of the earth in hopes that his armies would gain a slight advantage. *Damn the elves and their magic.* His armies were made of nothing but brute strength. And the dragons! How ironic that they served the Resistance. Ozmodion had assumed, as creatures of power, that they would join the stronger side—his. But he had been wrong; even the griffins had not accepted his placations.

A twig snapped. Ozmodion whipped his head toward the sound, tensing like a snake ready to strike. A large battalion of men who had sneaked around his dark troops now surrounded him. Two troll guards on either side of Ozmodion's throne made ready to unsheathe their swords, when Ozmodion raised his hand.

"No," he whispered, "I shall deal with them. No doubt they should prove amusing." His voice, deep and dark, sounded from everywhere and nowhere.

One of the soldiers stepped forward and raised his sword.

"Surrender Ozmodion" he commanded, "or prepare to die!"

Silence fell like shooting stars. Ozmodion laughed. The dark, sonorous sound echoed against the rocks and trees of the foothills. The man who had stepped forward lost his confidence, and he lowered his sword to eye level. Unease played blatantly across his pale face.

"And who is to bring about my death?" Ozmodion yelled down to the soldier, "Not you, I hope, or the Resistance is infinitely more foolish than I ever thought possible! You sorry, worthless piece of flesh! Allow me to teach you a lesson you shall not soon forget!"

He lifted his right hand, a grey and decayed thing with many scars, and waved it in the direction of the soldier, roaring a string of words in a strange tongue.

No sooner had the spell left his unseen lips than a dazzling ray of red light emitted from the warlock's hand. It rocketed through the night and collided with the lone soldier.

A blood-chilling scream followed as the soldier dropped his sword and clutched at his sides. Deafening cracks filled the air, as every bone in the man's body broke. The soldier shrieked and writhed in agony. And as quickly as he fell, the screams died, along with the man.

Ozmodion chuckled as he looked at the body, and then at the stunned soldiers.

"Who dares to challenge me next? Fools! Do you think yourselves the Guard of Aelïne? For even they were as nothing to me! I smote them upon the Black Fallows! And where are the Legions of the Yuln Clan? I do not see them present in this onslaught! Could it be that even the mighty Lord Daio quakes before me? Does he fear to share his father's fate? And yet you, lowly foot soldiers, mortal *men*, dare to raise your swords to me? I ask once more: who challenges me?"

The sorcerer's voice rose with passion and intensity, and he had even risen from his seat. Still, calm emanated from him. It was this calm which shook the soldiers the most. They were greatly disturbed at the thought of the fallen Guard of Aelïne, and they were painfully aware that the Yuln Clan had not come. But it was the sorcerer's ease shown even after such a fervent tirade that troubled the soldiers most, and there was a long pause before anyone made a move.

A boy, no older than fourteen years of age, stepped past the body of the broken soldier, whose eyes, cold and blank, stared blindly into the depths of the night. The boy did not make any grand gesture, nor did he seem the least bit formidable. The rest of the soldiers stared at him, bracing for another brutal murder.

"I challenge you," the boy yelled, his voice high and young. "Your tyranny has reached its end, and you will soon—"

"Yes, yes," interrupted Ozmodion in a tired manner, retaking his seat on his great throne. "There is little doubt you will astound me with your prowess and skill, and so on, and so forth, etcetera, etcetera. I trust you will be shocked to hear that I have heard that speech hundreds of times by men much larger, braver, wiser, and stronger than yourself. You might not even be a bit surprised to discover that I disposed of those would-be usurpers as though they were insects. Now, if you would be so kind as to save your heroic lines while I rid you and your pathetic comrades of this world."

He stood up from his throne and raised his finger, already savoring the soldiers' deaths.

At the same time, the boy who stepped forward unsheathed a sword. The blade glowed with a light blue, magical aura. Such swords were rare even then. How the boy had come across the sword was an entrancing mystery. Even the master who had forged it in days when such swords were a little more common could not tell.

The boy lunged at the Red Sovereign, sword aloft.

Ozmodion barked a syllable and sent another curse hurtling down at the soldiers. The red light returned, lividly illuminating the pale and frightened faces of the men. Then, the boy jumped in the air and swung at the spell with his sword.

Time slowed to a crawl as the spell was absorbed by the sword. The blue light of the blade merged with the red light of the curse in a brilliant conflagration of violet. Afterward, the spell shot out of the sword and hit the boy and soldiers, painting the scene with the same horrible red light that the dead soldier had seen before he died. Ozmodion laughed again, confident he had just ensured his victory.

But his laughter suddenly caught in his throat when he realized what the sword was, for he knew the sword and loathed it and hated more the one who wielded it. It had been almost two decades since he had seen it. Now, as he gazed at it once more, he again felt the long forgotten icy horror fill his innards.

He looked at the soldiers to see that his fears were affirmed. A soldier's sword sprouted metal branches. It was obvious he was not a mage or spell caster of any kind, for the soldier had thrown the possessed sword to the ground and screamed. Other oddities began to occur among the brigade. One soldier grew a third arm. Another sprouted wings. Armor absorbed into one of the soldier's skin, giving his face a metallic black look.

While Ozmodion watched this, the boy swiftly murdered the two guard trolls and jumped toward the Red Sovereign. Ozmodion barely had time to unsheathe his red sword and parry the attack, sending a shower of livid orange sparks into the air. The boy took another swing at the dark sorcerer and another, and yet another. Ozmodion growled at the boy's efforts, doubling his own forcefully.

"Damned be the one who dares to trifle with me," the Red Sovereign seethed, "You are lucky that I have not run you through."

The boy smirked. "As are you." He horizontally slashed at the sorcerer's side. Ozmodion deflected it easily.

"Fool," Ozmodion hissed. He swung his sword in an arc and prepared to bring it down on the boy's head, "I am Ozmodion, Iltari, the Demon Tamer, Advocate of Avria, King of Shadows, and the Shepherd of Forsaken Souls." He brought down his sword; the boy jumped to the right and skirted it.

"Lovely titles," the boy replied.

As their fight progressed, the boy talked to Ozmodion as though they were discussing matters calmly over dinner, his demeanor calm and casual.

"I see your jeers have ceased," he said coolly, "Perhaps you would have preferred my, oh what did you call it? My heroic lines?"

Ozmodion thrust his sword at the boy and said, "Silence!"

The boy sidestepped Ozmodion's blade. "Apparently the appearance of my sword has disabled your witty remarks."

Ozmodion growled as he parried another attack. "You would be a novice without it. And how does an urchin like yourself come across a sword like that?"

The boy smiled. "I am afraid we do not have time to exchange stories. I have come for one reason and one reason only: to kill you and return the lost concept of freedom to the world."

"Freedom?" Ozmodion laughed maliciously, slashed the boy's sword one last time, and brought the tip of his red blade to rest on his collarbone. The boy's smile disappeared as his muscles tightened. He dropped the sword.

"Some words of wisdom, worm," Ozmodion said, gripping his red sword's hilt, "Freedom has been, is, and always will be…a fantasy."

One of the human soldiers sent an arrow whizzing toward Ozmodion. It sank deep into his shoulder. Ozmodion roared with pain and lowered his blade. Reaching for his own sword, the boy swiftly slashed at Ozmodion's chest. The sorcerer cried out inaudible words, for the soldier's cheers for the boy drowned it out.

The last thing Ozmodion saw and heard was the shimmering of the blade and the swish of movement as the sword penetrated his skin under the cloak.

Chapter 2: The Mortals

Present Day

G**wen's eyes snapped open** as she rose from her bed, sweating and panting. She rarely ever had nightmares, but this one had been so vivid and real that she fought to wake.

Why had she such a far-fetched dream of elves, dwarves, and blood tinged magic, she wondered? Yet this dream had not been like others. It felt real. It *was* real. But how? How could that be?

As she woke, her mind grew clearer of the reassuring reality all around her. *Don't be silly*, she silently scolded. *I'm home, not in some medieval forest.* The dream, she determined, was nothing more than childish fantasy. She rubbed her eyes and pushed the images from her mind.

Her alarm clock suddenly blared to life. She jolted from her bed with excitement. A summer of waiting, and now the long anticipated day had come. Today, she would attend her first day at Greystone High as a freshman. Finally, the humdrum, cumbersome days of middle school were gone, and in their stead a new and exciting adventure awaited. Her three best friends were attending the school as well, and she looked forward to catching up with them. Maybe she'd even tell them about the bizarre dream.

Or maybe not.

She briskly walked out of her room, down the hall, and into the bathroom she shared with her brother. She grumbled at the disarray the little cretin had left it in after his last visit. Angrily, she showered, brushed her teeth, and combed her hair, all quicker than her usual habit.

After she was cleaned and dressed, she went downstairs to have her breakfast, still groggy with drowsiness; sleep had not come easily. Sunlight, muted by the thin clouds of the new morning, streamed through the windows of her house onto the chairs and sofas that were spread about her spacious living room, casting lengthy shadows across the carpet. She made her way to the kitchen, the heels of her shoes clopping on the white linoleum.

"Good morning, Sunshine!" Her parents rose from their seats at the table and greeted her with hugs. Her nine-year-old brother, Taran, however, greeted her with a long raspberry. She, in turn, made a face, and took her seat, finding that a steaming bowl of oatmeal was already awaiting her.

Her father returned to his seat at the head of the table. He ran a hand through his withered hair and sighed loudly, as though he had just been relieved of a great burden. A sharp glance at Taran, who was contorting his face in an attempt to make Gwen wretch, succeeding in only making her roll her eyes, and then he spoke while unfolding the business section of the newspaper.

"All right, settle down you two," he said in his constantly calm voice. He looked older than his forty-six years, but fifteen years of providing for a family had made him age quicker than usual. He was the president of Branders, a chain of department stores, and the stress from his position had been incorporated into his features in the shape of wrinkles. His hair was grey and receding. His eyes were colorless pools that often stared into infinity, and his face was gaunt, and pocked; it always had a worn, tired look. His skin on his hands and arms held a little too tightly to his bones, giving him a skeletal appearance.

Her mother, on the other hand, was quite the opposite. She was a plump woman of forty-nine, and always demanded the house to be perfectly tidy. One stray sock was enough to set her off. She was usually pleasant even if she was wound pretty tightly, and she always made time for her family.

Gwen's father smoothed his hair again, yielding no noticeable result, and then arched his fingers upwards. Then came a long string of phrases like, "The first day of school, oh we're so proud" and "you're growing up so fast."

Gwen hardly listened, choosing instead to imagine the day ahead. Toward the end of her father's monologue, she nodded and smiled. Her father then winked and turned back to the *Sacramento Bee*.

After she had finished her breakfast, her mother announced it was time to leave. Gwen hugged her father, punched her brother in the shoulder, and followed her mother to the car.

Twenty minutes later, after picking up the carpoolers, the car was abuzz with the chatter of excited freshmen.

Lea Pearson was Gwen's best friend. They had known each other since kindergarten when Gwen shared her peanut butter sandwich with Lea. She had radiant blue eyes and dark blond hair that attractively framed her incurable smirk.

Anthony Davis sat beside Lea, and on his other side sat Michael Force, local weatherman Gale Force's son. He was explaining to Anthony about how he planned to go to college and major in corporate marketing.

"That's where the money'll be in a few years, Anthony. You have to admit that." Michael's pompous, know-it-all behavior always annoyed Gwen. She had never liked him, and doubted she ever would.

"Yeah, sure Mike. Whatever." Anthony obviously wasn't buying into the theory. Anthony was just as intelligent as Michael, but he was much more quixotic; his humor shone through in everything he said and did.

Meanwhile, Gwen chanced seeming nuts, and shared her dream with Lea.

"There were these elves and dwarves," she said, eyes widening at the memory. "And goblins! And this dark wizard-like guy in red." Her voice rose and fell with excitement as she recounted the tale. "It was so *real!*"

Lea scoffed. "You do know that could never happen, right? I mean, c'mon, we're talking about a dream Gwen. Lay off the C.S. Lewis for a while, and I'm sure it'll pass."

"Oh sure," said Gwen, taken aback that her best friend wasn't as interested in her dream as she was. As Lea turned to jibe Michael with some cruel and perfectly applicable slight, Gwen looked to the window, sullen.

Outside, a hawk soared above them, and then perched on the branch of pine on the side of the road. As the car came to stop at an intersection, Gwen frowned, staring intently at the bird. Where had she seen it before? It's not like it was the only hawk around. Still it was looking at her. She felt sure of it. As the car took off again, the hawk pumped its powerful wings and took flight. Gwen's eye widened as the hawk soared right next to her window. For a brief moment, the hawk's eyes locked with hers. Gwen gasped as the hawk smiled and winked at her. Before she could rub her eyes and take a second look, the hawk took off and flew over a hill and out of sight.

"D-did any of you just see that?" Gwen stuttered, silencing the crew.

"See what?"

"The hawk."

All heads shook. "If you've seen one hawk, you've seen them all," Michael scoffed dismissively.

"I saw it," her mom chimed as she pulled into the school parking lot. "I thought it was going to come right into the car, the way it followed us."

But Gwen wasn't listening. She had seen the hawk before. She was sure of it. She slammed the door, waving absently to her mom, while everyone else mumbled their thanks for the ride.

☐

Greystone High School sat plunk in downtown Sacramento, California. It had been built many years ago, and the gray bricks from which it was made gave a dreary feeling to the place. The ancient structure seemed all the older as vine twined around the building's pillars and down its walls. It seemed oddly out of place, surrounded by the bustling metropolis of Sacramento, as though it had been plucked from another time and set down in another, left in stark contrast.

Upon entering, she was surprised to find how many students attended the old school. It was packed shoulder to shoulder with people talking and laughing loudly. There was a musty smell in the air, leftover from the school's empty summer. With a smile, Anthony set off into the throng; Michael parted from them without a word or even a glance.

When Gwen had first received their schedules a few weeks before, she and Lea were giddy to discover that they both all the same classes. First period was health with J. Garies, room twelve. They bumped and pushed their way to the classroom, taking in the small school and its myriad of students that flocked up and down the halls.

As the first bell rang, they arrived to find a small classroom covered in anti-drug posters and diagrams of organs, muscles, and bones. Its lone window was small, and the blinds were drawn, blocking any sun. Instead, the fluorescent lights above them filled the classroom with unnatural light, making it feel cold and unwelcoming. There were many desks, though most of them were bereft of occupants.

They took seats next to their good friends, Caitlyn Montressor and Kendal Bennet, who had taken desks toward the front of the classroom, where a large, white grease board had been fixed to the wall. Also in the room were a small group of boys in the far corner, Anthony among them, talking animatedly. Three other girls sat together in the middle, though none of them were talking to each other; apparently they did not know one another. Slowly the room filled, and at nine 'o' clock, the second bell rang and all went quiet as the teacher came in.

J. Garies turned out to be a young woman in her early thirties. She wore a black skirt with a pink blouse, and had tied her mouse brown hair up in the back, revealing her slightly too large ears.

"Hello class, and welcome to introductory health. You're very lucky to be having this class so early."

Someone in the back muttered something lowly, and several of those close to him laughed. J. Garies ignored them.

"Let's get to know each other," she continued. "My name is Jone Garies and I like Chinese food. How about you?" she asked the boys in the front of the class.

"I'm Tyler White, and I like basketball," said one of the short ones. Ms. Garies smiled and pointed to another. "Colin Myers," said he, "and I like swimming."

Ms. Garies continued through the class, until there was only one left; a boy with wavy brown hair, who Gwen hadn't noticed sitting in the back of the classroom.

"I am Eion Shifter," he said when Ms. Garies pointed at him.

Ms. Garies frowned when he said nothing else. "And what is something you like to do?"

Eion raised an eyebrow. He was quiet for a while longer, then he said, "Well, I do like to fly, I suppose." The class snickered.

Ms. Garies' frown deepened, "You mean flying in an airplane?"

The boy laughed. "Only mortals have need of such ridiculous technology. Really, how you people get along with your combustion engines and your lithium batteries is beyond—"

"Yes, well, let's save all that for English, Mr. Shifter," Ms. Garies interrupted. "This class deals with science. Not science *fiction*."

Eion opened his mouth, and then closed it. He nodded and smiled wryly, as though he knew something everyone else did not.

Gwen quickly looked the other way when his eyes turned to meet hers. She hadn't met him before, but his voice was familiar; confident, strong, but soothing at the same time.

☐

The next class was history. All the same people from health were in this class as well. Gwen caught up with Lea. Both girls were disappointed to find that their teacher, Mr. Stevens, had already made a seating chart. Gwen was even more disappointed to find that she had been assigned to the sit next to the strange Eion boy. She tried to make herself as small as possible at her desk, mentally hoping that he would not try to talk to her. She stole glances at his birdlike features, noting the muscles in his arms. With a body like his, it was a wonder he couldn't fly…

Mr. Stevens passed out a syllabus and began a speech about the class expectations, his monotonous voice lulling many to a dozy state; Tyler White, a tall, dark haired boy, actually fell asleep. Drool seeped from his mouth and spotted his spiral notebook.

"…One of the things I want you to learn this year is to separate history from myth. Ridiculous things like Atlantis will be unmasked as legends and you will—"

"Excuse me," Eion interrupted, waving a finger in the air to match the teacher's gesture, "but the story of Atlantis is no legend. It actually happened." The class turned to look on him with mild amusement. Already they were bored with Mr. Steven's lecture, and they were more than ready for an interruption. Tyler's eyes flitted open, and he raised his head, a curious smile played across his lips.

Annoyed, Mr. Stevens turned his attention to Eion. "Oh, really? I suppose then that you think it's possible for waves to sink an entire island?"

Eion scoffed. "Waves didn't sink it. A group of conjurers were trying to lower the sea level so the islanders could travel to the mainland on foot. They tried to make a land bridge, see. Unfortunately, one of them mispronounced a syllable, so the island sank instead of the water. This in turn led to the creation of Diab's Words of Commandment, a simpler way to control spirits and—"

"Enough," said Mr. Stevens. "If you seek to waste my time, Mr. Shifter, I will waste yours."

The boy snorted with laughter mirthlessly. "Waste *your* time? Forgive me if I try to help you differentiate between fact and fiction. This is *history*, isn't it?"

Mr. Stevens' eyes narrowed, his lip curling dangerously. "I'll speak with you after class, and we'll discuss just that."

"It will be my pleasure, I'm certain," replied Eion with blatant indifference.

The class snickered, whispering insults under their breaths. Eion disregarded them, and remained expressionless.

Who does this guy think he is? Gwen scoffed silently, half frowning, half laughing with the class.

Mr. Stevens continued as though there had been no interruption. "We will also look into the reasons and causes of events in history, like the natural volcanic activity of Vesuvius and why King—"

"Vesuvius, *sir*, had nothing to do with natural volcanic activity. And irritable elf, Ewlu the Cantankerous, had a reservation at one of the finest hotels in Pompeii, but when he arrived, they said that the reservation was never made. In turn, he pointed his staff at Vesuvius, uttered the Curse of Earth, one of the twenty-four elemental spells, and BOOM! There went Pompeii. Of course Ewlu died too; he never was much of a logical thinker."

"And apparently neither are you," said Mr. Stevens. "I think you'll enjoy a session of detention with me, and we'll see if we can force some discretion and sense into that skull of yours."

Eion only smiled. "I would be happy to return the favor, *sir*."

Although they clearly enjoyed his disruptions and admired his boldness, the class looked upon Eion as an outsider. Even Gwen shook her head in annoyance and turned back to the syllabus, completely embarrassed that she had been sat beside the boy whose mind was firmly rooted in some fantasy world. Her dream sprang to mind briefly, but she pushed it from her thoughts and tried to focus on the lecture.

After history came art class. Gwen always loved to paint and draw. She knew that she was not particularly good, but the mindless creation allowed her to let her mind wander. She had painted a fairly good canvas in elementary school, and had enjoyed art ever since.

They stood at long black desks in a classroom full of paintings on canvas. The room was well lit with a single window in the far corner of the room; sunlight streamed through brightly and reflected off the highly polished linoleum floor. There were no stools or chairs in the room; even the teacher's desk was bereft of a seat. At the front of the room, beneath the white grease board, stood a table littered with fruit and figurines and sundry objects too varied to list, all assumedly for still-life's that the class would later be expected to draw. Another table stood in the back of the classroom, this one burdened with mounds of paper of different sizes. There were plenty of cabinets and shelves lining the walls, all stuffed and piled with paints, charcoal, pens, pencils, and goodness knows what else.

Gwen was so preoccupied looking around that she jumped when the teacher came in. When she first laid eyes on the instructor, Mr. Alez, she immediately realized he might take the fun out of art. He was a large, Native American man, with his hair tied in a long braid that only missed the floor by fragments of an inch. His black eyes were narrowed, flashing from student to student as he scrutinized the class. Gwen quickly resolved to avoid making this man angry

"TOO LOUD, PLEASE," he said with a booming voice so thunderous that several of the students started in alarm. Colin actually fell to the floor from surprise. A quiet series of giggles quickly ensued as Colin picked himself up and dusted himself off, but the giggles immediately ceased at Mr. Alez's harsh glare.

He brought out a sheet of canvas and set it on an easel facing the class. Painted on the canvas was the most abstract piece of art Gwen had ever seen. It was easy to tell by the look on his face that Mr. Alez was very proud of the painting. He beamed and looked around the room, waiting for someone to compliment it. When no one did, he cleared his throat and addressed the class.

"Okay, so what I'm looking for is feedback, positive or negative. I want to hear what you think."

It was very apparent what everybody thought of it, but no one was stupid enough to start off on the wrong foot with a new teacher on the first day.

Well, all but one.

"What's it supposed to be?" asked Eion, his brow furrowed.

Mr. Alez's smile disappeared. "A wolf," he said quietly.

"A WOLF? Where's its ears?"

He pointed to some faded lines. "Right here."

"Oh…okay. I think I see its snout but why does it have two tongues?"

Mr. Alez grew pensive. "Two tongues? You see a forked tongue?"

Eion shrugged. "I suppose. Either that, or it is having a major conniption fit."

Mr. Alez grinned. "Why is that, do you think? Why do you see that?"

Eion started to respond, but stopped short as his brow furrowed in confusion. Dumbfounded for the first time that day, he shrugged.

"You see, Mr…"

"Shifter, Eion Shifter," Eion answered.

"Shifter, yes, well I ask what you see because, to my people, the forked tongue represents the snake, the trickster, the liar. Not too many people see the snake anymore; they're moving too fast to get a good look at it. Those who can spot the snake are wise…but untrusting. Soon, they see the snake everywhere, and withdraw into themselves.

Mr. Alez turned his full attention to Eion. "Perhaps, you have seen the snake so much that you've forgotten how to trust? That's why you see it in my painting. Where else do you see it?"

For the first time Gwen saw retreat in Eion's expression, as if Mr. Alez had hit close to home. Eion mumbled something, but no one clearly heard it, and Mr. Alez laughed.

"Ah, maybe you need to learn to trust again, Shifter. If you're always looking for the snake, you'll never see anything else."

For the first time that day, Eion didn't have a sly response. He blinked a couple times, mouth parted in thought. Then, his eyes widened, as some comeback or some remark or some revelation came to mind. He didn't say anything though; he nodded slowly and averted his eyes, lost in wondering.

Later, in math, while the class was taking notes on the key terms that would be appearing on their first test, Gwen was struggling to see the white board, but Eion's head was blocking the way.

Bristling with irritation, she leaned over and whispered, "Um, excuse me."

Eion slowly turned his head, and she made eye contact. His eyes were strange and unlike anything she had ever seen before. His iris was gray, with just a hint of blue, but the odd thing was that they seemed to circle his pupils, which were deep and unnaturally black. Gwen felt herself drawn into them. If it wasn't for the class's conversations, she wouldn't have been able to bring herself back.

Eion didn't seem to notice. "Yes?" he asked.

"Uh, never mind," she quickly said. She turned back to her notebook and hastily scribbled down the rest of the definitions.

Lunch period finally came. After she had been dismissed from her class, she rushed to her locker to grab the lunch she had brought from home. She then made her way to the cafeteria, a small room with only six tables, and took a seat at the table that Lea, Kendal, and Caitlyn were sitting at.

Immediately, they dove into a stream of name-dropping, trash-talking, and general gossip. A girl came up in the conversation, and after many opinions were given, Gwen brought the discussion to a close by saying, "Yeah, I hate her."

But just as she said this, Eion Shifter walked by.

"No, you do not," he said quietly, stopping beside the table. Gwen looked up at him in surprise, careful not to look *directly* into his eyes.

"No you do not," Eion repeated, quieter than before. "You do not *hate* her. You do not hate *anything*. I am sure you have the capacity; most people do. But, you do not *hate*. You do not know how…yet."

With a nod, he left, and went to sit by himself at the end of one of the tables. He ate quietly, looking out through the window placed opposite of him. An air of wisdom seemed to hang upon him, and he ate with a look of shrewd knowing.

Suddenly, Gwen hated him.

Whether it was his cool confidence, or his sardonic tone, or his blatant arrogance, Gwen couldn't get her head around him. But there was something unsettling about him. Something that made her afraid, as if he had the power to change her world, which right now was the best it had ever been.

Still, there was something about him that interested her as well, something she couldn't place.

Without a word, she got up from her seat and, leaving her lunch and her friends behind, and approached Eion's table.

She sat down across from him and watched him eat. He either didn't notice her or he chose to ignore her, because he did not look up or speak. Finally, after he had finished eating, he flopped open a book. "What do you want?" Not bothering to look up, he directed his attention to the book that now lay open before him.

"Who are you?" asked Gwen incredibly. It wasn't polite, and she sounded petulant. Still, her mind was such a torrent of questions that it was the only thing she could think to say.

He looked up from his book, his eyes betraying some sort of exasperation that Gwen couldn't credit. "Do you really care? What does the life of a stranger mean to you?"

"Let's just say you bug me, and I want to know why," she replied acidly.

He laughed at that. "Well, flattered as I may be, I am not about to share with you my story. It is too long, for one thing, and you would not understand most of it."

Eyes narrowed with intense dislike, Gwen challenged, "Try me."

"Please," he said, rolling his eyes. "Try to rise above my expectations. Foolish people, all of you. Whatever you do not understand, you treat with disdain. You build your lives upon the superficial and the unreal, and pride yourselves on being self righteous. Yet, you wave your crosses and stars in each other's faces and wander aimlessly through life. No wonder you were excluded from the New World. You are all so *dense*."

Gwen stared, her mouth open, unable to think of a response. Eion only turned back to his book, indicating that he was finished.

After a few minutes of stunned silence, Gwen recovered from her shock and laughed. "You're delusional! Who are you to make moral judgments on all people everywhere? You talk like you're perfect. You talk like you're...like you're...like you're not *human*."

Eion chuckled as he turned the page. "Well, funny you should bring that up. Actually—"

"Oh, shut up," she interjected coldly. "You're just a high-and-mighty snob."

He laughed at that, his eyes boring through her. "Oh, now who is making judgments?" He rose from his seat and leaned forward, speaking his next words in a livid whisper. "Grip on to your false convictions while you still can. I have seen things that would rock them to the very core. Take comfort in your ignorance. You. Know. *Nothing*."

With that, he walked away, depositing his trash in the bin as he left the cafeteria. He had left his book on the table.

Gwen, unnerved, and not too sure of what had just happened, left the book and walked back to her friends.

☐

Gwen didn't talk too much to Eion after that. In fact, no one did. School continued and Gwen, Lea, Kendal, and Caitlyn soon became very good friends with Tyler, Colin, Ryan, Eric, Brad, and Anthony. They became inseparably close, while Eion—Eion stayed alone, marked an outcast. Not that this seemed to bother him, nor did their constant ridicule of his stories. If ever someone would bother to make fun of him, he would only smile and return to what he had been doing.

The school year passed silently without any great incident as Gwen had so hoped for at the beginning. She turned fifteen in the middle of May, and had a spectacular party that was the thing to talk about for weeks. Later, the first of June came, and it was time for summer vacation. Now, on the last day of school, Gwen said her goodbyes and looked forward to seeing them all again next year. All spring she had ridden her bike to school, and now she felt fit and strong and ready to face the summer.

She went into the restroom and changed out of her uniform and into some plain jeans and a top. Then, she left the building, unlocked her bike, and prepared to ride home when, out of the corner of her eye, she saw the hawk that had been taunting her all year, walk out of the school. It didn't even seem to nudge the glass doors open. In truth, the doors seemed to disappear as the bird walked through, but when Gwen took a second look, she clearly saw the sun reflecting off the glass.

Regardless of the optical illusion, it was still a mystery as to what the bird was doing inside the school. She looked around to see if anyone besides her had noticed, but everyone seemed oblivious. Before she could grapple with the anomaly, the great bird spread its wings and begun to run. Flapping with great force, it took to the skies.

Gwen knew that nobody would be home, so she decided to follow the great bird. She hopped on her bike and quickly peddled after the hawk, visions of her dreams and nightmares flashing through her mind.

☐

Sixty minutes of hard peddling on the side of the road, and still the hawk soared. It had almost led her to the first hills of the Sierra Nevada Mountains; she had already passed three signs saying how far it was to

Reno. She needed to stop and rest. Maybe it would be best if she just turned back now. The evening was getting on, and soon her family would be coming home to find her missing.

As if it had read her mind, the bird began to descend, making great, downward spirals in a graceful fashion. Gwen turned away from the sight from fear of getting dizzy.

Unfortunately, it seemed as if it was going to land somewhere in the pine trees on the right side of the highway. Gwen let out an exasperated sigh, got off her bike, and walked it into the forest.

The high branches of the pines were so thick and dense that all sunlight was blotted out. The stillness gripped her. She had hiked through the forest many times with family or friends, and always it had been alive with the call of birds and the sound of wildlife. On some days, light breezes brought the sweet scents of blossoming trees and flowers. But now, it was quiet; there was no birdsong, there was no breeze. The silence permeated everything and did not wish to be disturbed.

She leaned the bike up against a boulder, for the trees had become big and closer together; it would be difficult to navigate through the wood while guiding a bike. She'd walk without it the rest of the way.

Uncounted minutes passed and still she hadn't found the hawk. Just when she thought of turning back, she tripped over a rock that had snagged her looped shoelace, and fell painfully to the ground. It took her a few minutes to get up, but before she did, she took a close look at the soil she had fallen in. She saw prints that were unmistakably a bird's. They were fresh, too. She got up and followed them, but not even five feet away the tracks stopped. There a new trail began, but these were a human's shoe tracks. Maybe a hunter had found the hawk. Concerned, she quickly ran after the trail.

She followed the footprints to a cave of granite that stood beside a small, grassy hill. Here, there was a space in the tree boughs that allowed the light to stream through, illuminating the cave eerily in the dusty forest. Waving a few mosquitoes away from her face, she stepped around to the mouth of the cavern and stepped quietly inside. Her heart pounded so hard she was sure it could be heard echoing off the walls.

The air was cool and musky, rank with the smell of fermenting moss and mushrooms. Feeling the wall for guidance, she felt a sticky coating of some kind of spider web. She resisted the temptation to shriek and instead wiped her hand on her jeans.

Upon taking only two steps more, a brilliant blue light sprang to life. Gwen hid behind a boulder next to the left side of the cave, crouching into a little ball so no one would be able to see her. She then heard voices close by, one she recognized as Eion Shifter's.

"Lord Fairskin," said Eion, "I have spent a bloody four years in this mortal world. I have traveled far and wide, and still there is no sign of anybody with the least amount of potential to be one of the Prophesied Ten."

"Eion," said a gentle voice, "I know that cannot be true. You have spent almost a year in the same place. This is where they are. It is where you have been led to find them. What has kept you if you've found nothing?"

Eion sighed, a little perturbed at being caught in a lie. "All right, all right. Yes I have not only found one person, I have found *ten*. And the prophecy clearly said '*One to lead, eight to follow, one to rebel*'. But they just do not seem orthodox."

"How so?" asked the other voice.

"They are *children*. Gods, Lord Fairskin, how can the Prophesied be *children?*"

"Do not try and tell me the young are not capable of great things. You were a child once too, Eion. And if memory serves, you accomplished more greatness than many adults ever do in a lifetime."

"Yes, but there was a slight difference. I had grown up...differently. These fools all but laughed themselves to death at the thought of the existence of Atlantis."

"Well, what do you expect? Humans have not had any magical influences in over one thousand years. Of course they forgotten that magic is real; they have been taught to believe in logic and that we are just fairy tales and the spawn of myth. Even adults would not have believed you. Besides, how do you know Atlantis existed? Plato himself rather doubted it."

"Do not patronize me, Lord Fairskin. I am far too old for it. You were vacationing there when it happened, and I believe it was you who warned those conjurers not to do it. You got off the island right before it sank. And anyway, Plato was a mere second-rate mage of no great talent; I have no idea why humans play him up so much."

"Yes, people are strange that way." The second voice chuckled merrily.

"I am glad you think this is funny," said Eion, agitated, "We have two years before that spell takes effect. Then someone else will be laughing, and if Vundin's prophecy is true, as every one prior has been, I shudder to think of what will happen if we are without the Prophesied."

"Very well," said the other voice with newfound seriousness, "I think it is best if you stay and get to know these ten mortals before you leave. They may be our salvation."

Eion sighed tiredly. "All right. Tell my officers to get my troops ready. I think this is going to start sooner than we think."

"Oh, I forgot to ask you: no one knows what you are, correct?"

"Of course not. They would not believe me anyway."

"Your words hearten me. I was worried you might have revealed yourself; you do have a tendency to prove yourself right. And another thing, have you found the third Iltari?"

Eion next words sounded hesitant. "Well, possibly. It is so hard to tell here with the mortals' grim reality. But two of the ten have the potential, and they both appear to look and act exactly as Garon said the Iltari would. Perhaps if you could tell me which one conceived the Third?"

"Garon did not furnish me with that information either. I believe he wants only the Iltari to know first."

Again, Eion sighed. "In that case, we must venture a chance on these ten."

"Very well then. Bring them here when the time comes, Eion."

"Aye. I shall contact you later through the gem. This guise is already old. Farewell!"

"Farewell, Eion." The blue light blinked out.

Silence filled the cave, broken only by Gwen's racing pulse. Confused, she quickly crawled out of the cave. She stood once she exited, and arched her back to loosen the cramp that had been building in her spine. Questions zipped through her head. She looked back up the trail she had come down, immediately freezing when she saw that she was not alone in the glade.

In front of her was a wolf, one unlike any she had ever seen. Foam dripped from its mouth. Leathery skin hugged its ribs; it looked as though it hadn't eaten in weeks. Its red eyes glinted like two small flames dancing inside its skull. Perhaps it was just her fear, but she two ram horns curling around the wolf's head. Its pointed ears pricked up when it saw her, and it growled softly.

All common sense left her. She screamed, turned to the left, and ran. She ran fast, but the starved wolf was faster. She looked over her shoulder, just in time to see a figure emerge from the mouth of the cave and sprint after her. Unfortunately, the wolf jumped and bit the back of her leg. She screamed with pain, stumbled, and hit her head on a rock.

As consciousness left her, she had a sense of soaring. Floating in the air. And a voice telling her everything would be all right.

☐

When she next awoke in what seemed like years later, she found herself in a hospital bed with a terrible headache. She sat up and looked at the table next to her, dots painting her vision. On the table laid countless get well cards and her father's head, fast asleep. She felt a pinching on her thumb. Looking down, she saw that she was hooked up to a monitor, which recorded her heartbeat with the rise and fall of the cardiograph. She moaned, sore for some reason she couldn't place.

Suddenly, she remembered the wolf. In a trice, she lifted her covers and examined her leg. No wound, not even a scratch. But she was sure the wolf had torn open her leg. She got out of bed on wobbly legs and looked in the mirror on the left side of her room. She had a nasty bump on her forehead and there was dried blood in her hair and on her hospital gown, but no wound, no gash.

She sat on the edge of her bed. *How could this be?* She remembered the wolf biting her so vividly. She knew there should've been a gash inches deep, but instead, there was only smooth, unharmed skin.

Deeply confused, she climbed under the covers to brood. She was so deep in thought she was barely aware of her father waking up, barely aware of him telling her that she had had an accident on her bike, barely aware of being reprimanded for acting so carelessly.

☐

She was visited the next day by her friends. Lea was wide eyed with worry as she set a large vase full of laburnums and lilies on the small dresser beside Gwen's bed.

"What were you thinking, Gwen," she said, "worrying me like that. What happened?"

Gwen wondered if she should tell them the story of the wolf. Did it happen? Or was it just another nightmare?

"Fell off my bike," she said with a shrug, "knocked me out."

"In the mountains?" asked Anthony. He eyed her doubtfully.

Gwen shrugged in a non-committing sort of way, hoping to look convincing. "Yeah, I had a lot of stuff to think about. I thought I just take a ride around Auburn's foothills."

Unconvinced, her friends left her with flowers and cards, but not five minutes after they had left, the door to her hospital room opened.

"Hello." Eion entered, adorned in jeans, a white t-shirt, and a zip up hoodie. His hands were tucked casually in his pockets, and he was smiling, as if amused.

Gwen looked up from her book in surprise. She wanted to say hello, but what came out was, "Was it real?"

Eion just smiled wider. "Perhaps, perhaps not. We might not ever know."

Gwen raised her eyebrows, and then returned his smile. While things were still a little unclear, she accepted Eion, eccentric or not.

"Thank you," she said.

He gave a slight nod, and walked out quietly.

☐

Upon getting out of the hospital, she phoned her friends to report Eion was not bad at all. No matter how Gwen had sustained her injuries, Eion had helped her in her time of need.

Sophomore year came and went. With Gwen's encouragement, the rest of the group accepted Eion. They became good friends, and their friendship only grew more as they went through many months, blissfully unaware of what lay ahead. And if Eion had any idea of what was coming, he certainly didn't let on.

☐

Gwen returned one gray morning in January to Greystone High. As in the past, the school was packed with hundreds of students. Gwen quickly found Lea, Kendal and Caitlyn at their usual meeting place: the vending machines. The three greeted Gwen and together they all set off to find the rest of their group.

They found everyone but Eion and Brad gathered around Tyler's locker, laughing and telling jokes as was their custom.

"Where's Eion?" asked Caitlyn. Colin shrugged and returned to his conversation with Anthony about the ridiculous assembly schedule for the end of Homecoming Week. This year's theme was a "Tribute to the

Eighties"; all week, people had come to school dressed as though they had stepped out of "The Breakfast Club", giving fuel to their cynically cruel amusement.

"There he is," said Ryan, pointing. The group turned as one.

There was Eion with a tired but smiling face. He didn't look well. He was very pale, and his hair was disheveled. A great weariness showed in his eyes, and they seemed much greyer than they ever had been. His breathing was different too; short and quick as though he were waiting for something to happen.

Only Gwen noticed this. She'd taken a liking to Eion after what happened with the wolf, though she never mentioned the experience to him ever again.

The rest of the group welcomed him but Gwen whispered in his ear, "What's wrong?"

He beamed at the question strangely. His grey eyes were a torrent of excitement as he chuckled and whispered something that Gwen did not fully understand.

Come are we to the beginning
And we are off to the reach the end
The road is far, the way is long
With many twists and bends
But the sun is high, the day is new
And we are to meet the horizon
So with a fond farewell to lands well known
Our journey now begins

Gwen frowned, but dropped the matter. Eion had always acted a little odd, and he had an abiding love of poetry and verse. There was no point in asking him to repeat himself, and even less of a chance that he would explain himself. So, without any questioning, the ten friends all went into math class together.

Mr. Tekin, their Turkish math teacher, sat at his desk as they came in. His bushy eyebrows were furrowed together. His forehead was lined with many wrinkles that snaked from each other like a series of forking streams.

"You're all late!" His heavy accent was deep, guttural, and laced with annoyance.

"Sorry" they said at the same time, smirking and giggling amongst themselves. It was hard to take Mr. Tekin seriously. Though he would've liked to have been menacing and controlling, the effect was somehow ruined by the teacher's lack of height and vocabulary.

"Take your seats," he added, with more unsuppressed irritation, as though he had been interrupted during as long lecture when he actually hadn't even begun to take attendance yet.

With a few more snickers, the group of friends took the variety of empty seats sprawled across the room, careful not to sit too close to one another in prevention of another Tekin Tirade. Michael shot them all smiles from his seat across the classroom, relishing the thrill of watching the friends being reprimanded. He received a quick series of rude gestures in return, which quickly ridded his face of his smile and replaced it with a disapproving frown.

"Take out your notebooks please," said Mr. Tekin, oblivious to all of this as he often was. "We will continue our discussion on polynomials and their use in—"

At that moment, Brad Thomas burst through the door.

"Sorry I'm late," he cried, "got stuck in traffic"

"That's not my fault," said Mr. Tekin, beyond annoyance and now angry. "This is becoming a habit with you. Detention Brad."

"WHAT?" Brad slammed his books onto the desk.

Mr. Tekin gave him a look.

"I mean, Yes Mr. Tekin."

Eion coughed something that sounded a lot like "mortals", but Gwen felt sure she must have heard wrong

Furious, Brad plunked in this seat and slammed his book open.

☐

The last class of the day was American History. Ms. Robbins had been gone on maternity leave for the past few weeks, and she was not due back until the end of the following month. Thus, to the dismay of all, Mr. Tekin was substituting.

Though the class had been lively and interactive with their regular teacher, Mr. Tekin insisted on spreading his malignant lethargy, forcing them to silently summarize chapters from their textbooks.

While taking notes on the Industrial Revolution, Gwen felt a strange rumble under her feet. She looked up to see if anything else was shaking.

"Do you feel that?" she whispered hoarsely to Brad.

"Feel what?"

"The earth moving."

"I didn't know I had that effect on you." Brad grinned, but the grin disappeared when he looked at Gwen's narrowed eyes.

"I'm serious. You can't feel it?"

"I feel we might be having an earthquake," Mr. Tekin began, when all at once the door to the classroom flew open exposing an ugly, gray creature with gnarled horns. It raced into the room.

"Where is he?" it roared, saliva dripping from its curling fangs. Mats of black hair hung lank on his head, growing in thatches around its horns. The body, clasped in black armor, was adorned with a single, red half-circle on the breastplate.

Students dove under desks, screaming. Many of those close to the front of the class, where the monster swung his mighty head, jumped from their seats and raced to the back of the room, cowering. Others tried to make themselves look as small as possible at their desks, unable to move. Faces paled. Tina Watt, a small, nervous-looking girl, actually fainted.

"What do you want?" demanded Mr. Tekin, standing up bravely, though the color was completely drained from his face. He barely reached the creature's shoulder.

Grabbing Mr. Tekin by the throat, the monster smiled wickedly. "I am here to find a boy named Shifter," it said with a hiss.

Mr. Tekin raised a shaking finger and pointed it at Eion, his nobleness seemingly spent.

Eion continued to read his book, apparently unfazed by the creature's appearance. Without looking up, he simply said, "Took you long enough, Belzorg. I think age is catching up with you old friend, if it takes you this long to track someone."

"How was I to know you were hiding in the Mortal Realm?" the creature snarled, ignoring the last statement and releasing Mr. Tekin, whose eyes were so wide that they looked as though they were about to pop from his head.

"I assure you I do not know, but it does not matter" stated Eion, still looking at the book with mild interest. "You're still getting slow."

Belzorg looked evilly at Eion and whispered, "He has returned."

"He?" Eion glanced at the beast, then looked away.

"The Red Sovereign has returned."

"Oh has he?" asked Eion brightly as he turned the page and readjusted his reading glasses. "I was wondering how much longer it would take. I was the only one who heard him mutter that incantation that night I struck him down all those years ago. My, time does fly."

Belzorg smiled. "He sent me to kill you".

"Kill me?" Eion looked up from his book and stared at the creature. He took off his glasses and placed them in his book bag and smiled broadly. "*Really*? How foolish of him."

Belzorg's smile widened. "Why? You think I am not able?"

Eion shrugged. "You said it, not me. But, if we care to look on times gone by, I believe that scar on you forehead still stands as a merit to your swordplay.'

Belzorg growled with anger as he ran a claw down the ropy scar that disfigured his scalp. "Time has made me forget how much I loathe, hate, despise, and abhor your kind."

"Tsk, tsk," said Eion calmly. He closed his book and gathered his papers. "You really should learn to control your anger Belzorg. That is why you failed so many years ago. The Ozra were always too reckless."

"Hardly."

"Think, old friend. Do you think it was a terribly clever thing to split your forces three ways in the Battle of the Silver Ice Sea? Come, come Belzorg, a blind man could have countered such a strategy."

While Belzorg growled his retort, Gwen finally recovered from the shock of the sight of the creature and found her voice again.

"Eion," she asked, "What *is* that? And *why* do you *know it*?"

Eion chuckled. "I will answer your second question first. Belzorg and I go way back. Old friends, eh Zorgy?"

Belzorg scoffed. "Me? Friends with a shifter? *Never.*"

Eion smiled placidly and turned to Gwen and said, "As for your first question, Belzorg is a goblin. Not just any goblin though. He is the Commander and Chief of all Ozmodion's Goblin Armies, or at least I believe so, now that your father, Grungloch, is dead?" The question was directed at the goblin.

"Quite an important job," nodded Belzorg, puffing his chest out proudly.

"And a delicate one," Eion said cleverly while he flicked his nose in a knowing way.

"A goblin?" Gwen asked, trying to remain calm. She had to be dreaming, yet Belzorg's stench screamed otherwise. *More nightmares*, she thought.

Eion nodded his head. "Mm. A goblin. If I had my way, it would be a long time before you saw one. Still, I suppose it is better this way; it gives one courage to look evil in the eye."

"But goblins aren't real," Gwen insisted. She had grown up with very realistic parents who had not permitted many fairytales to enter their walls. Gwen's childhood had been reinforced with dismal reality since she was five.

Eion scoffed. "Says who? Mum and Dad?"

Taken aback at Eion's bitterness, she nodded. Eion tutted and shook his head. "Well, as there is a goblin standing right in front of you, I would say that your parents are wrong. Goblins are indeed real, along with a great myriad of other things that human society has always found too inconvenient to accept. It is much easier to say that they do not exist. But exist they do, as you can so plainly see." He gestured at Belzorg as he spoke. The goblin, meanwhile, chuckled with twisted amusement.

"Like this girl, eh Shifter?" His smile revealed yellowed, holey teeth, "Maybe I should kill her as well."

"Oh, yes. If you wish yourself free of the burden that is your head, by all means give it a try," replied Eion coldly, his eyes quickly narrowing.

"Thank you, I will," said Belzorg, his comprehension of threats seeming to stretch only so far. He unsheathed his bent rapier and lunged at Gwen.

Gwen screamed as the blade came inches away from her face. Suddenly, Eion's arm shot in front of the sword. Gwen expected his arm to fall off, but no. She couldn't tell what was happening to his arm because his sleeve was down, but he seemed to be fighting the sword away, judging from the strain on his face. Belzorg smiled and took a slash at Eion.

Clang!

Eion again blocked the blow with his arm. With inhuman speed, Eion put his other arm against the goblin's neck. Belzorg eyes widened and he dropped his rapier, loudly gulping in surprise and distress.

"A costly mistake, old friend," Eion said happily. He flexed his fingers experimentally, as though he were preparing to make a final move.

"Kill me now, eh?" asked Belzorg calmly, but the beads of sweat trickling down his face betrayed his terror.

"Tempting, but not now, no. Not in front of so many innocents," Eion waved at the class with his free hand. All of them were even more pale and blanched then they had been when Belzorg first appeared. Tina was still unconscious on the floor; no one had gone to bring her into the safety of the huddled group, their fright too paralyzing. "There will be plenty of time for that in the coming months I'm sure. However, I think I can persuade you to go back pleading to Ozmodion without further incident."

"Really? How?" asked Belzorg, slightly amused and greatly relieved. His breathing, which had been deep and shaky for the last few moments, regained its calm and steadiness.

Eion raised his free hand. All his fingers were outstretched and pointing to the goblin. A final smile and a whispered phrase the Gwen did not make out, and Belzorg started to shrink

"NO!" the creature shouted, clutching at his hair and sides as if he were trying to prevent the process. "I WILL GET YOU FOR THIS SHIFTER! ON MY KIN'S SOULS, I SWEAR IT!" He tried to speak more, but his voice was growing more ragged and raspy. His features contorted and twisted violently, and Gwen was almost sick, when suddenly she realized what was happening. Belzorg was turning into a frog. Now green and less hairy, he sat hunched on all fours; his eyes bulged and his horns retreated into his head. Within a moment, gone were all signs that the creature had ever been a goblin, and instead a fat, forlorn frog looked up with blatant indignation. Gwen had never seen an indignant frog, and despite her fear and shock, she found the sight deeply amusing.

"Go on Belzorg," said Eion, head inclined and his eyes sparkling with laughter, "unless you would like to stay. Mr. Janca's classes are performing dissections today, and I'm sure he would appreciate another vict—, excuse me, specimen."

The frog opened its mouth to respond, but all that it managed was an offensive croak. Embarrassed, it retreated. An embarrassed frog is almost as interesting as an indignant one.

With that, the frog hopped out of the classroom, croaking as it went. Eion shook his head "Goblins," he muttered. He then turned to the class. Upon seeing their frightened faces, he smiled calmly.

"I would not bother about *him*," he said casually. "If it had been Kahn, then you *certainly* would have had reason to tremble. Trolls are not as intelligent as goblins, but they are much bigger and they have considerably less restraint. He might have thought it fun to knock you all senseless with a club. Still, no sense in worrying about him now; he has not come, and we have other matters to attend to. For now, I think I will collect the Prophesied and be on my way." He walked back to his desk and set about putting everything away. When nothing was said for a long time, Eric spoke up.

"What do you mean 'the Prophesied'?" he asked timidly from his crouched position in the back.

"Mercy! Another idle question!" Eion exclaimed grandly, not looking away from the sundry items littered across his desk. He picked up the book he had been reading and sighed loudly.

"Mortal rubbish," he said with a shake of his head as he carelessly threw the book aside. "Automobiles? How do you people live like this?" He cleared his throat and faced the cowering students. "All right, now we really can't waste any more time. I had not counted on Belzorg coming; it is rather out of character for Ozmodion to send an assassin *out* of the Magic Realm, though he is very used to sending them around it. And now, after all that effort, Belzorg will return with nothing to show for it. Ooh, I do not envy him. But now, we are late. Lord Fairskin has been expecting us, and we really must go."

"Who's '*we*'?" asked Kendal, still ducked under her desk with her arms over her head.

"Hm? Oh, yes, I forgot...the Prophesied...well, Gwen, Lea, Kendal, Caitlyn, Tyler, Colin, Ryan, Eric, Brad, and Anthony, will you all stand up? Do not bother collecting your things; you will have no need of textbooks and pencils where we are going. But go we must, and quickly, because I really would not want to put out the rear guard for nothing. Mind you, I would not mind seeing Steel and Fletch. It has been years, and I am sure they were included in the reinforcements. But there will be time enough for that later. And now, we must go."

No one moved. Looks of doubt, disbelief, and fear filled the room. No one made a noise, and the sounds of breathing seemed uncommonly loud.

Eion waited, but quickly lost his patience. With a roll of his eyes, he said, "Frogs are horribly trivial for me. I can manage much more uncomfortable things."

His five fingers on his right hand instantly turned into snakes. They twisted and hissed while still connected to his hand. Whether out of fear or surprise, the ten that were called stood up. As soon as they did, the snakes hissed and changed back into fingers.

"Good. Let's go, then." Eion flexed his fingers as though he had been oblivious to the transformation. He then reached into the pockets of his jacket and pulled out a gem. Gwen stared in wonder, having never seen such beauty and craftsmanship in a jewel. The gem sparkled with colors that never stayed the same. Blue became green between blinks of the eye. It was impossible to define its shape, for there were so many facets that one couldn't concentrate long enough to decide whether it was cubic or round. A white orb was glowing on the inside, pulsing occasionally.

"Mr. Shifter," Mr. Tekin sputtered, apparently regaining his composure, "I want an explanation of what just happened."

Eion didn't answer. Instead, he held the gem to his mouth and whispered something. It then melted into a multi-colored vapor and expanded and dissipated into the room. As it stretched to the walls, a little nexus was formed. Air was pulled into the center, creating a strong breeze in the room.

Everybody in the class gawked at it, save Eion. He just pulled some silver powder out of another pocket. He threw it at the class and Mr. Tekin and said, "Sleep well."

The silvery dust floated through the air, capturing the eyes and attention of the remaining students and the teacher. As soon as it reached their eyes, they nodded off and, one by one, they fell asleep.

"When they wake, they will not remember a thing," he explained to his friends. "Though I expect they would have thought it a bad dream. Silly creatures, humans; seeing is believing, they say, yet even when they see it, they still refuse to believe it.

"But look now: the nexus calls. So, at your leisure…" he left it at that, motioning toward the center of the red mist.

Eric shook his head vigorously. Brad lost all the color in his face and squeaked. Colin trembled violently.

Eion sighed with exasperation. "Come, come. I swear no harm will befall you." There was great assurance in his voice, but the swirling nexus was not so convincing.

"How do we know we can trust you?" Gwen dared ask.

"I would not have expected that question of you, given how I have twice now saved your life."

Humbled, Gwen allowed him to shepherd her in with the horrible finger snakes. The others followed. Red mist shrouded Gwen's vision as she stepped into the center. For a brief moment, she felt the cool vapor on her skin, and there was a sweet scent in the air. Then, all at once, she felt the floor give way beneath her feet, and she fell away from the world.

Chapter 3

The Flight

T**hey were falling.** That was Gwen's first realization. They were falling. Wind rushed past her face, and when she looked down, she saw herself plummeting passed layers upon layers of clouds. The cold air chilled her, and she felt the water collecting on her skin turn to ice.

Kendal screamed once she had dared to open her eyes. "Gwen! Eion! We're falling!"

Eion faced her, eyes full of excitement. "Thank you Kendal, keep me posted." He turned around, muttering, "'We're falling', honestly…"

"What happens when we reach the ground?" shouted Eric; his shirt billowed about him and threatened to fly off his back.

"We stop, I presume." Eion frowned, seeming remarkably at ease despite plunging at an alarming speed. After a moment of thought, he shouted back, "I suppose I will just have to call Breeog and a few others."

"Breeog?" hollered Anthony over the rushing wind, tumbling in a somersault over and over again. "What's a Breeog?"

But all Eion did was point a finger at his throat. Though no visible changes were made, Eion was able to open his mouth and yell "BREEOG!" with a magnified voice that echoed throughout the sky. Eion pointed a finger at his throat once more, and then the group waited a minute or so before someone spoke.

"L-Look!" Caitlyn pointed as well as one could point under the circumstances to the distance; her hair whipped wildly about her face.

Gwen and the others turned and stared. Gwen turned green. Kendal screamed Everyone else seemed at a lost for words.

Closing in, were eleven airborne creatures. Their bodies were huge, and their wings colossal; Gwen and the others could've all crouched under them and still there'd be room for more. Their four legs were relatively short but their claws looked as sharp as spears. Their necks were very long, and rippled with muscle. They had shimmering scales of varied colors that danced in the sunlight. Their jaws were about two feet long and protruded from their faces. Their facial features varied; some had tufts of fur underneath their chins, others had spikes poking out around their nostrils, and others still had twisted horns protruding from their heads. Some were roaring while others were spouting flame from their wide jaws.

A chill shot down Gwen's neck. "Dragons!"

The mythical beasts circled the falling humans, regarding them wryly. The largest of the dragons was grinning with a mouth full of razor-sharp, golden teeth. His red, black, and silver scales shined so brilliantly that it looked as though the dragon was wearing a coat of gems. Then, while Gwen was still trying to take all of it in, the dragon spoke with a bellowing voice.

"WELCOME HOME, EION SHIFTER!" it roared. "It has been too long since we last met."

"Friends," said Eion to his ten terrified human companions, his voice returned to its usual volume, "meet His Majesty, Breeog, King of the Dragons." He gestured at the important beast before them.

"Hahaha," laughed the dragon, flicking his tongue. "Forget the formalities, Shifter. I have known you since you were sixteen years old."

"Oh, you must be mistaken," squeaked Lea as loudly as she dared, "Eion is only fifteen. We all celebrated his birthday six months ago." She shrank back at Breeog's hard glare.

"I'll explain later, Lea," smiled Eion, patting her on the shoulder reassuringly. She still eyed the dragon nervously.

"Well, now come on. The day is getting on and all," said Breeog graciously, grinning one last time at Lea. She gulped audibly as he finished with, "I have not eaten all day, and will certainly starve if we waste any more time. Climb on"

Mounting a dragon while plummeting toward earth is not as simple as it sounds, and it took many tries before each of them had securely straddled one of the winged beasts. After all the mortals had been taken care of, Eion climbed onto Breeog's back, smiling as he said, "It has been too long, old friend."

Once they were all astride a mount, the dragons inhaled and leveled off, declining in altitude only marginally. Still the deep murk of the clouds surrounded them, and though the dragons were swift, they seemed to be forever trapped in the silver fug.

Gwen had climbed onto the back of a blue-green dragon, whose scales sparkled in the sunlight like the moon on the sea.

"Greetings," said the dragon, his voice deep and rumbling, "My name is Gorbon." His eyes were bright and his smile was sincere, though the rows of jagged teeth slightly ruined the effect.

"Hi, I'm Gwen," she responded, quite unsure of how to talk to a dragon. She discovered that she had no need to be worried, for Gorbon was still smiling genially.

"Well, Lady Gwen, let me show you the Magic Realm."

Gwen looked down. They had finally pierced the clouds, and she could now see the land far below. Such natural beauty Gwen had never seen. They were flying over green hills and deep forests, lakes and cascading waterfalls. In the distance, Gwen could see endless mountain ranges that touched the blue sky seamlessly. The sun was high, and she savored its warmth; her clothes were now completely drenched by the moisture trapped in the clouds. The air was sweet and the scent of flowers hung heavily about it. She barely had time to take it all in; the dragons could fly surprisingly fast for their size.

Gorbon soared close behind Breeog, and Gwen could here the dragon talking to Eion over the wind.

"It is good to see you again Breeog," said Eion genuinely, if a little stiffly. "How goes the fight on this side?"

"Well," replied the dragon loudly, "every creature of the Resistance has been called to assemble in a twenty-mile radius around the Esialan

River, and the leaders of each race are to report to Fairskin Manor with their head officers."

"Any sign of the Ozra?" asked Eion, pulling his shirt closer about him, most likely in an effort to quell the cold.

"Aye. Reports state that they have left their hiding places in the mountains and woods and are all making their way back to Saurindon, bearing the Standard of Ozmodion high. The goblins were there first; I hear Belzorg went looking for you on *his* orders."

"Yes, I took care of him before we left. Poor Belzorg; a fool will always be a fool." He paused uncomfortably. "Have there been any signs of…. him?"

Breeog bowed his head. "He, alone, murdered the remainder of your family," he answered sadly, "He was looking for you. We got there just in time to see him cast the Eclipse."

"What! Why couldn't you do anthing?" Grief filled Eion's face.

Breeog spoke solemnly. "He was escorted by a legion of sixteen hundred goblins. Our patrols would have been butchered. The ones guarding the house were slain…Tactics along with them."

"More tragedy, I see..." Eion's voice cracked. He turned to check on the rest of the flight, and Gwen saw he had tears in his eyes.

Eion turned back to Breeog. It was a while before he spoke.

"I am going to kill him," he said finally, "Once and for all I am going to *slaughter* him. He has hurt me for the last time."

Breeog growled. "Gods willing."

Confused and sad, Gwen held back her own tears as questions quickly plagued her mind. Who killed Eion's family? Why? Who was looking for Eion anyway?

And how did she and her friends fit into all of this?

She gasped as they rose above a series of hills and saw what lay hidden behind them. Set in a wide vale ahead was a town medieval-like cottages, with thatched roofs and thin walls. Coming out of them were people with snow-white skin and golden hair. None seemed the least bit surprised that a flight of dragons soared overhead; they went about their business without any disruption.

But a little farther on past the village was and even bigger valley. In it were dragons, thousands of them, though they were hardly alone. There were legions of men with golden hair and blue eyes. Also among them were four-foot tall men with beards. Everyone was ready for battle; armor and helms glinted in the sunlight, and many swords and axes were being sharpened.

Then Gwen looked past the valley. Several hundred yards away on a green hill was a white castle. It had several turrets, hundreds of windows, and dozens of balconies. Its white visage glistened in the bright sun, standing as a monument to every fairytale Gwen had missed as a child. Beside the hill that it stood on was a beautiful, blue-green river, perhaps a half-mile wide. It sparkled beautifully as the light reflected off its surface. On the other shore was a temple situated in the mouth of a forest. A beautiful statue depicting a robed god stood at the entrance, welcoming all in.

The dragons landed right in front of the moat surrounding the castle. Gwen and the rest dismounted slowly, careful to avoid the razor sharp tip of the dragon wings. Eric shirt caught on his dragon's scales as he slid down his side, ripping it clean off. The dragon roared with laughter, and Eric, his face blushing, stepped away from the beast, covering his chest with folded arms.

Breeog and Eion led the group to the front of the castle, where an oak drawbridge was raised. Gorbon stayed with them. The other nine dragons took off to join the dragon ranks, roaring goodbyes in parting.

"Stand back," instructed Breeog.

The group backed up several paces, rank with trepidation and excitement.

Breeog then sang something that was not of the humans' language. Its splendor was unmatched by anything they had ever heard. As the melody filled the whole of her body, Gwen began to feel a wave of peaceful exhaustion.

When Breeog finished the song, the drawbridge lowered.

Across the bridge was a very old man, with a long silver-gold beard and lengthy, wispy hair of the same color. His white, bushy eyebrows met in the middle, giving character to his bright eyes. He was hunched over and used a staff to walk around.

"Welcome, welcome," he said, "Welcome old and new faces. Some of you already know my name. For those of you that don't, allow me to introduce myself. I am Lord Fairskin, master of this home. Please come in. We have much to do."

Chapter 4

The Explanation

*E**ion stepped forth*, and embraced the old man like he might a father. Once they had broken away, the old man turned and receded into the castle. The newcomers followed into a high ceilinged entrance hall, lit by candelabras and torches lining the wall. The floor beneath them was stony, but covered with an ornate rug that stretched down the passageway and out of sight.

The group was led to a large room with a very large table, around which sat about twenty people. There were enough chairs left to seat all the newcomers, save Breeog and Gorbon. Their bodies remained in the hall while their long necks snaked through the door.

The rest of the newcomers, though, found empty seats about the table. Gwen and her friends mostly sat together, but Eion took a chair near Lord Fairskin and another important looking man, though he seemed younger than Fairskin and very much shorter. His face was completely hidden by a bristly, grey beard, and two, black eyes stared out from under his very wrinkled brow. He seemed a cold sort, an indescribable grimness hanging about him like storm clouds atop a mountain.

Now Lord Fairskin stood from his seat at the head of the table, and he raised his hands. All conversation immediately ceased, and the old man opened his mouth to speak.

"Welcome all members of the Resistance," he said, "It has been long since we last met. May the bonds we once shared never break!"

"Hear, hear!" all sounded around the table. Some raised glasses half filled with wine, but all the short, bearded man raised flagons that were filled with a brown liquid that Gwen supposed was mead.

"And I believe we owe a special welcome to the Prophesied Ten!" continued Lord Fairskin grandly and with great vigor.

At this there was enthusiastic applause. Some even stood from their seats, while other shouted their cheers. There were bows, and calls, and whistles, and much fervor.

"Please introduce yourselves," Lord Fairskin prompted, once the ovation had died down.

The group awkwardly told the company their names. Caitlyn was the last to introduce herself; the crowd gasped upon hearing her surname.

A man with bright gold hair walked up to her. "I was familiar with one of your earliest grandfathers," said he.

"Really?" asked Caitlyn brightly.

"Yes, and never have I seen a worse case of cowardice then that of Lieutenant Bowen Montressor," said the golden haired man, "Although he did kill those three trolls all by himself in the battle of the Vectl Gonta valley, a fluke when you think about the Grand Griffin's…"

"Enough, Tirmal Goldhair," said Lord Fairskin, frowning. "Do not fill their heads with epics and tales of evil until they understand our story". The golden haired man bowed respectfully, whispering his apology. He then returned to his seat.

Lord Fairskin nodded and turned to the ten humans. "Since I asked Eion and King Breeog not to explain anything to you until you arrived, I suppose now you would like some clarification. The floor is yours." He sat back in his seat at the head of the table.

Many awkward glances were exchanged before the silence was broken by Eric. "All right, all right, this has got to be one of those dreams I have every time I have leftover meatloaf before bed. I've never had one this realistic though, so I'll play along."

Eion chuckled at this and then, standing from his seat, walked over to Eric, and punched him square in the shoulder.

"Oww!" shouted Eric, leaping back defensively, "What was that for?"

"Did you feel that?" asked Eion as he smiled. It was a strange, disconcerting smile, one Gwen had never seen on him before.

"Of course I felt it." Eric massaged his shoulder, eyeing Eion carefully.

"Then you are indeed awake," replied Eion with a shrug. "You have left behind the comfortable realm of dreams. You have come to a reality like none you've ever known, and you can be sure it will be one wild ride. Now to explain how it all happened, I suppose I should start at the beginning." He paused. "Well, my beginning, to be precise."

He walked back to his seat, but he did not sit. Instead, he turned from the table and, facing the one wall in the room that had no window, spoke with slow reflection. "I was born one thousand one hundred and twenty nine years ago. That is right. I am old. I am much older than all of you. I am even older than Biblical figures such as Methuselah. I was born in 878 A.D., and I lived a peaceful life with my family. Ten years passed without a single war. Ah, but I remember those golden times. Times when magics and mortals lived in peace," he paused, his voice becoming sadder, "Then the black years came."

Gwen shivered, as if through her dreams she knew what was coming.

"A sorcerer of great power gathered together dark creatures for an army. Goblins, trolls, shadow wolves, nightshades, all went to serve him. This sorcerer set out to dominate the entire globe. This sorcerer's name was *Ozmodion*."

"Ozmodion burnt forests and ruined towns. His troops slew innocents and mortals. He corrupted or killed people with his mastery of the heartless magic the world calls Black. The world seemed a doomed place, a mere toy for the Red Sovereign."

"There was one last hope; to consolidate together, surmount the insurmountable, and destroy Ozmodion and his evil minions.

"Elves and dwarves, accepted rivals, put aside their differences and fought side by side. Men and dragons, notorious enemies, found it in their hearts to be peaceful toward one another and vanquish their foes together. Thus the Resistance was born.

"Much blood was shed over the next four years, but we were able to keep Ozmodion at bay. Many souls gave their lives for the cause.

"Then, one night, one thousand, one hundred and fifteen years ago last week, one of our spies learned that Ozmodion was going to march out of

Saurindon that is his home, over the Mountains of Midnight, and launch a full scale attack with every creature in his army. We defended with every creature in our own army.

"I went with a troop of men, who were to search for the Red Sovereign and capture him or slay him if we could. We found him, and he laughed at our attempt. Just as he was about to unleash a spell that would've killed us all, I unsheathed my sword. *This* sword."

Eion turned to face the table again, and now he reached in midair. In a moment, a key appeared. Eion grasped the key, thrust it in midair, and turned it as though he were unlocking a door. The key began to change. In a moment, it had become an ancient sword, four feet long and very sharp. The hilt was unadorned with any decoration; in fact, it would have been absolutely ordinary if it wasn't for the bright blue aura that pulsed from the blade, tingeing the room with color.

"This," continued Eion, "is *Raz'atr,* the spell master. It was made to take spells and alter their intended purpose or reflect it back at its originator.

"As Ozmodion cast his magic, I jumped and hit the spell with the sword.

"Then something happened that no one had intended or foreseen. The two magics merged. Ozmodion's spell, which was supposed to kill us, was consumed as *Raz'atr* gave us its power, the power of change.

Gwen stared, mezmorized by the glowing blade.

"We could now change things. We could alter our appearance, our form. We could shift shape without magic. We had split away from the human race and had been changed into a new species: the shape shifter, or shifter once abbreviated.

"At that point I took a swing at Ozmodion, but before I could kill him, he yelled a spell into the night. Roughly translated it meant, 'I'll return in one year for each man who witnessed my death.' There had been one thousand, one hundred and fifteen of us that night.

"With that, Ozmodion was slain, but not dead."

Eric leaned to Caitlyn. "How can someone be dead, but not dead?"

Caitlyn shrugged. "Guess we're about to find out," she answered.

"The one thousand, one hundred and fifteen years ended three days ago. I was aware of it, and I knew I had to act soon. But forgive me; I am getting ahead of my story.

"With Ozmodion gone, the creatures of his army were afraid of the Resistance's power. They went into hiding. Peace and relief swept the earth.

"At first, the years passed uneventfully. But unfortunately, as Man grew in intelligence, he started to fear magic; the New Religion marked it as unholy and ungodly. Logic was the newfound alternative, and with it, Man created weapons, weapons that he used to destroy magical beings.

"The magical lords of the Resistance consolidated their powers to help the magic population. They created a Reflection, a replica of our world; one identical to the old one, except ours had the blessing of magic. The landscape and scenery was the same, but man was no longer a part of our world. No man lives here now."

"Wait, I don't understand.," Ryan interrupted, plainly lost. "A replica of the world? So does that mean we're on another planet?"

"No, no, no," replied Lord Fairskin calmly, "A Reflection, in this sense, is a world overlapping another, as though they are on two planes of existence. Imagine looking at a mirror. Theoretically, another world exists on the other side, a reflection of your world. Still, you cannot cross over to the other side, because the glass still stands in your way. It is a complicated magic, and it will take a lot of time to fully explain its principles."

Ryan nodded slowly, seeming more confused than he had been before he asked the question.

"And so passed the birth of the two realms," Eion continued with his narrative, "Magical borders were put up so mortals could not enter the Magic Realm, and safeguards were placed to restrict entrance into the Mortal Realm. Man took over the old realm and sculpted it to his liking, renaming old mountains, building new towns, and destroying all records of the old world.

"Six years ago, we were aware that the one thousand, one hundred and fifteen years were drawing to a close. Yet we were still missing the one weapon that could end Ozmodion forever. It was said long ago by the seers of old that the Red Sovereign could only be defeated with the help of a group of people named the Prophesied Mortals. As you might expect, most thought the prophecy to be wrong, for mortal men had already proven their hatred for magic. Still, when Vundin, the God of Time, made a similar prophecy, we were convinced."

> *A leader born divine*
> *And different from the rest*
> *Helped by another nine*
> *Eager for their test*
> *Eight to follow*
> *One to rebel*
> *The first to lead*

"Shortly after this divination, I was sent to the other realm to look for the fabled ten."

Eion paused. He gestured at Gwen and the others.

"And I found them. You are to help us. We will immediately begin your training, and, once you are prepared, you must march to Saurindon and slay Ozmodion. Allow me to introduce you to the Kings and Masters of the Resistance. That dwarf over there is King Barthol, King of the Dwarves of the Zanasha Mountains." He gestured at the short, grim-looking, bearded man that did not change expression as he inclined his head in acknowledgement. "Those are his generals and captains." Here, Eion motioned at some other short men with beards, though they all look much younger and less grim. "You know Breeog. Lord Fairskin rules his clan of elves, the Vra. Most of the people here command his army." Here he waved at the many fair-haired people who surrounded the table. They smiled and waved and trilled with musical laughter.

"Now," Eion hesitated, and he smiled slightly at his next words, as though he found some irony deep within them. "As for me, I am the Master of Shifters, for I was the first."

Eion took his seat once more. An uncomfortable silence fell over the table. They all waited for the mortal's reply, but they remained obstinately taciturn. They exchanged looks and doubtful glances, and everyone around the table jumped as the quiet was broken.

"Why didn't you tell us from the beginning?" sobbed Caitlyn suddenly, her eyes wild and intense.

"Yeah!" piped Ryan, who quickly recovered from his alarm, "We're your best friends and you couldn't find the time to tell us that you're not human?"

"Well, it would hardly make for good dinner conversation," replied Eion with a troubled frown. "Anyway, do you really think you would have believed me? Come now, don't live up to your humanity completely."

"None of this is real," said Brad defiantly, crossing his arms with a scoff. "Sorcerers? Magic? Those are fairy tales we hear when we're kids, like witches, and trolls, and—" He stopped, staring at Breeog warily.

"Dragons?" the dragon king offered with a smile. "I would be cautious if I were you; your mouth moves faster than your mind. Coincidentally, so does mine." He winked, driving the point home. Beside him, Gorbon's head sniggered

Eion frowned at the dragons, then turning back to Gwen and the other nine, he said "I know you find this hard to accept, but believe me, this is all real. Deny it, and you doom an entire world."

"Prove you are a shifter than," said Kendal, both assertive and shaken.

Eion glared angrily. "That is the human way, isn't it? 'Seeing is believing,' Man says, and yet he never opens his eyes. Very well, but someday you will have to learn that not all things will yield their secrets, no matter how much you force them." He sighed and pointed his finger at himself.

Eion turned into a dog, the dog turned into a dragon, a goblin, a human girl, a fish, a black creature that stood on his hind legs, and then finally into a hawk.

"That was you," Gwen gasped, as the hawk winked and smiled at her.

The hawk turned back into Eion. He then pointed his finger at all his human friends, and they underwent the same series of changes he had. Gwen felt a strange sensation as her innards moved and shifted around inside her. It was not a painful feeling; it was actually quite soothing.

Between the changes, she felt a wonderful sense of openness, as though she could float away and have no self.

When they all changed back into their regular selves, they stared at the shifter for a long time. Gwen quickly realized her awe was shown plainly on her face, and she replaced it with an attentive stare.

Lord Fairskin showed no expression. "Reckless," he mumbled, shaking his head tiredly. He sighed.

Gwen, after looking around and seeing the astonishment had not left her fellow mortals yet, finally spoke. "I believe you, Eion"

"Thank you. You all do, though you will not admit it."

"I still don't," said Brad, "This has been very elaborate, Eion, and I congratulate you on a job well done. But now, I'm tired, and I'm going home. I don't have time for anymore stupid magic tricks."

"Cheeky little guttersnipe, isn't he?" said Breeog lazily, "Want I should change the prophecy into the Great Nine and roast him now?" He grinned his golden grin and allowed some smoke to drift through his teeth. A slight flame ignited inside his nostrils, making his eyes flash malevolently.

Brad cowered and squeaked something incoherently. He took a few steps backwards, his teeth now chattering.

"Calm yourself, Breeog," said Eion, who seemed to be hiding his amusement, "he's just confused."

"Ah, then allow me to offer him some clarity." The dragon opened his maw and then snapped it closed loudly.

"Enough of this!" Lord Fairskin shouted, rising from his seat. "Shame Breeog; I would have expected better from you."

Breeog, unmoved, only shrugged.

The old elf shook his head, and then gestured grandly around the table. "A feast has been prepared in the Prophesied's honor, one big enough for each member of the Resistance to eat their fill. Come, to the dining hall. I will have someone bring the troops inside."

He turned to face the golden haired man on the right side of the table. "Tirmal, would you be so kind as to fetch them?"

The elf nodded. He raised a staff and mumbled a word. There was a flash of light and the elf was gone; a wisp of smoke rose from his now empty seat. The ten humans stared at the spot for a while, and then Lord Fairskin interrupted their awe.

"Honestly, these young elves always go in for theatrics. Strength lays in subtlety, children, remember that. Please follow me," he said as he got up from the seat and left the room. The others slowly stood up and prepared to follow him. There was much grumbling and talking and chatter of things Gwen either knew nothing about or simply didn't understand. As they passed the mortals, they bowed lowly and made signs of welcome with their hands. After he addressed her as "m'lady" several times, Gwen wondered again if she, like Eric felt earlier, was only dreaming.

Chapter 5

The Feast

L**ord Fairskin led the way** out of the conference room and through the labyrinth of corridors that filled the whole of the castle. There were staircases scattered everywhere; some led up, some led down, and some spiraled in both directions. There were doors of every shape and size lined on either side of the halls. Gwen was amazed that they hadn't gotten lost, but Lord Fairskin was certain of the way, never pausing even once.

Eventually, they passed through a high archway of marble that led into a gigantic room that was entirely constructed of gold. The ceiling was so high; five dragons would have had to stand on each other's shoulders to reach the top. Chandeliers and candelabras lit the room, making the gold glint and sparkle in the firelight. In the center was a table so long and so wide, it seemed to go on and never stop. It must have had some magic in it, because, though there was now a stream of creatures pouring into the room, the table never ran out of space.

They sat down to find that the food was already set out for them. Looking around, Gwen saw that they were sharing the table with creatures of every different size and specie. Dragons, with huge piles of food on their plates, amused themselves by setting the salads on fire, which angered many of those sitting next to them. Elves sat and conversed with each other, while the dwarves ate savagely and without pause.

As Gwen reached for a piece of bread, Lea tapped her on the shoulder. "So what do you think?" she asked.

"Of what?" Gwen grew distracted by Tirmal's sudden reappearance. He came forth from a sudden burst of blue flame and joined several talking elves that did not seem the least bit surprised by his magical entrance.

"What do you mean 'Of what'? Of all this!"

"To tell you the truth, I've felt as though some place like this existed the whole time."

"Really? Why?"

She shrugged, and then proceeded to butter the roll. "I don't know. It was nice to think of a place where that rat race back home couldn't touch," Gwen paused. "Did you hear what Breeog and Eion were talking about on the flight over here?" she asked.

"No, what?" Lea poured a generous amount of gravy onto her potatoes.

Gwen quickly retold what she had heard, though she was interrupted a few times as the dwarves nearest them argued loudly over whose beard was longer. One was already threatening to end the debate by unsheathing a small dagger from his belt. Still, Gwen ignored them, and managed to retell everything.

"Oh no, really?" cried Lea, once Gwen had finished. "Who do you think did it?"

"Oh, come on Lea," exclaimed Gwen, irritated. "It's obvious. It must have been Ozmod—"

"How goes the feast, m'ladies?" Eion had walked over and took a seat next to the girls, careful to avoid the flying vegetables that flew past. The fight abruptly came to a halt when a tomato was impaled on the dagger. The dwarf holding the weapon looked at it dubiously for a moment, and then the whole group of them laughed and called for another round of ale.

"Great," choked Lea in response. She resumed her meal taciturnly, but Gwen was wondering about something. A question prodded her mind, an uncomfortable question, and she was not quite sure how to ask it.

"Eion, come here," said Gwen, "I need to talk to you."

They got up from the table and walked over to a corner of the large hall near a potted oak tree with silver leaves and a burgundy trunk. Gwen pulled Eion behind the tree so they would be seen or heard.

"When Belzorg tried to kill me," she said, "how was it your arm didn't fall off when you put it in front of the blade?"

"Ah, why avoid what is really on your mind?" replied Eion, amused. "But I will answer anyway. I shifted my arm into a blade itself"

Eion rolled up his right sleeve and pointed a finger toward his elbow. It began to change. His fingers merged together and the tip became sharp. The whole of his arm went rigid. It changed from flesh to steel. The sides of his arm became saw-edged. Eion allowed Gwen to stare for a couple of moments, and he then changed his arm back to normal.

"Now," said Eion, "what did you really want to talk about?"

"Well," Gwen caressed a stray leaf, "I overheard your conversation with Breeog on the flight over here."

"And?"

"I'm sorry. I shouldn't have eavesdropped."

"No worries. I would have told you eventually." His eyes misted, as if he was in deep thought.

"But he killed—," Gwen hesitated, "Breeog said 'remains of' your family."

"Yes. One night, long, long ago, Ozmodion's troops attacked my village. Four goblins raided our cabin. My father and older brother were able to slay three of them. The other goblin killed both of them with one swipe. He then moved onto my other brothers. Goblins show no mercy. This one, name of Sronka, was no exception. Luckily at age ten, I was already an able swordsman. I couldn't kill him, but I did chase him off. I saved my mother and my sisters, for what it was worth."

"What happened to Sronka?" asked Gwen

"I joined the Resistance shortly after this incident, and he was the first goblin I ever killed. I avenged part of my family. But now I must avenge the other half. Ozmodion's days are numbered." His fists clenched and he smiled grimly. It was unlike any look Gwen had seen on him before; it was confidence, it was conviction, and it was anger.

It was hate.

She didn't know what to say. She mumbled something about "letting it go" but Eion shook her off angrily, his smile gone.

"Let it go?" he asked wildly, eyes wide. "*Let it go*? There are times when revenge is the only thing that keeps me going. Hate, Gwen, may not nourish, but it does fill. Ozmodion cut me in such a way that I will never fully heal. I may be callused and old, but that wound is still fresh with me. Such a hole *needs* filling. Such a hole *needs* hate."

Gwen, unconsciously, took a small step back.

"Scares you, does it? Ah, well, I could not make you understand even if I tried. You see Gwen, people fear hate because it can consume them. What they do not realize is that it is a tool. When used properly, it is a thing of power. Terrible, yes…but then, most truths are."

Gwen shook her head. "But like you said, it doesn't nourish. You can hate all you want, but it won't make anything different."

Eion narrowed his eyes irritably, but then he smiled. "Perhaps not, but…" He stopped. Shaking his head, he said. "No use in arguing. I just hope, Gwen, that you never understand the usefulness of hate…I hope you will never have need to."

She wanted to know more, but he would not go on. He simply guided her back to her set at the table. Now a choir of elf maidens was gathered on the far side of the Great Hall, trying to sing sweet melodies composed by elven musicians long dead, but were interrupted by a wide-eyed Brad, who seemed to be in awe of their beauty.

The feast itself was going splendidly. Kendal, Caitlyn, and Lea were talking and giggling with some more elf maidens, these even more beautiful then those trying to sing. They were all the daughters of Lord Fairskin, so Eion whispered to Gwen. Colin and Ryan told wild stories with a group of dragons. Every couple of seconds, the whole group would laugh wildly, the dragons sending bursts of flame to the rafters. Eric and Tyler, who were a little on the short side, talked to the dwarves who had been arguing. The two listened in awe as the dwarves recapped great battles the Resistance had undergone.

The party lasted for hours. The food kept coming, and the entertainment increased in magic with each new act. The dragons put on a spectacular fireworks show with the help of Lord Fairskin, who pointed his staff at the flames and transformed them into a wide variety of colors and shapes. The dwarves performed some kind of wild dance while chanting in their deep, gruff voices, bolstered by the mead they had been steadily drinking for the last few hours. Later, the elf maidens were finally dismissed and were replaced by a band of minstrels, who, with Brad's coaxing, played an upbeat sort of jig. Soon, even the drunkest of dwarves was on the dance floor waltzing through the night.

Around eleven o'clock, the festivities died down. The troops headed out for their camps outside, and the dragons taxied everyone to their designated camp.

Lord Fairskin walked up to Eion, Gwen and the others. "I have had your rooms prepared," he said, "Eion, will you please guide them to their chambers?"

The shifter nodded. He led them out of the Great Hall and to a gigantic staircase of silver. They climbed them until they arrived to an endless, torch-lit hallway with hundreds of doors. Eion led each one of the company into rooms with beds. The last one left was Gwen. Eion opened her door.

"Pleasant dreams," he murmured, winking at Gwen.

He turned on his heel and started to walk down the hall.

"Eion," Gwen motioned for him to stop.

Gwen ran up to him, leaned toward him, and kissed him on the cheek. She couldn't tell if Eion was actually blushing, or if it was merely a trick of the flickering of the torches on the wall.

"What was that for?" he asked, smilingly slightly.

"To thank you," replied Gwen, returning the grin, "for this adventure."

"Well, you are welcome," said Eion, "If you think today was something, wait and see what is in store for tomorrow!"

With that he headed for the silver staircase. Gwen watched him till he was out of sight.

Chapter 6

The Enemy

*H**undreds of leagues away* from where Gwen slept in Fairskin Manor, across the Emerald Plains, past the Silver Ice Sea, through the forest of Ÿalnz Dàr, was the Mountains of Midnight. There the sun never rose, and there was always a visible moon in the night sky. Over the mountains, lies Saurindon, a huge wasteland of red sand. This barren desert was a breeding ground of nightmares and was infested with indescribable monsters. And in the very center of the valley, was Taronest, the Fortress of Ozmodion. Its nine black towers seemed to stare sinisterly down on everything below them, covering the red sand in black shadow. On most occasions, the perimeter was simply stiff with minions of Ozmodion, but today on his orders, all the creatures in his armies were off training in some far reach of the valley. There were only several guards in the fortress and two goblins guarding the gate.

Fyras and Wozkarn were each about seventy-five years old (very young by goblin terms). Even though they were young, they were experienced in the ways of battle. They had fought in the Two Century War when the Resistance had tried to exterminate the last of the Ozra. When the Resistance's death toll became too high, the Resistance had let the Ozra be.

The goblins half dozed. Their post was almost redundant; none had ever gained entrance to the valley without the Ozra's leave. Far away to the north, they saw the red Gates of Angar Vûn, great and foreboding, deterring anyone foolish enough to cross into Saurindon. The goblins were about to drift into full sleep, when suddenly, Fyras saw something.

"Wozkarn," he shook the goblin's shoulder. "Do you see that frog in the distance?"

"Tough fellow," replied Wozkarn, rubbing the sleep from his eyes lethargically. "Must be if he scaled the mountains and trekked the valley."

"Yea', but what the blazes is it doin' here? They ain't stupid, frogs. They knows they got to have water, and they knows where to find it. Mountains and deserts? Nah, they steer clear of them."

"Bah, who cares? So the frog's a little loony. No matter; it will taste the same. I've not eaten since mornin'. I will gladly split it with ya, Fyras.

Fyras cackled joyously. Grinning, they both pulled out bows and nocked arrows against the frames, taking aim for the distant frog.

Surprisingly, the frog increased its speed and dodged two of their black arrows by hopping in ways frogs should not be able to hop. It jumped past the goblins, and squeezed under the very black gate they had been guarding

"""How'd it do that?" asked Fyras.

"Wha's it matter?" said Wozkarn, "More than our lives are worth to let a frog in! Oh, Captain Sarnor will have us hangin' in the dungeons by our ankles, and that's only if he don't kill us first! Come on!"

Wozkarn pulled out a black key from his pocket. He shoved it into a hole in the gate and turned. As he did, the gate creaked and opened slowly. Once they were beyond the portcullis, they used a different key on the iron doors beyond; they moaned ominously as they swung inward.

The goblins raced into the black abyss behind the doors, now absolutely sweating with panic. They grabbed torches that had been placed on the walls and ignited them with the flints they kept in their breast pockets. They then set off into the labyrinth that was Taronest. Straining their ears to hear for the sounds of the frog, they directed their torches in all directions, searching in vain.

"Oh, we're doomed, says I," moaned Fyras.

"Here now, wha's got you two in such a fuss?" a sinister voice boomed.

The goblins wheeled around. There behind them was Gornl. He was twelve feet tall, towering over the goblins by a good four feet. His legs and arms were so muscular that they looked like tree trunks. His jaw protruded a foot away from his face, and on either side of his mouth grew ivory tusks tusks. His black hair was wild and stuck out in unexpected places, and his eyes were black and cold.

He was a troll.

"A frog got 'round the gate," explained Wozkarn timidly, bracing himself for the inevitable jeers.

"Bleedin' hell, amphibians too difficult for ya?" laughed Gornl. "Ya're spent, says I. Save the executioner the trouble and go die now."

"Ya let it get past your post, too," smiled Fyras, exposing his sharp, yet rotting teeth.

Gornl's grin faded. "Ah, right ya be. Nothin' to do but to find it, then."

The three of them ran down the corridor, careful to make as little noise as possible, though this proved a difficult task for one so big and as so armed as Gornl. He lumbered along in the stupid way that all trolls do while his sword banged loudly on the side of his armor.

"Careful, now, you tryin' to bring ol' Blackheart on us?" hissed the goblins angrily, their eyes darting to and fro for any movement.

They turned a corner and came to a place where four corridors met. Following a whim, they turned left. They took five paces before Wozkarn ran into something solid and unseen.

"What was that?" roared the goblin, rubbing his nose gingerly.

"Who do ya think, ya sod?" said a voice in front of them.

Gornl raised his torch. There in front of them was a dark looking creature named Ulurn. He was standing on two legs. The whole of his body was covered in black, spiky hair. Each of his arms looked strong, and on the end of each of his eight thick fingers were foot long, purple, sharp claws. His face, also covered with fur, looked like that of a cat's. He had no visible ears and had glistening red eyes with violet, cat-like pupils.

Ulurn was a nightshade.

"What's wrong with you?" yelled Gornl, "Can't you give us fair warning when you're in front of us? That bloody black fur of yours is like a patch of shadows; can't see you in this damnable gloom."

"Ya're worse than a cowerin' shadow wolf, Gornl," said Ulurn. He flicked a non-existent piece of dust off his arm.

"Ulurn, you've an exceptionally loose tongue," said yet another voice behind them, "It will get you into trouble one of these days."

The group turned around to see where the voice had come from. In front of them was a wolf, a wolf with strong looking legs and fur blacker than a moonless, starless night; a shadow wolf.

"Gods, Shrar! Give us a scare like that; you be as bad Ulurn!" roared Fyras, doing the best he could to hide his fright.

"It is not my fault you are so excitable," said Shrar with indifference, "Oh, and Ulurn, I suggest you take back that witty comment concerning shadow wolves." Shadow wolves, as you might have noted, are a bit more eloquent than goblins, trolls, and nightshades. Still, you must not mistake vulgarity as stupidity when it comes to nightshades; they are exceptionally wry and clever, as you will come to see.

"Or ya'll do what?" asked Ulurn. "Give me yar temper? Speakin' of which, you might wanna wipe yar mouth there, Shrar; bit foamy, ya are."

Shrar growled and let out a snarl as he lunged and collided with the nightshade, sending them both to the stony floor of the fortress. The two wrestled and slashed each other for a moment until Wozkarn walked up and kicked them in their sides.

"Enough, we have to find that frog, or we are all done for," he said.

"Eh? What, what?" asked Ulurn slyly, as he collected himself from the cold stone floor. "A frog? Aw, Wozkarn too soft to do in the little toady? So sweet."

"Look you," replied Wozkarn angrily, his hands clenched into fists, "I'll do you a good 'un, I will. Let us see how chatty ya are when I put my boot up yar arse."

The nightshade flexed his fingers experimentally. "Let's." He grinned unpleasantly.

"Kill each other later," Fyras said hotly. "We've got that frog to find, or it's our skins."

The battle of threats immediately subsided, and the five of them continued down the corridor. Shadow wolves have a keen sense of smell, and soon Shrar had smelled him out. He led them all to a great, jewel encrusted door, the entrance to Ozmodion's chambers.

There was the frog, hopping in the same place over and over, as though he were going to press the five point star-shaped ruby in the center of the door. Fyras pulled out a crossbow, aimed, and pulled the trigger. The arrow sped toward the frog, missed, and pushed the ruby inward. The door slowly creaked into the chambers beyond. With that, the frog croaked triumphantly and hopped inside.

"Cheeky blighter, ain't he?" said Gornl as he pushed his way past the small group and stepped after the frog. The nightshade, the shadow wolf, and the goblins followed him through the doorway, exchanging tense glances.

Inside was a gigantic room of glistening red stone. Torches were lined across the wall. The ceiling seemed unreachable by any means. A large window was situated on the right side of the room, its black curtains drawn

There, in the center of the room was the frog, at the base of a series of steps that led to a red and gold throne. And in the throne sat Ozmodion, cloaked in glowing red. The unseen eyes under the hood seemed to stare at the frog. He raised a finger, pointed it at the frog and mumbled a few words in the dark language that he alone spoke.

The frog, swallowed by a blast of green light, underwent an amazing change. Fyras and Wozkarn gawked, for the frog had transformed into Belzorg, the Commander and Chief of Ozmodion's Goblin Armies.

To the others, this meant nothing. The goblin general had no power over the trolls, the nightshades, or the shadow wolves; such was the hierarchy of the Ozra. But when the guards had first walked in, they were so preoccupied that they had not noticed the other occupants in the room.

On Ozmodion's left side stood the huge troll Kahn, Commander and Chief of Ozmodion's Troll Armies. "Bleedin' hell," mumbled Gornl frightfully when he saw him, taking a few steps back, as if preparing to run. On Ozmodion's right stood the bear-sized shadow wolf Olarn and the sinister looking nightshade Gorez, Commanders and Chiefs of Ozmodion's Shadow wolf/Nightshade Armies. Ulurn and Shrar flinched involuntarily, sharing a look of vexation and absolute terror.

"So, you thought you would just eat me, eh?" Belzorg roared as Fyras and Wozkarn exchanged looks of terror.

"We're sorry sir," began Fyras. "We didn't know you had gone and had yourself turned into a frog."

"Not a productive pastime, I will agree," whispered Olarn to Gorez. The two sniggered cruelly.

"And you," Kahn reprimanded Gornl, "How could you let a frog pass your post?"

"I didn' mean to, sir, it is just tha' the halls be so dark and I be so tall I couldn't see the wretch go by."

Belzorg harrumphed, and Gornl started nervously. "No offense meant, sir, I meant no offense."

"Do him a good one for me, Kahn," said Belzorg wickedly.

Kahn grinned and nodded. He walked up to Gornl and raised his fist to hit the unfortunate troll, when Ozmodion spoke.

"Hit them not," he said darkly, "I will deal with them."

He turned to the group of his slaves. "You have failed me. The Red Sovereign does not forgive failures. Nor does he forget. Forty lashes each, I think, and thank your stars that that is all. I suggest that you report to the drill instructors at the other side of the valley. If ever I meet you again, if I so much as hear the whisper of your names, it will be, indeed, disagreeable. Now…*go*."

The group jumped in the air and ran to the door, tripping over themselves as they went. The doors slammed behind them loudly, catching Shrar's tail. An agonized yelp was heard; the four captains chuckled to themselves. Ozmodion snapped his fingers, and the doors opened wide enough to free the shadow wolf's tail. They closed once it was clear, and the captains shared another round of laughter.

Ozmodion raised a hand to silence them. He then turned to his captains, studying them critically, laughing quietly. "Quite a bunch you have trained for me," was all he said.

"'S'not my doin' that made that imp into the nightshade warrior he is," said Gorez indifferently, clicking his long claws together in emphasis.

"Ultimately, it is. Performance reflects leadership Gorez, remember that," replied Ozmodion, unfazed by the nightshade's vulgar speaking.

He turned to his goblin captain. "Belzorg, I realize it is fruitless to expect good news from you as you returned to us in such an amusing manner, yet I would enjoy hearing your report. "

"I failed sir," replied the goblin as he bowed his head, too ashamed to elaborate.

"Pathetic," mumbled Olarn, "Outwitted by a shifter."

"I would not be so cocky," said Kahn, "You have never met this particular shifter. In battle, his power is titanic; he can bring ogres to their knees with the unsheathing of his sword. He is merciless when he wants to be, and so slippery, always changing. Sadly, I can hardly say that I am surprised that Belzorg forgot about that, his intellectual span matching that of a pile of bricks."

Though Belzorg might not have been bright enough to understand the insult, he did recognize the condescending sneer. His face contorted into livid rage, his anger beyond words. He unsheathed his sword and ran at Kahn. The troll was equally as fast as the goblin. He unsheathed his sword. The two fought on for a few minutes. Then Ozmodion raised a finger, and spoke another spell in livid whispers.

Belzorg and Kahn were swallowed by orange light. When it lifted, the two of them were standing as still as statues, their faces caught in looks of surprised fear. Only their eyes moved, darting back and forth madly.

Ozmodion snapped his finger. Kahn and Belzorg fell on top of each other. They got up, put away their swords, and dusted themselves off, then turned to face Ozmodion.

"If you fought like that against the Resistance, this war would be finished and I would have long conquered the Magic Realm," he exclaimed sarcastically. He chuckled, waiting to hear a defensive reply. There was none.

He turned to Gorez. "Take three of your swiftest nightshades to Fairskin Manor. Bring me one of the fabled Great Ten Mortals. Bring the one that stands alone among her fellows. I tire of the Resistance's antics, and the aid of another Iltari will finish this war before it begins. Away! All of you!"

Gorez bowed, and exited the chamber first, eager to follow the sorcerer's command. The other three exchanged looks of hurt dignity, but said nothing and followed the nightshade out of the great chamber.

Ozmodion sat alone in the silence, watching the torches flicker on the walls, casting sickly red light across his chambers.

"Gone are the days of the Resistance," he said, speaking in the ancient evil tongue. "Their alliance will crumble, their power diminish. Now come the age of the Ozra, and the Red Sovereign."

He snapped his fingers and the torches went out.

Chapter 7

The Training

G*wen snuggled against the sheets.* Her bed was very large and very comfortable. There were layers and layers of cloth of the softest kind, enveloping her in warmth. There were two very large and very full pillows, and the headboard was beautifully crafted with ornate roses and lilies carved into the wood mahogany. The room itself was wonderful, vaulted with a high ceiling. A fair sized balcony lay just outside her window, and the hard, stony flow was covered with a great, squashy rug.

Still, Gwen did not sleep very well that night; she was haunted by some very strange dreams. First, she was standing on a stool as elf maidens presented with gorgeous gowns while they argued over which she should wear today. Then the elves were replaced by dwarves, who clasped hands and danced around her and sing in their gruff voices. As their song grew in volume and tempo, the dwarves melted away into the dream that Gwen had had before; the epic battle fought in a mystical land, and the fall of a terrible red sorcerer. She tried to scream, but like in all bad nightmares, she had no voice to do so.

Abruptly, she awoke to Lea shaking her violently. At first, she did not recognize her, her vision still blurry with sleep. When things came into focus, she saw her friend hovering inches above her face with eyes full of worry.

"What?" asked Gwen, stifling a yawn.

"You were screaming" replied Lea, concern still written on her face. "You were having a nightmare."

In a flash, the dream popped back into her mind, and Gwen shuddered reflexively. When she saw that Lea was now even more frightened, she smiled and with a shrug she said, "Yeah, I guess it was all that food last night; I don't think the wild boar agreed with me very well."

Lea's expression quickly softened and she allowed herself a giggle. "Me either. The goose was a little undercooked, too. But, come on, Gwen," she said, "They're serving breakfast.

"What time is it?" whispered Gwen, rubbing the sleep from her eyes.

Lea checked her watch. "Seven-thirty, our time. I wonder if it is the same here…" she added thoughtfully. Unsure herself, Gwen didn't answer.

She instead got out of bed and went to the closet, which itself was a separate room, large enough to walk into and fully equipped with a mirror and bench. She stepped inside and closed the doors. As soon as she did, the closet was illuminated with a yellow light that seemed to come from nowhere. She saw tunics and breeches and dresses of all kinds hanging from the rack. Uncertain of what to wear, she chose a simple tunic with leggings to match. After she had changed into the outfit, she noticed a chest of drawers set into the wall. In it she found soft shoes of leather. She found a pair in her size and slipped them on her feet.

After she stepped out, she noticed Lea was still wearing the clothes from the mortal world. Gwen smiled and offered her the closet. Lea thanked her, stepped inside, and a few moments later she stepped out wearing a green tunic with brown leggings. Satisfied, the two left the room and set off down the long corridor. They came to the grand, silver staircase and walked down it in wonder. The bright morning light streamed through the stained glass of the high windows, painting the room with a myriad of color.

They entered the great hall and found it almost completely empty; apparently, with the feast over, the great host of soldiers was back to living under rations and out in the camps. They did, however, find the other eight mortals already at the table. They all said their tired greetings between great spoonfuls of thick porridge that smelt strongly of cinnamon.

"Sleep well?" Lea asked everyone, as she and Gwen took their spots on the bench. As soon as they sat down, two bowls full of porridge appeared in front of them along with folded napkins and spoons. They kept their surprise in check, and instead began eating as though they hadn't in days.

"Not me. I couldn't get Belzorg's face out of my mind," said Colin. He shivered and he took a tug on his tea, to which he added so much sugar that it was almost white.

"No doubt, man," said Anthony with a nod and his mouth full. "I had nightmares not to be believed. I woke up twice sweating and panting."

"Really? I didn't have any trouble," mused Caitlyn, who was playing with her food rather than eating it. She stirred it with her spoon, making valleys and hills in the bowl. "That bed was wonderful. And those sheets were *so* soft; it was like sleeping between clouds."

They continued to talk and laugh and joke all throughout their meal. They saw nothing of their host, Eion, or any other being of any kind. As soon as they had finished, however, Eion stepped in, clad in a loose shirt, black breeches, and boots made of very worn leather.

"Are you all ready?" he asked while he slipped on a pair of gloves.

"For what?" asked Brad, draining his cup of tea.

The shifter grinned boyishly. "Training," replied Eion.

"Training?" asked Colin. "What do you mean training?"

Eion raised an eyebrow as he chuckled, "Really, you did not think we would march to war when you have had absolutely no knowledge of the ways of battle? Goodness, you would be cut to ribbons before we would have gone a mile. You will learn swordplay, archery, and healing. We will teach you to find chinks in armor and see flaws in technique. Ah, you will be soldiers before you know it."

"We have to *learn*?" groaned Eric. "Man, just when I get excited about missing school, you spring this on us."

Eion smiled and he patted Eric on the shoulder. "The cost of ignorance, my friend, is rather pricy if you value your head."

A strange look passed over Eric's face at Eion's words as though he had just swallowed mud or some other unpleasant thing. He gulped loudly and then gave a nervous kind of laugh.

Gwen shared his apprehension. Her nightmare came springing back to mind, and now she imagined herself in armor and wielding a sword, battling monsters like Belzorg. It wasn't a happy thought, and she began to wonder what she had gotten into.

"Still," continued Eion, clasping his hands together loudly, "that is the risk you run in adventures. They can lead to glory as easily as ruin, but they always lead somewhere. Yes indeed. They *always* lead *somewhere*."

He then made his way out of the great hall, gesturing for them to follow. With exchanged looks and a few shrugs, they got up and set out after him. They exited the castle through the main gate and across the oaken drawbridge. The brilliance of the day was astounding. The sky was of the same hue it had been the day before, and absolutely no clouds hung in the sky. And it was quiet; without all the noise from cars and electronics and factories and other bothersome technologies, all that could be heard was the birds' song and the rushing of the river.

Eion led over a knoll behind Fairskin manor, which led to a nice sized field tucked between the green hills. Under the shade of a large aspen that grew in the center of the glade waited Gorbon, along with an elf and a dwarf.

"Hello!" exclaimed Gorbon as they approached. "I hope the morning finds you well?"

"As always." Eion arched his back in a stretch. "Really, there is no such thing as a poor night's sleep here. Tirmal, I thank you and all elves everywhere for the comforts and luxuries you have extended."

The elf bowed lowly so that his long, golden hair swept the grass. "Our pleasure." He straightened, and then said, "You cannot allow yourself to grow accustomed to it though, Eion; the hospitality of the elves can only reach so far into the wilds of the world."

"Bah!" spat the dwarf, who was leaning on a great double bladed axe carelessly. "Elvish hospitality! Give me a dwarf mine any day over these silly ivory towers and green meadows. It has been long since you have come to our home in the mountains, Eion, and you are indeed sorely missed."

"One adventure at a time, I think, old friend. Maybe after this journey's over, I will pay a visit to the Zanashas."

"That will be a long time coming," mused the elf with a grave look, "unless we are very fortunate."

"Always so grim, Tirmal!" barked the dwarf in rough laughter. "And you elves are supposed to be all cheer and giggles!"

The elf smiled placidly. "And you dwarves are supposed to be all greed and avarice. I am glad to see that you, at least, do not disappoint."

The dwarf's face soured. He lifted his axe when Eion cut him off.

"Apologies, friends, I have forgotten my manners." He turned to face the ten mortals. "Allow me to introduce Tirmal Goldhair, Captain of the Elf Armies of the Resistance. And this is Varez, same position for the dwarves."

They had seen Tirmal before, but Varez was new to them. He was awfully tall for a dwarf, perhaps five foot four inches. He had a long red-silver beard, with green-gray eyes. He was attired with a sword, armor, and a crossbow. Tirmal was also dressed for battle, though his armor was much more elegant and clean.

"If you two are done with your usual banter," said Gorbon tiredly, though he eyed the dwarf and the elf in warning, "perhaps we can begin the Prophesied's training, eh?"

"Aye, Gorbon. We shall begin with swordplay," said Varez. As Tirmal passed out double bladed swords to the ten, Eion unsheathed *Raz'atr*.

Varez and Eion walked to a wide, bare patch in the grass, where they stood twenty feet opposite each other. Swords drawn, they stared intently for a few moments, then Varez raised his blade over his head and ran toward the shifter. Without hesitating, Eion slashed at Varez's sword forcefully, without extorting much effort. Varez spun away from the shifter and arced his sword toward Eion's head. Again the shifter parried, smiling now as a mischievous glint sparked to life in his eyes. *Clang clang.* As the swords connected, sparks flew into the air from the blades' friction. The fight was cut short, though, as Eion clashed *Raz'atr* against Varez's hilt, and the sword landed at the dwarf's feet. Before he could bend down to retrieve it, Eion brought *Raz'atr*'s tip to the bottom of Varez's goiter. There was no fear in Varez's face, only disappointment.

"Will we ever spar longer than a few moments, Shifter? Am I so easy to best?"

Eion laughed, lowering *Raz'atr* and allowing Varez to retrieve his blade. "Peace, my friend; I have only met a handful of fighters as fierce as you."

"Save any elf in the Magic Realm," called Tirmal, who stood just outside the bare patch, leaning on his staff in a bored manner.

Varez whipped his head around, his long beard following after his face. "You would be hard pressed to match me or any other dwarf, Razor Lobes."

Tirmal frowned and ran a hand over his pointed ears. Setting his staff down, he unsheathed his sword and jumped into the air. Before he descended, he flipped in a forward somersault. Awe, Varez did not even realize he was attacking before the elf had landed and brought his sword to rest on the dwarf's shoulder. Tirmal chuckled, revealing his fullest satisfaction.

"Really, Father Longbeard, if you do not check that tongue of yours you are going to lose your head. It is a small loss, I realize, but I am sure you hold it in a rather higher regard than I do."

Varez opened his mouth to retort, but he was interrupted as Gorbon sent a stream of fire into the air, roaring deafeningly. A hare that had been hopping cross the field started in fear and went lunging off into the opposite direction.

"If you interrupt one more time, I will eat the both of you," he said once he had stopped. His face seemed so vicious that Gwen was sure he wasn't joking. Tirmal, an elf and thus full of his confidence, shrugged and sheathed his sword. Varez was not quite as composed; he seemed very blanched from Gorbon's tirade, but he managed to nod and mumble some nonsense that Gwen took to be an affirmation.

Eion, shaking his head in delight, sheathed his sword and he addressed The Prophesied Ten again. "Well," he said to the group, "it is your turn."

Such a display was rarely seen. Within in five minutes, they had all sustained scrapes and deep cuts. As Eion was tending them, he said, "Ah, maybe we should start with poles." With an intent stare at the swords, he rounded their edges and dulled their points.

"There now," Eion said, smiling at his work, "No more eviscerations to be afraid of. However, they will still crack skulls and break bones, so please be careful."

Well, it did prevent external injuries, a very good thing too, for they would have mutilated each other had it not been for the safety precautions. Still, they managed to bruise and batter each other pretty nicely even without the sharp edges.

"Come now, Ryan, parry!" Tirmal said exasperatedly, who was sparring toward the outer edge of the bare patch. "Your enemies will tear you to shreds in real battle; my sisters handle swords better." In anger, Ryan took a swipe at Tirmal's head. The elf parried the blow with unnatural speed and poked Ryan in the stomach with so much force that Ryan fell to the ground.

As poor as Eric, Anthony, and the rest were doing, the boys' troubles were nothing compared to the girls'.

"OWW," screamed Caitlyn after her shoulder had been brutally bashed by a pole. "Lea! That hurt!"

"Well, you're the one swinging that pole all around like you're trying to catch butterflies with a net. You nearly took out my eye a moment ago."

Gwen, distracted by the argument, couldn't stop Kendal from slamming her pole against Gwen's shoulder until it was too late.

Eion, Varez, and Tirmal tried to help as much as they could. Gorbon, being a dragon, wasn't much help with swordplay and took the liberty to lean up against a tree and laugh loudly at their attempts, spouting short bursts of flame into the air.

As the sun sank past the distant mountains, the group headed inside with bumps and bruises. They sat down to a dinner much like the last one, though this one was somehow less enjoyable. Sore and tired, they limped up to bed.

☐

They awoke the next day to a very gray morning. After eating a hurried breakfast of porridge, they returned, weary and sore, to the field. There Eion stood with the others.

"Another key asset to war is archery," said the shifter, as though the lesson had never stopped. He shifted bows and arrows for everyone's use. As Tirmal passed them around, Gorbon growled and took off to the skies. Eion took little notice, only smiling to himself slightly. After they had all been armed, Tirmal raised his staff and sent five jets of light to the end of the field. Five little targets appeared where the blasts stopped.

"Now then," said Eion, shifting a bow for his own use, "watch closely."

He shifted a black arrow with red fletching right into the bow. In a split second, he had pulled the string back as far as it would go and had released his grip. The arrow flew straight and fast. It hit the middle of the closest target with a *fwwt*. Not but a moment after the arrow had hit the target had Eion shifted another arrow and shot it towards one of the other targets. It too hit the bulls-eye. Eion shifted yet another arrow. It also hit the middle of one of the targets after he had launched it. He continued to do this until each of the targets had an arrow in their center.

Eion turned to the group once more. "Now you try."

The group feebly attempted to hit the center of the targets. Every arrow fell short about fifty feet. The second and third volleys yielded no better results.

They practiced with the targets for hours, grumbling and moaning as Eion, Tirmal, and Varez gave advice and help.

Eion then shifted rocks into animals and watched the ten try and hit moving targets. Only Anthony made an improvement by shooting a doe in the rear. Out of sympathy, Gorbon swooped down and devoured the crazed beast.

Airborne targets were next. Eion released thousands of geese lose from a cage Varez had rolled to the field. Six birds fell after the whole group had let loose their arrows

Soon, the golden-red sun sank behind the green hills again, signaling the end of another painfully long day.

"That is enough for today everyone," said Eion. "We have barely begun your training. We will continue tomorrow."

They all returned to Fairskin Manor and slept through the night, heedless to their many aches and bruises. Gwen felt the swelling of a large welt that was rising on her forearm, grimacing as she touched it. A hot bath did little to ease her pain, though it did help her sore muscles to relax.

The next morning they all returned to the clearing, but instead of picking up their swords and fighting each other or firing arrows, Eion spoke to them all.

"When the time comes," he said, "you will not fight against each other, but against Ozmodion's forces. It is time you became familiar with them."

"We've already seen goblins," Ryan pointed out candidly.

"Ozmodion employs other foul things beside goblins into his ranks," said Varez darkly.

"It is also time to meet some of my closest friends and captains," said Eion. He cupped his hands over his mouth and called, "Steel, Fletch, Armor, Beast, Flame!"

The group waited. In a moment, a group of people came walking into the clearing. They all seemed about Gwen and Eion's age. One was burdened with many swords, yet he did not struggle from the weight. He had brown hair much like Eion, except Eion's was short and wavy and this person's was long and tied in the back. He had high cheekbones, and angled features that accented his green eyes perfectly.

Another had two bows and a quiver full of arrows on his back. He had shoulder length black hair, with a strong jaw, a heavy brow, and luminescent blue eyes. His short sleeves revealed his strong arms that were tanned and rippled with lean muscle. Many deep scrapes and scars marred his skin.

The third figure, attired with armor head to toe, adjusted the helmet that rested on his head. His pointed nose dominated his face, seeming to drain any other detail around his visage.

The fourth bore no weapons and simply wore a brown tunic. His hair was brown and wild, and his eyes were so brown that they were almost black. There was a strange glint in his eyes; it was not malicious, nor was it kind. It was simply there. Fine lines around his mouth suggested that he had known hardship, recently or long ago no one could say.

The last one was unburdened with swords or arrows as well. His hair was spiked and flaming red. He was smiling slightly, making him seem like a child who had a secret. His fingers had shiny welts and burns on his fingers and hands, though he did not seem to be inhibited by the injuries.

The five of them formed a half circle around the group, saluting Eion, who saluted back formally, though the effect was somehow diminished as he went to hug them and clasp their shoulders in a brotherly way. Then Eion turned back to face his ten mortal friends while the five men behind him waited silently.

"These are the captains of my army," said Eion, "This one," he gestured at the one with multiple swords, "is Steel. He commands my swordsmen. And this," he gestured at the one with bows, "is Fletch, who captains my archers. This," he pointed at the one with the helmet and breastplate, "is Armor, whose ten shifters shape and perfect our shields, helms, and other defensive weapons. This," he gestured at the one with wild hair, "is Beast, whose troop specializes in animal transformation. And finally this is Flame, who leads a legion of shifters who specialize in elemental shifts," he pointed at the one with red hair.

Gwen and the others introduced themselves. They found Steel, Fletch, and Flame to be open and cheerful, Beast to be gruff and short, and Armor was withdrawn, saying nothing at all.

"As I said, Beast captains a platoon of shifters who specialize in the transformation of animals," explained Eion, "He will show you the other minions of Ozmodion. The biggest and strongest of these are trolls. They are huge, stinking monsters with skin like leather and muscles as big and thick as tree trunks."

Beast changed into a twelve-foot tall creature, armed with a nine-foot long sword, with every inch of his body covered in two-inch thick armor. His face was horrific, with his jaw protruding a foot away from his face. He had multiple, sharp teeth and black, sinister eyes.

He roared and swung his sword at Eion. Eion wasted no time in unsheathing *Raz'atr*. He parried Beast's sword. The troll roared once more and shifted back into Beast.

Eion sheathed *Raz'atr* and turned to the group. "Another one of Ozmodion's miscreants is the shadow wolf. With four paws, they cannot wield swords, not that they need to with their razor sharp teeth and claws. They will jump on you, pin you to the ground, and finish you with such speed that reaction is impossible unless you are prepared long before they make their charge."

As Eion explained all of this, Beast shifted again, this time into a giant black wolf, as black and as dark as a midnight bereft of starlight. His teeth were stained red, the last remains of a victim no doubt. His body was very large and built, covered with fur black and slick, and his yellow eyes seemed to pierce all they gazed on. He let out an ear-shattering howl and lunged toward Eion.

Instead of attacking with *Raz'atr,* Eion shifted into his hawk form and took to the skies. Beast growled and changed to his usual form.

"The last," said Eion, returning to earth and his usual form, "is the nightshade. These are the swiftest and most agile of Ozmodion's minions."

Beast changed once more, this time into a black beast standing on its hind legs. He had a broad, long, purple claw on the each of his fingers. His black, spiky fur covered the whole of his body.

Beast slashed at Eion, but he had already unsheathed *Raz'atr.* Eion parried the attack. Beast growled and resumed usual form

Eion turned to the Gwen and the rest. "My captains and I will transform into these creatures while Tirmal and Varez help with your swordsmanship and archery."

"But we'll cut you down with these five foot long pieces of steel you'll have us using," pointed out Caitlyn. They had been given real double edged swords today, and they were fatally sharp.

"We will have a chance to stop you before you do," replied Steel in his surprisingly deep voice, those his eyes and expression remained kind.

And so the shifter began to change. Flame and Armor became goblins. Steel became a nightshade. Fletch and Beast became shadow wolves, and Eion became a troll.

Steel lunged at Tyler, claws outstretched. Tyler crouched down into a fetal position, covering his head. Flame and Armor ran toward Lea, Kendal, and Caitlyn with bent swords. The girls screamed and took cover behind Ryan, Brad, Colin, and Eric who were busy fending off the nightshade Steel. Tirmal and Varez exchanged smiles, and Gorbon covered his face with his claws to disguise his laughter.

Their training branched as they honed their skills. Swordplay and archery were practiced every other day. Other days, Lord Fairskin taught the ten the geography of the country of the Magic Realm they were in, Arconia. Tirmal taught the ten about magical herbs and plants with the help of two other elves, teaching the Ten how to tell the difference between poisons and antidotes. Breeog was gracious enough to allow them flights on dragons' backs occasionally.

And so their training continued on like this for weeks. The Prophesied Ten improved their fighting skills, and soon they knew the names of the neighboring mountains and glades and rivers by heart now.

One day, when they had finished all their training for the day, Eion stopped them before they set off for the castle.

"Lord Fairskin has called council again," he said, "Follow me."

Chapter 8

The Decision

*T**hey all met in the same room* as they had when they first arrived at the Magic Realm. The company was the same as well, but gone was the air of joyous celebration that had been so permeating before. Grim faces now surrounded the table, wreathed in shadow, for the drapes were drawn.

Lord Fairskin again sat at the head of the table, and he again raised his hands to talk. "The time has come to make a decision. The Prophesied has begun training and our armies are rallied."

"How many serve in our army by the way?" asked Varez.

"Twelve thousand five hundred from each race," said Lord Fairskin, "totaling in at fifty thousand strong. The forces of Ozmodion are four times greater."

"What!" exclaimed King Barthol, choking on the wine that he drank from an ornate goblet forged from bronze. He mopped the liquid from his beard with a handkerchief that Varez offered him before continuing. "Two hundred thousand followers plus the strongest sorcerer the world has ever known?'

"Oh yes," said Lord Fairskin grimly, "Since his death his minions have returned in increasing numbers. But we have to decide what to do. Ozmodion and his dark forces are like a lingering shadow spoiling all that is good in this realm. If they succeed to defeat the Resistance, Ozmodion will move on to dominate the Mortal Realm. We must stop him. The question is *how?*"

King Barthol spoke again. "We must bring the end to Ozmodion in some other way than death, for he is the first Iltari. If he is killed, the Magic Realm will change dramatically. The echoes of a fallen Iltari will reverberate long and devastatingly across the world, and the very order of magic will be disrupted."

"That is a chance we decided to make a *long* time ago," said Eion pointedly. "There cannot be any changes of heart now; Ozmodion dies."

"Of course," King Barthol retorted, "your race is more than willing to take this risk. There is little or nothing magic about you. You cannot even perform the simplest spells."

"May I remind your Majesty," Eion replied coolly, "that dwarves can not wield magic either? This is an art that can now only be performed by elves and a handful of other creatures that are either too few and scattered or too rare and nasty to be named. Why else do the elves all carry staffs?

Also, allow me to point out two other Iltari sit at this table, and neither one of them seem as frightened as you, O Dwarven King."

The dwarf king's face contorted in anger but, though he glowered venomously, he said nothing.

"I vote we march our army into Saurindon," continued Eion, ignoring Barthol's rage. "There we will confront Ozmodion's forces, while I lead the Great Prophesied to Taronest and destroy the Red Sovereign."

"This is a dangerous move for the Resistance," said Breeog, his head snaking through the door way beside Gorbon's. "But the Dragon Race and I second the motion." Gorbon's head nodded vigorously next to Breeog's.

"As do I and the Vra," said Lord Fairskin, "It is a risk we will have to take."

King Barthol was silent for a while, but he soon agreed. Now every eye at the table turned toward the Prophesied.

"Well," said Breeog, "What say you? Your word is as important as the rest of us."

Gwen looked at the rest of the group. They all nodded.

"We're ready," said Brad.

The rest all murmured their agreement.

"Then it is settled," said Breeog, "To war!"

"But we should at least try negotiations one last time with Ozmodion," said Lord Fairskin tiredly.

"Bah! The Blackheart does not reason anymore than the seas do," scoffed Breeog, but he did not argue.

Lord Fairskin pointed his staff at the table and muttered a few words. A flash of white light emitted from the tip, and when it passed, a glass ball laid before the old elf. He put his hand over it and again said some nonsense words that meant nothing to Gwen. The ball went very dark, and then it quickly became a cloudy color red. A voice echoed from the center of the ball.

"Impressive," it said, "I see one millennium has not seen your power reduced." The voice was very dark and malignant and brought disturbing images to mind.

Suddenly, the torches and candelabra inside the room were extinguished, and the room went unnaturally dark and silent. Then, a bright red flame erupted from the middle of the table. It flickered menacingly and a deep whisper resounded from its center.

"Though that hardly means much," the voice continued. "I see we are all ready for battle, aren't we?"

"This is your last chance to sign a treaty Ozmodion!" roared Breeog, his scaly claws clenched into tight fists. Tendrils of smoke drifted from his gritted teeth and his eyes were narrowed in concentrated hatred.

"We have been very reasonable up to this point Ozmodion," said Lord Fairskin in a strong voice.

The flame flickered for a moment, then rose to the ceiling and crackled loudly.

"Reasonable is not the word. Foolish, weak, stupid, all fit very nicely. This is your last chance to raise the white flag and surrender to me. My power flourishes! I will win whether you yield or you attempt to fight my immense power as the slow decay of time rots the whole of the world. *Your death I will savor greatly, Fairskin.*"

With a cry of fury, Tirmal jumped from his seat and raised his staff. He concentrated as a dark blue light blasted from the staff's tip and shot towards the flame, roaring with a sound like cannon fire.

The dark voice shouted some foreign words that Gwen did not understand. Tirmal's spell halted and became a black flame. It whirled around and launched itself back at its caster. The elf stood still, hypnotized by the spell's sudden appearance. Eion ran to Tirmal, unsheathed *Raz'atr*, and blocked with the sword before the spell collided with his heart. A flash of light exploded when the blade and the magic met. It passed, revealing Raz'atr to be glowing with a livid red. As it dimmed to its usual blue tint, Eion said coldly, "We will never surrender."

The flame screeched and roared. It expanded to the borders of the table, and the roof creaked and cracked in response to the heat being radiated. It underwent several color changes, and though the flame itself roared, the voice was as calm as ever.

"Well if it is not Eion *Shifter*," He pronounced the last word with a horribly venomous hiss, "I see you kept that sword well polished."

"Yes, but I look forward to seeing it stained with your blood," replied Eion casually.

Ozmodion laughed a terribly shadowy laugh. "Confident, are you not? Remind me to give you a lesson in manners when next we meet." The flame shrank to its original size then addressed the rest of the table. "If you will not surrender, then die. Every last one of you. I will cover the lands in shadow and flame, and while you all rot in your graves, your descendants will live to see the darkest age the world has ever known. You need not worry though, O Glorious Eion Shifter. I will spare you. It will do my heart good to see you tortured into madness until the earth, the sun, and the moon cease to exist and all life is lost. Oh, how I relish the thought."

Again the room darkened. The ceiling above them became transparent, to reveal a dark black overcast and occasional flashes of red lightning. Ozmodion's flame loomed over them, looking even more sinister than it had a few moments ago.

"Farewell, O Resistance! I wait for you at journey's end, fists clenched and sword drawn!" he said in a booming voice.

Another flash of red lightning and the flame was extinguished. The ceiling was no longer transparent and the torches had reignited.

"Can he be stopped?" Brad asked with a note of panic in his voice. Apparently, the sorcerer's words had really shaken him.

"Let us hope," whispered Lord Fairskin. He suddenly seemed much older and more worn than he had a few moments before. Gwen could not tell in the poor light, but it also seemed that new worry lines had crept across his forehead, adding to the network of wrinkles that already crisscrossed his face.

Eion stared at the empty space Ozmodion had occupied moments ago. He raised his sword above his head as he climbed on top of the table to address them all.

"My Lords and Kings, the shifters march to war with or without the support of the Resistance," he said.

Breeog spoke up. "The dragons march right along side you. Goblins taste delicious and my troops hunger for meat." His forked tongue flitted out with a hiss.

King Barthol unsheathed his sword and held it above his head as well. "The dwarves, too, are your allies."

"Then it is decided," said Lord Fairskin grimly. "We march off to war."

"So be it," said Eion. He turned toward his ten human friends. "And so begins your greatest adventure."

Gwen went to bed that night with many confusing thoughts on her mind. Would she survive this adventure? Would her friends? Why does Eion keep sending her looks of care and concern? And *what* was an Iltari?

She had remembered that Eion had listed it among his titles when she first met him. And now she had discovered that, not only were there two at the table today, Ozmodion was one as well.

She didn't have long to wonder before she drifted off into a fitful sleep full of unpleasant dreams.

Chapter 9

The Attack

G*orez had chosen his three nightshades* very carefully. He had brought the idiot who had abandoned his post in the castle, who, before the incident with the frog, had proven to be fierce in battle, as well as two others who had achieved high-ranking positions. Their plan was simple: kidnap the third Iltari and then make for the magic portal Ozmodion had left for them. They soon approached Fairskin Manor, after being magically teleported by the Red Sovereign himself. They found themselves on the banks of the Esialan River. The water was swift and yet it made little sound as it rushed passed. High above, thin tendrils of clouds roped about and twined across the sky, obscuring the full moon. *No Eclipse,* mused Gorez. *The Red Sovereign's pride will have to wait.*

He then turned and whispered something to his followers in the horrible language that only the nightshades could speak. They began their slow ascent up to the castle, blending in with the darkness like stalking patches of night.

⬜

Gwen stirred in her sleep, as uncomfortable thoughts plagued her dreams. Try as she might, she could not push the nightmares away. Thus she awoke, looking about her room for comfort from her dreams. Silver light from the moon poured in through her balcony window, casting the room in a dreamlike haze. For a moment, she thought she was still sleeping. Looking out the window, she saw some movement. She rubbed her eyes and looked again, only to find a hideous surprise waiting for her.

Outside, four shadows with red eyes tried to claw their way in with long, scythe-like talons that curved from their thick fingers. They made no noise, so deft were they with their dagger hands.

Gwen tried to scream but no sound would come. She reached for the sword underneath her bed and retreated into the darkness.

The shadows saw the movement. They screeched with glee and increased their effort. When they wedged the window open, they all jumped in with less noise then a small breeze passing across grass.

"We don't need light to see you, my dear," said one of the shadows lowly as he stalked the room. "Be good and come with us quietly."

They advanced toward Gwen. She tried to run away but they soon surrounded her. With out hope of escape, she slashed at them violently, but they parried her efforts with their long purple claws. She attempted to slay one of them again, and this time misfortune met her. One of the nightshades slashed the sword out of her hands, cackling wickedly. She gasped in surprise. Her pulse quickened.

The leader gestured at Gwen, and with a chuckle, one of the shadows stalked his way over to her, placing his claws against her throat. "Now be a good little girl, and say goodnight," he hissed slowly, revealing a black tongue that ended in a fork. She felt his claws tense up.

Then suddenly the nightshade inhaled sharply. His claws lost their firm grip. His eyes rolled upwards. He fell to the floor. "Goodnight," said a voice. Gwen turned to the doorway, where Eion stood, with an empty bow in his hand. Gwen looked at the nightshade. She had a good idea where the arrow was.

She ran toward the shifter to hug him. He greeted her with open arms.

"Are you okay?" he asked.

"I'm fine, now" Gwen replied, "But what about the others?"

One of the other nightshades lunged at the two. Eion didn't hesitate. He unshifted his bow, pushed Gwen behind him, and unsheathed *Raz'atr*. He parried the creature's claws and stabbed him in the chest. The nightshade fell, and the last two retreated out the window. Eion pointed a finger at one of them. His claws quickly shrank into his fingers. The unfortunate nightshade yelped in panic and tried to grip the side of the castle, but to no avail. He fell.

Eion rushed to the window. He looked down the castle in time to see the last nightshade jump from the wall and merge into the shadows.

"Leaving so early Gorez?" shouted Eion into the night. "Would your master approve of such cowardice?"

A dark voice answered. "You fight well against four of us, Shifter. But wait until the hour comes when you must fight an army of two hundred thousand. You will fall and we will laugh as you watch your comrades and friends die before you. I look forward to it, Kinslayer! Farewell!" No more was said

Eion reshifted his bow and sent a shower of arrows into the darkness. Admitting defeat, he unshifted his bow. He then concentrated in the window until it was sealed by bars. He studied his work for a moment, then, unsatisfied, he shook his head and instead filled the window with bricks and mortar. He nodded and returned to Gwen. She didn't notice him; she was too preoccupied with the corpses.

Following her gaze, Eion said, "Forked tongue. Hmm. Mr. Alez was right; I do see them everywhere."

"How am I going to help you?" Gwen asked in whispers. "I'd only be killed in battle; this proves it."

Eion eyes showed no expression, his face calm and bereft of feeling. His next words were strong, yet quiet: "Gwen, I gave you a very heavy burden when I brought you here to help us. For that I apologize. But, as the seed must someday turn into a mighty tree, so too must you carry this charge. Fate is a tricky thing; we will never really understand it. You can pretend to, but deep down, you know you are guessing along with the rest of us. You were *meant* to be here Gwen, to fight, to change the course of things. Few have such grand lots in life."

"I'd rather a simpler one, "Gwen replied, sullen.

Eion now shrugged. "Hopes and thoughts are not useless, but they cannot change things by themselves. All the wishing in the world cannot do anything to change the ways things are. Do not be afraid though; you are not alone. You have your friends, your memories, and, now, me. I promise I will help you on this long road you have been set on. You will not see its end for a long time…but no journey worth taking is ever short."

Eion bowed deeply, his deep, knowing eyes staying on Gwen's. He then straightened, turned on his heel, and left the room, closing the door gently behind him.

Chapter 10

The Resurrection

*G**orez had returned to the valley swiftly*; Ozmodion had transported the nightshade by magic. He knew he was in trouble and that Ozmodion was aware of his failure; the idea of explaining the story to his master made him sick.

When the transportation spell was complete, Gorez found himself standing in front of the doors of Ozmodion's Chambers in Taronest. He knocked, and trembled as it opened menacingly slow.

He stepped toward the middle of the room, where the series of steps led up to the golden red throne, in which sat Ozmodion. The black under the hood stared at Gorez. The sorcerer's gray fingers were arched upwards, tapping lightly against each other

"Well?" he asked quietly.

"I am sorry my lord," replied the nightshade captain, kneeling to the floor. "They ambushed me. Shifter was more than ready for a surprise attack; he slaughtered three of my finest nightshades without remorse. But I did manage to find who the third Iltari is. It is that dark-haired girl. Her aura, my lord, blinds. There is a boy, too, who seems as though he could be the Spoken One, but…there is something odd about this girl, a strangeness that I think even she is not aware of…"

Ozmodion hissed lowly. "I already know that, you blithering imbecile. I have known all along whom it was I was looking for, but that does not aid my cause if she is not here at my disposal. I told you to bring her here!"

Gorez looked at his feet. "I tried," he mumbled.

"You might remember, Gorez, that I do not forgive failures…" He let the words hang, and the sorcerer chuckled as Gorez gulped loudly.

"Oh, my lord!" cried the nightshade as he threw himself at Ozmodion's feet. The wretched creature kissed the floor underneath the warlock's robes. Ozmodion returned the gesture by kicking Gorez across the mouth, ignoring the yelp of pain that ensued. The nightshade took several paces back and rubbed his chin tenderly, careful of avoiding the long, dagger-like claws that obtruded from his fingers.

Ozmodion sighed, "No matter. I will just have to resort to different tactics. Leave now, and make *sure* I am not disturbed." He paused, and chuckled. "And Gorez, should you *ever* fail me again, you will certainly feel my…displeasure."

The point hit home. With another bow, Gorez stalked out of the room, slamming the great doors shut behind him.

Alone now, the red sorcerer rose from his seat, and hissed a syllable. With a loud crack, a black cauldron appeared in the center of the chamber.

With a few claps and a nod, tendrils of silver smoke snaked from the cauldron as a bubbling sound resonated inside of it.

Now, Ozmodion rolled his sleeves up to his elbows, and from his mouth poured a stream of old rites and incantations. The light of the chamber seemed to dim, and an eerie red glow emitted from Ozmodion. The cauldron hissed and popped; it too was shining with some inner aura.

From his now outstretched palms, a green flame ignited and, leaving his hands, floated over the cauldron, where it sunk into the contents.

Immediately, a great dark green flame spouted from the cauldron. Slowly, laughing with satisfaction, Ozmodion walked toward it, uttering a final string of words.

Upon the last syllable, a blast of blue light engulfed the cauldron. Then, with a sound like a volcanic eruption, the cauldron exploded and went up in a wisp of thick black smoke. Ozmodion stepped back and waited for the haze to clear.

When it did, a large black dragon emerged from the smoldering ruin of the cauldron. He had piercing red eyes and a long horn protruding right above his nostrils, with wings gigantic and dark; they loomed like clouds blocking the sun.

"Vaeirnïr," said Ozmodion, "my old general."

The dragon looked around the chamber, swiveling his head slowly and taking everything in. His red eyes were filled with a curious, analytical look, as though he were trying to recognize where he was. His neck then arched forward as he examined himself with particular interest.

"Do I live again?" he asked, as he felt his underbelly with his claws.

"Yes," hissed the Red Sovereign. He laughed quietly. "Yes, you live again. Thus am I a generous sovereign."

Vaeirnïr inclined his long neck in a bow. "I am forever in your debt, O Master."

Ozmodion chuckled. "Indeed you are. Are you prepared to resume your post as my second-in-command?"

Raising his head, the dragon seemed to hesitate. "My lord, I do not want to seem ungrateful, but—"

"I shall be blunt," interjected Ozmodion testily. "I do not present you with a choice. I gave you your life; I can easily take it back. Besides, do you not crave revenge? Will you suffer a treacherous usurper to live? Would you not return to your throne as Dragon King?"

A snarl, and then the dragon looked down at the red sorcerer, its eyes a red flame. "Yes."

Ozmodion laughed forebodingly. "Good. Remember, Vaeirnïr, the Red Sovereign remembers those who help. Your service will not be forgotten."

Ozmodion cleared his throat and continued. "Now then, I want you to fly the Mountain of Antiquity. A few hundred gnomes and hobgoblins guard its insides, but I trust that will not be too difficult. Go to the Forbidden Archives, and bring me back the Scrolls of the Necromancer."

The black dragon flinched upon hearing the name. "The Scrolls? Why, oh, why the Scrolls my lord? Those bewitched documents have brought the fall of countless empires; pestilence has always followed them throughout the ages. Why ever would you risk it?"

Ozmodion hissed once more. "Vaeirnïr, do not question me. I am ordained by gods; why would I fear the Scrolls? Their power holds something I dearly covet, and I will tap the magic they hold. They are crucial to this war. Would you have the Resistance rise up and quell all that we have worked so hard to achieve?"

This was Ozmodion's way, of course; he had learned the dragons' trick of beguiling and manipulating with words. It was this talent that made him so powerful, not his magic. He could make day seem night with a few well placed sentences. In the days of his uprising, he swayed and corrupted many without use of his magical powers, and though his magic was very great indeed, greater still was his tongue.

"I ask again, would you be a slave to the Lord Fairskin?" pressed the sorcerer, elated as he watched the dragon's temper rise. "Would you bend a knee to that broken elf that uses his staff for a crutch more than a weapon? Would you have the dwarves mine and desecrate the earth for their gems? Would you have the shifters, descendants of men and dragon slayers, chain your kin and treat them as monsters?"

Vaeirnïr, now very angry, let out a great spout of flame as he roared, "Nay! Let sun be quenched and moon be crushed before any such evil comes to pass!"

Ozmodion chuckled once more. "Go, then."

With that, Vaeirnïr left. He jumped out of Ozmodion's window, and soared over the mountains and out of sight. Ozmodion watched the great dragon until it could no longer be seen. He then returned to his red throne, chuckling with pleasure.

Chapter 11

The Journey

***G**wen woke up long before the sun rose*. She lay awake staring at the ceiling, thinking of what the day would hold. She'd be marching off to war. It was likely that she'd see some newfound friends die. This was not a fantasy book where good always triumphs. Evil *can* prevail.

After a good long while of contemplating and pondering, the sun rose. She got up, washed her face at the basin, dressed in a blue tunic with matching leggings, put her sword belt on, draped a cloak over it all with a hood, and left her room.

When she arrived at the great hall, she found all her friends were dressed much like her. They had had only a few moments to talk as they ate breakfast when Eion walked in, clad in shiny new armor with just a little bit of leather wrapped around his arms and shins where there was no metal protecting them. His chest plate slipped over his head and buckled at the sides. No helmet was present, and his brown hair seemed out of place compared to his armor. He seemed a little taller as well. He smiled as he surveyed the group.

"Ah, granted those clothes are comfortable, but they are not too effective at blocking swords and arrows. You are much better off being fitted. ARMOR!"

The shifter came clanking into the hall, his armor colored a traditional gray. As usual, his face was hidden behind the helm and scarf, and as usual he remained silent.

"Suit them up," instructed Eion, "Lord Fairskin wishes to see us all, so make it quick."

Eion walked out of the room. Armor raised a finger and pointed it at Tyler. In a blink of the eye he was wearing a light-blue suit of armor. While he examined the protective covering, Armor repeated the process until everyone had breastplates and helmets. Gwen emerged from the transportation with a chain mail shirt that was so light she could hardly feel its weight. She grimaced and slipped her cloak on over it.

After they had all been suited, Eion poked his head through the doorway to check on them.

"Good, you are ready," he said. "Armor, join ranks. As for you lot, follow me."

Eion led them into the entranceway. There they came to a halt. "Brace yourselves for a sight you will find hard to forget."

He opened the doors, and immediately, their jaws fell as Armor, unfazed, made his way past, leaving them to goggle.

The grassy field they had arrived at so long ago was now covered with soldiers of the Resistance. Dragons, elves, dwarves, and shifters were all standing in formation, ready for battle. Banners and swords were held aloft as rows of armor sparkled in the sunlight. Only the dragons were unadorned with weapons, though their claws and teeth, glistening with ivory, onyx, gold, silver, and diamond, would serve the same purpose.

Eion led them to the shifter brigade to face the castle, situating the ten mortals into ranks. He then joined Breeog, Barthol, and Lord Fairskin, who stood gazing upon the troops from a raised knoll.

As the shifter joined them, Lord Fairskin raised his hand to speak. "Today we march off to do Heavens, and possibly Hell's, work and vanquish the festering malignancy known as Ozmodion." At this there was a roar of cheers that rippled across the armies with a resounding pulse. "Before we leave though, I have some distressing news. The Head Hobgoblin of the Mountain of Antiquity sent me urgent news via telepathy this morning. The mountains highest security vaults were broken into last night. Though hundreds of the mountains guards were murdered, a few survivors confirmed the culprit's identity. It was a great black dragon with piercing red eyes. At that I worried. I looked into the past to see what it was Ozmodion was up to yester eve. I picked up traces of a strong Resurrection Spell. So beware, for Vaeirnïr Bloodshedder has returned."

At that, a furious series of roars erupted from the dragon division. The other armies seemed livid too, but the dragons reacted with such a rage that Gwen, for the first time, was afraid of them.

Lord Fairskin raised his staff into the air, releasing a dark red orb the size of a beach ball from its tip. It exploded with a deafening *boom,* and the roars ceased immediately as the four armies whipped their heads in search for the source of the noise, finding only Lord Fairskin with his hands raised again.

"Enough. That will not help. We will just have to deal with that particular…" he paused for lack of word. "…atrocity," he decided. "I trust our objective is well known to us all. Therefore we begin our march. Be wary though, for we face months of hardship and travel."

He nodded to Tirmal, while the other three leaders nodded at their captains. As one, they acted, signaling their buglers, who responded by placing their instruments to their lips and making one, high note. Quickly, the humongous force mounted horses and ponies, while the dragons took to the skies. Another round of trumpets, and they set off, their heavy footfalls seeming to shake the very core of the earth. They veered to the south, and in a short while they passed through the village Gwen had flown over on the day of her arrival so long ago. There were banners overhead and bouquets in the street; cheers erupted from the sidelines and houses as the elves cried their farewells. From one of the balconies, a lone, mandolin-playing minstrel sang:

I sing of a story
Both sad and sadly true
An epic with tainted glory
So listen as the characters pass through
Two wills fight for power
As they have since time's dawn
Each hath the strength of a tower
But neither the sight from beyond
Like spiders they spin a web
Of change and of shifting shape

Always they will spin whilst harmony shall ebb
Trusts are broken; there are dreams of escape
Backwards and forwards their song ever sways
Good and evil locked in titanic clash
While we lament for better days
In their wake we flounder and splash
Will the ending ever be in view?
Or shall the world know its end?
For against these opposing powers
Which force of arms can contend?

The words echoed hauntingly in Gwen's ears. Before she could get a good look at the minstrel, he had disappeared from the balcony

Eventually, they left the cheers and banners behind, and that was the last time that the company ever saw the beautiful village and their fair inhabitants, though Gwen was unaware of this as she looked over her shoulder and watched it sink into the distance.

As the sun traveled across the sky, so did the company across the land. Soon, Fairskin Manor was only a very small dot on a hill, and the Esialan River was thin blue line that bordered the horizon. Eion halted his horse to look once more on the place he had temporarily called home. He sighed, and then smiled as if he felt a sense of adventure and daring well up inside, feelings that had long been dormant.

"Onward!" he shouted, and wheeled his steed around to lead the shifter troops again.

And so the beginning of the "Ten Century Unrest", as it would come to be called, began.

Chapter 12

The Questions

*S**everal long weeks passed* uneventfully. Though the landscape changed and they left Fairskin Manor a long time ago, progress was unnoticed. At first, they passed through friendly lands, full of cheerful beings and luxuries such as bed and food. But soon, they left those lands behind, and traveled to places with people who spoke with strange voices and in queer languages. Then they came to places with no people at all, with nothing but the road to accompany them.

Each night, the Prophesied Ten continued their training regimen, and they grew stronger and quicker. The sword that Gwen had found so heavy now felt lighter, and while night after night she was defeated in the soaring, she was pleased with her improvement. The others too made progress, but only Ryan seemed to match Gwen.

Despite all of this, Gwen was still tired and irritable. It had been almost two months since she and her friends had left the mortal world. She missed her family, she missed her home, and she missed her life. As she rode beside the soldiers of the Resistance, she wondered what her parents were doing without her, if they were worried, if they had given up hope of her return, and if they all missed her, short of her brother, perhaps, who now had the bathroom all to himself.

These gloomy thoughts ate many miles of the march away, but still, progress almost went unseen, except for the fatigue and pain of riding, as the unchanging land merged into a great expanse that seemed to have no end. Then one day, long after the minstrel had played his song, the armies came to a halt.

They had reached the Emerald Plains. Gwen had pictured it to be a small field, but in reality, that was not true. They had just climbed a large set of hills that were placed leagues upon leagues away from the Esialan River, just to arrive in an endless sea of green that stretched in every direction. To some, the endless expanse of grass was uplifting, as though their journey was progressing smoothly. To others, it was just another place to march.

"We've ridden for miles and miles," Gwen stated to anyone who would listen, "but for what? Saurindon is barely any closer than it was when we began. We've marched for weeks at a breakneck speed! The majority of you are immortal, but we definitely aren't. We just might die from exhaustion." The other mortals silently agreed.

The hawk that Gwen had seen so many times before soared overhead and swooped down to land on her shoulder.

"Keep in mind," it said in Eion's voice, "when your heart wants lifting, it does not need its burdens pointed out."

With that, he winked and flew off to resume his lead in the ranks. Gwen just stared at the groups of shifters in front of her. She then recognized Steel and rode her way over to him to talk.

"Steel, you're Eion's oldest friend; can you tell me about him? I've known him for two years as one of my closest friends, and now I feel like he's a complete stranger."

Steel laughed. "There is not a lot to know, or rather there is simply not a lot known at all. Still, there is nothing like asking when you want to learn something. I say talk to him yourself."

Gwen frowned, but she knew she wasn't going to get anything more from him. She nodded her thanks and took off to follow his advice.

She raced to the front of the line, dodging and weaving around the many horses that bore the soldiers of the Resistance. There were many whinnies and brays, and the soldiers grumbled and grunted their protest, but, ignoring it all, she pressed through. When she finally came to the front, she stopped and stared in wonder. Without a swarm of soldiers obstructing her view, she could see the Plains. The grass was knee high and smelt sweet and in the distance, Gwen could hear a brook babble on as it went over rocks and stones. The mountains at the far edge of the valley seemed distant and small.

To Gwen's left, Eion rode on a brown steed with a black mane. Its magnificence made Gwen's mount look like a mule, though she wouldn't have been surprised if Eion had shifted his horse from an old mare. Perhaps she could do the same. Eion's eyes were firmly fixed on the horizon, and he took no notice of her.

"Um, Eion?"

He turned to fix her with that disconcerting stare. His irises still rotated and his pupils were still deep. But before she could become hypnotized, she, averting her gaze, said, "I have some questions for you."

"Questions? And what are they?" he asked, smiling slightly. There was a new look in his eyes, one of peaceful tranquility instead of deep thought.

"Well," she began uncomfortably, remembering the conversation on dragonback so very long ago, "Who was Tactics?"

Eion's face fell. He tore his stare from her to look ahead. He quietly answered, "He was my general in charge of battle strategy. He was guarding my mother when Ozmodion came."

Gwen nodded sadly and, sensing Eion's anguish, she moved onto another question, this one stemmed from curiosity of the new world she found herself in. "Where did the elves come from?"

Eion laughed, the cheer in his face returning quickly. "Ah, see now, that is a story that I cannot fully tell without a few hours. The elves are the creation of the gods, and the gods cherish the elves more than anything else that lives on this earth. They are not as old as the dwarves, the dragons, or even humans. They are the perfection of all forms of life. They are all, as you can see, fairer than regular people. They live extraordinarily long lives and they are one of the few creatures born with natural immortality. Magic comes to them innately, and both genders are trained in combat and enchantment. The elves are divided into eleven kinds, and are therefore placed in eleven clans. Each clan is independent of each other, and functions under the rule of their lord or lady. The Vra is the only clan native to Arconia, thus they are the only clan to fight with us."

Shocked, Gwen asked, "But why? Surely all the clans would unite if they were all threatened."

"Aye, but they were *not* all threatened. Ozmodion only succeeded in terrorizing Arconia and its surrounding countries, none of which are home to the other clans."

"Why?" Gwen asked again, "I would have thought he would want to rule the entire world?"

"I have no doubt that is what he planned, but he did not intend to be resisted on such a large scale. See how much good the Resistance has done?"

"So why does he believe he can do it again?"

Eion's face darkened. "Ozmodion is corrupt in many ways, but he is still sane in one: he learns from his mistakes. Every time we faced the Ozra, it became harder to defeat them, because Ozmodion found flaws in our strategy each time we fought his forces. They were practically invincible the last time we clashed with them. We would not have survived the battle if Ozmodion had not been struck down that night. His forces are much stronger this time, and I fear that he may have new and better plans. Plans that could insure his victory."

The news deeply troubled Gwen. "Is there any hope, then?"

Eion turned to watch the horizon. "There is always hope, no matter how weak. Without hope, we would not march. Without hope, Ozmodion has already won."

The wise insight startled Gwen, and for the first time she forced herself to realize just how old Eion was. The friend she thought she knew so well was gone and instead she rode next to a man who was completely strange to her. And then it dawned on her; she was not dreaming, and these mysteries were all real. She felt very ignorant as she thought of how she had been raised. It all seemed so superfluous and unimportant when compared to the black evil she knew lay at the journey's end. She felt sick at the thought of the lies she'd been told, lies spawned from the ancient civilizations of men who hunted down the ancestors of her new friends as though they were vermin.

Gwen pushed it from her mind and moved onto her next question. "And what about the dwarves? Where did they come from?"

Eion laughed again and turned back to face her. "Oh, theirs is a story worth the telling." A dragon flew overhead, roaring in his wake. Eion took a moment to think again. "The dwarves came from the heart of the earth, or so they say, after they were created by the Earth God, Joao. They dug and dug upwards for years and years, and when they finally reached the surface, they found a vast collection of hills and mountains, which they mined to their hearts content. They found a fortune of jewels beyond measure or price, and they built cities beneath the hills with gates of gold and pillars of silver. Even the poorest of them had enough to spend their money on nonsense. Oh, they had the occasional problem of plundering dragons and picking the next king when a royal line was dead but those were their largest problems and were easily remedied. Now the dwarves that we march with are from the Zanasha mountain range to the far north."

Gwen nodded. "What about the dragons?"

"What about them?"

"Where did they all come from? They're supposed to be mythical."

"*That* is the ignorant statement made by one who has grown up with the damnable dribble of frightened mortals. But in any case, the dragons were created right after the earth was, and they are the oldest living creatures on the face of the planet. They too first appeared underground at the very core of the earth. It is said that they were spawned from both the God of Fire and the Goddess of Wind. They flew to the surface up volcanoes and cracks in the ground. They do not take any long-term mates, but rather just breed once a year. They love gems and gold and delight in the hording of treasure. A dragon's importance was and is decided by the size of his or her horde, which they keep in their caves and guard jealously.

"The dwarves have long despised them, for the dragons slaughtered many of them for their wealth. They are inclined to take young noblewomen as hostage and have them serve them in their cave, and they enjoy fighting knights or princes or whoever else thinks their self capable of challenging a dragon, but that was of course in the days before the Resistance. They have always been intelligent and cunning and they adore riddles and they love to be admired and flattered. They enjoy being mysterious and often say things that have hidden meanings. Their libraries are fountains of knowledge and they always leave you feeling as though they know more than they let on, which they usually do."

Gwen nodded vaguely, stunned that so much of the dragon-lore she had heard in the Mortal Realm was true. "And how is it they fly?"

"They fly because of a build up of hydrogen in their ribs. Hydrogen is lighter than air, and gives lift. Many believe that dragons fly by beating their wings. But that is not the case. Their wings are no more than a turning device, with the tail as the rudder."

"How does the hydrogen build up?"

"After eating, dragons swallow limestone to grind their food. When the calcium in limestone mixes with their stomach acid, hydrogen is formed."

"Oh...but then how do they breathe fire?"

"Some of the hydrogen absorbs into a third lung. When they contract that lung hydrogen is released."

"But then they'd just be exhaling gas."

"But hydrogen is flammable. Dragons have certain magics in their throat that generates extreme temperatures. When the hydrogen passes the throat, it ignites and thus, fiery breath."

Gwen thought about this for a moment, trying to let it all soak in. "Where do dragons live, then?"

"Many live on the Mirithin Plateau. There is a series of caves up there where a large population of them can live comfortably. Some choose to live a solitary life and are scattered across the globe. Their politics are very unique; they are the only race that has one king. Their cousins, the wyverns, have never consented to this hierarchy, and thus the two don't get on well"

"And who was the first dragon king?"

"When the land was dark and unshaped, the dragons were un-united and without leadership. Fights were common. They killed each other so often that they seemed a dying race. Then one dragon claimed Mirithin for himself, and he defeated anyone who challenged him for it. He was a fierce fighter and was unmatched by any creature the world had known. He soon gained respect from his entire race, and they later appointed him king and he ruled for thousands of years."

"What was the dragon's name?"

Eion bowed his head and sighed. "Vaeirnïr."

Gwen whipped her head around to face him as recognition struck her. "Isn't that the name of the dragon who invaded the Mountain of Antiquity? Why was everyone so furious? You'd think they'd be happy the first dragon king had returned."

"During Ozmodion's rise to power, all the races were scared. He was beginning to dominate all life, and Ozmodion offered positions of power to the leaders of the races if they would join the Ozra. None accepted…except Vaeirnïr. He pledged his entire army. Well, the dragons on a whole are not so easily swayed. They turned their backs on Vaeirnïr, appointing his great-grandson king. Vaeirnïr in turn betrayed his fellows. With his newfound position as Ozmodion's second in command, he attacked the Mirithin. Trolls caught dragons in their sleep and slaughtered them, earning Vaeirnïr the title "Bloodshedder". This angered the new dragon king greatly. He went to the elves for magics and spells. The next time Vaeirnïr dared to approach the Plateau, the dragon king placed the terrible Life Drain Curse on him. Vaeirnïr's soul was ripped from his body and mind, left to die. Ozmodion locked Vaeirnïr's body into a vortex of dark spirits. Where his soul went, no one knows. But Ozmodion has resurrected Vaeirnïr's body and soul, and I will wager he is stronger than ever and seeking revenge on his heir."

Gwen shivered with fright. "Who's his great grandson? Does he still live?"

"Oh yes. In fact, he still rules the dragons."

"You mean it's Breeog!"

"That is right. But do not let your heart be troubled. He is not too worried. Even though Ozmodion cursed the dragons crippling their power to wield magic long ago, Breeog still has the entire dragon army at his disposal."

That all makes sense, thought Gwen. Then another question prodded her mind, though this one was difficult and very awkward to ask.

"May I ask you one more question?"

Eion chuckled. "You just did, but you may ask another."

"How did Ozmodion come to be?"

Eion's smile faded. The shine in his eyes darkened, and the happy note in his voice disappeared entirely.

"Now *that is* a story." He paused and looked over his shoulder to check on the troops. Gwen looked into the distance. They had reached the center of the Emerald Plains.

"Halt!" Eion raised his arm high. The great company responded; the Plains sounded eerily quiet without the thunderous marching of feet and the clang of armor and weapons. Breeog swooped down next to Eion, and Lord Fairskin and King Barthol, after repeating the order to stop, joined the other two. They gathered in a circle, obviously debating about something. For a short time, they spoke in quick but soft whispers. Gwen tried to hear what they were saying, but they were just out of earshot. Eventually, Eion nodded and, stepping away from the circle, pointed a finger at his throat. When he spoke, he did so with the magnified voice he had used to call Breeog to their aid on the day of the mortals' arrival.

"We camp here tonight."

The captains and lieutenants nodded, and gave the order to their troops and patrols. Like a melting block of ice, the great mass of soldiers broke apart, spreading out as they broke open their packs and prepared to set up camp. They pulled out blankets and sheets of canvas, and pretty soon, a sea of tents sprung from the ground like a fires woken from cinders.

Eion turned to Gwen. "Lord Fairskin and I alone know that story, beside Ozmodion himself, of course. I shall tell it to you all around the fire tonight."

Gwen nodded and set out to help erect large tents that would house all but the dragons, who would be content to form a perimeter around the camp and sleep on the ground. Gwen would share a tent with the rest of The Prophesied Ten, and she expected nothing else. She watched as a patrol of dwarves was sent into the far reaches of the plains to look for fallen trees or stumps to be used as firewood. Hours later they came back with what seemed to be an entire forest in their hands. Thousands of mounds of wood were piled up. As the dwarves made rings of stones around them, the dragons ignited the mounds with their newly explained fiery breaths.

As twilight crept into the sky, the giant company began to surround the fires. The Prophesied Ten, Eion, Breeog, Gorbon, Varez, Barthol, Tirmal, and Lord Fairskin gathered around the largest one. Finally, when dinner had been cooked, eaten, and cleaned up, Eion pointed a finger at the flame. Though it did not change by any visible means, Eion stepped into its center without flinching. He began to speak.

"I have been requested to tell a story, an epic that has its beginning and ending...and ends at a beginning. Many, many ages ago, before the Reflection was created, and long, long before the shifter race was born, a fateful event occurred. Vundin, the God of Time, peered into the future as he often does, and saw a vision that depicted unrest between the races and the end of magic forever. Avria, the Goddess of Death, took it upon herself to ensure the continuance of magic, and she conceived the idea of a mighty sorcerer to pass the wonders of magic on. For millennia, she honed her plan, leaving nothing to chance. When she was ready, she planted her seed into a young noblewoman. Outraged to see her pregnant and not yet wed, the noblewoman's family abandoned her and stripped her of her titles. Alone and frightened, she fled.

"The required nine months passed. Avria's patience would soon be rewarded. One dark night, in a small cottage on the outskirts of the golden town of Maerna, the baby boy was born. Alas, the mother passed away while giving birth, leaving the child to its own fate. Hours later, Haurn Serpenteyes, a shadowy sorcerer, entered the cabin seeking shelter for the night and found the boy. By means of magic he nourished the child as well as the mother could. Haurn lived a lonely life, and this child would make a suitable companion. He vowed to teach him the mysteries of magic and the arts of the sword. He named the child . . . *Ciroth Avilvin.*" At this the flames rose, making Eion look dark and powerful. "See how the flame stirs at the name, for it is cursed with horrors I could not begin to describe. Even the elements loathe its sound. Haurn raised Ciroth in the deep wilds of the world, favoring the dark forest of Ÿalnz Dàr above all else. Ciroth was taught many forms of magic. Haurn bewitched elves to teach Ciroth how to communicate with spirits of power. Ciroth quickly became a master with the blade. At seventeen, not even the elite elf forces could challenge him and live to tell the tale. Avria's creation was quickly becoming all she'd hoped it be.

"Then something happened that Avria did not intend. Haurn conjured a great spirit for a task unmanageable by any means. Ciroth wished to see his mother. Resurrection is impossible once the soul has left the world; no one will ever find an enchantment capable of accomplishing it. The spirit listened to the command carefully, then it laughed and, instead of renewing Ciroth's mother's life, it claimed Haurn's. Ciroth screamed in pain, for he had lost the only parent-like figure he had ever known. He turned to the spirit and unleashed a very dark spell. Where he had learned it, no one knows, for elves do not practice such magics and even Haurn hadn't the power to perform a spell that could harm a spirit from the other side. Perhaps he had invented it himself. Or, more likely I think, perhaps such things came natural to anyone conceived by Avria's magic.

"The spirit was locked into a vortex, doomed to wander it alone for eternity until the door was opened again and Ciroth summoned it. With that, madness reached its ascension.

"Ciroth wandered the world, alone and in despair. Then he came upon a valley; Saurindon. In those days it was lush and full of life, a place of wonder and beauty, but it no longer held any charm for Ciroth. In his grief, Ciroth ruined the valley, replacing life with death and light with dark. His magic was so strong, a single spell transformed the thriving valley into the red wasteland it is now. With another curse, he took hold of the moon and changed its nature as well. Half of it darkened, but the other half played host to, not a pearly white color, but a dark red hue. And thus passed the birth of the Crimson Eclipse, Ozmodion's battle insignia. Due to this celestial change, though reasons that have n ever been fully explained, Saurindon's perimeter is constantly in a state of night. Ciroth stared at his work; his spell had provoked cosmic metamorphosis.

"He then cried to the heavens, asking why he alone was so damned and why the world seemed to mock his pain. The thought was enough to allow Avria to become a whisper in his mind, ensnaring and imprisoning him like a serpent does a rat.

"Ciroth claimed Saurindon for himself. He masked himself with a cloak of terrible power of his ungodly creation. It glows red with hate and loss and is bonded with his very life. He gave himself a new name: *Ozmodion*. In the evil tongue, it means forsaken.

"And still this not the end of the tale. He summoned a host of dark entities with his terrible branch of magic. He was prepared to deal with shadowy spirits by now. Under his influence, the spirits flew to the Mountains of Vazg in the far south. There dwelled Grungloch and the goblins. The spirits forced malignant spells on the goblins to enmesh their minds and will. Helplessly, the goblins were forced to march to Saurindon to meet Ozmodion, and their doom. Ozmodion also sent the dark spirits to enslave other races; the trolls from the Shadaras Hills, the nightshades from the Il'lion Plains, and the shadow wolves from the Black Veil Woods. With his minions congregated, he banished the demonic entities he summoned into the vortex where Haurn's murderer still roamed. The spirits' spells of control on the dark creatures minds broke. Ozmodion offered them to join him freely, but he was dealing with creatures just as cunning as he. But they were, unfortunately, not as powerful as the sorcerer whom they now had come to hate. They tried to attack and bring his downfall, but at this point, Ozmodion was too powerful to be overcome by means of brute force. He again entangled their minds and dominated their will with spells and incantations the world should have long forgot. Helpless to his power, they fell slave to his rule.

"For years, his minions toiled on his black fortress. When it was finished, Ozmodion named it the Stronghold of Resurgence in the black speech: Taronest.

"Avria no longer needed to whisper to Ozmodion's thoughts, for his devotion to her was unwavering, and his madness fueled itself, though she was always there to see through his doubts and to set him on course when he wandered away from her plans.

"We are all too familiar with what follows: the Dark Times and the long struggle between Ozmodion's forces, the Ozra, and the Resistance. Thus, the tale of the Enemy is told."

A dark veil of silence surrounded the fire. Eion looked around as the fire crackled on loudly without remorse. When nobody said anything for a long period of time, Eion walked away slowly, leaving them all deep in thought.

Chapter 13

The Creation

*A**ngered by the struggle*** shown at the Mountain of Antiquity, Vaeirnïr returned to the valley swiftly. In the red-hot blaze of the sun, the valley looked more desolate than usual, but Taronest, The Dark Fortress of Ozmodion, looked cold and grave in the distance. Vaeirnïr angled toward the highest tower and flew through its lone window, which led to Ozmodion's Chambers.

He landed on the cool stone floor of the chamber and found the sorcerer sitting on his high throne, gazing deep into a red orb that rested on his lap.

"I trust everything went accordingly?" asked Ozmodion, without looking up.

"Precisely my lord," replied Vaeirnïr, folding his wings against his scaly hide. "They put up a little bit of a fight but nothing I could not handle. Here are…" he gulped, as he extended his claws, in which rested several rolls of aged papyrus. "the Scrolls."

With a flick of Ozmodion's wrist, the scrolls flew out of Vaeirnïr's claws and into the sorcerer's hands. He opened the scrolls and eyed them carefully. Then he laughed his deep, dark laugh that resounded in the chamber long after it had subsided.

"Excellent," he whispered, "This is an ancient bit of dark magic that the masters of old laid down. When they discovered that they couldn't control the magic they had summoned, they locked the secrets into that cursed mountain. But those wizards and magicians were weak and brittle. But not I…I will have complete control over these spells, and none will defy me."

At this, he mumbled a few words and waved his hand. The large, black cauldron appeared in the middle of the room once more. Ozmodion stood up and walked toward the cauldron with the scrolls in hand. Again he eyed them carefully. With a brief nod he spoke a lengthy stream of incantations in that evil speech of old. Continuous jets of light of various colors emitted from the Sovereign's hands and poured into the cauldron. The contents inside began to bubble and hiss as it released steam that rose to the ceiling and slowly disappeared. Ozmodion paused.

"In order to obtain the desired result," he whispered, "I need to somehow mix a Death Curse with a Changing Spell. Hmm. Ah-ha! I know." He uttered the right words lowly. Black vapor emerged from the tips of the warlock's fingers and snaked into the cauldron.

"One last thing," muttered Ozmodion. He spoke a syllable, only one rough syllable, but the effect was instantaneous.

A sound like ice shattering, then a tremble passed through the air, and in the center of the chamber, a tear seemed to form, in the very air around them. Through the tear, horrible sounds echoed, and from it, shadows emerged. They slipped through it like fugitives fleeing in the blackest of nights, seamlessly merged with the dark. Soon the shadows occupied the whole of the room, the red slits that were their eyes staring fixed on Ozmodion.

"Your wish?" they all asked with booming voices.

Ozmodion chuckled and pointed at the cauldron. "Give them life."

The shadows bowed and leapt into the air, swirling in great circles. Then the cyclone of shade then touched down in the center of the cauldron, quickly pouring into it. A strong breeze swept through the chamber; Ozmodion's robes flapped around him wildly, heightening his sorcerous aura impressively. After a few brief seconds, the last of the shadows disappeared into the cauldron's contents, which then released a deafening *boom*. Dark rays of green light exploded over the sides, destroying chunks of ceiling when they collided with the rafters. Vaeirnïr was nearly hit by one of the rays, but dodged at the last moment with a growl of alarm.

Then the bodies began to climb out of the cauldron. They looked human, and would've been human too if their skin had not been as black as a starless night and if their eyes hadn't been gray and sinister red. They examined their hands and fingers closely and with interest, and all the while more and more of the creatures poured out of the cauldron. All of them looked the same; not one feature was different. As the last of them crawled from the steaming cauldron, they turned to look at the sorcerer and the dragons with their awful, demonic eyes.

Ozmodion muttered a few more words and pointed his fingers at the creatures, and with a flash of light, the creatures emerged with black armor and hooded faces. Long red swords with black hilts were at their sides, and quivers full of black arrows rested at their backs.

Ozmodion hissed as he looked them over. "Welcome my shadow-shifters." He paused for a long while, and studied the creatures. "Two hundred of you, I would guess. That will be more than enough. You are the second to receive this great gift from me. Oh yes, I have given it before, though the last time was an accident and counted against me. But this time, things are different. Allow me to introduce myself. I am Ozmodion, Iltari, Avria's Advocate…and master of you…unless there are any objections?"

One of the shadow-shifters approached Ozmodion, kneeling to the ground to kiss the hem of the Red Sovereign's robes.

"We live to serve you, sire," he said in a dark, sexless whisper.

"Good," replied Ozmodion. "With Vaeirnïr's lead, you will fly to the Nalarti Mountains and wait for the Resistance to pass you. Attack them from behind; they won't expect anything. Oh, and Vaeirnïr, stop by our little friend in the forest and remind her of her loyalties…and obligations."

Vaeirnïr nodded. "Let's go, you lot," he said to the shadow-shifters as he made his way to the window. Out he soared, and the shadow-shifters, changing into black falcons, followed. Ozmodion watched them until they became little specks dotted against the horizon.

Chapter 14

The Ascent

*T**he story of the enemy.*** Gwen shivered in her tent, as Eion's tale ran through her mind over and over again. *Ciroth Avilvin,* she thought, *a name that would be entirely innocent if fate wasn't so cruel.*

She found little sleep that night.

☐

The Resistance broke camp long before the sun rose. The soldiers' breaths could be seen against the cold, crisp air. Breakfast was meager, consisting of cold rabbit and some concoction made up of flowers and grass. It was filling, though the taste left much to be desired. Gwen packed her things and joined ranks. Rubbing the sleep from her eyes, she rode alongside Eion once more. Then questions began to prod her mind once more.

"Eion," she asked, "if Ozmodion was controlled by Avria, does that mean he really isn't evil?"

Eion turned to look at her strangely. His eyes were scrutinizing, and she could feel him sizing her up.

"What is evil, Gwen?" he asked finally, not taking his deep stare off her.

She returned it with a look of her own, one of confusion. "What do you mean?"

"What I mean is can evil really be defined? And if it can, who defines it? You? Me?"

Gwen didn't really know what Eion was getting at. She knew what evil was: murderers and those who fed off the pain and suffering of others; oppressors who slaughtered and wronged for power; liars and thieves who cheated and stole from innocents.

When she told Eion this, he smiled sadly and shook his head.

"No, Gwen. That is only your interpretation of evil. In another light, those murderers, oppressors, liars, and thieves could be hailed as heroes. There are always two sides to any story."

"And Ozmodion?" Gwen challenged, annoyed. "What about him? Who'll hail him as a hero?"

Eion shrugged, inhaling deeply. "I do not know Gwen. Vundin's vision of magic disappearing is a frightening one, and I am sure no one wants to see it pass. But, if it is to pass, there is nothing we can do about it. I have as much reason to hate Ozmodion as anyone else, but, in his mind, in Avria's mind, he is doing something good, something great. That conviction is so great that, even if the entire world opposes him, he will never back down from it. I suppose, if no one else does, he will applaud himself in the end, whatever that end may be."

Gwen didn't take that in; at the mention of Avira's name, she reeled that the goddess had purposely created Ozmodion for his malignant nature. When she asked how the gods could allow such an abomination to live, Eion laughed grimly and answered with a question of his own.

"Answer me this: like all things, evil is a part of life. Wouldn't good seem entirely redundant without the contrast of evil?"

Gwen thought for a moment, realizing he was making sense. But still, the image of Ozmodion's flame that day of the leader's council at Fairskin Manor haunted her memory. She shivered.

A host of eagles flew overhead, cawing in their wake.

"I sent Beast to scout ahead," explained Eion, seeing her surprise. Gwen nodded. He smiled and looked ahead once more. He then began to sing, or recite, or chant, for his words had no discernible tune at first, but there was a certain rhythm.

The wind moved swift across the moor
Sweeping from some distant shore
It howled, it moaned, 'cross fields 'twas blown
And brought with it days come before

It stirred the young and frail leaves
That rested on the sleeping trees
It froze and chilled and warmth it killed
Gaily roaming 'cross the land and seas

It moved the clouds o'er sky
And hid the stars from men to die
It whistled, cried, loudly sighed
And down the valley it quickly dived

    Gwen listened to his poem and smiled. He glanced at her from the corner of his eyes, smirked, and spurred his mount ahead.

☐

    The sun moved slowly across the sky, casting the great army's shadows on all sides of them. There were more songs sung and more stories told, and the great din of their voices echoed throughout the huge glade. Soon, the sun touched the crests of the distant mountains that laid to the west. In the fading twilight, Gwen saw that to the south more mountains rose, close now, and she also noticed that the great peaks formed a ring all about them, encasing the Emerald Plains in a huge valley leagues across.
    Again, the sea of tents was erected and a host of fires lit the night air with sparks and flame. There was food and drink and laughter for many hours after sunset, but Gwen, too tired to join the merriment, crawled inside her tent and fell into a sleep haunted by dreams of Ozmodion.
    The morning met them refreshed and revived, and camp was broken as quickly as it was made. And then, almost regrettably, they turned their sights to the south and set off once more.
    By midday, they were approaching the end of the Emerald Plains, and the mountains loomed ominously. Their peaks glistened with snow, and

their slopes were craggy and wild; such mountains Gwen had only imagined in dreams.

"The Nalarti Mountains," spoke Eion quietly. Gwen started at his words; she had been so absorbed by the mountains' enormity that she hadn't noticed him approach.

"Are we near Saurindon now?" Gwen asked nervously, her eyes still held by the rocky giants before her.

Eion smiled and put a hand on her shoulder. "Not even close. Beyond these mountains is the Silver Ice Sea, a lake so vast that the opposite shore can't even be seen. Past that is the Waning Waste, a short heath that separates the sea from the immense forest of Ÿalnz Dàr, and even then we will have to cross the fallow Ozra Gap if we are to come to the Mountains of Midnight and storm the Gates of Angar Vûn. *Then* and only then will we be close to Saurindon."

Gen looked away from the mountains. She sighed heavily and thought once more of her distant home. *Had they written her off as dead? Planned a memorial, perhaps?*

Eion left her to brood. He rode his way to the head of the column and dismounted. Lord Fairskin, Breeog, and King Barthol all gathered around the shifter, and they whispered and nodded in a huddle. When they broke apart, Eion again pointed at his throat.

"We climb the mountains," he boomed with his magnified voice. "Release your horses; they'll find their way back. Shoulder your packs, lads. It will be long before you see level ground again."

The massive party was quick to act as they broke into fourths as the different races congregated. They spread out all across the foot of the mountain range, each preparing to take a different pass, all, judging by the faint brown that crisscrossed their way up the mountains, about three miles apart. The Prophesied Ten were divided up among the shifters and elves. Only Gwen, Lea, Ryan, Brad, and Eric remained with the shifters. Eion sent Beast, Armor, and Flame to the other races to act as his surrogates while Gorbon, Varez, and Tirmal joined the shifters.

The horses were unsaddled, and there was much grumbling as the soldiers of the Resistance were forced to stow all the extra supplies into their packs until they staggered under the weight. Once they had been relieved of their burden, the horses were reluctant to leave, but a slap on the hindquarters sent them galloping away. Still, once the shock and pain had subsided, they stopped to graze on the high grasses of the Plains. Too busy to be concerned, Eion did nothing to pursue them.

Horns were blown, and they began the slow climb up the mountains. Weighted by the weapons, armor, and provision, the hike to the passes were slow and tiring. Soon, the separate passes wound so far apart that Eion could no longer see the other three races. He shivered and climbed on.

It was very steep and the higher they went the icier and snowier it became. Altitude sickness became common, forcing the great company to stop at several points. They camped at different heights of the mountains, allowing their lungs to get used to the thin air.

Eion cursed at The Prophesied Ten's human limitations. Three days were wasted each time they acclimatized. Even the patient Fletch quickly lost his temper. Still, acclimatization was necessary; Lea had already passed out twice from the thin air, and Eric suffered from a perpetual headache.

Up they climbed for three more days, stopping only to sleep and eat. The company's mood quickly turned sour, and Varez's pathetic attempts to raise the morale only escaladed the tension. There was no more song, there was no more laughter. There was only

On the fourth day, a horrible blizzard came as they reached the summit of the first of the mountains, Eaen Peak. A cloud of misfortune had always hung around the mountain when it was mentioned in the stories Eion had heard, and they proved to be true, for the storm was the most horrendous Eion had ever seen. The shifters found or made shelters under rocks and caves. Gwen found herself tightly cramped under a boulder with Lea and Brad. The wind howled and the snow blew throughout the night, making sleep difficult to find, but the cold slowed Gwen's body and mind and eventually she drifted off into a deep slumber.

When Gwen awoke the next morning, the terrain was covered in three feet of snow. She groaned, shivering from the frigidity. Ryan was already up, and he had cleared a patch in the snow and had started a fire. He muttered his good morning irritably, the cold quelling his cheer. Gwen grunted in response and got up to join him. She placed her hands over the fire. Slowly, the numbness wore off and she felt the tips of her fingers again.

A shifter with a great black kettle approached them. He shifted two bowls and plopped whatever thick substance was simmering in the pot into the dishes with a large steel ladle. Whatever it was, it was brown, syrupy, and steamy. It did not seem that appetizing, but after three bites, Gwen was sure she had never eaten anything so good. Whether this was because the cold or altitude, she wasn't sure, but she devoured the bowl's contents in less than three minutes. After that, the familiar horns sounded again. With a sigh, she shouldered her pack and joined the ranks to march again.

They hiked well into the night. She trekked beside Eion because Lea had become more than irritable in the constant cold. There was little conversation; a deathly silence had fallen around them, and it did not like to be disturbed.

After an indefinite amount of hours, Gwen suddenly felt the slope lessening, leveling off into a sight that momentarily stunned her.

They had come to a secluded little valley made from walls of sheer rock. There were only two entrances, the one they had come through, and one straight ahead of them. The ground was uneven and made of black stone that was strangely free of snow. Eion found it unsettling and cleared his mind of everything but the valley hoping to detect anything dangerous.

As the great host of shifters entered the valley, Gwen gazed at the clear sky, amazed by the bright stars. In the mortal world, Gwen lived deep within the borders of the capitol, and the many lights blotted out the stars. Here, though, the stars were bright and blazing blue. The sheer numbers staggered her, and she found it impossible to imagine a night without them. As she absorbed their unearthly beauty, she thought she saw two pinpricks of red light shining through the dark. She shook her head and pulled her cloak tighter around her. She was tired and worn from the journey, surely.

They were soon crossing the center of the valley, and Eion's unease now emanated from him and he barely drew any breath. Suddenly, he heard something and stopped short; it sounded like wings.

"What's wrong?" asked Gwen, thinking of the lights.

Eion shrugged. Had he imagined the sound from his strain of concentrating? "Nothing," he answered and continued to walk slowly.

Gwen felt a strong gust of wind. She turned around and put her hand to the hilt of her sword. She again saw two points of red light in the air that again disappeared as soon as she saw them. She unsheathed her sword. Eion did so as well. Brad strung his bow. Lea pulled out her two single blade swords. Ryan took out a dagger, looking quickly side to side.

A blinding flash of red light sprang to life.

"Get down!" Eion pushed Gwen to the ground.

A black dragon flew over them, bellowing flame as he went. His red eyes glistened with malice as they locked on Gwen's. Her whole body grew rigid, paralyzed by fear. Then she heard Eion curse under his breath.

"Vaeïrnïr Bloodshedder," whispered Eion, "Gods help us."

Vaeirnïr shouted something in the dark language, and though Gwen did not understand it, it was horrible to listen to. Almost instantly, dozens of black falcons dived from the sky, screeching in their wake. As Vaeirnïr landed, the falcons changed. They morphed into human-like creatures with deep black skin and flaming red eyes. They wore heavy gray cloaks, and everything but their scarlet eyes were hidden by a scarf and helmet. They were all identical, with nothing standing out among them. They had thin red swords that had already been drawn. On their backs were quivers of black arrows with red fletching blazing in contrast.

Eion stared at them in trepidation; he had never seen anything like these strangers. "Stay close," he whispered to Gwen and the others, then shouted, "Steel! Right side now! Fletch, position yourself on those stones. Tirmal, take Troop B to the left. Varez, Troop D and right. Gorbon—" but Gorbon had already taken to the sky and set off toward Vaeirnïr. Vaeirnïr smiled a smile filled with silver teeth. He angled himself toward the heavens and soared upwards. Gorbon followed.

Eion swore under his breath; he would have to take Gorbon's troop. Beast usually commanded them, and if they intended on facing the swords as animals, Eion could not see how they would live. He turned to address them, quickly forming a strategy.

"Shift bows, arrows, and swords now!" They obeyed but they looked a little worried, for they were long out of practice with such things.

"String bows!" the shifters pulled out three arrows, stuck two in the ground, and nocked one in the bow. To Eion's surprise, the black swordsmen who were facing them had not moved since they changed. They just stood holding their swords in a defensive stance.

Eion felt uncomfortable. Surely they would've attack if they were dangerous by now? Yet they were traveling with Vaeirnïr, and therefore they were a threat. He nodded and strung his own bow.

"Aim!" Eion yelled. The company pulled back on their bowstrings, their arrows placed against the frames and poised to kill. Still the swordsmen did not move.

"FIR-!" But Eion was stopped short. The swords men gestured confidently with their hands. Eion looked down at his arrow. It seemed to be evaporating into the air. But Eion knew better. The arrows were *shifting into* air.

The swordsmen were shifters.

Eion stood dumbfounded. He looked around. Everybody else's arrows were gone now too, as though they were nothing but dust in a breeze. Bows were cast aside and swords were unsheathed. Eion held *Raz'atr* aloft and ran next to Gwen, growling his war cry savagely.

The shadow shifters took up their swords slashed madly at the chargers. The clangs of steel against steel reverberated off the stone walls. Gwen swung at her enemy, but it parried with unnatural speed. Beside her, Eion blocked an attack effortlessly then slew his opponent, quickly moving on to another. Gwen was too evenly matched with her attacker; they were performing and intricate dance full of clangs and slashes, and neither seemed to be gaining an advantage. Gwen took a chance and lunged at her opponent, but the shifter brought his sword down hard on hers and knocked it out of her hand. Then, with inhuman speed, he brought his sword tip up to her neck. The shifter let out a low hiss as he prepared to shove the sword through her throat. Gwen inhaled sharply.

Suddenly, the shifter's eyes widened. Gwen looked down and saw the blue tip of *Raz'atr* sticking out of the shadow shifter's stomach. The sword withdrew and the shifter crumpled to the ground. With a quick sigh of relief, Gwen yelled her thanks to Eion as she moved on to the next shifter.

□

High in the skies, the two dragons were battling mercilessly.

"Death to you all!" screeched Vaeirnïr as he slashed at Gorbon with his ivory claws, missing the green dragon's face by fragments of an inch.

Gorbon in turn spouted flame at the black dragon's wings, but Vaeirnïr only closed them and sank into a beautiful dive. He pulled himself upright and charged Gorbon. Gorbon turned and sent his tail slamming into Vaeirnïr's chest. The black dragon roared with pain.

"What a pitiful excuse for a Dragon King!" Gorbon shouted at Vaeirnïr, "It is truly amazing to think the Mighty Breeog was spawned from you!"

Vaeirnïr snarled. "Impudent speck, allow me to show you how I took the Mirithin Plateau!"

He inhaled, letting his inner chambers fill with hydrogen. He rose with his claws outstretched and caught Gorbon by the neck.

Vaeirnïr stared at the green dragon wildly. Gorbon adopted a defiant look and stared back. "Die, grandson's servant!" His claws constricted as he bellowed flame into Gorbon's face.

Gorbon's eyes rolled into his head and Vaeirnïr felt the green dragon's body go limp. Bloodshedder laughed in his dark roar.

"May the fall crush your skull!" And he let loose Gorbon's neck.

☐

Down below the fight was not going well. The shadow shifters were as competent in swordplay as the Resistance's shifters were. Only Steel's flank was making headway, but there victories were rare and sporadic.

Eion was fighting with what seemed the leader as he had a strip of red clothe with the Crimson Eclipse embroidered into it around his arm. Eion had rarely seen so fierce a fighter; he had not had this kind of a challenge since he brought down Ozmodion himself, and that itself was a stroke of luck.

Eion barked a command, and a swarm of silver arrows with blue shafts arched from the stone wall's top. Fletch's troop had finally scaled the wall and joined the fray. About fifty or so shadow shifters fell. Others parried the arrows, directing them to the ground or cleaving them in half. While they were distracted, the Resistance's shifters took their chance. Seconds later, another one hundred were slain. "Fire at will!" bellowed Fletch, and his brigade sent a never-ending volley of arrows down to the battle. Tirmal Goldhair launched Death and Coma spells in all directions. And all the while, the shadow shifters' numbers were slowly decreasing. Eion's heart lifted; they would surely win.

Then the Eclipse formed in the sky. At first it seemed as though the left side of the moon was being erased. Then the right side shimmered and darkened into a bloody scarlet color.

Eion cursed. This was Ozmodion's way of heartening his soldiers and urging them to press on.

The remaining shadow shifters—a mere twenty—whooped and cheered. They regrouped and began making a glorious comeback, despite their pathetic numbers.

Distracted by the Eclipse, Gwen found herself up against the walls of rock that encircled the valley. She was about to rejoin with the shifters when she heard a twig snap to her left. She whipped her head around and saw a shadow shifter charging toward her with a red sword held aloft. Knowing she could not parry at that speed, Gwen took off to get to higher ground. She ran toward the end of the small valley, her chest swelling with heaving breathes, and squeezed through the exit, small crevice in the rocks. The shifter was closely pursuing her. It shifted a rock into its hand and lobbed it at Gwen.

Before the stone hit, she was faintly aware of a green dragon falling from the sky and landing deep in the forest in the mountains. Then, a dull thud left her expecting to feel great pain, but she felt nothing. Everything went black.

Chapter 15

The Conjuror

G*wen awoke what seemed years later*. Her head throbbed and she felt very cold. She sat up and looked around. She was lying in about two feet of snow in the same spot she had fallen last night. She shielded her eyes as the sun climbed over the mountains to the east.

She tried to stand up and stumbled back into the snow. Her head swam; she felt horribly dizzy. After a few moments of resting, she tried to stand again, this time she moved slowly.

Well, she thought, *what now? Did the Resistance just walk past me, leaving me for dead?*

She walked back to the stone valley and gasped. A fresh blanket of snow had buried the previous night's battleground; hundreds of large, red splashes blazed clearly against the white scenery, and the smell of blood filled her nostrils, making her stomach nauseous. She promptly wretched to her left. When she was done and had caught her breath, she left the valley, trudging slowly, trying to forget what she had just seen.

As she walked away from the secluded valley, she vaguely remembered a green dragon falling to earth before she had been knocked out. She looked to the small valley to get her bearings, and realized that the dragon must lay to the east if it was still there.

She went through a patch of bushes, pushed her way past some shrubs, walked through a small clutter of trees, and found a small meadow. And there was a sight so awful, Gwen almost screamed.

There lay Gorbon, bloody and bruised. His wings had slight tears in the thin blue membranes. His face was adorned with long, deep gashes, and his underside was rising and falling, quickly and shakily. He was covered in a snowdrift with crimson blotches strikingly similar to those she just had left behind in the stone valley.

Gwen rushed to his side. His breaths were short and raspy. She stroked his large head. His eyes flickered and then were still again.

"Oh, Gorbon. Don't die. Please." She looked around, tears burning her eyes. "I must find fresh meat for you."

Grabbing her bow from the quiver, she strung an arrow then stalked to the other side of the meadow and disappeared through a small clump of trees. On the other side was a small, iced over stream. After breaking through the sheet of ice and filling her flask she hid behind a blackberry bush, eating a few of the cold, frozen berries that she'd found. She waited for about three quarters of an hour when a small doe came to take a drink. As it leaned its head to the stream, Gwen sent an arrow whizzing toward its head. It missed by a finger's width. The doe bolted away. Gwen swore and ran after it, when she heard a loud voice behind her yell, *"Kill!"*

Gwen felt a strong wind rush past her and collide with the deer. It stumbled and lay still.

It took all her strength to restrain a scream. She quickly looked over her shoulder, taking aim with her bow. No one was there. Heart throbbing madly, she turned around to see that the doe was a lifeless figure on the ground.

Confusion, mingled with gripping fear, took her. She looked in all directions, straining her ears for the slightest sound. She didn't find anything; she didn't hear anything. She was alone in the woods, with a slain doe lying not but twenty feet away. She shook her head and walked over to the dead animal. She took one more look about her, and then replaced her bow in the quiver. She then bent down and, grabbing the doe by its legs, dragged it through the still forest.

A quarter of an hour later, she had returned to the meadows, scraped and tired from lugging the carcass. Gorbon still lay there, bruised and bloody. She held back any emotion this time and hauled the body of the doe to where the dragon rested. She then knelt beside him, and ran her hand down the side of his face; his scales were cold, and the edges were crusted with ice. They were not the vivid blue-green that they ought to have been, either.

After five minutes of stroking his face, his eyes flickered, and in another moment, they opened. Gwen could have cried with relief. "You're back!" she said, trying very hard to hide her worry.

The dragon gave a weak smile, and though he tried to reply, he only managed a choking cough. Puffs of smoke ejected from his mouth, and a spray of red flew through the air to bury itself in the white powder, tingeing it with the sickly color.

"What happened?" Gwen asked, watching all this in horror.

"Bloodshedder," Gorbon whispered quietly, so as not to provoke the coughing spasm again. He extended his neck, took a bite out of the doe, and then fell back asleep.

☐

Gorbon didn't stir again until early evening. When finally he woke, he saw that Gwen had downed two more deer and a couple of rabbits. On a makeshift stool roughly carved from a dead tree stump, she sat and watched him anxiously.

She smiled when he opened his eyes. "How are you feeling?"

Gorbon managed a weak laugh, which nearly threatened to become another seizure of coughing. "I will not last through the night," he said in a raspy voice once he recovered.

"Don't say things like that! You'll make it long after that."

"No, Lady Gwen, I die tonight. My wounds are beyond your ability to heal. Before I leave you, hear my last words and heed them. To the northeast you'll find a cave. The one who lives in it can help you, even if he refuses at first. Tell him that if he helps you, the Duranz will consider his dept fulfilled. He will then bring you into his home without any other objections. This is all I can give you before I go."

Gwen cried silently, doing all in her power to keep the tears from flowing, but they relentlessly streamed from her eyes. She sniffled loudly, and the dragon smiled.

"Do not let my last sight be your tears; it is the way of things. To the well-organized mind, death is just another path to walk down. Have you not heard the stories of Garon's Heaven?"

Gwen sniffed again, and shook here head. A look of absolute content crossed Gorbon's face.

"There the stars speak and the sun smiles on all. The quarrels of the dragons and the wyverns, the hippogriffs and the griffins, and the fomariuns and the elves are quelled, and peace truly reigns. Garon watches over his heaven and his blessed whispers are heard everlastingly.

"I do not fear death; why shy from that which is inevitable? Fear, Gwen: that is the true disaster. Caution would not go astray in this dark, wide world, but you cannot allow it to shape you. If you do, you will be left with nothing more than a ghost of a life, a feeble imitation that is not worth having."

"I will say no more. With sorrow or joy, I must leave you. Forget me not, Gwen Talbot. My one regret is that in the centuries of my life, I only knew you for a short part of our journey together. You are destined for great things; know that you will be sung about for eternity, and I shall hear of your deeds even from the Necroverse. For now, farewell." Gorbon closed his eyes, and exhaled deeply.

One final sniffle, and then Gwen threw her arms around the dragon's neck. She cried for many hours, and it was long after the fall of night before she drifted into sleep, tearstains marking her face.

☐

Morning came too soon, and Gwen's first thought upon stirring from her sleep, which had done little to rest her, was that Gorbon was gone. She sat up and checked for breathing. There was none, but Gwen held back her tears, too exhausted to cry anymore. She had a cold breakfast of leftover deer, though the raw meat did not seem to fill her. She then collected leaves and grass and covered Gorbon with them. She would've liked much more to bury him, but she was ill equipped and Gorbon was much too big. When the crude burial mound was completed, Gwen bowed her head; upset and unable to channel her grief, she looked to the northeast. More of the Nalarti Mountains loomed in front of her, like hooded strangers staring blankly. She shuddered as she registered their enormity. With a sigh and a final look at Gorbon's resting place, she set off into the wild.

The forest and rocky slopes hindered her progress, and hours later she felt that she had made little headway. She continued to check her bearing, judging the position of the sun and using Eaen Peak as a landmark. Enclosed now in a valley tucked away between the mountains, she was utterly lost and could no more guess at where she was then grow wings and fly away. With a tired sigh and a tug at her hip flask, she continued on her way.

As the sun touched the mountains in the west, setting the sky alight with orange twilight, she came to a treacherous cliff face of granite and limestone. She saw that a small cave mouth was set into the rock. She had no way of being sure if this was the mountain Gorbon had intended her to find, but in any case, night was falling, and she would soon need a place to shelter from the elements. She walked up and over the rocky crevices till she came to the mouth of the cavern

"Hello?" she called into it. There was no answer. "Hello?" she called again. Still no answer. Gwen took one step inside when she heard a loud voice behind her.

"Here, now, what do you think you're doing invading my home?"

Gwen whirled around. She gasped. In front of her was a man, no, a goat, no, both. Below the man's torso were goat legs and tail. Above it was a man's body and head with two gnarled horns sticking out of his temples.

"W-What are you?" Gwen asked. It wasn't polite, but at the moment it was the only thing she could think to say. She was very tired, you must remember.

The man-goat frowned. "If you must know, I am a satyr: half man, half goat. I am also an accomplished conjuror. But I know who I am. Who are you that tries to enter my home without any invitation, or without my knowing of who you are?"

Gwen still gawked at the satyr, which stared at her severely and tapped its hoof on the stone beneath their feet. She reveled in his presence. Before they had left the mortal world, they had been studying Shakespeare's *A Midsummer Night's Dream* in English, and she was stunned to meet one of the many creatures described in the play. In a moment, she found her voice.

"M-My name is Gwen Talbot."

The satyr raised an eyebrow. "*The* Gwenivere Talbot? The *third* Iltari? I suppose you're trying to be funny? Get out of my way and leave my home." The satyr pushed its way passed Gwen, sinking into the shadows in the cave.

Gwen paused at being referred to as an Iltari, but then remembered what Gorbon had told her to say.

"I was a friend of the Dragon Gorbon," she called into the mouth of the cave. "He died this morning. He told me that if you help me the Duranz would consider your dept repaid."

The silence from the cave echoed in her ears. Then she heard hooffalls approaching her. The satyr reappeared from the mouth of the cave.

"The Duranz?" he said in a strained voice, his eyes now misty and questioning. "You are a friend of Gorbon?"

Gwen felt tears well up inside her eyes. "I *was* a friend of Gorbon. He was attacked…no, *slaughtered* by the Dragon Vaeirnïr. I tended his wounds the best I could, and I—"

"Stole the deer I killed," the satyr whispered. "I thought it strange that it disappeared when I so plainly saw my spirit smite it." He blinked and then smiled at Gwen.

"Well, this changes everything. Gorbon did me a great service many years ago. Won't you come in? My name is Axunrult."

Axunrult beckoned Gwen to follow him into the cave. She gave a slight nod and advanced into the deep dark.

Gwen walked in the direction of the sound of Axunrult's hooves. She occasionally bumped into a wall or got her foot caught on a rock or loose stone, but for the most part, the passage was clean and free of clutter; whoever had made it was very skilled.

After a quarter of an hour of walking, a dim red light poured into the passage around the corner. Axunrult took a right, and Gwen followed him into a very large series of caverns. They stood, then, in the largest one. Strange red fires were crackling in torches on the marble walls. There were many tables cluttered with strange books, chalks, and incense. On the floor were rugs and carpets and blankets made of animal furs. A large fireplace made of black brick lay on the other side of the cavern. What furniture that was in the room was occupied by scrolls and strangely tinged bottles. A blue-gray smoke hung in the air, which smelled strongly of sulfur.

Gwen gaped for a moment as the satyr disappeared into another cave. Closing her mouth and repressing any awe, she walked to one of the desks and picked up an old sheet of parchment. Etched in red ink were runes of several languages, none of which she could read. She set it down.

"Can I offer you anything?" called Axunrult from the other cavern, "Tea, coffee? I believe I have some mulled mead resting in the deep cellars beneath our feet?"

"Tea will be fine, thanks," Gwen said, walking into the new cavern. Gwen was surprised to see a crude but definite kitchen. Another fireplace was set into the wall; this one had a cauldron set on top of it. A cupboard had been etched into the wall, and on it sat jars of pickled and salted meat. Another stone seemed to rest on hinge drilled into the stone. Axunrult was busy dipping tea bags into a kettle.

"What's that?" Gwen asked gesturing at the stone.

Axunrult turned quickly, chuckled, and then turned back to the cups. "It is called an ice box in the mortal world. I put a freezing spell into the very rock so everything inside is kept cold."

Gwen let the fascination show on her face, but it quickly left as an uneasy feeling began to well up inside her. A question prodded her mind, and she knew asking it would be painful for the both of them. Still, she knew she had to ask if she was to find any peace.

"Axunrult?" she said.

"Yes?" The satyr put the tea kettle over the fire.

"May I ask you something?"

"I dare say I know the question, but you will have to wait for the answer. I suggest you get some sleep. In the morning, I will explain everything. Please follow me."

Gwen sighed, but Axunrult said nothing more as he led her to another cave with a decent sized bed. The satyr said goodnight, bowed and extinguished his candle and left her to her slumber, which came swiftly as her fatigue finally bested her.

☐

When Gwen awakened the next morning, she wondered if she truly had, so dark were the caves of Axunrult. She got out of bed, rubbed her eyes, and entered the passage that led to the main cavern, where she found the conjuror at one of his many desks reading a scroll. Gwen cleared her throat. The satyr started and stared at her with wild eyes. Upon seeing Gwen he sighed and smile.

"I just put some tea on the fire. Care to join me?"

Gwen shook her head. "My questions?"

"Yes, yes, ask away," he said as he turned his eyes back to his scroll.

Grabbing a stool by a near desk, she cleared her throat. She sat down and tried to make herself as comfortable as possible, but the impending questions allowed no comfort.

"Well, first of all, are there many satyrs left, and if so, how many are conjurors like yourself?"

"There are many satyrs," he said, not looking up, "but the majority of them live in the Valley of the Weres in the west. And I am, as far as I know, the only one that is a man, a goat, and a conjuror. But you procrastinate; ask the real question so I can give you the real answer."

"How did you know Gorbon?" Gwen asked sadly, shifting in her seat awkwardly.

Axunrult rubbed his eyes and looked up at Gwen. He stood up and walked over to the fireplace after rolling the scroll up and setting it on the desk top. As he stared at the flames, he spoke to Gwen.

"Did you know that satyrs used to be a part of the Resistance? Yes, we made the greatest of spies; so quiet are we when we want to be. Yes, for the first ten months, the Resistance had five races serving it.

"I was a young lad then, very impressionable at that age. I marched alongside elves, and their magic enthralled me. I was fascinated by their spell weaving and the way there confidence seemed unbreakable. I wanted so badly to learn magic. But, being that I was a fomariun, a creature that is half human and half beast, I was thought too lowly to learn the secrets of magic.

"But I wanted it so badly it became a burning obsession. I thought I would die if I could not have it, for in my mind, I thought I could only be happy if I was a spell caster.

"A young dragon took pity on me. In the dead of night, he would fly me to the Mountain of Antiquity to read the scrolls. For six years, I read the documents in the Mountain. I gave the dragon the name the Duranz, the name of the great wizard Duranz Oljurish, and I swore to repay my dept."

"'Think nothing of it my friend,' said the dragon, and he flew away.

"Two years later, a group of satyrs were charged with selling Resistance plans to the Ozra, Ozmodion's armies. Although they were never found guilty, the entire satyr race were decommissioned and banished from Arconia. Dragon patrols were sent to pursue us to the borders. One such patrol was led by Gorbon. He spared my troop's lives when we camped out five miles away from the border. He acted as though he had not seen us.

"The satyr race then marched into the Valley of the Weres, where they took refuge in the Rashadel Woods."

"Were the satyrs guilty?" asked Gwen.

"No, they were not, though the Resistance did not want to risk more betrayal. But in my mind, the satyrs gave up too easily. I on the other hand wanted to help the Resistance. I traveled secretly to the Mountain of Antiquity. With the help of certain spirits, I was able to disguise myself as an elder hobgoblin, allowing myself to studying the secrets of magic. The more I practiced, the more competent I became. I unearthed Continual Resurrection spells, and cast them upon myself. When I get old, I die but then start over again as an infant. Rather phoenix-like, I thought.

"I then took an interest in scrying. I began to meet Gorbon in secret in the Waning Waste to tell him what the Ozra had been doing. In return he kept the fact that I was hiding in the Mountain to himself, so I had not really full-filled my dept.

"Unfortunately, King Breeog was patrolling the Mountain one day, and recognized my scent. He charged me to tell him who had helped me. I did not say anything, and Breeog, in turn, put an order in for my execution. Gorbon himself volunteered for the job. He gathered me in his claws and roared with such ferocity that I was sure I was going to die. I was wrong. He then dropped me off at this mountain, bidding me to never leave its slopes ever again. I suppose he later assured Breeog he had killed me, for I have not seen any trace of the Resistance for many centuries. I vowed to fulfill my dept ten times over for his acts of kindness. I think helping you is the least I can do."

Gwen sat and stared at the old satyr. When she didn't say anything, he left the room, mumbling under his breath.

Eion flapped his wings hard, his hawk eyes searching the ground. His vision was superb in this guise; he could make out every detail on the ground two miles in the air in the dead of night. He welcomed the wind passing under his wings, the freedom that filled his being. But the joy was muted tonight, for he had a mission to fulfill.

The shadow shifters and put only a small dent in the troop; a mere fifty of the Resistance's shifters had died. Thanks to Steel's troop's quick tactics, they were able to drive the shadow shifters back; none survived.

But Gorbon and Gwen were missing and the entire Shifter Legion was scouring the mountains in a vain search for them. Eion could have killed himself; losing one of the Prophesied and Breeog's second-in-command. If he didn't find them soon, they would be late to reach the rendezvous point. Not only that, but it was now common knowledge throughout the Resistance that Gwen was the third Iltari in five millennia. If Lord Fairskin found out... Eion dared not think about it.

It was then that Steel, in his hawk form, glided beside him, eyes wide with apprehension.

"Eion, we've found something," he said in hawkish. "I think you should see this."

Eion gave a nod and followed Steel to a small meadow on the southern side of the mountain they had been scouring. As they closed in on the meadow, Eion made out a mound of leaves and twigs.

The pair landed, and shifted into their usual forms. They walked to the mound, which was now surrounded by a host of shifters, Tirmal, and Varez. The shifters all saluted Eion, but, too edgy to take notice, he only stalked to the nearest officer.

"Well?" Eion asked the lieutenant shifter.

"We believe there is something underneath," the officer replied, a little uncomfortable under Eion's harsh stare, "but it could be dangerous, a trap set by the shadow shifters."

Eion pushed passed him and knelt next to the mound. He concentrated on the air around it, shifting it away from him, at first lightly, and then with all his might. The leaves and twigs were swept away with the strong wind, revealing the bloodied and bashed body of a green dragon.

Eion gasped. Gorbon. Half of his fears were confirmed.

He threw his head back and yelled into the sky. "Assassins! Murderers! Fire!" Ozmodion had claimed another one of his friends! If Gwen was found dead too…curse Avria for touching the whelp!

"Get a fire going," Eion ordered, after the outburst had passed, "Make it big. His ashes will be placated for council from the gods."

☐

Two weeks had passed, and still Gwen was a guest to Axunrult's caverns. When he had asked her why she was on the mountain, she had been hesitant to share with him everything, but she rationalized that he meant the Resistance no harm, so she relayed the story, and the satyr listened intently, offering plenty of insights to the motives of both the Resistance and Ozmodion. When she finished, he vowed to help her any way that he could. Gwen soon found herself regarding the old hermit as a friend, and felt very much at ease in those hidden caverns.

He would tell her satyr-lore, and she would tell him about her home in the Mortal Realm, about which he had a surprising knowledge, though he still asked many questions, particularly about human politics.

Back and forth they would ask each other questions, and they would tell stories, and make jokes until the days had grown into weeks. Those were some of the happiest days of Gwen's life; inwardly, she was tired of adventuring, and the battle with the shadow-shifters had discouraged her. The prospect of the impending war had only worried her before, but now it terrified her and haunted her waking hours. Somewhere, a little part of her hoped she would never be found.

Not that she was without distraction; the old satyr's stories fueled her imagination, and she had plenty of questions she wanted answered.

"What is a conjuror?" she asked one evening at dinner.

The old satyr chuckled. "It's a type of spell caster that does not rely on his own magic, but on the magic of spirits. The more spirits a conjuror ensnares the more magic he is able to do. I have seventy two and a half spirits serving me at this time, and I can summon more if I wish, but it is not necessary."

Gwen raised her eyebrows. "Seventy two *and a half?*"

"I do not enjoy servants who show their cheek, and, well, he pushed me a little too far. I suppose that was cruel, but I have very few reasons to laugh on this old mountain, and the sight of him always provides the comic release I need." He chuckled again.

"You mean you can see them?" Gwen asked in awe. She found it hard to picture what a spirit would look like, much less one that had been cut in half.

"Of course I can. How would I be able to see what they were doing if I could not? Unless you give them a strict charge no to harm you, they will as soon as they get the chance. But yes, I can see them. You cannot because you did not summon them. Only the Summoner can see the Summoned."

"How do you control them?"

"Oh, it is very simple," Axunrult answered excitedly. "You simply tell them what to do with a word." He gestured at an unoccupied chair. "Lift," said he. The chair miraculously rose three feet in the air. "Lower," commanded Axunrult. The chair returned to the ground.

Gwen stared in wonder. A powerful, envious feeling welled up inside her. She'd been fascinated by the elves' magic too, and now this. A jealous desire rose up, and it quickly spilled forth.

"How can I learn magic?" Gwen blurted before she could catch herself. She averted her gaze, hastily looking down at the floor to hide her embarrassment.

When she dared to look up again, she did not see Axunrult staring at her in surprise. Instead, he was smiling warmly, a look of empathy gleaming in his old eyes. "Well, enchanting would be the easiest way for you to learn. But I have no idea where I would find an enchanter. But you cannot march into Saurindon Gorge without some slight skill in magic. How strange of Lord Fairskin to not think of that…" He paused, as if considering the elf's oversight, then, with a shake of his head, pushed the matter away. "Well, I will at least give you a look into the ways of magic. Come, to my workshop." He got up and beckoned her to follow. Gwen raised an eyebrow, but followed him.

He led her down a staircase made of gemstones. So enthralled was Gwen by its beauty that she stumbled once or twice and nearly fell. Looking back on it years later, she wished she had asked Axunrult how he had made it, but she had been too awed to even think of it.

She would've liked to marvel that staircase longer, but soon, the torches that lined the walls disappeared, and they and the staircase were swathed in blackness. Again Gwen had to follow the sound of the satyr's footfalls. She bumped into the wall a few times, and then collided with the satyr's pointy horns when he suddenly stopped, mercilessly poking her stomach.

"I have to open the door first," he said irritably. Gwen stepped back, rubbing her new inflicted bruises, and heard the rattling of keys and the opening of the latch. Torchlight poured from the open threshold, and her eyes were, for a moment, dazed. When the flickering spots left her vision though, she saw why Axunrult had brought her here.

Gwen walked into a high ceiling cavern with tables of clutter much like up stairs. Axunrult clapped and a chandelier that hung form the ceiling ignited, illuminating the cavern even more. There were many desks, and worktables, and counters, and shelves. And all were filled with scrolls, books, and pieces of parchment with foreign runes scrawled messily across. The walls and floor were nothing like the ornate staircase that led to the room; cold black stone, rough and unkempt. Above, stalactites hung down like stony icicles, ending in very, very sharp points.

As she took this all in, Axunrult brought an old, dusty tome to one of the many tables, flipping through it in search for a page. Gwen came to stand over his shoulder, looking at the hand-drawn and often gruesome illustrations.

"Do you understand death, Gwen?" the satyr asked, as he kept looking in the book.

Gwen cocked her head. "What do you mean?"

"Do you know what it means to die?"

Shrugging, she replied, "I don't know, I guess it just means that life as you know it is over."

Axunrult nodded enthusiastically. "Exactly. That is it. That is exactly it. Once you die, there is nothing like life that follows. Even in Garon's

Heaven, existence is not living. It is...*being*, more like. But, dying and being dead are two very different things, as Ozmodion's already proven."

An involuntary shiver ran down Gwen's neck; she had almost forgotten that Ozmodion existed. The mention of his name broke that illusion instantly, though.

"There are those who avoid or choose to leave the Necroverse: spirits unbound to this world or the one after it. These have incredible energy potential, and if you can learn to manipulate and control the magic they store, you can have unfathomable power at your hands." Here he grinned, like he was just realizing what he was capable of.

Gwen frowned. "That seems kind of dark, don't you think?"

Axunrult only made a non-committal shrug as he finally found the page he was looking for. On it, a picture of a skeleton and a man shaking hands had been drawn on the old parchment. Both of them were grinning disconcertingly.

"There are worse things," Axunrult said quietly.

☐

Olarn led the pack up the slopes of the Nalarti Mountains, savoring the hunt as he had not done in years. He was in his element, stalking an unsuspecting prey for endless miles. Ordinarily he would have already been on his quarry, but he was not alone and unable to move at his fastest pace.

Ozmodion had only allowed him a legion of two hundred shadow wolves, but their victory did not depend on strength, only stealth. They had to be swift and silent; if the Resistance found them they would surely be killed.

Olarn stopped short. The pack halted with him, and the great wolf raised his snout to the sky. A satyr's stench hung on the air. Perfect. The Red Sovereign had been correct; the old conjuror still dwelled in the hills. Olarn raised his snout again and let out a deep, blood-curdling howl. The pack did the same, filling the hills and valleys with the awful sound.

"Onward!" Olarn roared as he surged forward. With many yips and barks of glee, the pack followed, straining to keep up with the bear-sized wolf.

High above them, Beast, in an eagle guise, saw all this. He screeched and swiftly made his way back to Breeog's encampment.

☐

Gwen felt unnerved as she flipped through the book Axunrult left on the table. There were more drawings and diagrams, along with rites and spells to bring spirits and magic to the conjuror. Axunrult, who was now flipping through other books as though he had not read them in years, would every now and then stop to laugh. Gwen couldn't help but notice that it was a rather wicked sound.

She was about to mention this, when a high, blaring screech resounded in the cavern. Axunrult stiffened; his eyes widened. With a clap of his hands and a stomp of his right hoof, the blaring died, and then he uttered a string of words in some harsh language, one full of clicks and guttural sounds. After he had finished, Gwen felt a stir in the air, and the cavern suddenly felt much colder. She shivered, and rubbed her palms against her arms to warm up.

Axunrult took no heed of the cold. He listened carefully to some unseen speaker, nodding and furrowing his wrinkled brow all the while.

He was very grim by the time he clapped his hands again to dismiss whatever had been speaking to him. Gravely, he turned to Gwen.

"My spirits have just informed me that a pack of wolves are swiftly approaching this cave."

It was now Gwen's turn to stiffen.

"Wolves?" she asked fearfully, dreading the very worst. "You mean wolves native to the mountain, right?"

Axunrult nodded bleakly. "And apparently, Ozmodion has charmed them against my branch of magic. Five of my best spirits shriveled upon touching them. You are not safe here."

"How can they have known I was here? Those shadow shifters must have thought I was dead, and even if they didn't, they don't know about you."

"True, the shifters did not know of my existence. Sadly, Ozmodion does. I once scryed deep into the very bowels of his fortress, into his inner chambers. He felt my presence and grabbed a hold on the tendril of magic connecting me to the room. He looked deep into my mind, finding the secrets of my life, and found I acted for the good of the Resistance. It would have been so easy for him to kill me, but he did not. He knew my power was negligible, so he let me live. Since then, wards have been erected around Saurindon, and I have never been able to get through again. I know my actions angered him greatly, still, I do not know why he would bother with me, I am nothing compared to his might. Unless—" he stopped short. A long shuddering howl resounded outside the door, and Axunrult was gripped with panic.

"They are here! Gwen, you must hide!" He clapped his hand twice more and whistled.

Gwen shivered and looked at herself. Though nothing visible had happened, Gwen looked to Axunrult and watched him look past her with unseeing eyes. Gwen then felt strong arms lifting her high, high above the ground, almost to the ceiling. She screamed as she saw the floor fall away underneath her, but no one heard her cries.

The door then burst open, and twenty some black wolves prowled into the room, quickly forming a tight ring around Axunrult and blocking any escape. The biggest wolf approached Axunrult as a cat does a mouse, its teeth bared in a menacing snarl. It then spoke.

"Are you the conjuror known as Axunrult?" it growled.

"I am," the satyr said boldly. He crossed his arms in a gesture of defiance. A soft laugh ran through the wolves. The leader did not share in it.

"The Red Sovereign requests your presence immediately," it continued with a hard voice. Authority lay thick on his words, which complemented his colossal size terrifyingly.

"And may I inquire as to the reason?" asked Axunrult in a strained counterfeit of cool easiness. Gwen knew he was frightened, and she didn't need to see the sweat on his brow to know that the wolves knew it too.

The wolf laughed icily at the request. "Arrogant formariun…it should be enough for you to be thought so highly by the Red Sovereign. His intentions are none of your concern, you who is not fit to breathe the same air as him. Still…I see no harm in letting you know your fate. The Red Sovereign is the only being in Saurindon capable of magic. He wishes to build an army of mages and wizards. Since you are the only one save Lord Fairskin who dared to infiltrate the magical wards surrounding Saurindon, the Red Sovereign wishes you to lead this battalion."

The satyr threw his head back and laughed defiantly. "I would rather die."

"Undoubtedly you will if you do not consent. But, no matter. You have no choice in the matter for now. You are to be taken to Ozmodion…alive. Now, whether or not you wish to serve him after hearing him speak is your business. Of course, you will be promptly terminated if you refuse." The wolf smiled wickedly.

"You have my answer."

"Do you think it wise to tempt us? We have just run many leagues, and my pack is hungry." The other wolves growled menacingly.

Axunrult snorted. "A bigger group of ragtag ruffians I have never seen. I would suspect they are all flea-ridden, too."

"Flea-ridden, is it?" the wolf whispered dangerously, licking his lips. "My, you are very thick. I will not envy you when you awake from our journey. Nuntra, Koshcel, if you please?"

Two shadow wolves advanced on Axunrult. Quickly, one jumped on his chest, pinning him to the ground, and then the other stepped on his neck with one strong leg, blocking blood from getting to his brain, and any attempts he may have made to cast magic. A few moments of gurgling sounds, then the satyr's eyes rolled into the back of his head and he went limp. The wolf standing on his windpipe stepped off him, sniffed him, and then nodded to the other wolf. It stepped off him and dragged him through the door.

Gwen stifled a scream, not that any of the wolves could hear her. Exiting the room, they left her in darkness. The biggest was the last to leave. It raised its snout to the air and sniffed, and for one, agonizing minute, Gwen thought it knew she was there.

Then the wolf snorted, and, shaking his head, left the cavern, and Gwen in the dark, with only an unseen spirit for company.

☐

Olarn led the way down the mountain, picking up speed as he sprinted downhill. Behind him, Nuntra and Koshcel, aided by Shrar, were carrying the unconscious satyr. The thuds of their footfall were thunderous, resonating in the night air, but Olarn barely heard it; he was too busy savoring his victory.

How happy Ozmodion would be. The first step of the gathering of the mages was successful. This victory would be strategic as well as triumphant; it would help greatly to have Ozmodion's favor, which would allow him to maneuver around Belzorg, Ulurn, and Kahn. The mere thought of rising above his rivals was so heartening that Olarn couldn't help but lift his head and howl to the silver orb that was the moon. But as he did, he saw a sight that stopped his breath.

A flight of dragons was circling overhead.

Olarn roared. He could not let them undo what he just did; in his mind, he saw his victory turn into excruciating failure, and he imagined his three rivals building on his defeat. Spurred by fear and hypothetical shame, he began to run faster down the mountain. The pack followed his example, but still the dragons gained on them. If only they could reach the rendezvous point with some of Belzorg's soldiers, they'd be safe; goblins could fire arrows.

The first of the dragons sped down toward them. To the dismay of Olam, it was the Dragon King Breeog. The great beast's maw was parted, and tendrils of smoke drifted through his teeth. He inhaled.

"Faster!" Olarn roared, but it was too late. Breeog had emitted a stream of fire. The burning cyclone of flame licked at the heels of the wolves, spurring them on with a series of pained yelps. The brigade bearing the satyr was unharmed, though they, like the rest of the pack, were wide-eyed with fear. Olarn surged ahead, forcing the pack to move before Breeog could fire again.

The mountain was leveling off now, right to the shores of the Silver Ice Sea. The outline of the Mountain of Antiquity could be seen clearly against the starlit horizon.

On the rocky shore, the waves lapped loudly, bolstered by the breezes sweeping across the water. There the goblins waited with crossbows in hand.

"Fire!" Olarn roared at them. The lumbering monsters took aim stupidly, and sent a stream of arrows whizzing through the moonlit night. Dodging the deadly missiles, Breeog changed the flight's direction, but they quickly regrouped.

Olarn ran past the goblins and plunged into the sea. Icy water enveloped him, but he preferred it much to Breeog's fire. The pack quickly followed, making large splashes and waves as they dove into the sea. The three carrying the satyr called for the aid of more wolves to keep him afloat, leaving the goblins to stand bewildered on the beach.

"What are we supposed to do now?" they called out to the sea.

Olarn smiled and howled back to them, "Swim!" knowing perfectly well that they could not. He turned away and watched the icy sea reflect the red light of the dragon's fiery breaths as they descended on the wretched goblins.

Though it was long cold, and wind and snow had raged on the trail for many nights, the wolf quickly followed the scent. Its long snout passed over rocks and bushes and rose up as it breathed deep the air. It blinked in surprise and began to pant. The trail stopped. Confused, Eion sat down on his hind legs and began to scratch behind his head.

The hills swarmed with shifters scouring for Gwen; many of the animals roaming the mountains that night were not animals at all, but rather soldiers of Eion's army, carefully seeking the lost mortal. Above, a great host of hawks, eagles, and falcons soared high with searching eyes flitting to and fro. Lea, Ryan, Brad, and Eric were left among the few shifters who had not changed shape; they stood a few hundred yards away from where Eion sat, their faces tired and frightened.

Eion raised his snout to the air again, and yelped with glee when he picked up on the trail. He howled, signaling a small brigade of hawks to follow him as he set off after the scent.

He followed it to the mouth of a cave. He stopped at its entrance, and the hawks alighted on boulders above and beside it.

"Trail lead here, sir?" asked one with bronze plumage.

"Aye," answered Eion, not taking his gaze away from the open mouth of the cavern.

"It could be dangerous, sir" continued the shifter. He flapped his wings once in apprehension as the others nodded their heads and clicked their beaks fervently.

Eion snarled, baring his teeth. "Let me worry about that, Lieutenant. Stay here; if I am not back in ten minutes, follow me."

"Yes sir," replied the lieutenant hawk, snubbed. Eion ignored his indignation and set off into the dark of the cave.

It was quiet, but that only worried Eion. It was far from a natural silence; it was unhealthy and far too prolonged. He sniffed the air, and found a myriad of smells hung on it like flies in a web. He quickened his pace, his padded footfalls alone breaking the stillness.

The scent was stronger the farther down he went. Soon he came to caverns furnished and decorated, all filled with scrolls and odd bits of parchment inscribed with scrawled runes. Gwen's scent was now mingled with incense and smoke…and some strange odor of some creature that Eion dimly remembered but could not quite place. He shook his head, clearing his mind. He raised his head and breathed deeply. Penetrating the foreign smell, he picked up on Gwen's trail once more. He followed it through a small passageway that led to a series of stairs carved from the finest gemstones. Ordinarily, he would have stopped to admire it, but he was too pressed to find Gwen to take in its wonder. He sprinted down the rest of the way.

Eventually, he came to a humongous cavern, reeking of shadow wolf with a strong trace of human. Tables were placed against its walls; these too were piled with rolls of parchment and papyrus. Candles and incense covered almost every inch of the floor. Eion shuddered at the implication; this was the home of a conjuror.

He shifted to his usual form and drew *Raz'atr* from its sheath.

"Hello!" he called. "Anyone? Show yourself!"

Silence was his only answer. He took a readier grip on the sword hilt and shouted, "Show yourself!" again.

This time, a rustling sound greeted him. A shadow dropped to the ground, landing with a loud, "Oof!" Eion took a step nearer with *Raz'atr*'s tip pointed toward the dark form of the figure. He drew very little breath, and reached out with his free hand to the burning pentagram. Shifting the air, the flame rose, brightly casting light on the shadowed form.

It was Gwen, massaging her thighs, onto which she had landed painfully. She looked up at him first fearfully, but the fear melted into tears when she registered who it was standing over her.

"Eion?" Her voice was rich with some odd emotion Eion had never heard in her before.

He sighed with relief. "Yes."

Gwen stood shakily (she really had landed hard) and rushed to the shifter, throwing her arms around his neck. "Oh, Eion, it's horrible. They took him! They kidnapped him!"

Eion pulled himself away from her and looked her straight in her eyes. She was tearing. "Who did they kidnap?" he asked, disturbed.

Between long raspy bawls, she managed, "Axunrult."

"The conjuror Axunrult?"

But Gwen was beyond words. She just leaned on his shoulder and cried. Seeing that he would get nothing out of her for now, he put his arm around her shoulder and together they made their way out of the caves.

☐

When they exited through the mouth of the cavern, they were met by the entire battalion of shifters, who had gathered outside at behest of the shifter Eion had stationed by the cave. All of them had taken their usual forms again, so needless to say they were pretty cramped in the small space. At the front of the congregation was Lea, Ryan, Brad, Eric, Tirmal, Varez, Steel, and Fletch, all of whom ran toward them and embraced Gwen in one big group hug. There were tears and there was laughter; even

Varez, perhaps the gruffest of the present company, sniffled once or twice in his happiness.

"We thought we had lost you." whispered Steel, who was fighting Fletch for his place. The many swords and knives that hung from his belt and baldric clinked together noisily with the struggle.

Eion would have allowed this emotional reunion to continue further, but Gwen's words would not permit any delay. "Steel, Fletch," Eion said urgently, "Make ready the troops. Tirmal, transport Varez and yourself to the Resistance's camp on the Silver Ice Sea. We leave for the rendezvous point tonight."

"But Eion—" Fletch faltered, as they broke apart from Gwen, all deeply confused.

Eion whirled around, looking at Fletch in an angry way. "Tonight!" he said, with such finality to his command that there was no room for argument.

Steel strode past Fletch and asked, "In which guise do you wish us to take? Horse? Wolf?"

"Hawk," Eion said, changing as he spoke. "Take care of the girl." He screeched and took to the skies.

Fletch grumbled something then stalked away to give the order. Varez and Tirmal exchanged looks and shrugged. Then Tirmal raised his staff aloft and muttered an incantation. His staff's tip glowed for a minute, and in the next moment, he, the dwarf captain, and the other four mortals were gone, leaving behind a plume of smoke that reached high into the night air. No awe from any of the shifters, and Steel only chuckled as he addressed Gwen.

"Tirmal always has to add flair to his spells; sometimes I wonder if he was placed in the wrong clan, as he seems much more of the Vain Elves' type. Come, we travel on land," he said as he quickly transformed into a horse.

Gwen, still shuddering with sobs, climbed on his back, fumbling once or twice. Once she was stabilized, Steel galloped into the night.

☐

The great host of shifters soared gracefully, flying in a single formation in a very un-hawk-like way. Eion knew that they would seem conspicuous to any watching eyes, but he was no longer concerned with stealth or subtlety.

The night was calm and with little wind. No clouds cluttered the sky, allowing them the light of the crescent moon above them. They said nothing and made no sound except for the flapping of their wings.

One of the hawks glided over to the leader, with a perturbed manner about his flight.

"Eion," shrieked Fletch in hawkish voice, "why must we fly to the rendezvous point tonight? The troops are tired, they must be ready for anything, and if you insist on pushing them to their limits—"

Eion screeched, cutting him off sharply. "*Because*," he said irritably, "Gwen has just informed me that the shadow wolves kidnapped a *conjuror*."

Fletch shrugged as best as a hawk can shrug in mid-flight. "I still do not see why we must—"

"The wolves are not about to run the great many leagues from Saurindon to these mountains just to devour a conjuror. Ozmodion called for him. And if he is called for one spell caster, you can be sure he has sent for thousands more."

Fletch's hawk-eyes widened with understanding dread. And while hawks cannot gawk, but he managed the equivalent. "An army of magic! What are we to do?"

"Ozmodion will soon be sending envoys to Cassori and then Yerrin followed by Nunren, so needy is he for followers and strongholds. Should they refuse him, they will be conquered nonetheless. For now, we allow Ozmodion to divide his troops in this matter; 'tis all the easier for us. However, this increases our need for haste ten times over. Spell casters are easily bought; we are more than lucky we have the elves on our side. Should he mount an army large enough, we will all meet our doom."

"And what of those shadow shifters?" Fletch asked nervously.

"Another reason to hasten, I must have council."

"With whom? The other leaders?"

"With the gods. We will next cross the sea and make for the Mountain."

The shifter captain' trepidation was now replaced with awe. When nothing was said for a while, Fletch soared away from Eion, leaving him in his thoughts. Eion ignore him and instead focused on the horizon.

The Silver Ice Sea was now in view. Far below them, on a rocky beach, were thousands of campfires surrounded by dragons, dwarves, and elves. They were all celebrating, though what, Eion could not say. Grimly, he shock his head; they would have no cause for jubilation once his news was received.

Eion began the slow descending circle, the battalion of hawks following his lead. So great was the legion that it took nearly a half hour before they had all landed and shifted back to their usual forms. Once they did, all but Fletch ran to the fires eager for food and mead. Eion and his captain, instead, made their way to the center of the encampment, where the leader's tent would be.

As they made their way through the camp, skirting fires and tents, a galloping horse crossed their path, bearing Gwen.

"Put her to bed, Steel," Eion said wearily, massaging his temples with his forefingers, "then join us at the tent."

The horse grunted its affirmative and galloped away toward the fires. From one of them, Flame, Beast, and Armor strode over to Eion and Fletch, their faces visibly drawn even in the poor light.

"What took you so long?" asked Flame. Shadows circled his eyes; apparently he had gotten little sleep in the past few days. "We expected the worst."

"Then you expected right," Eion replied acidly. Seeing their confused faces, he apologized and said only, "I will explain later. Now, report on your adventures."

Beast was the first to speak. "Not but three hours ago, I spied a grand host of shadow wolves making its way up the mountains. Quickly I soared back to Breeog, and he aroused five hundred of his strongest dragons. By the time we returned, they were rocketing down the side of the mountain with a satyr captured. We killed a good three dozen, but the satyr and the rest plummeted into the sea, though we did dispose of the twenty goblins that waited for them on the shores."

Eion cursed loudly and strode even faster towards the tent, the other four straining to keep up; they were all still burdened with mail and weapons. Five minutes of taciturn marching later, Steel returned and jogged up alongside them.

"What is wrong?" he asked, but Eion said nothing. The other officers could only answer Steel with shrugs.

They came to the tent, a large, white erection with the Banner of Resistance fitted on top. Eion pushed aside the flaps and stepped in. His officers quietly followed

Chapter 16

The Complication

*I*nside a large round table had been set with ale and wine roasted meat. The smells were heavenly, and Eion's mouth watered. He repressed his hunger however, and focused on the tents occupants.

Breeog, Barthol, and Lord Fairskin all sat around table, laughing and talking in fruity voices. Varez and Tirmal were present too; they alone seemed dour.

"Enough!" Eion roared. At the outburst, Barthol choked on his drink, spurting ale down his front and across the table. Lord Fairskin was more composed, simply starting in surprise but calming down quickly into an attentive stare. Breeog's demeanor alone did not change, for it is very hard to catch a dragon unaware.

"Shifter," laughed the dragon king, his tongue scraping his lips in search of last remnants of his meal. "Whatever is the matter? We were about to set out to look for you, but we then vanquished some goblins, which is indeed cause for celebration."

"What *is* the matter, Eion?" slurred Barthol, now busy mopping up his shirt and face and beard, which was particularly drenched and dripping with the brown liquid.

"Oh, where to start?" mocked Eion, "The dragons' head officer's death should do nicely."

Breeog's grin vanished and was soon replaced by a snarl. "What a thing to speak about, even in jest. What is wrong, Eion?"

Eion shifted a chair for himself and sat in it. Steel, Fletch, Beast, Flame, and Armor did the same sitting uneasily as one.

"What is now a fortnight ago, my battalion was attacked on the high mountains by Vaeirnïr Bloodshedder and a host of black shifters, spawned from Ozmodion's black arts. We slaughtered the whole of them, but not before Vaeirnïr escaped after killing Gorbon. We found him dead in a field."

Breeog's snarl disappeared, and a look of distraught shock came over his face, which was soon followed by black fury.

"Very well," he said in a level tones, but his emotions were surrendered by the look in his eyes; those of loss and pain. "On Ozmodion's head is it."

"Oh, Dear Dragon King," said Eion with false casualty, "I have only begun. Beast informs me that you chased a pack of shadow wolves bearing a satyr this evening?"

"I did," Breeog started slowly, his forked tongue tasting the air with anger.

"Judging by Gwen's grief, I believe that she stayed with the satyr since Gorbon's death. She also informed me that said satyr is a conjuror."

At this, the whole table, save Eion and Fletch, gasped.

"Coincidence?" King Barthol began timidly, quickly sobering.

"I do not believe in coincidence," Eion said grimly. "True, shadow wolves have been known to hunt over great distances, but not, I think, when they are at war. I am sure that Ozmodion sent for the wretch."

"A satyr-conjuror, you say?" Breeog said, "I have only ever known of one satyr like that, and, until now, it was my belief that Gorbon killed him centuries ago."

"Where is the Lady Gwen?" asked Barthol, "We need her to help unravel this mystery."

Eion hesitated. "Must we? She has had a horrible stream of events pass in a short time, and now she sleeps."

It was Lord Fairskin's turn to speak. "This is a matter of gravest importance, Eion; the child's slumber will have to wait. Tirmal, bring her here."

The tall elf bowed and left the tent.

□

Leagues away, a dragon was screaming.

"Ahhhhh!" Vaeirnïr wriled in pain deep in the dungeons of Ozmodion's fortress where sunlight had never seen. "I am ever so sorry, my lord. I apologize ten thousand times over. Please spare me."

Ozmodion sat on his throne, directing his magic at Vaeirnïr. He watched as the dragon curled in agony and screamed with each passing spasm. The echoes of the dragon's cries reverberated off the walls and off the chains that hung from them.

"And you shall apologize ten thousand times more!" Ozmodion shouted over the din, "The night is young, and you shall wish for death before dawn!" Another jet of black magic was sent coursing through Vaeirnïr, and the dragon bellowed afresh.

Many hours later, Ozmodion tired and ceased the torture. Vaeirnïr cried with relief, as spasms racked his body in after effect.

"No matter," said Ozmodion, "I am not without other option. I will resort to other strategies. GOREZ!"

From the shadows of the dungeon, the nightshade stepped forth, as if peeled away from the darkness. He stalked across the room and knelt before the Red Sovereign's throne.

"Send a platoon of nightshades to the royal families of Yerrin, Nunren, and Cassori. Send word that I request their presence in three day's time. Should they refuse, I leave it to you to," he paused, *"persuade* them."

A horribly wicked grin split the nightshade's face. He bowed, and then climbed the staircase out of the dungeon, cackling with delight as he went.

"As for you," Ozmodion said, turning back to Vaeirnïr, "Did you know I keep a vortex with almost five hundred Qurs trapped inside? I think you will do well to visit it."

"No, my lord. I beg of you!" Vaeirnïr cried, but it was too late. A red nexus had already formed around the warlock's hand. Vaeirnïr clawed at the ground, trying to prevent being pulled in, but the force was too strong. He quickly drifted into the center and vanished into the vortex.

"For your sake," called Ozmodion, "I hope the next battle will find you greatly changed." The dragon's screams resonated one more time throughout the dungeon. Then, the vortex shut, the chains stopped their rattling, and all was quiet.

☐

Tirmal returned swiftly with the girl at his side. She looked tired and disoriented, with many tearstains running down her face, but she was very much awake. She took Tirmal's seat next to Lord Fairskin. Tirmal grumbled, but he summoned another chair with his staff and sat.

Lord Fairskin clasped Gwen's hand with both of his, running an old, bony finger across her palm gently. "Gwen, we need you to tell us everything about this satyr you so recently lost."

Gwen inhaled one slow, shuddering breath, and then began. "The satyr's name was Axunrult."

"AXUNRULT?" roared Breeog, now standing up with his wings spread and smoke seeping through his nostrils, "That is the name of the satyr that thought he could learn magic. I found him in the Mountain of Antiquity during a routine check, studying conjuring. Satyrs, as everyone knows, have been banished since before the Shifter Race. I sent Gorbon to dispose of him...I see now that he either failed or betrayed me."

Eion sighed and began to say something, but Gwen spoke up first.

"He did neither!" she exclaimed angrily, throwing off Lord Fairskin's hands. The old elf sighed and massaged the bridge of his nose. "He took it on himself to let a dreamer live a dream. From the beginning, all Axunrult wanted to do was help the Resistance! And he is now the prisoner of Ozmodion just because he wanted to help your cause!"

This aroused Eion's curiosity. "What do you mean?"

"One day he was scrying in Saurindon to get some information for the Resistance when Ozmodion felt his presence and learned of his existence. And now he is on his way to the blackest sorcerer the world has ever known, and you can only resent Gorbon for sparing him!" She then buried her face in her arms and began another silent fit of crying, unable to continue.

Igniring her sobs, Eion addressed the rest of the table. "He is mounting an army of spell casters, an army of magic. The elves' enchantments have always been one of our greatest advantages, while the Ozra's only strength rested in numbers and brawn. If Ozmodion secures a magical force large enough, we will be painfully overwhelmed."

"What do you suggest?" asked Breeog, still a little angry at Gwen's outburst.

Eion inhaled slowly. "I do not know. Lord Fairskin?"

The old elf sighed. "The need for haste is now greater than it ever had been. We must move now, swiftly and quietly, to the journey's end to stop this disaster from growing."

"Lord Fairskin," interrupted Eion, "I need council with those who dwell in the Mountain. I understand if the rest of you will not follow, but I will meet up with you later should you forge ahead."

Lord Fairskin considered a moment, and then shook his head. "No, we will go with you. Besides, it will do my troops good to study up on more magic while we are there. A short rest…yes. That is what we need before we go on ahead into the forest of Ÿalnz Dàr. In the morning, we make for the Mountain of Antiquity."

Eion nodded his appreciation. He looked over to Gwen, who was now fast asleep, tears seeping through her closed eyes.

"Fletch?" Eion began, but the arrow-burdened shifter had already walked over to the sleeping form and carried her out of the tent. Eion nodded again, then left to make way for his.

Chapter 17

The Crossing

Gwen awoke to the sounds of hammering, pounding, sawing, crunching, and yelling. She sat up inside her tent and looked around. Judging from the light outside, it was long before sunrise. She groaned and buried her head in the sheets, searching for sleep again.

☐

Outside, the enormous company was busy at work once again. On the rocky shores of the Silver Ice Sea, dragons cut down trees and were clawing at the wood, sculpting them into rough planks. Dwarves were shaving the planks so they were smooth, and shifters were hammering the planks into the frames of ships. Elves then magically sealed the ships so they would not leak drastically once they were set on the water.

By sunrise, forty ships had been made in this way. Afterward, the dragons set to work to setting them in the water, while the rest of the great company prepared for the short crossing to the Mountain. The Mountain was three days away, and they would need a fair amount of food to feed the four armies. Some set out back into the mountains to hunt for game, while others gathered fruits and leaves on the shoreline.

As he supervised this, Eion walked with his mind heavy with thoughts of something else. The dream had visited him again last night, causing him to wake from his sleep in a cold sweat.

He was in Saurindon, with the Prophesied following close behind him. Black and violet storm clouds darkened the valley, complementing every black story that had been told about the dreaded vally. Red lightning occasionally filled the air. Eion led the ten down the foothills of the Mountains of Midnight, a pained silence consuming them all. At the base of the mountains, an old stone temple stood, built of black rock. Eion signaled the ten to follow him in, ignoring their pale and scared faces. He made his way through the dark entrance. In the center of the gigantic room they were now in, was a torch, burning with a sickly red glow. Suddenly it grew into a flaming arm, which then snatched one of the ten and brought him back to the flame. One by one, they all disappeared, their screams echoing in Eion ears. Eion tried to scream but found he could not. Then the doors of the temple locked themselves, and the arm reached for Eion, beckoning for him to join his friends . . .

Eion grumpily made his way over to Gwen's tent, rapping on the canvas as he came to it. A groan and some rustling later, Gwen appeared from the tent's door, hair crumpled.

"Morning," Eion said brightly. "Ready for another chapter of adventure?"

Gwen stifled a yawn. "That depends. Is breakfast possible first?"

Eion held out his palm, and shifted a bowl full of fruit into his hand. Offering it to Gwen, who took it gratefully, he shifted a log for them to sit on. They took their seats next to each other, Gwen quickly biting into a plump apple.

The lull that followed was indistinguishably uncomfortable, and Eion felt obligated to break it. "So I suppose this conjuror…this Axunrult…was close to you?"

Gwen nodded slowly as she traded the apple for a banana, peeling it and then nibbling at the fruit inside.

"I promise you, I will do all in my power to return him safely."

She did not answer him, instead only stared bleakly out to the gray sea. When nothing was said for many minutes, Eion patted her on the shoulder consolingly and left to supervise the loading of the ships.

Gwen watched him go sighing regretfully as she finished the last of the banana was devoured. Mindlessly, she dug her fingers into the peel while images of the night before passed through her mind. She ran her hands over her face, shaking her head. Tears began to well up, but she wiped her eyes before they could stream down her face.

Inhaling shakily, she stood from her seat, deciding to walk around before she was forced to leave this place. The beach was covered with dark blue stones. Mist filled the air as the waves crashed upon the share. The magic of the sea consumed her; the thought that a place of such natural beauty could exist momentarily stunned her.

Her wonder and thoughts were interrupted, though, when Ryan approached her from behind. He stood next to her and absorbed the view, his face sharing her awe.

"You know, there are some things that can change your life forever," he whispered.

"What are you thinking?" she asked, seeing a strange look in his eye that she had never seen before.

"I'm thinking of my home, my family, my life. I wonder if I'll ever see them again." He paused, cocking his head. "I wonder…if I actually want to."

Deep down in Gwen's heart, she wondered the same thing.

A whistle then sounded, calling all to the ships. Gwen turned, and then, sharing a resigned look with Ryan, set off for the closest vessel.

They walked up the wobbly gangplank carefully, afraid of falling into the icy water below. They searched for the rest of the ten and joined them by the ship's stern near the helm. She saw Eion had boarded the ship as well, and was now busy giving orders to the crew, finalizing any last minute details. Gwen looked to the beach to see the rest of the Resistance file onto the rest of the forty ships, until the beaches were again empty, all remnants of the armies' tenancy gone except for the upturned stones and countless footprints. A battalion of dragons and shifter-hawks took to the skies, circling the fleet and watching for danger. When the last of the cargo had been loaded into the hold and the last of the crew had boarded the ships, whistles were sounded again and the anchors were raised.

Wind wafted through the great sails as they rose up the mast. The great fleet lunged through the water. Gwen set her sights to the horizon, fearing that she might become sick. The sea stretched on forever without the slightest hint of land on the other side, save a small triangle that she assumed was the Mountain of Antiquity. She felt another burst of speed as great oars sprouted from the sides of the ships and paddled.

They sailed on into the day. The sea air was briny and stale, and for along time she felt that she was going to be sick. She went to an unoccupied rail and hung over it in case she became nauseous, watching the rippling water slap against the hull.

As she dizzily watched the water lap against the hull, a scrappy cat jumped onto the rail, breaking her reflection. It was black and had gray patches around its eyes. Its fur was matted and, in places, clumped. Its eyes held a questioning look behind them, seeming to mask some sort of intelligence.

"Hello," said Gwen, straightening, surprised at its appearance, "Who are you?"

To her great astonishment, the cat answered.

"I am Curthlond," it said, "And you?"

It took her a while for her to find her voice. When she did, she replied, "I'm Gwen." Unsure of what to say next, she finished with, "Are you a shifter?"

"No, I was once an enchanter. I was cursed by fiancé into my current state." His eyes were vivid green, and his stare disconcerted her.

"Why did she curse you?" Mentally, she noted that had she been talking to a cat before coming to the Magic Realm, she would've thought herself insane. But now, after long getting used to the new world, she was unfazed.

"Lothilina is an extraordinary witch," answered the cat with a dreamy look of reminiscence in his eye. "Her beauty is unmatched by any I have ever seen. I had known her since our childhood, and we had grown up together. I proposed not but a year ago, and to my joy, she consented. Then everything fell apart. I came to visit her one day a few months ago, and I found her on the floor, bawling uncontrollably. "What is it, my love?" I asked. She looked to me with a face filled with horror. In a barely audible whisper, she said with a cry in the back of her throat, 'I never want to see you again; leave and never return'. And then, as though forced to, she placed this curse. With my heart and powers broken, I fled."

For a moment, the cat hung his head solemnly. Gwen had never seen a cat look solemn, and she found it almost as interesting as an embarrassed frog. But the sight was so pitiful that any entertainment Gwen found in it was short-lived. She wanted to comfort Curthlond, but she was uncertain of how to do it.

Curthlond straightened up without any consoling and continued on. "I set out to look for help. The hesitance in her curse set me thinking that she had acted against her own will, as though she'd been forced. I wandered the world for months, and my hope was beginning to run out. Then I saw these ships, and I thought I could get help here." He paused and looked around. "By the way, what *are* these ships for? This is one of the greatest armies I have ever seen."

Gwen cocked her head. "You mean you don't know?"

Curthlond shrugged. "I have been out of Arconia for a while; I am afraid I am a little behind on the times."

So Gwen relayed the story as best she could. It was a little abbreviated, and she purposely omitted the previous two weeks; she knew she could not handle retelling what had happened again.

Curthlond listened carefully, and remained silent throughout the entire telling, though his eyes widened as she went on, and in a few places he gasped in surprise. When she was done, he sat in absolute and terrified awe.

"They *dare* to try and stop the Red Sovereign? They will be obliterated. It has been more than one thousand years since Ozmodion fell, and his strength in magic as well as arms has only grown in that time. It's folly to even think to defeat him; he is unstoppable."

Gwen looked down at him, a little disgusted with this cowardly statement. "What else is there to do? Would you rather Ozmodion went unchecked? If no one challenges him, what do you think will happen? He will rise up and conquer this world. And after he's done laying it to waste, he'll move onto the other."

Curthlond sniffed. "Oh? And just how righteous is this Resistance, eh? Are they so just that they fight solely to throw off an oppressor?"

Stunned, Gwen didn't answer. She now gawked as the cat had done only minutes before. She knew she looked foolish, so she closed her mouth and gulped a little too audibly, for Curthlond chuckled and pressed onward.

"Never occurred to you, did it? Listen, no one is ever so virtuous that they act without ulterior motives. They just have not told you what those motives are yet, that's all."

Gwen bit her lip, unsure of how to address this. The idea that the Resistance, people who crowed how desperate they were for her help, could be hiding something from her was frightfully disturbing. The mere thought that Eion might be using her for some kind of gain…she rejected it immediately. It was just too unfathomable.

Eager to change the subject, she then asked, "You're an enchanter you say?" Axunrult had briefly mentioned the other ways of manipulating magic, but he had been vague in his descriptions and he had lacked a lot of details. She was keen to learn more.

"Yes, but I cannot cast any spells now," said Curthlond, his head cocked to the side in confusion.

He didn't elaborate any further. Impatient, she went on. "Is one born an enchanter, or can you learn?"

"With the right teacher, it is very easy to learn," he slowly answered. His tail flicked back and forth, though for what reason Gwen didn't know. And idea was forming in her mind, and she could barely keep her enthusiasm in control.

"I'll make you a deal, Curthlond. Do you promise to aid the Resistance?"

Now utterly lost, Curthlond opened his mouth, then, changing his mind, said, "Huh?"

Gwen rolled her eyes and sighed. "Listen, I think I, or at least, through me, the Resistance, can help you. What do you say?"

Curthlond scoffed, arching his back in a stretch. "What is the catch?"

Gwen gasped in false indignation. "Catch? Why, there is no catch at all!"

"Save the tripe. What do you want from me?"

A little disappointed, she dropped any pretense and told him the truth. "I want to learn magic. I think I could really help the Resistance if I was able to use it…and I've never dared dream of something so fascinating. You seem like the one to teach me. If you do, I'll make sure the Resistance gives you it's every protection as well as find a way to return you to your old form. What do you say?"

The cat's eyes narrowed suspiciously, and he hmphed with loud distrust. He didn't have to though; his eyes said it all.

Seeing this, she bent down close to his face and she added softly, "I don't have any ulterior motives, Curthlond. I want to help you, and I want you to help me. That's all. What do you say?"

Curthlond paused for another moment, but as she watched his hard look soften, Gwen could tell she had convinced him. In a moment, he was nodding with a very wide grin. "I will do it."

Gwen sighed, happy for the first time since last night. "Thank you, you won't regret it." An afterthought sprang to mind. With a smile that she feared looked devious, she added, "Oh, and I think it wise not to talk to anyone but me."

Curthlond returned the look with a wry grin of his own. "Ha! No ulterior motives my eye! What? You do not want anyone to know?"

Gwen shrugged. "I want something to myself, something Lord Fairskin, Eion, even my friends can't keep an eye on."

Curthlond shook his head, still smiling slightly. "I will agree, but you will have a hard time hiding it after a while. These things are very...*defining*."

Puzzled, Gwen opened her mouth to ask why, but Curthlond cut her off.

"I will explain it to you at a later time," he chuckled, as he jumped into Gwen's arms, "Come on now; it's time for lesson one."

☐

Ozmodion waited in the Great Hall, a large room constructed of polished black stone that had been cut as smooth as any glass. A bulky circular table occupied the whole of the chamber, positioned directly under a wooden candelabra which hung from a thick, rusty chain, one that had once been attached to a manacle in the dungeons, but had been retired. There was nothing decorative in the room, only the Red Sovereign, reclining in a red and gold seat, his long, bony fingers tapping impatiently on the wooden table.

A long and loud creaking sound from hinges that needed oiling, and then Gorez entered the room through the large, wooden doors at the far end of the chamber. He clicked his claws together, a grin of absolute glee "My lord," he said with a bow, "may I present the majesties King Jarul, Lord Danothen, and King Grang."

Three wizened old men now entered the room, each escorted by four nightshades who seemed a little remorseful; they would now have to find new victims to torment. The men wore robes of red, blue, and green, all of which were a little dirty and weather stained; they had come very far, after all.

The nightshades offered them seats, which they graciously took, despite the aura of fear that surrounded them. The nightshades pushed the seats in and then retreated to the shadows of the room, their eyes gleaming in the dark.

Ozmodion inclined his head in greeting, slowly hissing as he looked about them. "My lords, welcome to the noble Saurindon Gorge."

The man in red robes scoffed. "Noble indeed. I hoped myself dead before I had to set foot in this evil place. What is more, I hoped my entire country rotted before I had to meet you."

Ozmodion chuckled and raised a hand, palm up. He whispered a few words, and a brilliant, black flame ignited between his fingers, crackling and popping though it burned nothing. The three men gasped, and cowered into their chairs.

"Perhaps you forget why you fear me so, King Jarul?" he asked sinisterly, "Allow me to remind you!"

The sorcerer rose to his feet, raising his arms above his head. The black flame rose and expanded. In it, a feeble picture was seen, flickering dimly. As the black flame continued to swell, the picture became clearer.

It was a large town, full of everything from bazaars, markets, cottages, to towers, temples, and a castle. Many people were in the scene, walking, talking, buying, selling, laughing, and living. The sky was a magnificent color of blue, and the flowers and trees were lush and full of life. Birds flew through the cloudless sky, settling in the trees and singing in harmonious whistles.

The scene was of Vlairil, the Capitol of Nunren, King Jarul's kingdom. Laying far to the east, it was a peaceful city with an ancient history. For many years, it stood as a stronghold against marauding nomads and pirates, until Ozmodion had risen up over a thousand years ago and put them in his employ, causing the city to fall to the Ozra's might. After Ozmodion's death, it had fortified its defenses a hundredfold, and its army had grown to a formidable power.

Suddenly, horns blew from the towers. The townsfolk looked to the towers with pale faces. Bells rang loud and long, desperately alerting the people of the town to danger. The alarms did their jobs. All stopped what they were doing and gathered in the town square to find what was wrong. But all the king's heralds said nothing. They only raised trembling fingers and pointed to the southeast. The townspeople looked, and quickly realized the impending danger with horror.

On the horizon, and great storm of dust rose into the air, kicked up by the great host that was marching towards Vlairil. Already their footfalls could be heard off in the distance, like the great thunderclaps of a lightning storm. Wicked laughter and cries of battle were soon heard as they gained more ground.

As they came closer, the banner they held aloft could be clearly seen, and the city's worst fears were confirmed.

They carried the Red Standard of Ozmodion.

The city's soldiers were quickly marshaled. They ran through the streets, buckling their armor and tightening their helms as they went. They whistled and yelled and rallied each other to action. Some shepherded the women and children indoors, while other conscripted able-bodied men and forced them to the armories.

It was a chaos unlike anything King Jarul had ever seen before. Tears welled in his eyes as he watched people cry and scream as families were separated, sons and husbands taken to be fitted for armor and weapons.

When finally everyone was marshaled, sentries were posted at the entrances of the city, armed with swords and bows. The gates were closed and the portcullis dropped. Legions of soldiers and spell caster positioned themselves on the city's walls, waiting for the black force to come.

And come they did. The next few scenes were a blur of movement, but the three kings saw catapults level the walls of the city, breaching its main defense with a verocity not to be believed. Then, like a tub being drained, the fields outside the city were emptied as the army of monsters filtered into the capitol.

Nightshades ran through the alleys, slaughtering all as they went and ignoring the terrified screams their victims produced. Shadow wolves patrolled the streets, devouring all in their path. Trolls entered houses, slewing their occupants. Goblins set homes and stores on fire, cackling as they went.

A second brigade of trolls entered the city now, with a battering ram carved of red stone in the likeness of a great demon. They marched down the streets, ignoring as their fellows slew the town's people. They marched up to the gates of the castle in the center of the town. They smashed the ram into the gates, and again, and again, and again. On the fifth try, the doors crashed open. The ram was dropped, and the black army made their way into the castle. Screams from inside echoed in the ears of King Jarul as he watched the black scene in horror.

The Red Standard of Ozmodion was raised to the highest tower of the castle. One last horror-struck scream, and the black flame shrunk back into the palms of Ozmodion.

"This is what shall pass if you do not grant me control of your kingdoms," Ozmodion said darkly, as he lowered himself back into his throne-like chair, "I give you one month to decide. Return them to their thrones."

The nightshades led the three old men out of the room and left Ozmodion alone in the Hall to reflect.

□

"You just found it?" asked Lea incredulously.

Gwen nodded as she scratched Curthlond's ears. He closed his eyes and purred, shifting his position in Caitlyn's arms.

They all sat in a circle on some barrels that had been set outside the ship's galley. The air was moist, and the sun was hidden in the silvery mists. Gwen had never really enjoyed boating; she had nearly drowned once on an outing to the marina. Still, she found the Silver Ice Sea strangely soothing, though she expected that the prospect of learning magic largely contributed to the feeling.

"What are you calling him?" asked Caitlyn, taking a bite out of a green apple she had found in one of the barrels.

Gwen smiled maliciously. "I did consider Buttons…"

Curthlond hissed warningly, threatening to squirm out of Caitlyn's arms in protest.

"Oh, that's a great name!" squealed Kendal.

Gwen raised an eyebrow. "Oh, well, I was just kidding…but if you like it, why not?"

Curthlond's eyes widened as he gave Gwen the most pitiful look the world had ever known. He doubled his efforts to get free, partly in anger, but now mostly in humiliation.

"Ooh!" cooed Caitlyn, "what a perfect name for such an adorable kitty." She nuzzled her face between the cat's ears and was quickly met by another hiss and bared fangs. Caitlyn jolted in surprise but did not let go. She only laughed once she had gotten over the brief shock. Finally, with one last Herculean effort, Curthlond jumped from Caitlyn's arms and sauntered away behind a pile of crates. Gwen shared a final giggle with her friends, and then set off after him.

"I suppose you thought that was terribly funny?" he asked when she had found him sitting by a barrel full of pears with his tail lashing back and forth in agitation.

"I couldn't very well give you a name like Curthlond could I?" Gwen retorted.

Curthlond shrugged. "Fair point, but *Buttons*?"

"Spur of the moment thing. Doesn't matter though. Now, about those lessons."

Curthlond sighed and nodded. "Very well. Is there anywhere where we can be alone?"

They decided on Gwen's quarters. It was dark and secluded and, for the most part, uncluttered. It housed only two bunks; the Resistance saw no need for any other frills. Gwen and Lea usually shared the room, but Lea had no reason to come below when so much activity was on deck.

Curthlond jumped on Gwen's bunk, the bottom one, and made himself comfortable as he prepared her lesson.

Stretching his front paws, he curled into a ball, burrowing his face into the blankets. For a moment, Gwen thought he was going to purr.

"Enchanting demands you rely on words and will to carry out a magical task. You need not memorize all the words, for that would take far too long and you would most likely forget. They are written in the ancient tongue of elves, so they themselves have magic in every syllable."

Curthlond then sat up and began bathing himself.

"The simplest magical tasks do not require an incantation at all. All they need is strong concentratio. Again, the more sophisticated you're skills become, the simpler some tasks will seem. The lord of the Vra, Fairskin, could probably lift all the water in a pond just by thinking very hard about it. Ozmodion could fell an entire forest by imagining it in a dream."

Gwen dragged a stool over to the bunk. Clearly, this was going to take some effort.

"Now," continued Curthlond, "you cannot expect to turn an ancient forest into a roaring fire on your first day enchanting. No, you have to start by lighting a match. We will start with what is probably the simplest task that can be done magically."

He stopped bathing himself and looked around the room, his cat eyes picking out a quill in the dark.

"Can you see that quill on the floor?" Curthlond asked. Gwen turned her head and nodded. "Good," said Curthlond, "Stretch your hands out toward it."

Gwen nodded then did what she was told.

"Now, concentrate solely on that quill. Search yourself for a core of magic, if you can. It usually takes great discipline and practice to find it, but some are lucky and can find it without difficulty. Once you have done that, let the will to lift that quill fill you utterly. Focus only on that thought.

Gwen stared at the quill and stretched her arms out as far as they went. She focused only on the quill rising through the air. Nothing happened. She tried again, willing the quill to rise with all her strength, but it refused to even budge.

"Core of magic," Curthlond reminded.

Gwen nodded. Impatiently, she turned her thoughts inwards and began to search for some store of untapped magic. She felt pretty silly doing so; she had no idea where to look and she was certain she wouldn't be able to find it. After many minutes, she was about to give up, when suddenly, in a place she couldn't identify, she felt something she had never noticed before. It was strong, whatever it was, and she again focused on one, sole thought: raising the quill off the ground. She focused only on that idea with everything in her, ignoring everything else.

Then, abruptly, the strange feeling of energy expanded, and something surged through her arms and out her fingers. It lasted for only a fraction of a second, and when it passed the quill hovered about three feet in the air.

"Excellent!" crowed Curthlond in excitement, "Stupendous! Magnificent! Marvelous! Now control it!"

Gwen lowered one arm but kept the other extended. She gave it a quick jerk to the right. The quill sped over to where Gwen's arm was directed. Excited now, she raised her arm above her head, and the quill followed it, arcing upwards to hover where her outstretched fingers pointed.

"Wonderful!" exclaimed Curthlond. He was on his feet now and his tail was whipping around with his enthusiasm.

Emboldened, Gwen was about to make the quill spin while maneuvering it in a triangular pattern. As she prepare for this feat, however, a sharp pain traveled across her palm, so suddenly and so violently she jolted in surprise. Immediately, the quill dropped to the ground, the spell upon it broken.

Curthlond jumped from his bed and onto Gwen's lap. He examined her hand.

"Ah," exclaimed Curthlond, nodding his head with satisfaction, "I know what this is…it has been so long. I had almost completely forgotten about it…hm, this complicates some things. This will hinder a lot of the basics…but I can see no other way around it. We will just have to be patient until it passes."

Gwen looked from her hand to the cat.

"What is it?" she asked urgently, not sure what he was talking about.

"Oh, you will understand," smiled Curthlond, "in time."

He jumped from her lap and made his way out of the room.

"That is enough for today," he called from around the corner. Gwen called to ask him what he was talking about, but he was already gone.

Eion sighed as he hung on top of the mast, watching the sun sink below the west horizon. The sky was painted with brilliant hues of orange, pink, and violet, shading the clouds with a magnificent array of colors. The sea itself was tinged with red and yellow. Wind whipped his hair about and made his shirt hug cling tightly to his skin. For the first time since before they had left Fairskin Manor, he was content.

The fleet was now almost halfway across the sea. In another day, they would reach the other side, and then they would make their way to the Mountain. Eion wondered if he should just fly ahead, get council, then fly back. Gorbon's ashes were stored in a large leather pouch that he had tied to his belt. It felt somewhat dishonest to not have told Breeog that he had cremated Gorbon and that he was now going to sacrifice his ashes. But the gods rarely talked to someone who had not brought a strong magical artifact, and dragon ashes were extremely magical.

Eion knew that there were three gods he needed to talk to. If he could talk to more, he would be very thankful, but three was all he needed. The first had to be Garon, God of Life. He was the lord of the gods and would aid Eion greatly. He was wise and kind but strong and powerful.

The second would be Vundin, the God of Time. Eion now needed to see what the future held for the Resistance, and though there were plenty of seers throughout Ÿalnz Dàr, no one could compete with a vision from a god.

The third would be Avria, Goddess of Death and Queen of the Necroverse. It had long been common knowledge that Ozmodion worshiped her above all the other gods. A magnificent temple had been built in the Saurindon in her honor. Through her, Eion hoped for answers to his questions about Ozmodion's plans. She would tell if Eion offered her more of Gorbon's ashes.

In a way, he hoped for a long stay in the Mountain, and dreaded Ÿalnz Dàr. Even now, while he sat in the middle of the sea, Eion could sill see it in his mind, its dark trees towering into the sky, casting shadows sinister and forlorn. Though it still separated them from the Ozra's Gap by a great distance of leagues, it was, by all accounts, Ozmodion's territory. Eion admired the bravery of those who still dared to dwell in those untamed woods. Eion had even heard tell of a tribe of fomariuns living to the far eastern side of the forest. This was farfetched since almost all fomariuns now lived in the Valley of the Weres far to the east, but Eion could not discredit the rumor completely. It had been almost three centuries since he had crossed into the forest and now, as he neared it, he wished it could be another three centuries more.

Eion sighed and climbed down to the deck, his apprehension and anxiety shown plainly on his face. He made his way towards his cabin, looking forward to the end of the next day and ignoring his dread of the days to follow.

□

Axunrult laid on the rack in complete darkness and silence, his head pounding achingly. The wolves had not been gentle in his transportation from the mountain. He tried to move his arms and legs, but found they were tied to the rack.

Not a sound could be heard, not even his own breathing. As he was counting the minutes, torches on the wall lit themselves and the dungeon was filled with a shade of red that was so dark it was almost black.

Then, through the silence, a figure could be heard walking down the twisted spiral staircase that lay far past Axunrult's feet. As the figure approached the rack, more torches ignited themselves to reveal the figure as a tall man in a red cloak.

Ozmodion chuckled. "Welcome, fomariun, to Taronest, my home."

Axunrult put on a face of contempt, but remained silent.

"Tsk," reprimanded Ozmodion, walking to the left side of the rack, "Why the face? Here I am, trying to welcome a guest in my home, and this is the gratitude I receive? We shall have to fix this."

Ozmodion walked out of Axunrult's eye line. Second later, the sound of a crank being turned could be heard.

Immediately, Axunrult felt the chains shackled to his wrists and hooves tighten. It was not painful, but horribly uncomfortable.

Ozmodion returned, this time on Axunrult's right side. "Now, I trust my officer informed you of my proposition?"

Axunrult turned his head to stare at the black underneath the hood. "He did."

"And…?"

"I would rather die."

Again, Ozmodion laughed his dark laugh, "How fortunate for you! I would be most happy to secure such arrangements."

He waved his hand in, Axunrult assumed, the direction of the crank. He heard it click. Again the chain tightened, this time a small pain spread through his arms and legs.

"Now," Ozmodion continued, taking no notice of the pain in the satyr's face, "Surely you remember my power?"

Axunrult took a quick intake of breath, and said, "Unfortunately, yes."

Ozmodion waved his hand again. The crank clicked once again and the chain tightened once more. This time, a fiery ache erupted through all of Axunrult's nerves.

"Then you do realize that this kind of torture is horribly trivial? I could do much worse, yet I have found it in my heart to not only offer you a kindly position, but to give you mere medieval torture."

Axunrult's breathing was rapid. Sweat was trickled down his forehead. He watched as his bare chest moved up and down quickly. He again turned to Ozmodion.

"I did not know you had a heart."

Ozmodion sighed and waved his hand again. Axunrult almost cried when he heard the click. Pain like none he had never felt before exploded through his body. His vision blurred, and Ozmodion's next words seemed to echo.

"If you will not aid me willingly, I shall have to resort to other methods of persuasion."

Axunrult barely heard him, and as soon as the last syllable was spoken, he lost consciousness.

◻

"Ow!" yelped Gwen.

She and Curthlond had practiced well into the night and had woken early the next morning. But every time Gwen tried to lift the quill, the sharp pain flickered throughout her palm. Curthlond was sympathetic and assured her the same thing had happened to him and that it would pass, but he gave no explanation as to why it was happening.

Now, in the early morning, the pain had become more than sharp and quick, but brutal and lingering. The pain was so intense, Gwen found herself having to sit down and catch her breath.

Curthlond jumped onto her lap in attempt to soothe her, but she was too irritable. She pushed him off.

"Why is this happening?" she yelled, pointing at him and raising him into the air with magic.

Curthlond hissed in the middle of a somersault, "I cannot tell you! You will never become an enchantress if you discover the secret so soon!" He tried to appear composed, but the flips and spins made this impossible.

Angry with the pain as well as Curthlond's vague insinuations, Gwen dropped him abruptly. He hissed again, and this time a loud thud could be heard as he came back to earth. Body and dignity wounded, he stalked out of the room, muttering grouchily under his breath.

At that point, Lea awoke. She was an amazingly sound sleeper, and so the lesson had been conducted unheard. She greeted Gwen, and then went to the closet to change. Gwen sighed, arose, and made her way to the galley for breakfast.

☐

It was Eion's turn at the helm. He kept his eye on the horizon as he navigated through the lazy waters, listening as the white caps broke against the ship. They were now maybe a mile from the shoreline. Eion had a crew of shifters on every ship enlarge the sails so they would catch more wind and thus arrive there quicker.

But still they were moving too slow. Eion gave the order for the oars to be used, but Lord Fairskin had thought it foolish. Sighing, he resigned himself to nervously anticipate their arrival at the Mountain.

The Mountain of Antiquity loomed over them, piercing the very heavens. It cast a humongous shadow over the west that covered all the eye could see. Clouds, threatening rain and thunder, circled it in a foreboding way, despite the Mountain's benevolent nature.

Steel walked up beside Eion as he too stared at the Mountain. Eion ignored him, or rather he did not notice him; the Mountain seemed to demand all his attention.

Steel cleared his throat when nothing was said for a while.

"Get the ships ready to disembark," said Eion. "Have them close their sails. We will dematerialize the ships when we anchor; there is no reason to let them rot in the bay. Send Fletch and Beast to the other ships."

Steel nodded and made his way to relay the orders. Eion watched him shift to a hawk and jump into the skies, and then gave the command to close the sails; quickly, several shifters climbed to the top of the mast while several others handled the ropes on deck. Several minutes passed by, then the great sheets of canvas were pulled to a close. Eion felt the ship slow immediately, deprived of its driving wind.

Eion barked another command, this time with his shifted amplified voice so all the ships could hear. As one, the life boats were dropped into the sea, which, like ants, every soldier of the Resistance climbed into. The dragons, too bulky to fit inside the small crafts, took flight, and circled the ships while gliding hundreds of feet above the water

From Eion's place at the helm, he watched as Gwen made her way into the boats, followed by her scrappy black cat. Eion took a good look at it. It was unlike any cat he had ever seen. It carried itself in an odd way, as if it was human. It paused for a moment and turned its head. For a moment, its slit like pupils locked with Eion's eyes. It then smiled. Eion looked again to be sure, but the cat had definitely smiled. It then resumed trotting beside Gwen.

Eion made a mental note to himself to keep his eyes on the cat; something about it unsettled him.

There was nothing he could do about it now. He shifted into a hawk and took to the skies, circling the boat that bore Gwen and the cat. He would ask Breeog to take a look at it, for dragons were much more knowing about those kinds of things then Eion was.

The boats were paddled towards the Mountain. A good-sized cave could be seen on the north side. Eion squawked something to Steel, who was rowing in the lead boat, accompanied by Lord Fairskin and King Barthol. Steel nodded, and gave the order to the other boats.

Roars could be heard from behind. Eion swiveled his head around to see the dragons tearing the ships apart plank by plank, while shifters in hawk form circled above, shifting the wood into water, rocks, and air. Eion clicked his beak, and then made his way to the cave. He free-fell and then pulled up until he was soaring only inches above the water. He zoomed into the cave, and perched himself on a rock to the right side.

The inside of the cave was like a natural docking port, with room for many lifeboats to anchor. The ceiling was very high, though the entrance was only about ten feet tall. On the opposite side of the cave, gigantic, bronze doors marked the entrance into the Mountain. Granite stairs led up to them, crudely cut in intense contrast to the remarkable detail done upon the doors.

The boats now made their way into the caves, each entering its own port. As the long stream of boats slowly made its way in, Eion shifted back to his usual form. Dragons swooped in, barely missing the heads of the boats' occupants as they soared through the low entrance. Breeog was the last to come in, making his way in front of the doors. Eion climbed the stone steps to wait next to him. Barthol and Fairskin exited their boats and joined them. The stairs proved a nasty obstacle for Lord Fairskin; even with the combined help of his staff and Barthol, it still took him about five minutes to reach the top of the rocky steps.

The last of the boats were tied to the stony dock, though most of the army was forced to remain in the crafts; the port simply did not have space enough for them all to stand. Immediately, the temperature of the cavern, which had been cool upon entering, spiked as the warm breaths of the Resistance mingled with the salty air. The dragons flew in a circle high, high above the water, roaring lazily, awaiting an opportunity to land. It didn't come.

Breeog banged his tail against the grand brass doors. A loud *boom* followed, shaking the very air around them. The Dragon King nodded, satisfied with the sound, and hit the doors again. *Boom*. It was louder this time; Eion felt the floor beneath him quiver from the force of the sound. A third *boom*, and then Breeog stepped back, pleased.

The company waited in silence, save for the flapping of the dragons wings and the coughs and sneezes of some scattered soldiers. The water lapped against the rocks of the natural harbor, sending a spray of water vapor into the air, which did little to quell the rising temperature of the cavern.

Suddenly the doors opened, swinging easily on the moist hinges. Out of them came men even shorter than dwarves; their gnarled horns protruding from their temples much like goblins. They wore long, billowing robes made of the softest silk, decorated with stars and runes that Eion recognized from the language of the gods. Their eyes were sharp with small gleams reflecting from their pupils, gleams of thought and uncounted years. Their faces were long in comparison to their bodies, with wrinkles disfiguring their skin.

The head of the creatures was very old indeed. Like Lord Fairskin, he had a long, gray beard and depended on his staff to move around, though he did not emanate the same power as the old elf.

The Head Hobgoblin addressed the gigantic company, raising his hands into the air to quiet them. He need not have done so; the company had hushed as soon as the doors had opened.

"Welcome, members of the Resistance," he said. His voice was hoarse and scratchy, like cracked shale against steel. To Eion, it brought images of scouring ravens cawing while circling some dead animal. It wasn't pleasant. "You honor us with your presence; the Mountain has long expected your arrival." He gestured, trying to seem majestic and striking. However, the effect was rather muted as he nearly toppled when he raised his right arm too high and lost his balance. It took four of his attendants to right him, and his breathing was very quick and short for a long while after. When he had sufficiently recovered, he smiled and spoke to the Resistance one more time. "Please…come."

Chapter 18

The Mountain

L*ord Fairskin stepped forward* and shook the Head Hobgoblin's hand, and then turned to the Resistance, beckoning them to follow. He allowed the Head Hobgoblin to lead them into the mountain, even though the short man hobbled very slowly and several of his assistants had to follow closely to make sure he wouldn't stumble again.

Eion followed behind the hobgoblins. He entered through the brass doors into an extremely long hallway. The ceiling was just as high as that of the cavern they had found themselves in moments ago, although this cavern was made from bricks of gems. Sapphire, ruby, and gold sparkled on either side of them in an ornate manner, forming patterns and designs that cried some unnecessary gaudiness and a blatant frivolity while diminishing neither. Stalactites and stalagmites of silver hung from the ceiling and stuck up from the floor almost decoratively.

They walked for what seemed hours down the wondrous hallway, their awe turning the minutes into weeks. As they neared the end, they approached an emerald door that stretched at least thirty feet high. It too was engraved with runes, stars, moons, and the Arconia's seal: a series of circles that intersected with one triangle, representing the myriad of races that came to pay homage to the Mountain. Over the top of the door, bold runes had been engraved into the stone. Eion recognized the letters and the language. It read:

Cross the threshold, if you dare
And seek the mystery you desire
Though of the magics, thou take heed
Else be consumed by dark and fire

Eion frowned at the message, recalling that it had not been there the last time he had walked this corridor. Looking at its base, he saw crystalline powder sparkling. Apparently, the runes had been recently carved. Eion understood their meaning firmly; it was a barefaced reminder of the Mountain's true tenants: the gods.

The head of the hobgoblins made his way to the door, reaching inside his robes to produce a key made of polished jade, which he shoved into the keyhole in the direct center of the door. As he turned the key, he mumbled several words, first lowly, then loudly. With the incantation complete the door dissipated into a green mist. Eventually, it completely disappeared, leaving behind an archway that led to a new cavern. Satisfied, the Head Hobgoblin nodded and beckoned for the rest to follow.

They walked into the main hall of the Mountain. Eion had seen it several times before, each time renewing his wonder.

The ceiling expanded to a ridiculous height; the very top could not be seen. Balconies, staircases, and pillars filled the room, all surrounded by hobgoblins. Eion had always found them as the strangest of magical beings. All, save the Head Hobgoblin, looked exactly alike, not one feature different from another's. They had brown eyes, a hooked eagle nose, horns, and a horribly obvious cleft in the chin. On top of the physical conformity, Eion had never heard of a hobgoblin having a name.

They all paused at the sight of Breeog and the other dragons (all of whom were now walking), fear seizing their faces. Eion realized that Vaeirnïr's intrusion had left the Mountain with a false impression of the dragons' nature. As Eion looked around the cavern, he saw gigantic scorch marks ruining the beauty of the gemstone walls.

Like the cave they had just come from, the main cavern was constructed entirely of gems. The dwarves stared at the cavern in awe. As masters of carving rocks, they had always considered the Mountain to be the greatest subterranean architectural development in the Magic Realm. True it was not the dwarves that had built it (oddly enough it had been the ancient elves), though the precision was indeed notable.

Several other caverns branched from the Great Hall, each marked with a different rune. The greatest of these was carved into a golden plate and sparkled with every color in the spectrum. Eion inhaled deeply, thinking of what lay at the end of the corridor. He shook the hand of the Head Hobgoblin, and made his way towards the hallway, receding into its dark maw.

Gwen watched him go, wondering where the corridor led. She shrugged, knowing the only reason they were there was because Eion had business at the Mountain. She had no way of knowing, of course, that she herself would venture down that very hallway before they would leave the Mountain.

The hobgoblins now led them to one of the other hallways. It curved and turned so many times that Gwen found it impossible to recall all the changes in direction. This one, though still masterfully crafted, seemed plain after the entrance corridor, as it was unadorned with gems or jewels. Yet the walls were still as smooth as glass, and the floor clean of any rubble or rocks.

At the end they came to a spiral staircase. They went up about twenty steps, and then came to a large area where at least twelve staircases met. All but one of the Head Hobgoblin's aids split off and started up the staircases, beckoning large portions of the Resistance to follow. Meanwhile, the Head and his last aid led Lord Fairskin, King Barthol, Breeog, The Prophesied Ten, and the leading captains from each race up the last stairway.

The steps were made of shimmering ruby, so flawlessly cut it look like red ice. The banister was carved into the side of the cavern with intricate designing weaving on top of and around the rails. The ceiling was not half as high as the previous caverns, stretching maybe twenty feet from the ground. Breeog grumbled as he had to stoop on all four and crawl up the winding stairway, his wide body scratching the walls with his razor sharp scales.

What seemed hours later, they reached the top of stairs, which led them to a large cavern with a series of doors placed all around. The Head Hobgoblin spoke a syllable and, suddenly, hundreds of small, floating, glowing spheres ignited throughout the cave, casting it in a ghostly light that ill befitted it. To Gwen, it seemed like the unhealthy glow of the florescent lights in a hospital; sterile and false.

The cavern was tiered with three levels, all with many doors set into the stony walls. The Head Hobgoblin escorted each to his and her rooms. Gwen was placed on the second level in between Lord Fairskin and an empty room, which she assumed would be Eion's. Once they had all been sorted, the hobgoblins bowed (or rather the aid did; the Head was far to stiff to manage the feat) and withdrew from the eerily illuminated cavern

Gwen closed her door and looked around. The room was small, with little decoration save a mirror that hung across from a small bed with a carved, mahogany head post. The walls and floor were smooth and made of gray stone. The ceiling, however, was jagged, with stalactites hanging down so far that, in places, Gwen had to duck her head.

Curthlond jumped onto the bed and began to bathe himself.

Gwen laughed. "Why bother?"

"Just maintaining the illusion," he answered between licks, "Your friend Eion might suspect me now. In any case, now is a perfect time to continue our lessons."

Gwen groaned and looked at her hand tiredly. She was baffled that it was not red with irritation; the pain of casting spells had now become so intense that she felt as though someone was slitting her hand open with a fiery knife.

"Now," said Curthlond, finishing his bath and facing. "That pain in your hand will pass eventually. Small spells like levitating will just irritate it. It is better to cast a larger spell, thereby ending the pain. We willl start with fire spells. Fire has a large variety of uses. Once you master the incantation, you willl have time to discover them, but for now, we we will practice using it offensively. Find that magic force and shout clearly, '*Noro destrisa*'."

Gwen nodded reluctantly, but before she could look for the magic, a loud knock came from the door. Gwen went to open it, but a hobgoblin had already entered. Silently, he beckoned Gwen to come. She sighed tiredly and followed him out. Curthlond jumped form the bed and followed her out.

The lights that the Head Hobgoblin had called on were now glowing green. Why, Gwen couldn't imagine, but it was better than the hospital-like illumination. The leaders and the mortals had congregated outside in the large cavern, along with good deal of hobgoblins, all quietly whispering to each other while they waited for everyone to come. Watching them, Gwen saw that they were pretty inanimate. They made no expression while they talked; indeed, they all seemed so blank that Gwen would've thought they had all awoke from deep slumber only seconds ago. She decided that she didn't like them. They were just too bizarre.

After Gwen joined Stephanie, Caitlyn, and Kendal, the four dozen or so hobgoblins lead them through the long corridor, back through the Main Cavern, and up another, shorter, brighter tunnel. It led to another incredibly large cavern, one so big that the Great Hall in Fairskin Manor was dwarfed in comparison. And like the Great Hall, an enormous table had been prepared with what was going to be a colossal feast. Turkey, ham, whole sides of beef, mutton, and every game bird imaginable had been cooked to perfection and had been laid out on the table. Among them were salads, fruits, biscuits, and soups of every kind. Inhaling, she was struck by an overwhelming array of scents, so tempting that she felt her mouth water hungrily.

The hobgoblins, monotonous and blank the whole while, shepherded everyone into their seats. This took time, much as it had at the feast in Fairskin Manor. They had particular trouble with helping the dragons to their seats, who were so tall and so loud that they were unable to hear the hobgoblins; in one occasion, a group of dragons were so deep in conversation that, oblivious to the hobgoblin in front of him, they trampled the poor creature into the ground, not even pausing to look over their shoulders.

As four more of the hobgoblins rushed to peel their fellow from the highly polished floor, Gwen tried to look down the end of the table, but found out she could not. *Another enchantment,* she told herself. She had no idea how such a spell would be cast, and shuddered to think of what a magical toll that would take on her.

Slowly, the other members of the Resistance entered the room, their faces filled with awe by the grandeur of it all. When what seemed like an hour had passed and everyone had made their way in, The Head Hobgoblin made his way through the entrance way and gestured at the food, indicating it was time to eat.

Gwen had not had a meal this good since the great feast in Fairskin Manor on her first night in the Magic Realm. There was much laughter, story telling, entertainment, and merriment of all kinds. Gwen shared in all of the joy while feeding Curthlond small strips of meat and small bowls of wine. The cat meowed delightedly, apparently starved.

Throughout the feast, drinks were served by hundreds of people in tattered clothes, which did little to keep them warm or hide their bodies. The men only wore small loincloths around their waists and they had no shirts. The women too wore the loincloths and very ragged tops, leaving a large section of their midriff uncovered. They did not wear anything on their feet, showing their many calluses and cuts and scrapes. They were all, Gwen noticed, very young looking. Several hobgoblins were giving them instruction in cruel voices, as though they weren't fit to be courteous to.

Gwen leaned to her right and whispered to Tirmal, "Who are those people?"

Tirmal looked at them, disgust showing plainly on his face. "They are victims of one of the cruelest magics. They are blood-slaves."

Gwen looked confused. "Blood-slaves?"

Tirmal nodded, turning back to his food. "I am sure you know the general concept of a slave, a person who is property of another person and does their bidding out of fear and under threat. The one problem with regular slaves is that they are able to disobey orders or, if they dare, escape. Well, blood-mages long ago rectified this problem. A blood-slave is bound to its master with horrible enchantments. To make a blood-slave/blood-master relationship, each must have a cup of blood taken. A blood-mage then puts binding curses and merging spells on both cups of blood. Then, the master's blood must be put in the slave's body, and the slave's blood must be put in the master's body. Once this is done, the slave is bound to the will and life of its master. The slave feels its master's pain and dies along with the one it is bound to. The slave will forever seem to be the age at which it was imprisoned, so it is useful until its master's death."

Gwen looked at the slaves in horror. "Is their anyway to free them?"

"Usually, the blood-master must consent to break the bond. If he does not, there is still another way. The blood-mage who performed the ritual must break the enchantments on the master, for the slave is still the master's property and therefore untouchable without permission. There is one drawback to this, however. If ever the slave comes upon a relative or descendant of its former master, it will be doubly bound, and its freedom will be possible only if its new master consents to break the bond."

Gwen squinted at the closest slave, and then another, and another after. Each bore an expression of unspeakable sorrow, as though they were on the verge of tears, but unable to cry. "Do they still know who they are?"

Tirmal nodded grimly, following he gaze to one of the slaves. "They are constantly tortured by their true identities. They are haunted by the lives they could, and should, have."

"Who would allow themselves to be enslaved like that?"

"It is nothing any sensible person would assent to do. I am afraid the youths are overcome by spells, such as a simple immobilization curse. All they can do then is sit and watch helplessly as their lives are given away."

"Why are the hobgoblins doing this? I thought they were peaceful creatures?"

"Normally they are. The blood-slaves were not here the last time I was at the Mountain. I suspect that they brought them here because they are short on help since Vaeirnïr wreaked havoc on the Mountain; Lord Fairskin informed me the death toll was immense. They will probably have the bonds broken once more hobgoblins come to the Mountain. For now, all we can do is lament their losses and not let ourselves become accustomed to the service from those who have no life of their own."

Gwen nodded sadly as a blood-slave approached her with a bottle of wine.

"Some wine, m'lady?" Her long, black hair was tangled and dirty, its shine muted by years of service. Her skin was a very unhealthy white and Gwen wasn't surprised at all to see that her midriff hugged her ribs too tightly. Her eyes were gray and sad, and the only clean patches of skin on her face were framed by tearstains. She was someone, Gwen noticed, who was once pretty.

Gwen looked to Tirmal, biting her lip. The elf sighed, and nodded sadly. "Yes please," Gwen said painfully, turning back to the girl. She nodded good-naturedly, and began to pour the wine, but the glass fell over and the wine spilt onto Gwen's favorite tunic. Almost instantly, the purple liquid soaked through the cloth, and she jumped instinctively as she felt the cold touch her skin.

The girl looked terrified. "M'lady, I am ever so sorry," she cried desperately, as she tried to clean the glass and spilt wine up with her sad excuse for clothes.

"Not to worry," Gwen said, "Tirmal could you...?"

The elf snapped his fingers and the wine stains on Gwen's tunic disappeared. Curthlond jumped onto the table and licked up any wine the girl had missed. His eyes met Gwen's very quickly, but he quickly cast them down at her harsh, reproachful stare.

Still the fear did not leave the girl's eyes. She was now on her knees begging Gwen to forgive her. Her rough hands grasped Gwen's arms, as if searching for mercy. Wails of "Please!" echoed through the great cavern; all eyes of the table were on the girl by now.

"It's all right," Gwen began, but she was cut short by the approach of another hobgoblin. The sight of him had sent the girl into a spasm of writhing and agonized screams. She released her iron hold on Gwen's arms and now rolled about on the floor, seemingly made with distress.

"Well," said the hobgoblin that paid no attention to this, "another *accident*, Ria?"

At the sound of her name, the slave-girl stopped her fit and stood up hastily, a little clumsy from the exertion of her bawls and sobs. She wiped her eyes and, bowing awkwardly, clasped her hands in an imploring way.

"P-Please, s-s-sir," she begged, sobbing. "My m-m-master—"

"Has lent you to the Head Hobgoblin," finished the hobgoblin plainly, coldly unmoved, "who has in turn lent you to me. But you, I am afraid, are more than useless. I will contact your master, thank him for the gesture, and send you back," He now addressed Gwen, "I am sorry about that, m'lady. She will be dealt with."

The Hobgoblin turned to leave, but the girl had thrown herself at him and had grabbed the hem of his robes.

"Please!" she wailed, "My master will punish me horribly for disgracing him like this!"

The hobgoblin turned to her. "I am sorry," he said sincerely, "Go up to the kitchens and wait for your master there."

With that he left. The girl, still weeping, followed him. Gwen called to stop them, to tell the hobgoblin to leave the girl be, but he was already gone, far out of earshot. With a heavy heart, Gwen turned to Tirmal, who gave her a weak smile before turning back to her food.

The feast continued well into the night, and Eion never came to join them. Gwen now began to feel uneasy, as though a strange yet vaguely familiar presence lurked close at hand.

When finally the last scrap of food had been eaten and the last drop of wine had been drunk, the great table began to empty as the four armies slowly made their way to their beds. For many hours after, the tunnels of the Mountain were clogged with the slow, shuffling soldiers, full of meat and drink. Gwen, fueled by some fiery emotion, pushed her way through the drunken droves, ignoring their grumbles and yells of protest. Wide-eyed with nervousness, Curthlond followed at her heels.

When finally they made it back to the cavern which led to the rooms, the hovering lights had changed to a deep shade of red. This fitted Gwen's mood perfectly, and she quickly stalked to her door, opened it, and stepped inside. She was about to slam the door shut, but stopped as Curthlond squeezed his way in with a yowl. Scowling, she shoved the door the rest of the way once the cat was clear.

For the next hour, she ranted and raved fiercely of the injustice of the atrocity they had just seen. Curthlond tried to comment at first, but here rage was so intense that he let her carry on rhetorically. When she had gone on so long that she needed to take a draught of water from the washbasin, Curthlond plucked up the courage to speak.

"Yes, it is a terrible thing to own someone's life," he said tiredly, bracing himself in case she directed her fury at him. "Perhaps one day you will find a way to free them."

Gwen opened her mouth to begin her tirade again, when she stopped. She repeated his words in her head, but found she could make no sense of them. She raised her eyebrows as she sat on her bed, looking at him with her head cocked to the side. "How? After this war is over, I have to go back to the Mortal Realm. I won't be able to help them."

For some reason, Curthlond laughed at that. "Gwen, since you have left you have grown. Do you think you will ever be content with what *was* now that you have what *is*?"

He left it at that, and curled himself into a ball at the edge of her bed. She pondered over his words, but, drained from her rant, she could hardly keep her eyes open. She crawled under the covers and drifted off into sleep.

Sometime, later on that night, Curthlond's purring woke Gwen. As she stared into the blackness, she suddenly heard the sound of the creaking of hinges and the slamming of a door.

Eion had returned.

Chapter 19

The Library

When *Gwen woke the following day*, her anger and feeling of blatant injustice returned. Lingering images of the blood-slaves passed over her eyes. She clenched her fists. Quietly, she crept from her room, careful not to wake Curthlond.

When she entered the large cavern, she found a single hobgoblin dozing in a large, green armchair, his glasses askew and the book he was reading lay open on his lap. Why he was there and how he had got the chair up to the cavern, Gwen did not know. With a shrug, she approached him and shook him gently. After a moment, he yawned and opened his eyes. He started when he first saw her, but, removing his glasses and rubbing his eyes, he smiled warmly once his vision focused.

"Yes, m'lady?" he said, trying to stifle another yawn.

"I have not had a proper bath in ages," Gwen explained, "Is it possible I could…?"

"Oh certainly!" said the hobgoblin, "Come, follow me!"

He rose from his seat and grabbed her arm. He had a surprisingly strong grip for someone so small. They left the large cavern through a passage she had not noticed at first. In moments, Gwen felt a warm steam wafting through the air. The hobgoblin stopped in front of a crude archway, warm mist filtering through and dark filling its insides.

"The pools are just through here. I will go now to fetch you some fresh clothes and a towel. You will find everything else on the side ledges. I will also see to it that you are not disturbed. I must warn you though of that…oh never mind, he might not even bother."

He then turned a walked swiftly back through the passage. Puzzled, Gwen sighed and took off her clothes, revealing her petite self. She walked gingerly through the archway, catching her bare feet on a stone once or twice. After passing through into the darkness, two flickering flames ignited in the outstretched palms of a horned, closed-eyed gargoyle that was carved into the opposite wall maybe five feet up from a pool of steaming water. Gwen sighed and stepped into the water, feeling the warmth envelope her. The pool was deep and the floor was smooth. She looked to her left to see a bar of soap set on a small ledge. She swam to the side and picked up the soap. She submerged her head, and relished in the feeling for a moment. She then ran the soap through the hair, watching the dull brown become the shimmering black it was supposed to be. She was about to proceed to the rest of her body when she glanced up to look at the gargoyle to find it yawning. She screamed piercingly, but the gargoyle interrupted her.

"Now, now; none of that." As he let go of the flames he held in his hands. The flames stayed suspended in the air as the gargoyle rubbed his eyes. He then crossed his arms and looked at Gwen. He smiled maliciously, revealing many pointed and stony teeth.

"Well, what have we here?" he asked, raising his faint eyebrows, "I must say you are a much better sight then those horrid hobgoblins." At this, Gwen did the best she could do to hide her nakedness. "Yes, after waking up to find a dozen or so of them swimming around here in all there naked glory, you would be quite content to sit in the dark for the rest of your life too."

He yawned again, not taking his eyes off Gwen, who still tried to conceal herself.

"Hmm, this is unexpected," the gargoyle continued, "No one has come down here in a good while, I expect they use the other baths, not wanting to chat with an old gargoyle. Ho hum. It does get lonely. Oh, speaking of which, who might you be?"

Gwen cleared her throat. "I am Gwen," she said rather awkwardly.

"Charmed," the gargoyle said lazily, "Also, you might as well continue your bath. I am again rather tired and will not be awake to watch you. When you are done, would you be so kind as to send one of those foolish shortlings down here to scrape me clean? I have mold growing in my ears and I would not lament being rid of it. Thank you."

He uncrossed his arms and took hold of the flames again. He then again closed his eyes and said no more. Gwen did not move for a while, and when she did she finished her bath quickly, making sure the gargoyle was not feigning sleep. When she felt herself properly cleansed of the grime of the journey, she rinsed her hair one last time and then got out of the pool. The air she had thought to be warm moments ago now felt bone chilling. She quickly stepped through the archway and wrapped herself in the soft, white towels she had found set out for her. She quickly padded herself dry, and changed into the beautiful, white dress that had also been set out for her. Once it was on she set back through the tunnel that led to the large cavern.

She arrived to find the hobgoblin guarding the entranceway to the tunnel, but otherwise the cavern was empty save the floating lights, which were now orange. The hobgoblin turned to face her and smiled again.

"Everything satisfactory?" he asked.

"Yes," Gwen replied slowly, "but there was a point when the—"

"Oh dear, I knew we should have taken him out," interrupted the hobgoblin, "but the Head refuses to let us. No one has used those baths in ages because of that vulgar statue. Always making fun of us, he is, begging us to put our clothes back on and that he will forever be blinded. I thought he might be a little bit more polite with you, seeing as he has not had any company in several years."

Gwen then relayed the message the gargoyle had given her. The hobgoblin laughed shrilly.

"No, no, no, if he wants to be so rude, he can get rid of the mold himself. Now m'lady, I believe breakfast is ready. Would you like to have it in the Great Cavern or in your room?"

"My room please, and could you please bring something for my cat?"

"Of course." He quickly set off to the kitchens. Gwen sighed tiredly, and walked to her room. Upon entering, she found Curthlond lying down and rolled into a little ball, his slit-eyes locked on her. He yawned.

"And where have you been?" he asked, uncurling himself as he did. He arched his back and stretched.

"Bathing," she said simply as she knelt by her pack and found a brush. She went to stand in front of the mirror and ran it through her hair, untangling the knots that were already forming.

"Ah," said Curthlond, "And what is in store for us today, I wonder? I do not suppose you fancy more magic lessons?

Gwen grimaced at her own reflection and shook her head, thinking of her palm. Curthlond still refused to tell her why it pained her so much to perform simple spells, but instead only assured her that it would soon pass. Until she knew why it was happening and exactly as long as it would continue, she didn't care to continue her tutelage any further.

"I thought maybe we'd explore the Mountain, walk around the caverns and maybe even see the some of the fabled libraries," said Gwen, trying to cheer him up; he seemed a little disappointed by being shut down so quickly.

It worked. He brightened and she saw Curthlond nod in the mirror. He opened his mouth to say something else, but there came a knock from the door and he quickly rolled back into a ball. Gwen tossed her brush on the bed and went to open the door, finding a hobgoblin standing with a tray bearing fruits, eggs, bacon, a glass of water, a saucer of milk, and some sausage links. Gwen thanked him and took the tray. The hobgoblin bowed and turned on his heel to leave the cavern. Gwen shut the door, and walked to the bed to set the tray down. Curthlond stood up quickly, jumped off the bed, and sauntered over to the saucer of milk that Gwen had now laid on the floor. He slurped it loudly as Gwen began to eat the fruit. She threw a strip of bacon and a sausage link to Curthlond, who turned from the milk and ate the meat quickly. Gwen smiled and downed the water.

When they were done with their breakfast, they left the room together to find Ryan leaning against a far wall in a corner of the cavern. He smiled when he saw them.

"Morning, Gwen, you look nice today," he said warmly. He spoke the next words in a cooing baby voice, "Hi-hi, Buttons!"

Curthlond hissed at the sound of the name. Ryan raised his eyebrows and tried to pet the cat, but recoiled as Curthlond batted at him with a clawed paw.

"Cwabby today, aren't we Buttons?" Gwen also spoke in a baby voice, but with a warning tone. Curthlond scowled, and lowered his razor claws.

"So where're you off to?" Ryan said in his normal voice, recovered from his shock. "The others already left to get a tour of the Mountain from Fairskin."

"Well, we-I mean, I was going off to find some books in one of the libraries. Want to come?"

"Sure! I'd like to learn some more magic stuff."

Gwen frowned. "Magic stuff?"

"Yeah! How it all works; how to do it. Man, I'd love to be able to use it, wouldn't you?"

Inwardly, she smiled. "Yes," Gwen replied slowly, turning to look at Curthlond. He looked back and shrugged.

"Well, come on!" exclaimed Ryan, "Let's go!"

They set off through the passage that led to the Mountain's gigantic main chamber. Gwen and Ryan walked next to each other, while Curthlond trotted behind Gwen. He grumbled a couple of times, but it was too low for Gwen to catch what was said. She suspected he didn't like behaving like an ordinary cat, which, as per their agreement, he was bound to do in front of everyone else.

They reached the Main Chamber, there awe renewed. The sheer size of it was still enough to silence Gwen; she had seen many of the great cities back in the Mortal Realm, and none of them had anything that matched this. She felt quiet disappointment well up inside her, as though everything back home was farce imitation of everything in the Realm of Magic.

They found a hobgoblin jogging quickly while carrying a large, swaying tower of books in the center of the bustling cavern. Gwen and Ryan looked at each other with amused smiles and decided to follow him.

"Have you seen Eion today, Ryan?" Gwen asked as they walked quickly to keep up with the hobgoblin that walked swiftly for one so small. Curthlond, trying to seem as authentically cat-like as possible, trotted up beside him and played with a loose tassel that hung from the hobgoblin's robe.

"Yeah, he said that he would be in council with the other leaders today and that we will be leaving tomorrow."

Gwen sighed. "It's a shame really. I'd like to stay for awhile." She meant it, which surprised her. She had heard a lot about the Mountain and was very keen on exploring it. Also, she had very much enjoyed sleeping on a bed the previous night, a drastic change from her sleeping arrangement of the last months.

Ryan nodded, watching the hobgoblin begin to lose his balance as the tower of books leaned to the right. "Me too. I've been told Ÿalnz Dàr is a horrible place filled with monsters. And after that…God, after that's Saurindon."

He whispered the name. Gwen did not blame him; they were closer to it than ever they had been. It seemed wrong to speak it loudly, as though the mention of it would call shadows from the air, or some other unpleasant thing. Gwen didn't care to think of it.

"Yes, I know," she said slowly. She tried to brighten the mood. "But we still have a lot of leagues to go before we come to the Gap."

Ryan grunted, but said no more. Curthlond, looking over his shoulder, apparently bored with the tassel, meowed questioningly, but Gwen ignored him.

Just then, the hobgoblin was now hopping on one foot, trying to right himself and the books. Gwen and Ryan quickly rushed to his side and helped him regain his balance. He thanked them, attempted a bow, failed, and set off again at his quick pace, and, eventually, he turned right into an archway that had been set in the wall of the corridor. They followed him through it and into another enormous cavern, this one holding something far grander than the jeweled pillars and walls they had seen elsewhere in the mountain.

It was a library. That much was obvious, but it was unlike any library Gwen had ever seen. It was about five stories high, with each level built of some white stone that Gwen suspected to be marble. Great pillars, no less than twenty feet in diameter, held each level up, a mighty task as each level was burdened with *thousands* of books and scrolls that sat on silver shelves. And such books! Everything from small sheets of parchment that had been stitched together to great tomes that were bound in dusty black leathers could be found in it. Tables clustered the floors, filled with seats and scrolls. Gigantic chandeliers, some ornate and some plain, dangled far above them, hanging from the stony ceiling, casting rays of light on the huge trove of writings.

But all this was not as impressive as the other occupants in the library. There were tall old men wearing shimmering blue robes and had long hair and beards. They, like the elves, carried staffs, which they leaned against as they flipped through books. There were also tall men who wore black outfits with hoods who had pointed ears, though they were not elegant enough to be elves. There were women who wore robes of black and lopsided, pointy hats. Some were repulsive while others were beautiful, but they all seemed to have some kind of cat. Gwen saw black ones like Curthlona, which made up the majority, but she still saw some tabbies and tortoiseshells among the bunch. All of them took no notice of the newcomers and instead they were enthralled with their books. Some power emanated from them…some inexplicable power that seemed alien and foreign, as though it was almost tangible, as though she could almost reach out and…

The hobgoblin finally slipped and dropped his load, sending a shower of papers and pieces of parchment in the air, while the many books he had been carrying sent him to the ground, where he lay to be buried by them. A host of his fellows swarmed to him and began to excavate him from the mound of literature, choking on the cloud of dust kicked up by the ancient pages.

One of the rescuers looked up and saw Gwen and Ryan. Leaving it to the others to save the imprisoned hobgoblin, he rushed to where they stood in the archway. "Good day!" he said, as though he was unaware of what had just happened, which was completely unbelievable, because the muffled screams of the wretched creature were echoing in the library. Many of the people who were browsing the shelves were setting aside their reading materials to point and snigger.

Oblivious to this, the hobgoblin pressed them "How may we help you?"

"We would like it very much," Ryan answered, tearing his gaze from the commotion, "if we could find some books concerning magic, magic history, the Magic Realm's geography, and books about creatures native to

235

the Magic Realm." By the time he was finished, he was grinning ear to ear with excitement.

The hobgoblin returned his expression. "Quite a curious lad, are we not? I will see that--" But he was cut off as another hobgoblin, who had entered the library moments before with a similar tower of books and scrolls, tripped over the pile of tomes and papers, burying the first hobgoblin even more.

The hobgoblin who was attending to them, made no indication he had seen this, despite the cries of dismay of his fellows. "I will see that you get all that and more. Now, if you will please follow me, I will lead you to a table where you can read and not be disturbed."

He quickly trotted behind a bookcase on the left side of the library. They followed him, allowing themselves one last glance at the literary tomb of the fallen hobgoblin, to find him climbing up a spiral staircase. They quickly pursued him, climbing two steps at a time to keep up with his thunderous pace that had presumably been sparked by some humiliation. When all four reached the top of the staircase, the hobgoblin led them behind another bookcase where a small circular table filled with books. Three chairs appeared out of nowhere, supposedly at some silent spell from their frenzied host.

The hobgoblin beckoned them to take their seats. Ryan and Gwen sat across from each other, while Curthlond jumped on top of the table, where he proceeded to curl into a tight ball.

"There," said the hobgoblin, "I think you will find everything you want right there. If not, just call for one of us." With that he quickly disappeared behind the bookcase once more. Gwen suspected he was off to help in the mining

Ryan smiled eagerly and reached for the first book he could get his hands on. Gwen stared at him for a moment and then reached for a book called *Magic: a complete history of the ancient world*. It was, from what she was able to read in the short time she had, a fascinating read. As it seemed, Arconia was the property of the gods, a holy country, and recognized no king or lord or monarch or ruler of any kind. It was a place steeped in magic, mainly because it was the home of the Mountain. She read of wonderful legends that sang of many heroes who did great deeds while they traveled through Arconia. It was the home of a great many magical places, including the Healing Well, which would cure any ailment or magical infliction if drunk from the tin ladle that hung there. However, if the water was taken by the golden ladle the drinker would forever be cast in stone. There were pictures of many people who had obviously used the golden ladle. Gwen grimaced.

Another such magical place was that of the Peredri Caves. It lay deep in the forest of Ÿalnz Dàr, and few who passed through left it empty handed.

She turned the page and found a large history of the elves. She read the following:

There were twelve varieties of Elven Folk. The greatest of these were the High Elves, whose deeds cannot be listed in this publication alone. Arconia is their home, and they call themselves the Vra. They are led by the Lord Fairskin.

The second clan is that of the Wood Elves, who now live in the Orano Forest. Kji is their clan name. They are a proud race, but they never accomplished anything as mighty as that of the High Elves. They are governed by Lord Fairskin's cousin, Lord Rianl.

The Sea Elves, or the Yene, have always been fascinated by the oceans and lakes, and are often found on white ships sailing through the misty waters. They live in the elven port city of Une, and are led by the Lady Silvi, Fairskin and Rianl's third cousin.

The Clla, the Moon Elves, are a nocturnal race of elves that delight in the lunar cycles. They are steeped in magics of night and live in the elven city of Ollen. The ancient Lord Tresto has ruled the clan for an uncountable number of years.

The Sun Elves are quite different, for they love the sun and they worship its god, Mellao above all others. They are of the Clan Ghi. They have found contentment in the Ewunl Valley, and live in Saion. They are astronomers and stargazers, and are led by the Lady Ulna, Lady Silvi's sister.

The Mountain Elves are the keepers of the peaks and hills, and belong to the Rewu Clan. They love all natural structures from the lowest hill to the highest mountain. They live in the city Gunda, on the peaks of Mount Nol. Lord Arowo is their king.

The Wise Elves are the philosophers and great thinkers of the elves, and have dubbed themselves the Fwaen Clan. They are the scholars and students who will always be fascinated by the ways of magic and often invent new ways of manipulating it. They live in the southern elven city Bagine, and follow the Lord Vreo.

The Vain Elves love the beauty of everything, and in contrast hate ugliness. They are the lovers and they are the poets. They sculpt and paint and are the artists of the elven world. They live in the lush elven city Fwini, in the Valley Ils. Erme is their clan, and they are led by Lady Cela.

The Strong Elves are the warriors. They are of the Yuln Clan. They love war and are fierce in battle. Never have they lost a fight of any kind.

They will battle with all except elven kin. The ancient elven city Zanu is their home and the mighty Daio is their lord.

The Forging Elves are more dwarf then elf. Their clan is Liol. They are the blacksmiths of the elves and love to tinker with metal and fire. They build shields, swords, axes, pikes, daggers, scimitars, and spears with a mastery no one else can compete with. They live in the city Drans at the base of the Mountains of Starlight. The Lord Yalo is more of an equal to his people then a leader, for he himself loves the forging of swords.

The Holy Elves devote their lives to the study of religion. It is required of every elf of their clan, the Oao, to pay homage to a temple of every god by their three hundredth year. They are the priests of the elves. They live in the great elven temple in Cii and Lord Nain is their chief.

The twelfth clan had no name and did not have a named variety. They lived in the elven city Lian and they were led by the Lord Breenen. They are no more. In the Ravaging Years, or the rise of the Red Sovereign, only one king accepted Ozmodion's placations, the Dragon King Vaeirnïr. What is not known is that Lord Breenen was prepared to accept Ozmodion's offer as well. His entire clan was unanimously agreed with him. They set out for the dreaded Saurindon Gorge. When they reached the Three Peaks of Caagz, they were stopped by the other eleven of the Twelve Clan Chiefs. Confused, Breenen called to them and said, "Hail! My brothers, what want you?"

And the Lord Fairskin said, "Go back Breenen. Go back to your halls in Lian. Go back and never again set out to aid Ozmodion. Go back Breenen, or we will smite you now on these peaks."

Angered, Breenen said, "You have no right to interfere with me or my clan. The ancient law states we Twelve Clans shall live within our own rule, independent and free of one another. My word is law within this clan, and you have no say of our endeavors. Be gone and bother me no more!"

At this, all the opposing chiefs raised their staffs. And Fairskin spoke once more, "You have been warned, Breenen. Go back to Lian and you will live."

Breenen was now outraged. "Staffs ready!" he yelled to his clan and they did as he bade. He then turned back to his eleven fellows.

"Impudence! You are hopelessly outnumbered, Fairskin! Now move or it shall be you who will be smote!"

The Eleven Chiefs spoke a syllable, and their staffs emitted great magics and the scene was blinded with white light. When it passed, every elf in Breenen's clan, except for Breenen himself, lay on the stony ground of the Three Peaks, dead. Breenen now looked up at his fellows with pale fury.

"Traitors!" he called them, "Oath breakers! May you burn evermore in Avria's Five Hells and may your descendants be eaten by maggots!"

The Eleven shook their heads and then spoke in unison:

> No longer are we the Twelve Clan Chiefs
> No longer are we the Twelve Strong
> No longer will we follow our oaths
> The oaths we held so long
>
> We send you now to the Halls of Waiting
> As we warned you moments before
> Without you, O Lord Breenen
> We are the Eleven Chiefs evermore

With the curse completed, their eleven staffs lit up with magic once more, and the scene was once again bathed in white. And when it passed, Lord Breenen of Lian was cast in stone, a statue of an elven traitor. He stands there to this day, between the Three Peaks of Caagz, a curse formed in his snarl.

Thus there are Eleven Clans, and Eleven Kinds of elves; the Vra, the Kji, the Yene, the Clla, the Ghi, the Rewu, the Fwaen, the Erme, the Yuln, the Liol, and the Oao.

Gwen gawked at the story she had just read. Lord Fairskin a killer? It could not be. *But then*, Gwen thought, *it was Lord Breenen who would've been the true murderer, he and his clan.* Finding relaxation in that thought, she sat back in her chair and rubbed her eyes. When she opened them, she saw Curthlond looking at, no, reading the pages she just had. She then looked at Ryan to see him reading his book with a wide grin.

Gwen raised her eyebrows. "What's so interesting?" she asked him.

He jolted up quickly and stared at her with wild eyes as though he did not know she was there. His expression then relaxed when he realized who he was and he grinned again.

"I'm reading about the different kinds of magics," he answered excitedly, "It's amazing how diverse they are! There are of course those who use the magic from inside themselves, which falls under elven magic, enchanting, and sorcery. There is magery, which is when you use the magic around you. There is wizardry, when you store spells in an object and release them from there later. There's witchcraft, when you prepare potions and take them to give you their magic. There's conjuring—that's when you use spirits to carry out magical tasks. Magicians like to practice all of these forms. There's fire magic, which you use the magical potential of fire to perform spells. There's blood magic, which is kind of dark, you need blood to perform spells. And last but not least, there is übelancy, but I can't find out what's involved in that. Maybe I should call for help from one of those hobgoblins."

As though Ryan had called, a hobgoblin popped out from behind a bookcase so suddenly that he might've appeared magically. His abruptness startled Gwen and made Curthlond jump into her lap with a hiss.

The hobgoblin beamed at them. "How may I be of assistance?" he asked.

"Could you please tell me what übelancy is?" asked Ryan, "My book doesn't say."

The hobgoblin's smile disappeared and was replaced by a look of absolute horror. He made a sign and uttered a string of words in a harsh language that Gwen assumed was the hobgoblins' native tongue. He then studied Ryan with eyes full of terrorized suspicion

"The Evil Art!" he cried, "Death's Hand! What do you want to know of that...*practice*, and *why*?" His tone was accusing.

"I'm just curious," Ryan assured, clearly taken aback at the hobgoblin's change. "I'm just fascinated by magic and the different ways of wielding it."

The hobgoblin's expression softened only fractionally. After a pause, the hobgoblin said, "Know this then: übelancy is the darkest way of controlling magic. In order to perform it, one must take a life and destroy it. Unlike blood magery, in which the mage only takes energy from a cup or two of blood, übelancy demands that you kill the one in which holds the magic. It is a black art and it has been banned for along time. Not even the Red Sovereign practices it."

With that, the hobgoblin bowed, this time with a noticeable stiffness. He then shook his head crossly, and disappeared back into the forest of shelves. As soon as he did, Ryan turned to Gwen, his grin returned to his face.

"Isn't that *fascinating*?"

Gwen looked appalled and shook her head. "I think it's horrible."

Ryan grin disappeared and he shook his head wildly. "No, no, no, no, no. I'm not saying I'd ever use it, but don't you think it's interesting that it can be done?"

Gwen again shook her head, picked up Curthlond, stood up, and left the library. Before she could a hobgoblin jogged up beside her and said, "Wait, m'lady, I think you forgot this." He handed her a small golden necklace with a blue gem hanging from it. Gwen took it without question. The hobgoblin smiled curiously, revealing his small, impish teeth. He bowed, and returned to lurk among the bookshelves

When they had entered the main chamber again, Gwen was still a little shocked at Ryan's fascination by the ability to reap power through murder. The thought made her stomach churn.

Letting her anger wander, she noticed the passage that Eion had took the day before.

"Do you know what that corridor leads to?" Gwen asked Curthlond.

He shook his head. "I have never been to the Mountain. I learned my enchanting entirely from a crotchety old hermit who had dabbled in all kinds of magic. Interesting man. Quite the genius, really. He taught me all I thought I needed to know, and I never felt need to explore the old tomes that rested here."

Though this new fact of Curthlond had sparked a small ray of interest, her curiosity of the passage was greater. "Shall we explore it?"

"Very well, but be wary. The Mountain's magic should not be taken lightly. Underestimate it on your peril."

Gwen nodded and started down the hallway with Curthlond trotting closely behind. The corridor seemed ordinary at first; in fact it was oddly boring compared to the other hallways they had gone through. But farther on, it changed, not in appearance, but in feel. Some presence was felt, something Gwen couldn't pinpoint. She did not mention it to Curthlond or ask if he felt the same way.

When they came to the end of the passage, they then reached a plain, oak door with brass knockers. The mysterious feeling subsided and disappointment took its place. Gwen picked up Curthlond, opened the door and walked slowly into darkness. Then, the door behind them slammed shut.

Chapter 20

The Gods

G***wen wheeled around*** and slammed her free hand against the door and screamed wildly. There was, of course, no reply from the other side, but still she banged her fist against the wood until her hand and fingers were numb.

"Gwen," came the disembodied voice of Curthlond, which was steady and calm in contrast to her panic. "Use the magic."

She managed to calm down enough to find the innate magic. She spoke the incantation Curthlond told her and a small flame ignited in her right palm, though it did not burn her. She raised her arm to cast the light around her, when suddenly the pain flashed across her palm once again. She yelped and let the magic fade, but, though the flame instantly died out, the room stayed illuminated with silver light that came from nowhere. A silvery mist was rose and swirled from the smooth gray floor beneath her feet. Confused, she turned around to face the room she had walked into. The sight made her drop Curthlond, who screeched with anger as he fell to the floor. She hardly heard him.

She stood in another large cavern, this one with a domed ceiling. It was empty except for the mist, which was now violet, and a stone altar directly in front of her, cracked and stained with uncounted years. On top of it, a layer of thick dust rested; the altar had not been touched in centuries She walked up to it and stood on its step while Curthlond jumped onto its flat surface, wiping clean the coat of dust. Underneath were strange runes, much like those she had read on some of the spines of the library books.

I can't understand these, she thought, scanning here eyes over the writing, trying to make sense of it. As if the runes had heard her, they began to glow so brightly that Gwen had to shield her eyes with her palm. When she dared to look again, the runes had changed into spidery letters written in English. They simply said.

We accept with open arms
All your trinkets and your charms

She frowned and then remembered the necklace that the hobgoblin had given her. Had he meant her to find this place? Slowly, she took it out of her pocket and placed it on the flat, cold stone. Immediately it shimmered with a blue aura like that of *Raz'atr's,* and then it disappeared in a wisp of smoke that smelled of brimstone. Gagging, she held her nose and waved her hand through the putrid air to clear the horrible stench.

When the odor passed, Gwen looked at the top of the podium, half expecting to find the amulet again. But it was indeed gone. She turned to Curthlond, but he only shook his head, showing he did not know why it had disappeared either.

Gwen shrugged and looked past the podium. She screamed, for at the edge of the room, a silvery, robed figure of an old man sat in a throne that was not there before. His white eyes stared at her hazel. Thin line crisscrossed his bright face, telling of eons of cares and worries. His eyes were hard and distant, and she felt his gaze pierce her like a sword.

A light wind brushed against her face and she looked to the right of the old man, where another silvery figure sat, this one a woman whose face seemed old but her body seemed strong. Another wind touched her face, and another, and another. Curthlond hissed loudly and jumped from the podium to hide behind Gwen's legs. A blinding light emitted from somewhere in the cavern. When it passed, the room was filled with thrones occupied by more silvery figures, arranged so the old man sat in the very center. All of them seemed human, and they would've been if not for their silver form and the air of unnatural power they gave off. They were cloaked, robed, clad in armor, wearing beautiful gowns, loincloths, and tunics. Not one of them looked the same; some looked old and others young; some seemed kind and others cruel. But, old or young, kind or cruel, they all now stared at Gwen with intent, scrutinizing eyes. Gwen stared back at them for a long while, aware that the swirling mist continued to change colors. Curthlond could be felt at her feet, quivering like a leaf on a high wind. Finally, the figure of the old man that appeared first spoke.

"Welcome, Iltari Gwen," he said with a strong voice that conjured up images of a bright sun shining on a peaceful glen, "Why is it you call council with the gods?"

Gwen gaped at him for a moment. *Gods!* "I-I did not kn-know…" she began weakly, "I was j-just exploring the M-M-Mountain."

The old man closed his eyes and nodded, "Yes, those touched by gods always have a tendency to stumble on us unintentionally. But stumble on us they do, and after the encounter their lives are never again the same. I remember when the first Iltari met us. He gave us a phial of elven blood, unknowingly of course. He stuttered too, and it took a great deal of explaining to convince him of what he was. Sadly, he went on to cause the pain and grief of an endless stream of pour souls."

Ozmodion, Gwen thought as she stared at the old man. She looked down at the altar, repulsed by the very idea the black sorcerer had once stood where she was standing now. She took her hands from the ancient stone and shoved them into her pockets, afraid of placing her hands where Ozmodion's had rested.

The old man opened his eyes. "But what else can one expect from one conceived by Avria? My sister is very hard to control; as you can see she has not consented to join the rest of us in this council."

Gwen looked around, and saw no one who would fit the title of Goddess of Death. Granted, she had only description and wild imagination to paint Avria's image in her mind, but she could not picture any of the beings before her carrying the black reputations that Avria bore.

The old man continued. "Perhaps last night's council has given her more black thoughts that she feels she must act on. But yes, her Iltari was and is one who must leave this world. The next Iltari was of my make. He came to us knowing we were here, and left for us a pile of dragon scales. But he had no knowing of the knowledge we gave him. I remember that he fainted right at that altar you stand at right now. When he awoke, we gave him the Third Sword of the Five forged by the Nameless Master, *Raz'atr*."

Gwen gasped; the silvery man she was listening to was referring to Eion. She shuddered, thinking back on the first day she had met the shifter and how he had named himself Iltari along with several other titles. For some reason, the phantom connection between him and Ozmodion gave her chills.

"Yes, yes. Almost immediately afterward, he set out to destroy his fellow Iltari, and he almost succeeded, too. But the Third Iltari was not yet there to help him, and it took a great time for Hawore, the God of Magic, to conceive her. But when he did, we knew she would answer the prayers of many."

Gwen blinked, unsure of what he was trying to say.

"Yes. Allow me to introduce myself. I am Garon, the God of Life. I am the lord of the gods and the conceiver of your friend Eion."

The phantom connection hardened into reality, and Gwen now knew that Eion was not inhuman, he was immortal. Somewhere in the back of her throat, a hard lump formed, and she found it difficult to breathe.

Curthlond, however, had seemed to recover from his initial fear, and now he jumped atop the altar to address Garon. "My lord," he said as he bowed his head.

Cats, as you probably know, very rarely humble themselves for anyone, and they certainly never revere anything or anyone else. Thus, Gwen found it rather strange to see Curthlond bow his head with great and solemn respect.

Garon eyes narrowed. "And who are you? And how is it you speak but appear as a cat? Are you enchanted?"

"My name is Curthlond; I am a friend and teacher of the Iltari Gwen…" Here he paused, not wanting to answer the second question. "As for seeming like a cat…well, let's just say something went awry."

"And what is it you want?"

"To pay my respects and to pray for the return to my true form, and to promise you my aid to the Third Iltari."

Garon nodded, and made a sign with his hand. Curthlond raised his head, and thanked him again, while Gwen's perplexity had finally reached its pique.

"Excuse me, sir," she said to Garon. The god turned his head. "But I'm afraid I don't understand. What is an Iltari?"

The gods all laughed in one roaring voice. The cavern resounded with glee; she felt the stone floor shake under her feet. She frowned, and looked to Garon, who only smiled and raised a hand. A soon as he did, the laughter stopped.

"You do not know?" Garon asked, once the walls stopped vibrating and the air stopped humming. Gwen shook her head, her face reddening with embarrassment. The god chuckled softly then smiled again. "An Iltari is one who has no mortal father, but is instead conceived by a god. The gift has only been given four times, the first to give birth to the elves. A fair folk are they, and they are more than worthy to bear the title.

"The gift was given a second time by Avria to Ciroth Avilvin, as I have just described to you. Eion received the third gift…and the fourth, the fourth was given by Hawore to you."

Gwen stiffened. She knew she must have heard wrong.

"Hawore, step forth!" commanded Garon in a much different tone, a tone that could be spoken only by one who was used to authority.

A robed figure on the right of the podium stood up from his throne. He had a short beard, a furrowed brow, an eagle hooked nose, long flowing hair, and very kind eyes.

Gwen opened her mouth to speak, but the words died on her lips.

"Gwen," he said with an equally kind voice. His next words were softly spoken, but they still had enough force to knock the wind out of Gwen. "I planted my seed into your mother. The moment I did, magic lived once more in the Mortal Realm. You were destined to become steeped in magic, as all Iltari are."

"You lie," Gwen said with unintentional coldness. How dare this silvery man talking to her claim to be her father. "My father is in the Mortal Realm right now, worrying about me, wondering where I am—"

"No Gwen," said Hawore gently. A quiet sadness crept in his face, one mingled with sympathy and regret. "The man you speak of is not your true father, only the husband of your true mother. Gwen, I know this is hard for you to accept, but—"

"No," Gwen said, icy venom now seeping through her words. "It is not hard for me to accept it, because I refuse to accept it."

Hawore now looked worry. "But Gwen, you are destined—"

"Then I refuse my destiny!" Gwen cried, turning on her heels and racing to the door. Just before she reached it, however, Hawore shouted a string of words, and the room was momentarily bathed in orange light. When it passed, Gwen felt frozen; she tried to move but found she could not. She felt Curthlond brush against her leg and say, "Gwen, please wait." She tried to say something, but the spell was too strong; she could not even move her jaw to utter the words. She felt a strong force turning her to face the gods once more. They were all now standing up, lowering their hands as though they were about to make magical signs. Garon was leaning on a gnarled wooden staff with many tassels and ornaments dangling from its head. He slowly sat back in his seat. All the other gods, save Hawore, took their seats as well. Gwen was forced to face the God of Magic. His eyes were still kind and they were now also firm. He snapped his fingers and the force that kept Gwen immobilized seemed to recede like waves on the shore. Her right palm ached.

"One cannot throw one's destiny away, nor can one turn one's back on it," said Hawore, "It shall always be there, calling you. I have placed a heavy burden on you, and for that I apologize. But you are destined for great things, whether you will them or not."

The words stung her; she dimly remembered a similar speech given by Eion after he had saved her from the nightshade attack.

Hawore, taking no notice, went on. "I trust that this enchanter I see before me has taught you rudimentary magic?"

Gwen leaned down, picked up Curthlond, and walked back to the altar.

"He has," she said slowly.

"I take it she is progressing smoothly?" Hawore asked Curthlond.

Curthlond hesitated. "Well, my lord, there is a problem with the development of the—" He stopped and raised his right paw. Gwen could not see the skin under the paw, but Hawore nodded and said, "Ah."

"Well, now that you know what she is, I assume you will act fast to teach her?"

Curthlond nodded.

"Very well, then. When Ozmodion is purged of this earth, we promise to restore you."

Curthlond bowed his head in reverence and thanks. He then muttered a string of words that Gwen took to be a prayer, though she did not understand the language he spoke.

"Gwen," said Garon, gesturing for Hawore to take his seat. "You must not mention this to your fellow mortals, for among them is one who will join the Red Sovereign, and he will tell his soon-to-be-master of your existence."

Gwen stared at him. "No, none of them would *ever* join with—"

"It is true," interrupted Garon, "My brother, Vundin,"—he gestured at an equally old man on his left. His silver eyes stared blankly at nothing; he was blind.—"has foreseen it, and his visions are never wrong. Beware, for the longer he stays, the more dangerous he becomes to your cause. Now, go, Gwen. We shall see you again before the end."

All of the silvery figures vanish, their thrones with them. The mist had now receded back into the ground, and the light was extinguished.

"Come, Gwen," said Curthlond's voice, his cat eyes being able to see in the dark. She followed the sound of his words, trying to restrain herself. She waved her hands out in front of her and she felt the door. Opening it, she allowed Curthlond to go first. When she left the room, she walked to the wall on the right side of the passage, slumped against it, and let the tears flow.

No mortal father…

Chapter 21

The Council

G*wen now thought* she had unearthed all of Eion's secrets, yet there was one she was still unaware of: Eion's council with the Gods the previous night.

He quickly reached the plain oak door that he knew held more significance than any could have guessed. He pushed it gently and the door opened on its quiet hinges. As he stepped into the darkness of the cavern, he shifted his eyes so they were able to see through the black. Behind him, the door closed heavily.

Eion walked to the stone altar and, after making a sign with his hands, took out the leather sack that held the ashes of Gorbon. He placed it on the altar and watched as glowed with a light much like that of his sword. It then disappeared, and the cavern was bathed in the silver light he had come to know so well. He looked directly across the cavern to see the form of Garon sitting in his pearly throne and robed in silver. Eion felt a strong wind and there was the bright light. He shifted his eyes back to normal, averting them to avoid being blinded. When he was done and the light was extinguished, the room was filled with many silvery figures, and one black. More gods then he had dared to hope had come. There was Garon and Vundin and Hawore, Mellao the Sun God and his sister, Raia, the Moon Goddess. There was Hante, the Mountain God and next to him Joao, the God of the Earth. Joao's wife, Shiia the Nature Goddess sat on his right. Arnew the War God sat on Garon's left, and next to him was Eenva, the Goddess of Love and Beauty. On her left was Iwe, The God of Harvest. There was also Euno, God of the Sky and Weather. The Twin Gods of Fire and Sea, Leana and Leano, sat side by side, and on their left sat Avria, garbed in black armor with a black helm from which two goblin horns sprouted. She was just as beautiful as Eenva, but in a darker way. Her skin was whiter than bone and her eyes had no color in them at all. Her hair was silky black, but hung from her head like dead vines from a tree. Her hands were white as well, and long, black nails grew from her fingers and ended at fine points.

Eion tore his gaze from her and instead turned to Garon, who now spoke to him.

"Well met, Iltari Eion," he said with his strong voice. "Why do you seek council with the gods?"

The traditional greeting somehow annoyed Eion. "You do not know?" he said with a voice he reserved for Belzorg. "O Wise King of the Gods, why do you play games? Look, I know that nothing in this world happens without you knowing. Why do we have to play games?"

Garon smiled. "Bold words. Had they been spoken by anyone else, I would have set a plague upon their descendants."

Eion did not return his smile. "I am lost, Garon. The closer we get to Saurindon, the surer I am that we will not be returning. Ozmodion grows stronger in arms and power every day, and I feel as though there can be no victory against his wrath. I have discovered that he will soon be marshalling an army of spell weavers. If he does, we will be outnumbered like we never have been before. If the Resistance is broken, then Ozmodion will stand unopposed as he breaks the Reflection holding the two worlds apart, and the mortals of the New Religion will come to know his evil just as well as any in this realm. For the first time since Ozmodion fell, I do not know what to do."

There was a long pause, finally broken by Avria.

"And why have you not called on the aid of your fellow, the one I set my hellhound on?" she said with a sharp, cold voice.

Eion turned his gaze to her, and spoke his next words with equal iciness. "I hate to disappoint you, but that hound's long dead. I killed him, and Gwen lives. Avria, I now charge you to tell me of the doings of Ozmodion."

She laughed; it was a horrible sound, like nails being rippied against skin. "You forget your place, lowly one. I am a god and I answer to no one. I do not acknowledge your so-called status of equality that is to be placed on Iltari. Only Ciroth holds that right."

Eion pulled out another, leather pouch, this one a small size larger than the one he had place on the altar. He tossed it to Avria, who caught it without taking her eyes off of Eion's.

"He is sending legions to foreign lands to claim them for himself," she said coldly. "Cassori and Yerrin have already fallen, and Nunren is quickly losing ground. They shall yield to his rule soon enough." Her eyes narrowed as she chuckled cruelly. "I see your thoughts Eion, Master of Shifters," she spoke his title with a sneer, "and I will now dispel them. Saurindon still has a force greater than any marshaled before, waiting for you. They will spill from the red gates of Angar Vûn and meet you on the Ozra Gap. You shall fight, I have no doubt, but you will all fade into shadow and your kin will be enslaved. I have unleashed hydra, hellhounds, and papillions back into the world, and they will do as I will them. Yes, Ciroth will win, and magic will forever be immortalized. For now, Eion Iltari, I bid thee farewell." And she and her throne faded into nothingness. Eion stared at where she sat moments ago, anger boiling inside him. He turned back to Garon.

"Oddly enough, that did not help me," he said flatly.

Vundin turned to face him with unseeing eyes. He smiled and chuckled merrily. Then his face hardened and he spoke the next words in a strange and stony voice:

In the Caves of Illothin
Gorothar's shield you'll find
From all spells it shall protect you
Be them malignant or benign

The Flute of the Tamers
Rests in Hware
Follow the voices
But of the beasts beware

Lastly I'll tell you

Of the Fourth Blade
In the Lake of Roiva
It lies with Alidade

His face then softened and he remained silent. The other gods turned their heads, looks of surprise and even confusion showing on their faces. Eion himself furrowed his brow, pondering on what the god had meant. Vundin did not often speak, and when he did it was only to make prophecies, like the one he had just heard.

Garon broke the quiet. "Eion, Vundin has just told you of the Three Lost Weapons of Odin the Valiant, the elf who educated dragons and taught them to speak. The Caves of Illothin rest in the forest of Ÿalnz Dàr, and therefore you should be able to find the Shield of Gorothar before you face Ozmodion. I do not know why he has told you the location of the Flute and the Fourth blade; perhaps you will gain them before Ozmodion will fall."

Eion glared. "The Resistance will meet Ozmodion's forces, and they will not stop until they are victorious or dead."

Garon shook his head slowly. "Do not think so surely. Ozmodion is playing a black game which he intends to win. He has set the board and he is making his moves, as the Kji Clan will soon discover." At Eion's blank look, Garon said, "Have you not heard? Lord Rianl's son, Gwalin, has not been seen in a couple of months now. The Kji are not too concerned about it yet, for they are waiting for the Vra's pleas of help. I have reason to think Ozmodion has had something to do with his disappearance. If Gwalin is found dead, the Elven Nation will be outraged in a way they haven't been in for several millennia. The Eleven Clans will unite once more, and even an army of spell weavers will find it difficult, nigh impossible, to stand against their wrath."

"So you say we should wish for the doom of Gwalin?" Eion asked him wryly.

Garon shook his head. "No of course not, I am merely voicing my speculations."

"But Garon, apart from the spell casters, the armies of the countries Ozmodion has already vanquished will be forced to fight. Also, there is the always the possibility that Ozmodion will soon send placations to the other races of the world. Some might accept this time, and we shall be even more outnumbered. Ozmodion has one weapon we cannot compete with, and that is fear."

Then Garon spoke his next words with deliberate slowness and strength. "Then you must hasten to journey's end. Yoke the strength of your fellow Iltari, and that of the other mortals, for without them, you have no hope whatsoever. If you are not victorious in the upcoming battle, send placations to the other races as Ozmodion will, and hope they side with you. Go to the griffins, the hippogriffs, and the phoenixes, for they will surely help. Go to the Valley of the Weres and seek the fomariuns. Call on the wyverns and the varengan. Plea to the pegasi and the perytons. Your hope rests with your humility, Eion. Now go, and heed our words. Farewell."

The gods faded and the silvery light was smothered, leaving Eion to wonder in the dark.

Chapter 22

The Conquest

J*arul, the King of Nunren*, sat in his throne while massaging his temples with two index fingers. He usually enjoyed his throne room, and delighted in sitting in the comfortable chair that was reserved only for the leading royal. On better days, his throne room might be full of tables, with merry guests eating and laughing with him. The thought of sitting next to his departed wife while they shared in a feast still brought a tear to his eye and a smile to his face. On other days, he might have been sitting in his throne while his subjects approached him and told of their troubles and requests. He found great pleasure in helping them, turning Nunren into a golden country one peasant at a time. Or he might just sit in his throne and look upon the majestic room in which he sat. It was impressive, built entirely of white stones. Banners were hung throughout it, tingeing the room with the country's colors of green and white. A large window had been placed directly across from the throne that would've shown him his beautiful Fields of Daien when spring was in bloom.

But the throne room seemed less majestic today, and his throne was less comfortable. The window did not look out to his beautiful Fields, but on to burnt plains strewn with carnage. He saw little dots that were his soldiers, and little dots that were Ozmodion's. The hell of war had flawed the golden age of Nunren, and Jarul knew it; his armies were weakening as the Ozra slowly crippled his country's defenses.

He had not heeded Ozmodion's orders, pride and vanity forbidding him from giving the sorcerer such pleasure. He now hated himself for resisting, for the vision he had seen in Ozmodion's black flame had come true. Vlairil was now three days under siege, and the death toll reflected it.

He forced himself not to look through the window any longer, and instead turned to his page that was standing next to his throne.

"Bring me Captain Hiestin and Frendern," he said, his voice cracking. The page nodded quickly and ran to the door that was situated at the other end of the room to the right of the window. Jarul let his mind wander while he waited. He did not have to wait long, for two minutes later the Captain of the Guards, Hiestin, burst into the room along with Jarul's head wizard, Frendern. Hiestin was clad in armor with Nunren's crest embossed in the center of the chest plate while Frendern wore white robes that complimented his long white beard nicely. He had foregone his pointy hat but, as always, had brought his gnarled, white staff. The two men walked to the foot of the stairs that led to Jarul's throne and bowed. They then faced Jarul with solemn faces.

"You called for us my lord?" asked Hiestin.

"I did," replied Jarul, "How goes the fight, Captain Hiestin?"

Hiestin smiled, and said, "I think you know, Your Majesty. A force of less than four hundred is now battling on the outside of the gates, and one hundred more wait inside, ready to fight if the city is breached, which I think is not only a definite possibility, but also an inevitable certainty."

King Jarul sighed and turned to his wizard, who spoke before the question was asked.

"Fifty battle mages are joined with the four hundred soldiers outside, another thirty wait inside the city, and another twenty are here in the castle, churning out as many golems as they can, though they are quickly tiring," the wizard said in his slow, deep voice. "Your Majesty, I think it best if we take you to the rest of the nobles in the safety of the country. My three best magicians are working now on the finishing of a homunculus in your guise. We can place him on the throne and it will be weeks before Ozmodion's man sees it is not you."

Jarul raised a hand. "No, I will suffer along with my people. I will stay here to make sure Ozmodion's man does not harm my country. I suggest that you take the women, the children, and the old to safety in my stead Frendern, or can you handle that many?"

The wizard thought for a moment and then said, "Not all at once, but I could transport about five at a time and work my way through them all, though it will be a slow process."

"Just save as many as you can. Arouse my heralds and have them send for all but able-bodied men to come to the castle as quickly as possible."

Frendern bowed his head and disappeared in a thin wisp of smoke. Jarul turned his attention back to Hiestin.

"Do we know who Ozmodion has sent to lead this onslaught?" Jarul asked.

Hiestin grimace and nodded his head slowly as if it pained him. "Yerrin and Cassori are being led by officers no higher than lieutenants, but sadly Nunren is bigger than both countries, thus Ozmodion has sent the Troll Leader Kahn. He is colossal sir, even now he is fighting with the rest of Ozmocion's forces, slaying all in his path. Their catapults and archers have wreaked havoc on the town to a point where I don't think Frendern will have to concern himself with too many women and children. What's more, we see them carrying a large battering ram depicting a great demon to the Great Gates. The Gates are damaged enough as it is, and I do not think they will hold"

Jarul knew then that they had lost. "If that is the case, Hiestin, pull your men out from the fields. Our only hope is that we strengthen the Gates. Bring some spell casters with you, have them help you save the soldiers and brace the gateway."

Hiestin bowed once more and hurried out of the throne room. When he was gone, Jarul stood from his throne and walked to the window to gaze upon his capital city. Many large boulders had crushed the beautiful buildings and structures. The statue of Garon that rested in a fountain in the castle's courtyard was now headless and a stream of water towered above the ground. Many souls had been crushed under the rubble, their legs or arms reaching out from under large stones. Scores of people were now scrambling through the streets carrying possessions and heading towards the castle.

Jarul now turned his gaze out towards the battle, where he saw twenty dots carrying something long and red to the gate. They picked up speed. Suddenly they stopped and a deafening boom resonated from the gates. The dots backed up several paces, and then ran at the gate again.

Boom.

Again they backed up, again they charged.

Boom.

A hole had been put through the center of the gates. Many soldiers were now standing in front of it, shields raised and swords drawn.

Boom.

More and more citizens were running towards the castle, screaming as they went.

BOOM!

And the gates were broken, and the city was breached. The battering ram was dropped and Ozmodion's forces streamed through, slaughtering Jarul's soldiers and spreading chaos throughout the city.

Jarul's stomach twisted. Numbness overcame him. His mind drifted to all the people he could have saved had he but surrendered. But no, he had not. This was his fault and he could not shoulder the blame onto someone else. He wondered if the Resistance could help them, but he knew it was a weak hope for it was common knowledge that the Resistance was now marching to Saurindon. They could not help Jarul directly, and he knew he could only place his hope in the idea of Ozmodion being killed. He silently laughed at the thought.

Tthe door burst open once more and there Hiestin stood with a blank look. Jarul stared at him for a moment before an intense anger filled him

"What are you doing here?" Jarul demanded, "Do you not know that the city is—"

Jarul stopped short as Hiestin fell to the ground face down. Puzzled, Jarul look passed the doorway to see the hulking figure of a gigantic troll crouching down to squeeze through the door. He stood perhaps thirteen feet high and grinned wickedly.

"Breached?" he asked in a rumbling voice, "Yes, I am sure he knows. Hail King Jarul! I am Kahn, your successor."

Kahn walked passed Jarul to gaze out through the window, chuckling deeply.

"I daresay that your soldiers will surrender soon, with or without your consent. Though you will be happy to know your wizard managed to escape with fifteen of your citizens, but I doubt he will have the strength to come back seeing as we slashed his side before he disappeared."

Kahn then turned and faced the throne room, still grinning like a wolf.

"How marvelous, this greatly surpasses the tent I have had to make do with since we came here. However, those banners will not do, they will be replaced with Ozmodion's Standard."

He then walked to the throne and sat in it, sighing loudly.

"Oh, yes. I can see why you did not surrender as the Red Sovereign commanded; this chair alone is worth the fight." He laughed loudly.

Jarul's anger boiled, and he quickly approached his throne.

"Remove yourself from my seat." He demanded coldly.

Kahn locked his black eyes on Jarul and laughed again. "GORNL!" he called. Seconds later, another troll came thumping into the room, this one with chairs in one hand and a whip in the other.

"I think it would do His Majesty good to learn some respect for his betters," said Kahn to Gornl. "Do you not agree?"

"Yes sir!" Gornl dropped the chains and approached Jarul, who faced him bravely. But just as the troll raised his whip, Jarul said, "*Utn grondia.*"

Gornl laughed and tried to bring his arm down, but the whip stayed in place. Gornl tried again, and again, and again, but the whip would not budge. Finally, the troll let the whip go and the braided leather stayed suspended in midair.

"Extraordinary," said Kahn, rising from his seat, "An enchanter, eh? Well, we had not counted on that."

Jarul's expression did not lighten. "Now leave."

Kahn laughed again. "Oh Jarul, do you think we are frightened? I can see that simple spell has taxed you greatly. Gornl, chain him up by his wrists in the deepest, darkest cell you can find. No, never mind, instead put him in the stocks in the town square and let him see his own people grow to hate him. No food or water for a day, I think."

Gornl nodded and walked to his chains and picked them up. He brought them back to Jarul and bound the king's hands together.

"Move it," Gornl ordered, leading Jarul to the door. Jarul strained his neck to watch Kahn sit in his throne one last time, and then bowed his head, allowing self pity to consume him.

Chapter 22

The Conquest

*E**ion left the large cave* where the leaders held council, relieved to be out of the stuffy room. He stretched his wing-like arms and extended his neck, trying to wake all the things that had fallen asleep during the meeting. How pointless it had been; they had just reviewed plans of action that hey had long agreed on. None of the other leaders were too pleased to hear of Vundin's vision, for the Caves of Illothin would cause them to march twenty leagues in the wrong direction. Angered by their lack of respect towards a vision from a god, Eion suggested that they separate as they had in the Nalarti Mountains. Only Lord Fairskin was willing to agree outright, but Breeog and Barthol had finally given in.

Relieved that they would not be ignoring Vundin's prophecy, Eion went off to wander the Mountain. He flipped through some books in the library and scanned some scrolls of various subjects, but it soon began to bore him. He then moved onto a map of Arconia and Ÿalnz Dàr. He saw the Mountain next to the gigantic Silver Ice Sea. He looked towards the bottom of the map, quickly sweeping over the immense forest, and examined a range of mountains that he knew made up Saurindon's northern border. A gripping fear clawed at his insides like none he had felt since his family had been taken from him. Quickly following the fear was anger. *No*, he thought. *More than that.* It was a burning, liquid rage. Eion's hand quickly moved to the hilt of *Raz'atr*, his knuckles turning white as he gripped. He was suddenly back on the Ozra Gap at the base of the hill. The pale dead form of a soldier lay spread-eagled at his feet. And at the top of the hill was golden throne with red satin cushions. And in it sat the one who orphaned him, the one who was responsible for the ghost of a life he found himself leading, one haunted by tortured thoughts and spectral visions. Eion began to draw his sword, but then the vision melted away and he found himself back in the library facing the unrolled scroll.

Steady, he thought to himself wryly. *It would not be wise to undo things now.*

Disturbed, he made his way out of the library and to the humongous cavern in which the gigantic company had dined on the previous evening. Upon arriving, one quick sweep of the cavern told him Gwen was not present. Puzzled but not yet concerned, he went to sit next to his officers, whose cheeks were red and their tones were fruity, the wine and mead quickly taking effect.

"Eion!" Steel motioned for him, "Join us in a toast!"

Eion smiled and sat between Flame and Beast. He shifted a glass and some wine, and then asked, "What is it we are toasting to?"

"To anything and everything," Fletch answered merrily. "It is Steel's turn to pick something, I believe."

Steel hiccupped loudly, and then shouted, "To nymphs! To all pretty nymphs near and far!"

"To nymphs!" cried Flame and Beast.

"Yes, and to dryads, too!" yelled Fletch

"To dryads," whispered Eion, and he drained his glass, enjoying himself.

He proposed toasts along with his friends, some serious and some equally ridiculous. They toasted to fauns for their beautiful music and they toasted to flowers for keeping bees away. They toasted to elves for their fairness and strength. They toasted mead and wine. Soon Eion was as intoxicated as his friends, and forgot to worry why Gwen was not present at the feast.

The banquet itself was a blur of motion and light; for years afterward, Eion couldn't recall any of the details of that night. As the festivity began to slow, Eion grew sober enough to finally notice that Gwen was still not present. He looked to where the rest of the Ten sat. Neither Gwen nor Ryan sat with them.

Disturbed, Eion shifted any remaining alcohol out of his system. He excused himself and quickly left the dining cavern, concern now growing. He combed every nook and cranny of the Mountain, his worry escalading while he looked. He took the tunnel that led to the library. When he arrived at the end of the passage, he looked behind shelves, under tables, and around corners until he came upon Ryan, sitting at a table piled with books, a look of mad glee on his face.

"A little late for reading, isn't it?" asked Eion, Ryan jumped at his the sound of his voice but he smiled awkwardly when he realized who it was, "And those books are not exactly light, now are they?"

Ryan chuckled. "I'm sorry Eion, time flew away from me. These books are absolutely fascinating. Did you know that you could manipulate any form of fire simply by—"

"I haven't the time," Eion interrupted, "Gwen has disappeared. Do you know where she could be?"

Ryan shrugged, turning back to his book. "She and her cat were here a while ago, but she left when I mentioned how fascinating übelancy is."

"Well if you do see—Did you say übelancy?"

Ryan nodded.

Eion looked at him as though he would a murderer. "There is nothing fascinating nor natural about that art. Stay away from it, Ryan; it leads to a path that is very hard to turn away from. I suggest you go now to the feast, before there is nothing to eat."

Ryan nodded, but did not take his eyes off his book. There was a long silence, and eventually Eion left the library, now worried about Ryan's reaction to the evil skill. As he made his way out of the library, he looked back to the times following Ozmodion's fall. Übelancy had been growingly popular, and übelancers were often trying to take up the mantle of the Red Sovereign, though none had succeeded. The Resistance had fought back, along with the ferocious elven clan Yuln, and Lord Daio had broken the übelancers after a single battle. Since then, übelancy had not been practiced for a long while.

Eion knew that Ryan meant no harm, and was bound to be interested in all magic now that he had seen the Magic Realm. He, like Gwen, was strongly steeped in power. When Eion first met him, Ryan's aura was able to light up a room. The other eight of the Prophesied showed nothing amazing when compared to Ryan and Gwen, and Eion knew it, for they were the only reasons Eion had lingered with the group for two years. He had trouble seeing which one was the Iltari, until, of course, Avria sent the hellhound.

He eventually came to the tunnel he knew led to the Chamber of the Gods. Wonder gripped him, and he almost laughed at the possible irony. Then fear returned to him as he thought of what would happen if Gwen had found out the truth. Panicked, he hurried along the passageway, his apprehension rising. Worry moving him along, he quickly reached the oak door and found Gwen slouched up against it, a blank look on her face and her strange black cat next to her. Her eyes slowly moved up to look at Eion, her stare red and swollen.

"You," she said quietly, and she quickly stood up and walked to stand perhaps two feet in front of Eion.

"Yes, Gwen, I was concerned when you didn't come to the feast. After all, we will be leavi—" He was cut off as Gwen slapped him very hard and very loudly on his right cheek. Stunned, he shook his head, trying to shake of the numbing pain.

Eion cleared his throat. "Ahem, perhaps you would care to justify that—" Again he was cut short and again he was slapped. Eion felt his eyes water and his cheek sting as though it were on fire.

"Gwen what's wrong?" and he jumped back three feet, avoiding another slap. Gwen's face was now livid, her eyes burning like a furious blaze.

"You. First you lie to me about yourself, portraying yourself as a normal human, and now I find that you lied about me as well. An Iltari! Me! An Iltari! I trust that you know what that is Eion? Of course you do, but I did not know this time yesterday, and now I do. I, like you, am not human, am I?"

Eion's heart sank, knowing why he had found her down this corridor. He wanted to speak condolences, but instead he asked, "Who is it your father? Mellao? Leano? Joao? It could have been any of them, they would not tell me until you knew yourself—"

Again he was slapped. "You knew!" Gwen shouted to him, and her cat meowed inquisitively, "Eion, you knew! How could you? I would think you would be entirely open with me seeing that you dragged me off to this horrible place, forcing me to fight a war I never knew about. This isn't how things are supposed to be!"

Eion shook his head. "You are wrong, Gwen."

Gwen's eyes narrowed, and Eion prepared himself for another slap, though it did not come. "Wrong?" Gwen asked dangerously. "How am I wrong?"

Eion sighed and turned around so he was facing the passage that led back to the Main Chamber. He was quiet for a long time, and when he spoke his words were slow and deliberate.

"You only exist *because* you were meant to fight this war. You were *meant* to fight." He now turned to face her, her look was still cold. "It may sound cruel, but you were put here to aid the suffering of many, like I was. These worlds, yours and mine, gain thousands upon thousands of new people everyday, who go on to live their small lives. Many are forgotten and years from now their names will mean nothing. But you and I, Gwen, are meant for greater things. We are meant to do things that will be sung about for eternity. Years from now, our grandchildren's grandchildren will still speak of what we have done. To be an Iltari is to be one like no other.

The gods gave you life, and all they ask in return is to give hope back to those who have none."

Eion paused, letting her soak in his words. When her expression did not change he continued.

"I understand how you feel, Gwen, for I have faced the same hardship. I remember when I found out who exactly I was and remember how it shook me. My identity had been thrown completely and utterly into doubt, and I questioned myself about who and what I was. But, I've longed learned to accept it. I now realize that I was put here for something bigger, something better. And you were too."

Gwen's coldness faded, and she almost smiled. All she said was, "Will I live forever?"

Eion nodded. "If we choose to we can live our lives eternally, and only a blade through the heart will end us. Though if life begins to lose all it once held for us, then yes, we may choose to relinquish our god-given immortality and die."

Now Gwen turned around, talking to the oak door instead of him.

"Eion, we weren't meant to outlive our time. People are born, they live their life, and then they die. That's the way things are supposed to be."

Eion chuckled. "That is how your friends will live, that is how everyone you know from the other realm will live, and that may even be the way you choose to live. But we are not bound so tightly as the others in these worlds. We are meant to exceed our times."

There was a long silence that was only disturbed by the short intakes of breath Gwen took while she wept silently. Finally, Eion asked, "Who is your father?"

More sounds of weeping, then she said in a sound quieter than a whisper, "Hawore."

Eion's mouth dropped open. *"The God of Magic"* he whispered. Of all the gods that could have conceived Gwen, Hawore the least likely. "Does this mean you will—"

No he thought, *It should make no difference.*

Gwen continued to sob under her breath.

Eion tried to say something, but a scream echoed through the passage interrupting him. He turned his head quickly, straining his ears for another sound. He heard Gwen shuffle around, breathing heavily. He heard Gwen's cat take three steps, and then stop, hissing menacingly. Eion tried to block them out and tried to listen farther away. Another sharp scream resounded in his ears. Eion turned around and grabbed Gwen's hand, saying quietly, "Stay close." She nodded. Eion looked appraisingly at her cat, then unsheathed *Raz'atr* and set off through the tunnel.

While they more screams met them. Eion's grip on both *Raz'atr* and Gwen's hand tightened until he felt his knuckles turn white. Eion now saw flashes of light and heard the clash of sword against sword. An agonizing anticipation seized him, and he had already begun to shift armor around himself and Gwen, ignoring her gasp of surprise as she felt the unexpected weight come upon her.

They reached the mouth of the tunnel and found the Main Chamber was now playing host to a battalion of no less then seven hundred goblins. They carried bent swords, rapiers, broadswords, scimitars, pikes, axes, bows, spears, scythes, and tridents. They whooped and cheered as they brought down all the small little hobgoblins that were unfortunate enough to stand in their way. The Resistance was trying to rush into the chamber, but the solid wall of goblins was barricading the small passageways; Eion's face fell as he saw that reinforcements would be very hard to receive. He turned to Gwen who was feeling around her belt, searching for a sword hilt that was not there. Eion smiled and released Gwen's hand, and he shifted her a sword. He handed it to her and said, "Use it carefully." He winked and he set off into the battle, hoping Gwen's swordplay would help her.

"Tirmal!" he shouted to the passageway that the goblins were blocking, seeing the elf struggling to get through, "use a thrust spell!"

Almost immediately after Eion spoke, every goblin turned to face him, their ugly faces split into horrifying grins. They whooped, they cheered, they shouted, "Hurrah!" they raised their weapons above their heads and crowed excitedly. They banged their shields against one another's.

Suddenly, Belzorg's second-in-command, Sarnor, emerged from the treacherous horde. He raised his sword in a saluting manner, and then bowed just to aggravate Eion even more. Then Sarnor stood up straight once more and spoke to Eion.

"Well met Shifter!" His rough, high voice was enough to immediately silence the cheers and whoops from the other goblins. Their grins, though, remained.

"Well met, Sarnor," Eion said calmly, trying with all his might to keep his temper hidden, "To what do I owe the pleasure of seeing you here in the Mountain?"

Sarnor laughed coldly. "Eion, why do you play the fool when we all know you are wiser than most?"

Eion smiled. "Even the wise man plays the fool, occasionally, for wisdom can be so dull, though I am sure you would not know anything of that."

Sarnor's smiled flickered, but he continued to speak with indifference. "I see. Well, if you are determined to play the fool, I will tell you why we are here. We come bearing a message from His Exaltedness, the Red Sovereign. We are to deliver it to you after killing as many as we can."

Eion chuckled. "I see, so you are to die senselessly for Ozmodion and we are to pry the message from your cold, dead hands? I must say, Sarnor, Belzorg must be tiring of you if he has sent you to your death. Perhaps shifting him into a frog has done his addled brains some good."

Sarnor face contorted with rage, as were the other goblins'. "Impertinence!" Sarnor seethed. "Vanity! How dare you insult both the Red Sovereign and the Great Belzorg! We shall teach you some respect before this night is done! Attack!"

At this, the goblins' cheers began again with newfound merriment as they ran towards the lone shifter with their weapons raised. Eion made no move. Instead, he smiled. He saw the bloodthirsty looks of the goblins turn into looks of confusion and doubt. It wasn't until they were in reach of *Raz'atr*'s tip that he slashed three goblins through the heart with one thrust and then pulled his now bloodied sword out of their hollowed chests. The three crumpled to the ground, their eyes bulging with pained hate. Eion then cleaved another's skull as it ran towards him with a particularly sharp spear. The shifter grabbed the corpse with his left hand and hurled it into the large mass of goblins, smiling grimly as he heard one scream.

He killed all who were dim-witted enough to come to him. A pile of bodies steadily mounted beside him. Years of learning how precarious life was dulled his sympathy as he continued to slay his attackers. He did not care that their lives were being destroyed or that he was the one who was destroying them. They were just pieces in a game he was determined to win. His face was now unrecognizable, as he roared and shouted war cries with each new kill.

A flash of red light filled the Main Chamber and several dozen goblins were blown into the air. Eion looked to the passageway that the Resistance had been trapped in to see Tirmal leading a steady stream of soldiers amidst the throng. Eion was not surprised to see Lord Fairskin himself among his fellow elves, wielding his staff and broadsword with the strength of twelve elven soldiers.

Sarnor now approached Eion with his sword raised and a ferocious snarl on his face. He brought the sword down on Eion, who parried the blow quicker than thought. Clenched in the goblin's other fist was a rusted war axe, which Sarnor swung at Eion. Without thinking, Eion shifted into a hawk and rose above Sarnor's head, missing the axe by inches. Once he was over Sarnor, he shifted back to his usual form with *Raz'atr* pointing down. Sarnor screamed and moved to the left, skirting the blade by inches. He roared and swung the axe at Eion once more, who split the handle in half with one slash of his sword.

☐

Gwen gazed down at the battle raging in front of her, terror paralyzing her. She looked at Eion and the Goblin he fought and then to the passageway where the flow of Resistance soldiers was remaining steady. She gripped the sword Eion had given her so tightly her hand began to numb.

"What do I do, Curthlond?" she asked, not daring to look at the cat beside her.

"Become who you were born to be," Curthlond answered.

Gwen nodded and dropped the sword. She raised her right hand, pointing it at the mass of goblins. She delved into herself until she found the knot of energy. She took a deep breath, and then shouted the words Curthlond had taught her.

The knot of magic burst apart and filled every part of her body. The sensation was wonderful, almost freeing as she felt uncultivated power coarse through her. Just as quickly as it filled her, it left through her extended arm, turning into a wide stream of flame as it left her palm.

A pain like none she'd ever felt erupted in her right hand. She screamed loudly, but could not hear it. She wanted to collapse, to bring her arm to her side and let it rest, but the magic held her in place.

Through the mind numbing agony, she saw the stream of fire collide with the goblins. Their whoops became yelps and their cheers became cries as the fire ignited their hair and the cloth they wore under their armor. They spread out, crashing into each other and setting others ablaze. The Resistance's fighters took the opportunity and began to make magnificent headway. Soon the goblins were reduced to half of their original numbers, and, disheartened and sensing defeat, they retreated through the passageways and tunnels.

Finally, the stream of fire died and Gwen toppled backwards, quickly fading from consciousness. She was out cold before she reached the ground.

□

Eion did not see who cast the fire, and did not care for that matter. Sarnor had been distracted as he saw his troops being burnt alive, and Eion had stuck *Raz'atr* deep into the goblin's armpit until the tip was protruding from his opposite shoulder. The goblin howled and dropped to his knees, releasing both his sword and axe handle.

"So this is death?" he asked between heaving breaths, looking at the ground. "It is not as I expected it. It is, well, *liberating*. It feels as though yesterday's worries are nothing, and tomorrow will never come. Yes, this is wonderful. Eion, old friend, my message…"

With his good arm, the goblin reached into his armor and pulled from it a rolled piece of black parchment that had been tied with a red ribbon. Eion took it from the goblin and looked at him in disgust.

"Enjoy your last moments in this world," Eion said barely repressing his hatred, "for I shudder to think what the next life holds for you. I send you now to Avria's Five Hells to be tormented for eternity. May her hellhounds feast on your soul!"

Sarnor looked up into the eyes of Eion. Eion was shocked to see that the goblin's green eyes had now faded and were instead pearly white, staring unseeingly.

Blinded, the goblin spoke. "Now those words sound much more like the death I thought I would have. Eion, if you are still here, I will have you know this. I would have served thou had it be mine own choice. I beseech ye to forgive my fellows; they know not what they do. Deluded are they, for Ozmodion's filthy whispers are quite enticing. I beseech you more, nay, I plead that you will please free them of Ozmodion's malignancy. Fare thee well, O King of Shifters. May your kin live to see better days."

Then the goblin collapsed face first.

Eion stared at the corpse for a long while, pondering his last words. *And so passes Sarnor*, Eion thought, *son of Belzorg.*

He then turned his back on Sarnor's body and untied the red ribbon that was tied to the black parchment. The message was written in fiery red runes in the dark tongue. Eion read:

Greetings, Shifter.

As you are surely aware of, this was a useless maneuver on my part, one that has surely lost me many goblins. But as I can no longer hold this from you with good conscience, I feel it necessary. Your Great Ten Prophesied have not proved much merit yet, and already they betray you. One will forsake the Resistance before you reach Saurindon, though you will have no knowing of the identity of the traitor. He will not leave you in a clear manner; indeed you will think nothing of it when it happens.

The winds carry your stench already Eion; I will know you are here before you do. You have invoked a wrath you cannot begin to comprehend. Savor your petty victory on that hill, for it shall never happen again. Know this: your friends shall all die painfully, and only for the reason that your stubborn pride forced them march.

Let know Fairskin my tellings, and allow him comfort by informing him that Gwalin lives, though uncomfortably. These letters were written with his blood.

As Eion read the last word, the black parchment suddenly became bathed in flames. In surprise, the shifter threw the parchment to the ground, but before he could extinguish the fire, the parchment shriveled into dust.

Eion cursed loudly, ignoring the stares and gasps issued by the soldiers of the Resistance who were slowly filtering out of the tunnel. He then pondered on Ozmodion's vague hints and cryptic warnings. Making no sense of it, Eion turned to look at the Resistance, who were now filing into the tunnels to wipe out the remaining goblins that had retreated in the winding passages of the Mountain. With a heavy sigh, Eion set off to join them.

☐

Gwen awoke with a start, her hand still throbbing madly. She sat up, supporting herself with her left hand, while letting her right hand rest on her lap.

"Well," Curthlond said, and Gwen turned to see the cat sitting by her, "I was wondering how much longer I would have to wait."

Gwen rubbed her eyes and then massaged her head, all with her left hand, then said, "How long have I been out? It feels as though it's been days."

Curthlond chuckled then shook his head. "No, it's only been a few minutes, but I have never been the patient type. It's a cat thing."

Gwen turned to look at the rest of the Main Chamber. It was strewn with the bodies of dead goblins that had fallen at the swords of the Resistance. The sight made her stomach churn, and she promptly vomited to her right. When she was done and had wiped herself clean, she turned back to Curthlond and asked tiredly, "Where is Eion?"

Curthlond began to bathe himself, and then said, "He set out with the rest of the Resistance to comb the Mountain for any remaining goblins not three minutes ago. I do not see what Ozmodion had to gain by this attack; he knew he would be mortally outnumbered. Still, makes no difference to the Resistance; there are that many less goblins to fight in the upcoming war."

Gwen nodded, grimacing as her hand seared with pain once more. When the spasm passed, Gwen forced herself to look at her hand. The sight made her scream, for etched into her skin was a bloody five-point star with a crescent moon embossed in its center. It oozed with fresh blood, and, though she now tried to wrap in with a handkerchief, she found it too painful to bandage it.

"Ah, yes," Curthlond said as he climbed onto Gwen's lap to examine her palm, "Finally it is done."

Gwen turned now to look at Curthlond once more. "You knew about this?" she asked with more anger than she felt.

Curthlond nodded. "Of course, am I not an enchanter, too?" He raised his right paw, displaying a smaller silver mark, though it was shaped just like Gwen's. "The Vawn is the mark of the enchanter. Each spell castor has an insignia etched into their hand, depending on what magic the spell castor uses. *That* is why your hand hurt while you used magic, but I am afraid that small spells do nothing but aggravate. A large spell like the one you cast is required if one wishes to end the pain and acquire the mark."

"How do I stop it from bleeding?" she asked hurriedly, alarmed at the rate the blood was dripping from the mark.

Curthlond shrugged. "Give it a while; you have unleashed a lot of magic."

Gwen grew dizzy and strained her eyelids to keep them open.

Curthlond now shook his head amazingly. "I cannot believe how long you held that spell; even at the height of my power such a feat would have left me dead. If I did not know you were an Iltari, I would have thought you possessed."

Gwen flinched at the sound of her title, its meaning making her sick. "Will this mark always be bloody?"

Curthlond shook his head. "When it has fully healed, it will become faint and silver, nothing more than a scar. And perhaps best of all, magic will no longer pain you; your power will know no bounds!"

Gwen yawned, and Curthlond put on a disapproving face. "Not tonight, Curthlond. I am tired and want nothing besides a good night's rest."

Curthlond nodded, and set off, skirting all the bodies. Gwen took a deep breath as she got to her feet and followed him, becoming lightheaded as the smell of rotting flesh and open wounds wafted through the Main Chamber.

Chapter 24

The Forest

*E**ion returned late the following morning*, black goblin blood staining his clothes. He marched alongside Tirmal, but he spoke very few words, allowing the battle to really sink in.

Death, Eion thought. *The Mountain reeks of it.*

Years of watching friends die, watching loved ones' lives being wiped away, had somehow changed him. He had never been the same since his father and brothers had died, and he secretly blamed himself for their murders. Now, over one thousand years since it happened, Eion was unrecognizable from the small peasant boy he once was. He was no longer short and he was no longer dangerously thin, his height and muscles having been honed for a millennium. Eyes that once sparkled with life and joy, were now dull and almost bereft of color. His face had changed as well, though Eion did not know if it was due to shifting so often, or if it was because of the sad life he had led. But most of all, it was his thinking that was different. In his younger days, his philosophy was kill or be killed. But years of battle had taught him the power of mercy, and how the sparing of a life can indeed alter the course of the future.

He knew that the battle of the Mountain would soon fade from his memory and become just another scar in his mind.

As they reached the main chamber, they found a large group of the Resistance disposing of the mounds of goblins. Eion was sick to see that many hobgoblins had died before the Resistance could come.

"The Mountain will never again show us such open hospitality," stated Tirmal as he approached Eion from a platoon of elves who had been stacking the goblins. "They can not risk it."

"Mm," was all Eion could think to say as they made their way to help put the goblins' bodies from the tunnels in the pile. Large hills of the monsters were now made, and some dwarves were sent for wood and oil.

"I trust you gained what you needed from the gods?" Tirmal asked.

Eion did not look at him, but instead moved the hobgoblins' bodies away from the goblins'. They did not deserve to be cremated so unceremoniously. "I did," Eion replied simply.

"And what are we to do now?" pressed Tirmal as he helped Eion along with several other soldiers.

"Seek the help of those we protect," answered Eion, hoping the riddled response would cease the elf's questioning.

"I see," was all Tirmal said. There was a long pause, and then, "Is that all?"

285

"Tirmal, you forget your place!" Eion shouted and he picked up the frozen form of a dead Hobgoblin and carried him to the furnaces to be properly cremated. For his sake, the elf did not follow him.

☐

The cauldron was bubbling, and hissing much like it had before. But now Ozmodion was using different incantations, different methods. He abandoned the idea of another army of his black creations, but he would be satisfied if he could hone and perfect a smaller amount.

It was night in Saurindon, yet the red sand outside of the window in his chambers still glowed eerily in red. The stars, apparently too good and pure to be seen above the dreaded desert, could not be seen in the black sky. Only the moon, full and bright, shined on the evil place. It was quiet, too; the legions of the Ozra had apparently bunkered down for the night. Even the guards that Ozmodion knew would be patrolling the innards of the fortress and the Gates of Angar Vûn were silent.

The sorcerer nodded in satisfaction; the less distraction about, the better. He turned the cauldron's substance once more, and backed up as he spoke the final incantation. As before, a great plume of smoke erupted from the cauldron. Ozmodion was chuckling as he ascended the steps that led to golden red throne. By the time he took his seat, the smoke had cleared, and ten dark creatures with livid red eyes were staring up at him balefully.

"Shadow shifters," the Red Sovereign hissed with restrained delight. "Your forerunners have failed me…perhaps I aimed too high, perhaps I was too hasty. Still, I do not repeat my mistakes. I place you all under my mastery; from me, you shall receive the tutelage your fallen brethren so clearly lacked."

He paused and studied of them. "There are ten of you…enough to match the Resistance's so called 'salvation'. I suppose it is some kind of poetic justice. Yes, you shall be the Maurimim, the Rising Bane."

The ten shadow shifters, garbed in the black robes and scarves like the others had been, bowed in unison, hissing their thanks.

"To the armory with you," commanded Ozmodion, pointing to the door with his decrepit-looking hand. "The morrow will see you ready for some intense instruction indeed. Go."

More bows, and the Maurimim exited through the great red doors that led into the heart of Taronest. Ozmodion watched them close the doors behind them, and set about clearing his chambers of the broken fragments of cauldron that had resulted in his latest enchantment. He snapped his fingers, and they disappeared in a high wind.

☐

Gwen awoke from an uneasy dream. It took her a long time to realize where she was, but she remembered eventually. Her room was dimly lit in the early hours of the morning, though she could not understand how.

The previous day's events suddenly came back to mind painfully, and she again examined her right hand. The star and moon were still there, now crusted with dried blood. She did not know why, but somehow the knowing she could perform magic numbed the pain of knowing she was an Iltari. She resolved to tell none of her nine mortal friends, though she wondered if they knew as well. She now realized how different she was from her friends, more magic than mortal. Still, there was not much she would not give to become their equal once more.

But I never really was their equal, was I? Gwen mused. Eion's words still echoed hauntingly in her ears, as though she had heard them in a dream. Then there was Curthlond's advice. *Become who you were born to be*. Had she listened to him? What would've happened had she not cast the spell? The thought made her sick.

When the questions stopped prodding her mind, she realized that Curthlond was gone. Telling herself that he was not a cat and could do as he pleased, she tried not to worry. She lay back down and drifted into another uncomfortable sleep.

She awoke at the sound of scratching at her door. Puzzled, she got out of bed and robed herself, having been too tired to do anything last night but strip of her clothes and climb into bed. She walked to the door and opened it. At first she thought no one was there, but when she looked to the ground, she saw Curthlond dragging an immense and ancient book by a tassel stitched into the spine.

"Morning," he said through clenched teeth, "Bwought somethin' for you."

Gwen leaned down and picked up both the book and Curthlond, shutting the door as she did. She then walked to the bed, where she sat both things down.

"Blech," coughed Curthlond, "Five hundred years of accumulated dust does wonders for the mouth."

Gwen nodded, to busy looking at the book to say anything. She sat on the edge of the bed and asked, "What is this?"

"Isn't it obvious?" replied Curthlond as he started to bathe himself. "It's a spell book, the only one you will ever need, I'd wager."

Gwen picked up the book once more, seeing that runes were engraved on the back. "Curthlond, I can't read these letters."

"Tell that to the book; it will understand."

Confused, Gwen held the book to her mouth. "Book, I can't read these runes," she said, feeling ridiculous.

Like at the altar in the Chamber of the Gods, the letters on the cover and spine began to glow with blinding white light. When it passed, the runes had been replaced with letters written in English. Now, Gwen saw that the book's title was *The Guiding Tome*. As she read the name out loud, Curthlond nodded with a boyish grin on his face.

"There are perhaps only ten of these books in the world, and three of them are in the library. I am sure the hobgoblins will not notice it is gone, seeing as the section I found it in has not seen a duster in centuries. But this book exceeds every other spell book in the world because it keeps up with present day, recording more spells when new spells are discovered."

"But it's so big," Gwen pointed out, "I'll never read it all."

"You don't need to; you need only refer to it when you need a certain bit of knowledge. What is more, the book knows exactly what you need when you open it, and it will always bring you to the page you require. For instance, look up Fire Spells."

Gwen thought very hard about Fire Spells for a moment, and sure enough, when she opened the book it opened straight to a chapter filled with enchantments and charms of fire.

"Now, stow that in your pack, for I daresay we will need it in the forest of Ÿalnz Dàr."

Gwen gasped; she had completely forgotten that they would be leaving the Mountain today for the forest that lay to the south.

"What's the forest like, Curthlond?" she asked, knowing he had lived there, or close by anyway, before he had been turned into a cat.

Curthlond's eyes misted, as if had just looked into the past and gazed at his old home. "There is no place like Ÿalnz Dàr. Steeped in magic and full of danger, it is not a place for the faint of heart or weak of mind; every corner could spell disaster if you do not keep your wits about you. There are all sorts of things in there that will enchant you, bewitch you, or charm you if you are not wary. And I can't tell you how important manners are; you can't chance being rude in places where things can eat you."

Gwen stared at the cat, as it continued to stare blankly at nothing and smile as it described what Gwen believed to be a nasty hellhole.

When Gwen had finished stowing the book deep in her pack, she and Curthlond set out for the Great Hall. They walked slowly, while Gwen gazed at the Mountain and thought how she would not miss it at all; in fact she inwardly hoped to never see its wretched walls ever again.

They arrived at the Great Hall to see it again alive with the immense and hungry company. As she walked to her seat, she noticed the soldiers did not look at her, not in anger or in any shunning manner, but in respect. Even some of the dragons, the beasts who were so noble they considered none but their king above them, bowed their heads as she passed. Some might've found it enjoyable, maybe even granted, but Gwen found it unnerving.

She took her seat next to Lea, Kendal, and Caitlin, who fortunately, in their ignorance, still treated her as usual.

"Morning, Gwen." Lea said between mouthfuls of scrambled eggs.

"Morning," Gwen mumbled. Curthlond jumped on her lap and looked over the table showing only his head.

"Morning Buttons Baby!" Kendal cooed. She then returned to her conversation with Caitlin.

"Dense-headed twit," Curthlond responded quietly as he jumped onto the table and sniffed Gwen's plate of food; he still blamed Kendal for his ridiculous pseudonym.

As Gwen gave him a strip of bacon, Lea turned to face her and asked, "Where were you last night? You never came to the feast?"

Not wanting to tell the whole truth, Gwen said, "I was helping Eion in the battle." She quickly made sure her right palm could not be seen.

"*Really?*" Lea's eyes widened incredulously. Both Caitlin and Kendal stopped talking and turned to face Gwen as well. "Why?" all three asked.

Gwen shrugged. "I was at the right place at the right time, I guess."

"The *right* place at the *right* time?" Kendal repeated with emphasis, "You act like it was your job to fight."

Gwen raised an eyebrow as Curthlond finished with his bacon and moved onto her glass of milk, sizing it up and trying to think of a way to drink it. "Why else are we here if not to fight?"

Caitlin scoffed. "We are the Great Prophesied; why should we fight? We're only here to help Eion kill Ozmodion."

"And how are we to do that if not by fighting?" Gwen asked, confused.

"Gwen, with our combined power," Lea explained tiredly, "Ozmodion does not stand any chance in defeating Eion, and—"

"What power do you *have*?" Gwen interjected, "What power do you have that no one else in this realm does? Is that why you think that Eion has brought us here, so he could tap us for energy? You' right; we are the Prophesied. We are *meant* to fight."

The statement made Kendal snicker. "Fight? That's the soldiers' jobs."

It was Gwen's turn to laugh. Even Curthlond chortled as he stood on his hind legs and slurped inside the milk glass.

"So, what…" Gwen, cocked her head, anger boiling inside of her. "You think you're better than the soldiers? More important, maybe?"

The three nodded as though they were relieved Gwen finally understood.

"If you will not fight," Gwen said, all traces of giggles or laughter now replaced with cold deliberation, "then you are definitely not at all greater than these noble people who will risk their lives in battle. If you do not fight, you are cowards, and I will distance myself to a point where some will find it incredible I ever considered you friends. Do the others feel the same way?"

Stunned, the three girls did not say anything for a few moments.

"Well?" Gwen pressed hotly, "come on, I don't need you wasting my time."

Finally, Kendal spoke boldly, "Only you and Ryan seem to think we're wrong." She spoke the words with barely suppressed pride. "He called us cowards, too."

Gwen stared at the strangers in front of her, strangers who so shortly ago were her companions. She smiled faintly, then stood up, picked up Curthlond despite his protests, and stormed out of the Great Hall to make for her room to pack.

☐

Eion, surveyed the Great Hall to see that everyone had finished his or her breakfast, then rose from his seat and tapped his goblet with a spoon. The tinkling of the glass was not heard by the many voices ringing through the large Cavern. Eion turned to Lord Fairskin, Breeog, and King Barthol who all sat next to him at the head of the table. Breeog let out an ear-piercing roar that resounded through the cavern. When he stopped, the chatter ceased immediately.

"Thank you, Breeog," Eion said quietly. He then turned to face the soldiers at the table. "Today we make for the last barrier between us and our journey's end. We face days, weeks of hardship. Food will be scarce, and it is very unwise to hunt anything that lurks in those trees. Therefore, we will have to make do with half rations until we leave the forest."

Groans and angry mumbles punctuated the silence of Eion's audience, and it was a long time indeed before Eion was able to continue.

"Yes, yes, I know it will be difficult, but unless you wish to face enchantments of a terrible sort, I beg you to not hunt the game or eat the plants in that forest. Shifters, I discourage you further to try and shift food; the air you must use is just as thick with strange magic. We will rendezvous with both Captains Flora and Fauna in less than two hours, so prepare to march!"

With that, all of the soldiers in the Resistance filtered out of the Great Hall to pack their belongings and ready for another long march through the forest.

The other leaders stood from their chairs. Breeog and Barthol set out after the troops, but Lord Fairskin hobbled next to Eion.

"You seem uneasy," the old elf stated.

Eion grunted as the pair left the Great Hall as well.

"Is it the forest that troubles you?"

Another grunt, then, "Have you asked for the other clans' help?"

Lord Fairskin chuckled. "Why would I do that?"

"Lord Fairskin, we both know the odds aren't in our favor. With Gwalin now in Ozmodion's clutches, the Kji, at least, have reason to battle. We need all the help we can, and it would be most helpful indeed if you—"

"If my brethren have found it unnecessary to offer their help, then I will not bend my knees and beg for it."

Eion sighed. Knowing the elf's pride was an unshakable thing, he did not press the matter. Instead, he set out for his room, arriving to hear the sounds of packing in the other caves. He smiled then opened the door to his own quarters and packed what few belongings he had brought in a small pouch. He then unshifted his sword belt and then shifted a baldric, which he strapped over his shoulder. He then placed *Raz'atr* firmly in its scabbard. Satisfied, he left his room, and again made for the Main Chamber.

Packed with every soldier of the Resistance, armed and ready for battle, the room was abuzz with excitement. Eion scanned the colossal throng for Gwen and found her toward the front of the mass talking to Tirmal, and made note of her cat curled around on her shoulder and that Gwen was now wearing open fingertip gloves. Puzzled that Gwen was not with the other nine, Eion moved to the front of the company where the other three leaders waited. Breeog's face split with his golden grin as he saw the leading shifter approach.

"Shifter," he roared, "I would like you to meet my new captain, Brunariun. BRUNARIUN!"

His roar resonated through the immense cavern, and in moments, a bright orange dragon appeared in the sky and landed in front of them.

"Well met, Brunariun," Eion greeted Brunariun politely. Eion noticed she was a female dragon.

"Greetings, General Shifter," Brunariun responded in a definite female voice.

"Please call me Eion, if you don't mind." He hated being reminded of his title.

Brunariun nodded kindly, but her eyes were scanning him in the unsettling way all dragons stare. Flicking her tongue with a "Hum!" she turned to Breeog.

"Are we ready?" Breeog asked.

"Yes, Your Majesty, the dragons are ready to leave whenever you are."

Grinning, Breeog nodded, indicating Brunariun's dismissal. The female dragon bowed her head, took another look at Eion, and set off into the gathering throng

"And the shifters, Eion?" asked Lord Fairskin from the other side of Breeog.

"They, too, stand ready."

"Barthol?" Breeog asked the dwarf who stood beside Lord Fairskin. The dwarf king grunted, "Yes. And you, Fairskin?"

"The Vra are ready."

"Then let us be off," roared Breeog. "TO ŸALNZ DÁR!"

The Resistance cheered and applauded, but Eion could not feel the urge to join them. He turned on his heel to face one last tunnel, one that led to the base of the Mountain on the southern side. At the mouth of the tunnel stood the Head Hobgoblin and what few hobgoblins remained in the Mountain. Eion, Lord Fairskin, King Barthol, and Breeog motioned the Resistance to stay as they walked to the hobgoblins. They all took turns shaking the Head Hobgoblin's hand and speaking their condolences and apologies.

All the Head Hobgoblin said was, "Rid his filth of this earth." Then he and the other hobgoblins turned and walked into another tunnel, leaving the Resistance alone.

The leaders looked at each other, then sat off through the tunnel they knew would lead them outside. The cavern echoed loudly as the Resistance set off through the tunnel, leaving the Mountain behind.

The passageway was a difficult thing, for it twisted and turned and looped back on itself so it became a labyrinth. But as the Resistance's leaders had all been to the Mountain many times, the way was eventually found after twenty minutes of marching. They were momentarily blinded as bright, morning sunlight poured in through the mouth of the cave. Eion shifted his eyes so his pupils could dilate even farther. When the pain passed, Eion gazed around him, taking in the beauty.

The morning was calm and cool. The Silver Ice Sea was lapping against the shore, sending mist into the air that chilled them all the more; the sky was clear of clouds, but the sun's rays sent no warmth to the ground. As Eion slowly looked to the right, he became aware of the gargantuan mass of green that lay ahead of him. Across the short heath of grey stone they now found themselves on, the Waning Waste, Ÿalnz Dàr, the enchanted forest, stood perhaps one mile away from his right. Instinctively, Eion touched the pommel of *Raz'atr*. Lord Fairskin, who stood to his left, patted him on his shoulder. Eion shook him off and pressed on into the Waning Waste, feeling the ground rumble as the Resistance followed him.

Shortly after all the Resistance had left the cave, Gwen caught up to Eion and grabbed him on the arm. He turned to face her, startled.

"Something must be done about the other mortals, Eion," Gwen said softly. Eion was surprised, for Gwen did not sound her usual self, or even the self he had expected after their last episode. Eion appraised her quickly, his clever eyes seeing subtleties that disturbed him greatly. She was different in ways Eion found hard to accept. Gone was the mortal girl that had the impudence of accusing him of madness. In her stead was someone who now moved and spoke deliberately. She seemed wiser and, perhaps the most shocking revelation of all, tired. Her eyes were sunken a small bit and she was not smiling as she usually did. Even her cat, still wrapped around her shoulders Eion realized that he was staring, therefore he sputtered out a reply.

"W-What do you mean?"

Gwen shrugged, repositioning her cat and making him yowl tiredly. "They seemed to think their positions as ones of regality and they think themselves not meant to fight."

Eion gasped, knowing the enormity of the situation; tf the Prophesied fell apart, then the quest was lost.

Regaining his calm, he nodded in understanding. "So, what do you say we do about it?"

It was Gwen's turn to stutter. "M-Me? What does it matter what I think?"

Eion laughed. "You are more their friend than I am. I think it is better that you deal with this yourself."

"But I don't know *how* to deal with these kinds of problems."

"That is only true if *you think* it is. But do not worry; I believe matters like these tend to resolve themselves. The forest has a strange way of changing someone's mind about things."

He silently mused how true the statement was. The folk who lived in the forest were indeed outlandish and strange. There were monsters stalking through the trees as well, and Eion and heard very few tales of people who crossed them and lived. There were tribes of cyclopsi and cities of gnomes; there were giants and enchanted folk as well. And all of them *always* seemed to be in some kind of feud or fight with one another.

As Eion focused again, he realized that they were very close indeed to the forest, the monstrous trees looming not more than fifty feet away from them. Eion halted, as did the other leaders and eventually the company before them. He looked to Gwen, and with a wink, he whispered, "Follow me."

She nodded, though her eyes showed confusion. Eion took a step forward and motioned the other leaders and captains to follow. They nodded and set out a couple paces behind him.

Ahead, the forest loomed. The trunks were gnarled and black and were very close to one another, with branches that twisted and looped around themselves many times before ending in smaller branches with hand-sized, emerald green leaves. A breeze wafted towards them, carrying the smell of moss and fermenting grass. There was no sound as Eion came to stand at the base of the first tree of the forest of Ÿalnz Dàr.

Eion gulped loudly, then cupped his hands around his mouth and made a strange call that echoed throughout the trees until, once again, everything was still. Eion frowned; surely they would've heard his call. He again called into the forest, louder this time. It too echoed through the forest. Birds took flight from the leafy boughs in the trees, cawing as they flapped. Again, all was still, when suddenly, a willowy woman stepped from the shadows, taking slow, long, graceful steps. She was not quite as tall as Eion, but her eyes had the same gleam. She had long, flowing, black hair that came to her waist. She was dressed in a pearly white gown with long sleeves. Her skin was very white, paler than a full moon. She came to stand only a couple of inches away from Eion, who opened his arms to embrace her. They held each other for a few moments, then stopped and broke apart from each other.

"Flora, my dear," Eion said, "It has been much too long."

The woman laughed, a light and pleasant magnetic sound.

"It has," she said in a voice that rang long and sweet, as if someone strummed a harp to make her talk. "You are always too busy, off playing boy heroes. Really, Eion, it is very inconsiderate."

Eion laughed, and Flora turned her attention to the shifter captains. Her eyes came to rest on Beast.

"Beast, my old friend," Flora said pleasantly, "How are you?"

Beast grunted. Flora smiled even wider and said, "You have not changed. All well and good; Fauna has not either."

Beast now growled. "I see she is not here."

Flora laughed again. "She will be along. She was off talking to Nimé when Eion called."

Lord Fairskin now came forward. Flora bowed her head respectfully when she saw him and said, "My lord."

Lord Fairskin chuckled kindly. "Now Flora, you and I both know that I am indeed not your lord."

Flora now looked into the eyes of the old elf. "I believe it is my choice to decide whom I dub my lord, is it not?"

The elf chuckled again. Breeog, Barthol, Tirmal, and Varez all greeted Flora with vague familiarity. Nine of The Prophesied Ten then introduced themselves, and Flora looked at them with appraising eyes. Her glare then came to rest on Gwen, and she stared for a long while without saying anything. Finally she leaned close and said, "Undoubtedly, you are the one and only Gwen Talbot?"

Gwen nodded slowly.

Flora smiled. "You have quite a good amount to live up to."

Again Gwen nodded, this time with a grim smirk. Flora's smile widened, then her eyes came back to look at Eion.

"I take it the journey was pleasant?" she asked with false ignorance.

Eion scoffed. "Come now, Flora. You mean to tell me you missed a pack of shadow wolves tromping around the forest?"

Flora opened her mouth to say something, but she was stopped short by the whizzing of an arrow that landed at Eion's feet. Eion looked down at it and laughed, for pinned to the shaft was a bit of black wolf hide.

"Now Eion, one would hope that you would know us better than that," said a voice like Flora's. Eion turned to look in the direction of the voice. Walking swiftly towards the group was another woman identical to Flora. Her dress was the color of the sky before the sun sank past the hills, a golden red with orange hues. She came to stand next to flora and grinned widely.

"Hello Fauna," greeted Eion, "I see your aim is still true."

Fauna's smile faltered for a moment. She then nodded slowly and turned to face Beast, whose snarl was now as fierce as ever. Fauna only grinned wider.

"Why Beastie, my old friend, how are you?"

Beast did not reply, instead he only looked at the arrow with the impaled wolf skin. "I see your lofty ideals have changed. You do realize that that is animal skin?"

Fauna laughed. "Oh, Beast, you know very well that *that* is shadow wolf skin. A pack of them came stampeding through the forest a couple of days ago. Our troops fell maybe a quarter of them, but then the remainder split in three directions and we lost them. The odd thing is that a satyr was lashed to three of the wolves, as though they had taken him prisoner."

Eion chuckled darkly. "I will explain everything in full, later, when we have food and mead in our bellies."

Flora and Fauna laughed in unison. "Yes, yes, all in good time," said Fauna. "But first I would meet the Great Prophesied."

Beast muttered something about Fauna not being fit to lick their boots, but it seemed only Eion heard him. He knew that both Beast and Fauna were captains that led shifters who surpassed all in animal transformations, and they were prone to argue as both had different views on many things.

The twin sisters Fauna and Flora had long ago been placed in the forest with a legion of two hundred shifters each. Flora's troop excelled in the manipulation of plants; they were the best healers the Resistance had after the elves. Their understanding of antidotes and poisons made them some of the most useful shifters in Eion's ranks, though he never called on them for battle…until now.

The Prophesied now introduced themselves again to Fauna, who, like her sister, seemed to be sizing them up. Also like her sister, she paused when Gwen introduced herself, though Fauna did not smile but instead glared icily.

When everybody had met, Fauna went back to stand next to her sister, looking on Eion reservedly. Now, after Eion shouted "Onward!" with his magnified voice, the Resistance set off into the fringe of trees, quiet than before; they did not wish to disturb the forest's silence.

As they marched on the faded path covered with overgrowth and stones, the trees began to grow closer together and the branches became more gnarled and tangled. Feeble rays of sunlight shined through leafless patches in the trees, but beside that there was no other light in the forest, the bright entranceway fading as they walked farther on. Soon, there were no rays of light, and they were plunged into almost complete darkness.

Elves spoke a syllable and their staffs ignited with bright, white magics. Dragons broke tree branches off and set them aflame with their fiery breaths and held them aloft for all to see. Immediately, the smell of smoke replaced the damp smell of fungus that had wafted through the trees moments ago.

Eion marched with Gwen and Beast on one side and Flora and Fauna on the other. He spoke to his two, female captains, asking them how things went so close to Saurindon.

"The Red Sovereign knows we are here," reported Flora. Even in the gloom of the forest, Eion could see that her face was severe. "He has often tried to purge the forest of our presence. Fortunately, Nimé has enlisted the dryads to help us and they warn us long before any of the Ozra can get to us,"

Eion raised an eyebrow. Nimé, the forest's nymph, was a peaceful being and the fact that she had given the Resistance the help of the dryads proved how desperate their plight was.

"Sadly," said Fauna, continuing where her sister had left off, "a horde of trolls have been positioned on the other side of the forest and they often cut and burn the trees. We lose dryads by the hundreds each day."

Eion gasped and turned to Flora. She said not a word, but her fists were clenched so tightly her knuckles were turning white. Eion knew that she saw any undue harm to a plant of any kind was wickedness that could be given no forgiveness.

"Other than that, all is well. The people of the forest are living life as they always have. Frün, the chief of the cyclopsi, has moved his tribe to the westward edge and the gnomes are becoming restless, but other than that there is peace in Ÿalnz Dàr."

"And what of your troops?" pressed Eion.

Flora answered, seemingly recovered. "We have made camp in the Five Clearings. We shall arrive before nightfall."

Eion sighed. The Five Clearings were situated perhaps one week away from the Ozra Gap and three days from the Caves of Illothin near the slopes of the Mourning Mountains. If Vundin was correct, Gorothar's Shield would soon be recovered.

He left his thoughts behind when Fauna laughed as a doe crossed their path to graze on some moss. Beast shifted a bow and pulled back the string without nocking an arrow. He released it with a *twang*. The doe started and quickly pranced back into the trees.

Fauna now turned to look at Beast. "Oh Beastie, why did you not just kill it? Surely, because it crossed our path we should—"

"Silence," hissed Beast, "I have never struck a woman in my entire life, but if you say one more word to me, I will most certainly forget my manners."

Flora groaned tiredly, but her sister only laughed. She stepped over to stand in front of Beast, walking backwards and facing him. Eion looked at her edgily, waiting for her to make a move. Quicker than thought, her hand made a sign and a sword with rubies set in the pommel materialized into her hand. Before Beast could react, she had already brought the tip of her sword up to his throat. She grinned.

Beast growled in response. "I expect that was supposed to impress me?"

Fauna laughed quietly. "No, Beast. That was supposed to humble you." She concentrated on the sword and it shifted away to nothing.

Eion cleared his throat. "That is enough you two. We are quickly approaching the end of our journey; we must be ready to war with our enemies, not with each other."

"But of course." Fauna walked back to march alongside her sister, who was still shaking her head in disapproval. Beast growled quietly, but said no more.

Eion looked at Gwen, whose eyes, distant and unblinking, were glued to the path ahead. Eion sympathized; he had once felt the same way. He looked on how he had cursed every single one of the stars for choosing his fate. He had secretly wondered if it was his destiny's fault that had brought his family's death, for Iltari were ordained to be plagued with misfortune, shaping their minds and thoughts. *It is a lonely life*, he mused to himself. He was now pleased, however, that he could finally relate to someone else: Gwen. No more would he have an equal in only the enemy.

The enemy! How close they were now. Once the labyrinth of Ÿalnz Dàr was overcome, the true purpose of their journey would be at hand. Eion had been plagued with the same dream for many nights, waking in a cold sweat whenever the fiery hand reached for him. He knew all too well what it had symbolized, and he feared it to be a prophecy rather than a nightmare.

His thoughts occupied him for the remainder of the march. Then, when long hours of silent trekking had passed, the light became painfully strong once more, and it for a moment blinded Eion. When his eyes adjusted, he looked to find a wide expanse of trampled grass and wildflowers, laden with many tents and people in green tunics and leggings. The old shifter smiled; they had come to the first of the first of the Five Clearings.

The people in the green tunics stopped and looked to the newcomers, smiling upon seeing Eion and called for one another and rushed to where their leader stood. Eion spent the next many minutes hugging and shaking hands and greeting many shifters whom he'd not seen in years. There were many pats on the back and clasps on the shoulder, and Eion then gestured at his captains. Flame, Armor, Steel, Fletch, and Beast all spent a long time greeting familiar faces as well; there was much tearing and cries of joy. Lord Fairskin, Breeog, Barthol, Varez, and Tirmal also said their hellos and embraced many shifters, though not as many as Eion and company. The Prophesied stood to one side of the reunion, unsure what to do it amid the merriment.

When all had been greeted and reunited, Fauna asked the forest shifters to please return to what they were doing. They all bowed in unison and left, scrambling back to their duties.

Eion gazed at the city of tents for a few moments before turning back to Flora and Fauna and saying, "You have been busy."

Fauna nodded. "We owe much to Nimé; she has kept many of the forest's... less pleasant creatures away from our camps."

Eion nodded and looked to the sky. The sun was setting against the distant peaks of the Mourning Mountains, setting the sky ablaze with a frenzy of colors, and the first stars were beginning to twinkle.

It was strange, he thought; the forest had always unnerved him, but now it soothed him, relaxed, made him feel welcome and safe. There were few places like that in his world.

Flora clapped her hands twice, bringing Eion's attention back to the camp. At the sounds of the claps, the forest shifters cheered and shifted the tents into tables. In another moment, they had shifted bowls of fruits, and vegetables, breads, every food imaginable except meat. Fauna and Flora and their brigades refused to eat meat unless absolutely necessary. Eion sighed and welcomed the prospect of eating something other than the animals found on their trail.

He walked to a table with Flora, Fauna, The Prophesied, Lord Fairskin, Breeog, King Barthol, Varez, Tirmal, and Breeog's new second-in-command, Brunariun. The great host of soldiers slowly filed out of the forest and took their seats at the various tables. It took quite a while before they had all left the trees, but when they did there was much toast making and speech giving. Wine had been shifted into the glasses, along with meads and rums. They feasted for many hours, and it was long after the sun sank and the moon rose before any left the tables. There was much story telling and recitations of legends. There was music played as elves pulled out their harps, dwarves prepared their drums, and shifter strung their lutes. Their melodies echoed through the Five Clearings movingly.

Long after the large company had gone to set up camps in the other clearings and indeed long after all had gone to sleep, Eion was sitting on one of the branches of the tallest trees surrounding the Five Clearings, too anxious to go to sleep. He had made up his mind, and he and several others would set out for the Caves of Illothin. Certain members of the Prophesied would definitely be included, he thought, as would Tirmal and Varez and perhaps even Brunariun.

His thoughts wandered for a short time when he was suddenly interrupted. Gwen, cloaked and hooded, was climbing up the tree. Eion waited until she had sat down on the branch next to him before he said anything. When she was finally situated, he said, "An enchanting night, do you not agree?"

Gwen nodded and looked up to the skies. Eion followed her gaze and saw that the stars were shining very brightly. Before he could truly soak in their wonder though, Gwen spoke to him.

"What does Vundin's prophecy mean?"

Eion restated the prophecy and explained that they were obviously intended to find the three items.

"They belonged to Odin the Valiant," Eion continued, "an elf from the House of Fairskin, making him one of Lord Fairskin's earliest ancestors. Many ages ago, before the dragons had chosen a king, Odin sought the beasts out and attempted to tame them. In those days, the elves had just as much troubles with the dragons as the dwarves did. The lords of the elf clans decided that teaching the dragons to speak was the only way to avoid any more hostilities. They sent Odin off with only three items.

"The first was the Shield of Gorothar. Long ago, the United Wizarding Order, a society of spell casters who acted in unison, set out to overtake the small of country of Baelin. Baelin's enchanters quickly began to fortify the capital with all kinds of magical fortifications. They even went so far as to present the King of Baelin, Gorothar, with a sword that would make the wielder insubstantial—and thus prevent him from being captured. It wasn't a very good idea and also a magical shield that would deflect all magic. The sword was long ago lost and the shield, up until now, was thought to be destroyed after Odin passed on.

"The second item was the Flute of the Tamers. The Tamers were a small band of gypsy gnomes who were constantly trekking about in the deep wilds of the world. Their travels eventually led them to Mount Strontian, a goblin fortress. The goblins quickly captured them and brought them before their ruler. The Grand Goblin Velnost sentenced the gypsies to death, and they were taken by a band of goblin warriors to the Pelivor Crags, a breeding ground of the dragons. They bound the gnomes in chains and then, out of jest, left them only a plain, brass flute to ward off danger. One of the gnomes escaped from the binding chains, but refused to leave his imprisoned, and quite probably doomed, companions. He walked to the flute and examined it. He played a few notes and waited to see if anything would happen. Nothing did. Then a horrible, ferocious roar pierced the night. An angry growl answered it, then another, and another. Soon, out of the black of night, five vicious dragons swooped from the skies and landed only several yards away from the imprisoned gypsies.

As the dragons cocked their heads at the gnomes and growled to themselves, the free gnome began to mutter spells under his breath. His thinking was too muddled to think of any precise spell, so instead he uttered many until, unintentionally, the spells wound themselves together and melded into one. Suddenly, the flute began to burn in his hands until he had to drop it. Puzzled, he picked the flute up cautiously only to find that it was cool once more. He then remembered what he had heard about how music could soothe the savage beast. He realized it was a ridiculous notion, but the dragons were quickly beginning to cease their wondering.

The gnome brought the flute up and played the first tune that came to his mind. Instantly, the dragons ceased their growling and listened. Soon one collapsed to the ground. Another fell on top of the first, then a third, then a fourth, and eventually the fifth. Stunned, the free gnome stopped playing and walked slowly over to the mound of dragons. He found that they were all asleep; asleep in the deepest sleep he had ever seen. Later, after he had freed his fellows by using one of the dragon's claws to pick the locks, the gnomes From then on, the band was known as the Tamers, and they and their flute were renowned throughout the entire world and were often called to help with any dragon problems that arose.

"The third item was the Fourth Blade of the Nameless Master." He looked to Gwen, expecting Gwen to recognize the name. She returned his look with blank attention. Eion sighed, organizing the details of the legend in his mind before reciting it.

"Long before man recorded his history and even long before the elf clans were united, there was a master of forging who had no name. His swords were flawless, perfect, and unsurpassable. Whether or not he used magic in his forging, I cannot say, for his secrets disappeared along with him. All the kings and lords of the world begged him to serve them, but he refused to swear fealty to any one man.

"War broke upon the land as war often does. By now, the master was so well known that warriors who would have him make their weapons constantly assaulted him. Finally, the master proclaimed to all the kings and lords that he would make five swords more, and they would be the best weapons the world had ever seen. He told them each sword would take a year to forge and that if they wanted these blades they would not pester or anoy him until the end of the fifth year. The kings and lords swore they would not so much as mention the master and his blades.

"True to their words, the kings and lords left the master alone and discouraged anyone from seeking him. True to his word, the master made the swords, and placed upon each of them magical properties. The First Blade could control the elements and when it was wielded it would wreath itself in flames and brought the winds to its aid. The Second Blade could shatter any sword save its four brothers. It was said to have a will of its own. The Third Blade was made to reflect all magic and allowed the wielder to be impervious to curses and hexes. The Fourth Blade's powers were unknown, though it was said that it alone could choose its wielder. The Fifth Blade was the greatest of them all. It had powers of resurrection and would allow the wielder to defeat an entire army alone.

"When the five years had passed, the kings and lords set out to receive the swords from the master, only to find that he had disappeared, along with his swords. They found only a stone tablet saying that the swords *could* be found. Outraged, the kings and lords sent their best warriors to find the swords. The warriors never returned.

"The Five Swords of the Nameless Master became legends and were forgotten as time moved on. But, as fate would have it, three centuries after the Nameless Master disappeared, the Second Blade was found. It was claimed by the Elf Lord Valin, and he named it *Wergwuin*. The old enthusiasm returned, and more quests were made to find the swords. Shortly afterward, the First Blade was found in a stone. Many great nobles tried to pull it from the stone, but only a young boy prevailed. He went on to be king, with the First Blade, *Ororset*, at his side. Soon after the Third Blade was found by Valin's cousin, King Raoen. He dubbed it *Raz'atr*.

"The Fourth blade was discovered by a small group of woodland folk in what is now the Dead Woods. They guarded the blade jealously, and they eventually hid it from the rest of the world. The Fifth Blade was the most sought after of all the swords. It was discovered by a young soldier who went on to be king of his small country once he had obtained the sword. War came, and the sword was taken. It rested in the country of Cassori for a while, but was stolen and given to the King of Hware. For centuries it was fought over, gaining new masters quicker than thought. It never stayed in the same place for more than ten years, and eventually it was lost during a battle on the Silver Ice Sea.

"With these items, Odin spent five long years with the dragons. During that time, he educated the dragons and found that they were quite intelligent to begin with. Eventually they learned to speak, and became friendly with the elven race. What happened to Odin is not known; he, the Shield, the Flute, and the Blade all disappeared."

Gwen raised an eyebrow after Eion's narrative was over and said, "And how is it that you came by the Third Blade?"

Eion grinned. "Do you not know?"

Gwen smiled slightly, thinking back on her council with the gods, and nodded. "What happened to the other blades?"

"The Fourth and Fifth remain lost. I hold the Third. The First was locked away in the Mountain of Antiquity when the young king died."

"And what of the Second?"

Eion sighed, seeming deeply troubled. "I was afraid we would get there"

"During Ozmodion's uprising, the Five Blades were sought by the Ozra, and there were many raids on many castles and keeps to find them. I was at one such battle in Zanu. Lord Valin was the leader of the Yuln Clan in those days, and Ozmodion himself had accompanied the Ozra, using Vaeirnïr as a flying mount. He leaped into the fray, and hacked his way through the Elven guards and confronted Valin himself. I was busy fighting off a small group of goblins, but I was aware of the sounds of their titanic battle. Finally, Ozmodion slew Valin and claimed the Elf Lord's sword. He then disappeared from the battle in a burst of flames. Since then, the sword has been renamed *Uthu'rach,* and has become one of Ozmodion's deadliest weapons."

He paused for a moment to catch his breath, but Gwen took it as a stop and asked another question.

"Eion, I've read about the elven clans. Why is it that they are not uniting against Ozmodion?"

Eion inhaled deeply, organizing his thoughts; the explanation would be complex, no matter how he tried to simplify it.

"You say you have read of the elven clans? I wonder, did you read the story of Lord Breenen?"

Gwen nodded slowly.

"So you know then the strength of the consolidated power of the Elf Chiefs. Eleven elves are enough to lay low an entire army. An army of them is strong enough to create a Reflection, like the one we find ourselves in now. Now, they are only capable of these feats if they are unchecked, that is, if they are not distracted by battle. The Vra is large enough to help the Resistance, but small enough to keep their power under control in war.

Long before Ozmodion's rise, the elf clans would, in times of war, unite. Absolute destruction and desecration laid the surrounding area to waste, for the combined strength of the elven clans was too much to suppress. Though the elves have had thousands of years to learn to restrain their power, they greatly fear the ruin they wreaked last time, and therefore they will only come together under the direst need. Ozmodion is only newly returned to power, thus the elves won't risk an amalgamation until they are sure that he's not lost any of his potency."

Gwen looked perplexed. "Why would they think that he wouldn't?"

"The spell that Ozmodion cast when I brought him down still mystifies some of the most powerful magic users in the world. Ozmodion locked his soul into some sort of limbo, some sort of holding place where it would be safe. This branch of magic was and is considered extremely dangerous, consequently it has never been fully explored. Ozmodion could, in theory, have lost many of his powers as a result from his resurrection."

Gwen smiled wryly. "But you think that's a bunch of bull, don't you?"

Eion sighed and nodded slowly. "Ozmodion is way too clever to cast a spell he knows nothing about. He would have learned everything about it before he would even consider using it. No, I think Ozmodion is just as strong as he ever was…maybe even stronger."

A chilling breeze wafted through the forest. Gwen shivered. Eion smiled, concentrating intently. A navy blue shawl weaved itself around

Gwen's shoulders. She returned his smile and whispered her thanks. Eion nodded and turned his eyes to the stars.

The heavens were dazzlingly bright that evening. The new moon was wreathed in shadow, allowing the stars to light up the night air until it was more of a blue rather than black. A shooting star shot across the sky, illuminating the night even more. Eion breathed deeply, and softly sang:

Traveling a road
A long winding road
Unsure of where to go

Marks of the journey
The ever-tiring journey
Let my weariness show

Surely there is a haven
A good and peaceful haven
Where I can let my wanderings slow

But until I find it
Whereever I might find it
I journey the winding road

When he had finished, he turned to look at Gwen, but discovered that she had already climbed down from the tree. Eion blinked, then sat against the trunk and closed his eyes, letting his mind drift.

☐

Gwen walked quickly back to her tent, pulling the shawl tightly around her. The temperature was quickly plunging and the wind picking up speed. She quietly made her way through the camp set up in the first of the Five Clearings. All of the Resistance was now fast asleep, snoring loudly and occasionally belching. Gwen smiled dryly. She would not envy them in the morning; every barrel of ale had been drained. As she crept towards her tent, she saw that the tankards were strewn around the camp, left where their owners had dropped them.

She arrived at her tent. Upon climbing inside, she found Curthlond sitting on her pillow, his tail lashing side to side agitatedly. His slit eyes narrowed when she entered.

"A little late for a stroll, is it not?" he asked casually, but his eyes revealed his anger.

Gwen found the reprimand, coming from a cat, too much to bear. She hid a smile and scolded gently, "Don't be a parent, Curthlond." She looked away. "It's unattractive."

He hissed. "Unbecoming or not, I would appreciate if you would tell me when you decide to take off into the night. People were running around in their drunken glee, screaming, singing, and goodness knows what else. It's a small wonder I was concerned. I didn't know if you had gotten lost, or if you had got drunk and hurt yourself, or if—"

"I'm touched, Curthlond," interrupted Gwen, meaning it, "and I'm glad to know you. But I can look after myself now."

It was Curthlond's turn to chuckle. "You think because you can magically conjure some fire that you are completely capable of surviving in a world you know next to nothing about?"

Gwen smiled, and whispered, "*Brons aeolth*". Immediately, Curthlond froze, motionlessly suspended between a passive look and a gawk.

"Well, I'm not sure if I would word it *exactly* like that," Gwen said cleverly, "but I believe myself able, yes."

The spell wore off, and Curthlond, trying to retain some dignity, cleaned himself as though nothing had happened.

"I see you been reading the book," he said between licking his paw.

"Skimmed through it, yeah."

"Well, it takes more than a few simple charms like that to endure in Ÿalnz Dàr and Saurindon for that matter, and I hope very much that the knowledge of being an Iltari hasn't clouded your judgment."

He walked away from her pillow to the top right corner of the tent. There, he curled himself into a ball and loudly purred.

Gwen stared at him, giggled once more, then climbed between the sheets and drifted into a much-needed sleep.

Chapter 25

The Quest

*T**he dawn came quickly*, and the sun rose earlier than usual, peeking over the trees in a cheeky manner as though it had meant to stir the soldiers from their sleep. Its golden rays quickly melted the frost that had come the previous night. As it rose higher, the armies slowly crawled out of their tents with much moaning, groaning, yawning, and belching. Gwen was right; the after effects of the ale and mead were indeed taking their toll.

Eion climbed out of his tent and stretched his arms. He yawned, blinked his eyes, and studied the morning. The sunrise had brought a beautiful array of colors that danced in the skies and clouds. He smiled inwardly; it was a good omen to start an expedition on such a day break.

Rubbing his eyes once, he made his way to the center of the first clearing, where no tents had been erected. There, a fire pit, ten feet in diameter, crackled with cheery flames. Around the fire dwelt those who would be accompanying Eion to the Caves of Illothin. Brunariun was here, and Valdez too. Tirmal leaned casually on his staff as he nodded his head at Eion in greeting. Gwen, cloaked, stood ready, with her cat, Buttons, beside her. Ryan was also present, garbed in black robes. Four more of The Prophesied Ten were there, in addition: Lea, Anthony, Caitlyn, and Tyler. Fauna was among the throng as well, suited in a tunic with leggings. A baldric was slung over her shoulder, with a silver sword hilt protruding from the sheath. Flora would not be going; she would have to manage the forest shifters on her own. Beast, Steel, and Flame were also there.

Eion sighed with relief; more had come then he had been hoping for. He would not force anyone to accompany him on such a dangerous mission and it touched him that so many had come without needing too.

Lord Fairskin, King Barthol, Armor, Fletch, and Breeog were also in attendance, though they did not appear as though they would be accompanying them. Eion knew that they would have to stay behind to direct the Resistance in his absence, so he had no bitter feelings directed towards them.

Lord Fairskin smiled warmly, extending his hand to shake Eion's. Eion clasped it graciously, and then he winked at the old elf. He shook King Barthol's hand next, and then received a rib-splintering hug from Breeog. Eion shifted away any bruises he had received, and then said his goodbyes and farewells to the dragon king.

He then clasped hands and embraced the three captains who would stay behind: Fletch, Armor, and Flora.

"Look after yourselves," Fletch said, smiling.

"And you, my old friend," Eion said, returning the grin.

"Be wary, Eion," Flora advised gravely, "Ÿalnz Dàr has grown darker; many untold dangers separate you from the Caves of Illothin."

Not letting his apprehension show on his face, Eion nodded and turned on his heel, beckoning the rest of the hunting party to follow.

They made their way through the first clearing, with much hand shaking and shoulder clasping and cheering. The Resistance parted the way for the hunting party, lined on other side and calling their goodbyes. The second clearing held even more soldiers waiting to send them off with their good wishes. Eion led the group in such a way they skirted the other three of the Five Clearings, disappearing into the dark, ominous trees of the forest.

At first, they followed a faint trail, with Curthlond always trotting a couple of feet in front of the hunting party, his tail lashing back and forth madly. But eventually, the trail disappeared and they had to maneuver through the trees and bushes that littered the way. Eion, Fauna, Beast, Steel, and Flame shifted their eyes, allowing their selves to penetrate the shadow. Brunariun, being a dragon, had no difficulties with the blackness. Curthlond hadn't such inhibitions either. Gwen had to stop herself from casting a spell to light the way. Luckily, Tirmal ignited his staff before she made such a mistake.

They traveled for hours in a taciturn quiet; the veil of silence over the woods did not like to be disturbed. They did not see much, as though the forest was completely desolate. After a while, nighttime crept upon them, plunging them in to a darkness blacker than pitch. Eion consulted with everyone, and eventually they decided to make camp roughly two hours after nightfall. They attempted to light a fire, but it brought all manners of wildlife to them. Large, baleful, yellow eyes stared at them from the branches and bases of the trees. Long after they had doused the flames, they heard chatters, squawks, squeaks, howls, and roars of strange, faceless creatures and beasts. No one got very much sleep that night, and whatever sleep they did get was filled with disturbing dreams.

The next sunrise brought another frost, leaving the travelers to wake up to damp sleeping cloths and packs. They quickly lit a fire and prepared a meager breakfast that still left them empty after it had been eaten.

They broke camp in silence, a lack of rest making them irritable. They buried the ashes of the fire under a foot of earth, not wanting to leave a scent or trail.

The trees were still bunched together after hours of walking and Ÿalnz Dàr still seemed as it had been the previous night. There were now chatters in the darkness, much like there had been what seemed only a few hours ago. The party's eyes darted back and forth quickly, trying to find the noises' owners. Their attempts amounted to nothing.

As the day grew older, the trees grew bigger and farther apart, though the branches were still so immense that only a very faint light made it to the forest floor. The party breathed easier in the open space. They now saw some of the inhabitants of the forest. Flame recognized a hippogriff that he had known years ago, and Tirmal asked directions from a small gaggle of gnomes.

While they continued to walk through the forest, Gwen could hardly keep Curthlond from speaking. He persistently whispered to Gwen about the forest and the creatures they happened upon, a nostalgic gleam filling his eye. Gwen finally tried a new silencing spell she had read in her spell book. It must've worked, for ire now showed plainly on the cat's face. He snarled as though he was trying to hiss, but no sound was heard.

Later in the day, they came to a small clearing. The trees were still so large, only one small beam of light made it through the leafy boughs, falling on a lone boulder in the center of the meadow. On it, sat a creature that at first Gwen thought was a satyr, but she noticed it had the legs of a stag rather than the legs of a goat. The horns above its temples were also less prominent. Other than that, he had a toned body, long black hair tied in the back, and he was playing a haunting tune on a pan flute.

Eion approached the pan flutist quietly, but Gwen grabbed his arm before he could get close.

"Eion, what is that?" she whispered urgently.

He smiled warmly. "It is only a faun; half man, half stag. They are not evil, but they love riddles and are usually tricky. No worries, I am just going to make sure all is good and canny; Ozmodion has many eyes, even in this forest."

Gwen nodded and loosened her grip on his arm. Eion winked assuredly and resumed his approach toward the faun. As he did, the faun opened his radiant blue eyes and locked them on Eion's. Eion extended his hand in friendship, but the faun shrugged, closed his eyes, and continued his tune. Eion did not lower his hand; he knew that that would be a great insult to the faun.

After a while, the faun finished his song and set the flute next to him. He turned to face Eion and smiled in a mischievous way.

"Greetings," the faun said genuinely, "Who might you be?"

"I am Eion Shifter," Eion said bowing. When the faun said nothing, Eion continued. "I am the Master of Swords and the Keeper of Elements. I am Raja'gh Om Shifters, Iltari, and—"

"Eion's enough," the faun said, raising his hand to quiet him. His smile didn't leave his face.

"Ahem. And who might you be?" Eion inquired, taken aback at being cut off by a perfect stranger. Only now did he lower his extended hand, his pride a little bruised.

"Ah, I have many names," The faun chuckled, "but they don't matter much here. However"—he paused dramatically for effect. There was none.—"you may call me Rembas."

"Well met, Master Rembas," Steel said, approaching the boulder, his sword drawn in a saluting manner. "I am Captain Steel of the Shifters of the Resistance."

Rembas laughed so hard at this that he fell off his boulder and it was a long while before he could pull himself together. Steel's expression betrayed his anger, but Eion gave him a hard look, signaling him to let it go. When the faun had recovered and wiped the tears from his eyes, he climbed back onto the stone.

"Well met, Captain," he said with only the slightest trace of a snicker.

Flame introduced himself, and then Beast and Fauna simultaneously, followed by Tirmal and Varez, and then Gwen and the rest of The Prophesied Ten who had come. Rembas was wry and clever with all of them, until he laid eyes on Brunariun for the first time. The appearance of a dragon startled him, and even a faun, Eion mused silently to himself, would think twice about mocking a full-grown dragon. When all had introduced themselves, the faun pulled a pipe out of a satchel he had set behind the rock. Apparently it was already full, because he lit it without pulling out any tobacco.

"What brings you to these sleepy woods?" Rembas asked after a few puffs. "They hardly make for a nice weekend get away." He then eyed their weapons. "But I doubt that's what you had planned anyway."

Eion smiled dangerously. "Why the curiosity?"

Rembas's eyes again locked on Eion. "No fears, Mr. Shifter. I know all about your crusade. You haven't been keeping a low profile, and word has gotten around. I would be more careful if I were you; such indiscretion might get you in trouble one of these days."

Eion slowly unsheathed *Raz'atr*, but before he could fully pull the sword out, Rembas laughed again.

"Peace, Eion! Peace," he managed between gales of laughter. "I have no loyalty to Ozmodion or his Ozra. In fact, I would be happy to help you. Give me an adventure, and I'll get you to where you need to go."

Eion considered this for a moment, then nodded and took his hand off *Raz'atr*'s hilt.

"Much better," Rembas sighed, his obvious relief betraying him. "Now, where are you journeying to?" The faun smiled again.

"We make for the Caves of Illothin"

Rembas's smile faded. "Come again? I am sure I heard wrong?"

Eion shook his head and repeated himself. Rembas stared at the shifter with wide-eyed disbelief. He took out his pipe and set it aside, and then, his wickedly knowing smile returned.

"May I inquire as to the purpose of this little holiday to the caves?" he said in a would-be casual voice, though something in his tone suggested suspicion.

"We seek the Shield of—"

"I thought as much," Rembas said flatly. "Listen, Shifter, many come to this forest for quests and adventures. Unimaginative as they are, they usually go for the caves and the fabled Shield of Gorothar. But the caves have, along with most of this forest, grown darker since Ozmodion's rising. Spectral beasts haunt them, they say, and all who set foot in those caverns never again set foot outside. I'm sorry, Shifter, but it is a fool's errand. What's more, the shield is probably not even there."

"We act at the word of Vundin. We know it is there," Beast said darkly.

"Vundin, eh?" Rembas said, raising his eyebrows. "My, we do come prepared, don't we?"

Eion cleared his throat. "Do we have a deal then, Master Rembas?"

Rembas did not answer right away. He collected his pipe and set it back into his satchel. The faun then stepped down from his boulder, throwing the bag over his shoulder. He turned to face the hunting party, his eyes hard and resolved.

"As long as I never again hear "master" before my name," he said, smiling, "then yes, we do."

Eion smiled too and held out his hand to shake Rembas's. Rembas chuckled, and grasped it.

"To the caves?" Eion asked.

"To the caves," Rembas sighed, nodding.

☐

While following Rembas, they learned they were off course by several miles. The faun led them through more strange parts of the forest. First they passed several pools that changed colors every few moments, followed by a colony of pixies, and then a unicorn den.

As they traveled through the forest, Gwen and Curthlond marched beside Rembas, several paces in front of the rest of the party. At first, they marched silently, but then:

"It was Gwen, wasn't it?" Rembas asked, leaning down to look Gwen in the eyes.

Gwen nodded.

"Gwen *Talbot*?" Rembas pressed.

Gwen looked up sharply, and Curthlond meowed questionably at her feet.

"Secrets don't stay secrets long in the Magic Realm," the faun answered indifferently. "Hm, judging by your demeanor, I'd say you only found out very recently.

"You are perceptive, aren't you Rembas?"

"Please, my friends call me Rem."

Curthlond meowed again, this time with a hint of warning.

Rembas looked down to the cat. He blinked, and then grinned knowingly.

"Cute cat. What do you call him?"

"Er…Buttons."

Rembas laughed loudly once more.

"Buttons, eh? You're quite sure it's not…*Curthlond*?"

Gwen gasped, and turned to look over her shoulder. The rest of the party was conversing with each other and appeared not to have heard. Gwen then whipped her head to look at Rembas, then at Curthlond who, shockingly, did not appear the least bit fazed that the faun knew who he was.

"Took you long enough, you horned buffoon"

"Horned buffoon? Is that the best you got? I haven't seen you for years, and you haven't thought of *one* new slight, have you? Don't you have *any* panache?"

"Oh excuse me! But it is a little hard to be witty when you've been transformed into a cat!"

"Jarred your brain, did it?"

"No it didn't jar my brain! It's just—"

"Temper, temper, old friend. You haven't changed at all. This is just like that time with the dwarves from Vazi Mountain—"

"We have been through this a thousand times; that was NOT MY FAULT! *You* are the one who made that wager and—"

"And who gave them 10-1 odds? Even I would not be so dense as to—"

"Nonsense, Rembas, you are dense enough to do just about anything."

"See? There you go! Bravo, Curthlond! You thought of a new one! Granted, you will repeat it several hundred times, but—"

"*Enough.*" Gwen nervously turned to look at the hunting party. They were still occupied with their conversations and the forest trail.

"Curthlond," Gwen said confusedly, "I take it you know Rembas?"

Curthlond sighed with aggravation. "Yes, before I was…ahem, altered, Rembas and I were, uh, acquaintances."

"Bah! We've known each other since our childhood," Rembas interjected. "Ever since Curthy here annoyed that elderly centaur and was almost turned into a bush. Remember him, Curthlond? Old man Romis? Ah, those were the—"

"You're rambling, Rem," Curthlond said testily.

"Rem, *please* don't tell the others," Gwen pleaded quietly. "They might stop me from learning magic."

"Why would they do that?" Rembas asked confusedly. "You're an Iltari; they certainly wouldn't deny you magic?"

"*Please*, Rembas," Gwen said again, her eyes blinking in an imploring way.

Rembas exhaled loudly, and then nodded. "It dies with me." He smiled sincerely.

☐

The day grew darker until the light was extinguished, and they made camp in a small clearing. Rembas suggested they collect wood for a fire, but Eion wouldn't have it. The faun then proposed that they would heat their food with Brunariun's flame. Brunariun was hesitant at first, but she consented in the end. When all had had their meager rations, for they were quickly running low on food, and the addition of a new comrade and put even more strictures on their meals, they climbed into their sheets and drifted into sleep.

They rested easier that night; there were less cries and noises, and the nightmares from the previous night did not disturb them.

They woke early again the next morning. This day's sunrise had brought no frost, but the air was still cold enough for them to see their breaths. The newly risen sun's rays were too weak to penetrate the boughs of the trees, and Ÿalnz Dàr was still enveloped in an extended darkness.

By midday, they had come to a clearing so large and spaced out that there were no tree branches to obscure the light. They all had to block their eyes from fear of blinding. The shifters readjusted their eyes, and Tirmal released a cloud of smoke from his staff to temporarily dim the light. When the haze passed, they surveyed the meadow.

It was full of all kinds of wildlife; from deer to squirrels to rabbits to birds. The sky above was a radiant blue, free of any clouds, turning the heaven into what seemed an upside-down ocean. They then noticed that in the center of the field was a gigantic slab of granite, and, in it, a mouth to a cavern.

They had arrived at the Caves of Illothin.

Chapter 26

The Caves

"*As requested, Shifter,*" Rembas said blandly, "the Caves of Illothin. Enjoy, take care, be wary, don't answer anything that calls to you, and remember…have fun."

Eion turned to face the faun slowly. "You are talking like you are not coming with us."

"Heavens, dear boy, of course I'm not!"

"Our agreement…" Eion reminded warningly, perturbed at being called a boy by a creature whom he was sure was several hundred years younger than him.

"…conveniently omitted any obligations pertaining to my entrance into the caves," Rembas finished cleverly. A vividly blue butterfly floated passed his face. He waved it away, smiling his wry smile. "Sorry, but I will not be accompanying you into those black caverns. Please don't bother with souvenirs, either; I can assure you I do not need any. Give a call if you need help, and I will see what I can do. Goodbye! Believe me when I say I hope to see you soon, and preferably whole."

Eion breathed in very slowly, letting the frustration on his face melt away into a grin. "Certainly, Rembas, we dare not overstep the parameters of our agreement. Feel free to wait out here for us." He took several steps towards the caves, halted, and then muttered under his breath, "Although I hope the. .no, of course not, they would probably just kill you."

"Pardon?" Rembas called.

Eion turned to face the party once more. "Oh, it is nothing, I was just wondering what would happen if the Ozra set spies to follow us, and if they might come to call."

The faun paled. "Are they likely to do so?"

"You can never tell with Ozmodion's forces, can you?" Eion said, shrugging. "This forest is essentially within the borders of his domain. You never know who might be watching and listening. There *is* safety in numbers, but I admire your courage. Not everyone in the Resistance would be willing to take on a pack of Ozra trained goblins or trolls. I know that you can do it, Rem, and godspee—"

"Enough, enough," said Rembas in a resigned voice. "Very well Shifter. You might very well be bluffing, as I suspect you are, but I'm not thick enough to gamble with my life."

Gwen's cat, who was perched on her shoulder, made coughing noises that sounded strangely like laughs. Rembas glared at him icily, and then faced Eion once more. "Very well, I'll join you. But remember, I warned you about the caves' dangers."

Eion nodded in grim satisfaction, and then turned and hiked toward the gaping mouth of the cave. The rest of the party reluctantly followed.

Eion smiled slightly as he came closer to the entrance of the Caves of Illothin. He, too, had heard the wild stories about the caves and their black nature. Perhaps that was why they had been chosen to be the hiding place of the shield. Perhaps that was why so many had failed to retrieve Gorothar's ancient weapon. None of this bothered Eion though, he welcomed the challenge. Too many sleepy years had passed since he had last had a real battle for his life. The previous encounters with the Ozra that he had had since Ozmodion's return had aroused his venturous nature, though they had not really appeased it.

But the caves were a different proposition. They were not some armored foe with a sword. They were a great entity, a monstrous being that couldn't be killed.

They now were a foot away from the mouth to the cavern. Eion halted, and looked around. The party had all turned their eyes unto him. Lea, Anthony, Caitlyn, and Tyler all looked at him with faces of fear and uncertainty. Gwen's look could not be interpreted, but he sensed her restlessness. Ryan, too, seemed ill at ease. Steel, Flame, Beast, and Fauna looked upon him with eyes full of encouragement and fealty. Bruanriun's large green eyes were contemplative, as though she were sizing Eion up. Tirmal and Valdez smiled faintly, but it was clear that they were both tense. The only one that seemed at ease was Rembas. He smiled broadly at Eion in a casual manner, as though his previous apprehension of the caves was nonexistent.

"Come, come, now," he said coolly, "We mustn't waste time."

Eion narrowed his eyes, revealing his irritation, but said nothing. He looked passed the faun and onto the green meadow once more; he hadn't really taken in much of its beauty before now, and he regretted it, for it really was a place of wondrous splendor. He looked to the brilliantly blue sky, too, already missing the sun. Silently, he rued the prospect of the darkness of the caves.

The shifter sighed as he turned to face the black abyss. Shifting his eyes so they would be able to penetrate the darkness, he plunged into the gloom, the party wordlessly following behind him.

As he crossed the threshold, he felt the temperature quickly drop; the cold stone of the caves had no light to be warmed by. This passage was narrow, so narrow that Eion was unsure if Brunariun would be able to squeeze through, but somehow the dragon managed to make her the way through. The way widened further on, and soon the shifter found himself in an immense chamber.

Eion was disappointed; the caves seemed entirely ordinary. Black stalactites and stalagmites lined the floor and the roof of the cavern. Common-looking boulders were scattered messily around the cavern, and only one lone passage, besides the one they had just passed through, led out of the first chamber.

Eion frowned uncertainly for a moment. He knew very well that the caves were treacherous and mysterious, but he sensed nothing unordinary among the rocks. The Caves of Illothin were supposed to be a place steeped in magic, but something did not feel right.

His disappointment became confusion; his confusion became concern; and finally his concern became fear. It wasn't unheard of for someone or something to lose innate magic, but it was extremely rare. It had only happened several times in recorded history of the Magic Realm, and Eion knew even less of the processes one had to go through in order to drain natural magic.

As though he knew what he was thinking, Tirmal fell into step beside Eion and whispered, "You sense it, too?"

"How normal it all is? Yes…"

"Queer, eh?"

"Mm."

Eion glanced at Tirmal to find him rolling up his sleeves and preparing to wave his staff. He raised it above his head, and with a fluid sweeping motion, he spoke a an incantation.

The tip of the staff glowed with a pinkish tint, and then dulled into a red. Eion stared at the tip with puzzlement. If any magic had been present in the cave, the tip would have grown brighter until it was a blinding white, but as the spell had revealed, there was nothing extraordinary here.

"This is wrong," said the shifter as he shifted a boulder into an armchair and sat in it, "Something most definitely strange…It is as though…ugh! This doesn't make sense."

"I don't like this, Eion," said Tirmal as he tapped his staff against the floor of the cave, "I have been to these caves before, and they always been a place of wild enchantments."

Eion massaged the bridge of his nose, perplexed by the mystery.

"There's an odd scent here, too," Brunariun said slowly, her snout directed to the roof of the chamber. Eion hadn't noticed her come in, and if he hadn't been so preoccupied, he'd have asked her how she got through the narrow passageway. "I cannot place it though…"

"Animal?" Beast growled lowly.

"No…mineral…"

"You're all fussed because your pet dragon smells a strange rock?" Rembas asked skeptically.

Brunariun lowered her head and swung her neck to look at the faun, a bored tone played across her face.

"I would choose my words a little wiser if I were as small as you," she said placidly, though something in her eyes suggested her offense.

Rembas smiled slightly, a blatant display of his indifference, and then walked slowly to the cave's corner, the *clip-clopping* of his hooves echoing throughout the cavern.

"But Rembas is right, isn't he?" Anthony asked, "It's a cave; everything's mineral."

Brunariun chuckled lowly in her throat. "It is a mineral not native to these caves. The scent seems strangely familiar, but I cannot place it." She raised herself to full height once more, and resumed her sniffing.

"Hm, look here," Flame mumbled, as he sat crouched on the cave floor, examining a pile of bizarrely colored dust. "Is this what you smelled, Brunariun?"

Brunariun turned to face where Flame was stooped and stretched her neck to get a better view of the powder. She inhaled deeply, recoiled, and nodded.

"Yes, that's it," she said disgustedly, "though it is much more pungent when so close."

Flame scooped some of the dust into his hand and studied it closely. He was silent for a moment, and then his eyes bulged and he dropped the powder in surprise.

"*An Emerald of Alexander*," he whispered faintly.

"WHAT?!" Eion rushed to kneel by Flame. "Flame, are you sure?"

"Positive," the red-haired shifter said weakly, "Look at the consistency. And the grain. And let us not forget the color."

"Bloody hell..." Eion cursed quietly

"An emerald of whom?" Gwen asked softly, slowly approaching the two crouched shifters.

"An Emerald of Alexander," Tirmal moaned, as he too came to stand beside Eion and Flame. "I do not know if you are familiar with the story of Alexander the Great?"

Gwen nodded, as did almost everyone else. Only Caitlyn shook her head, flushing with embarrassment.

"I'm sorry…" she said apologetically, "I could never pay attention in world history class. I mean, come on, Zackery Phillips sat beside me, you can't really blame—"

"Ahem," Tirmal coughed, cutting Caitlyn off, "Allow me to explain. Alexander was perhaps the greatest conqueror of his time. By the age of thirty-three, he was the King of Macedonia, Champion of Greece, Pharaoh of Egypt, King of Persia, King of Caria, and King of Bactria. Much of this was due to his brilliance in command and battle, but, as the centuries passed, it has been forgotten that large amounts of the credit would be given to his spell casters.

"The Battle Mages of Athens were some of the fiercest magic warriors in history, and they helped Alexander to conquer his Ten Alexandria's. However, during their battles with Egypt, the Pharaoh's magicians sent Homunculi and Golems to oppose the Battle Mages. They, the Pharaoh's magicians, were victorious. The loss left Alexander in dire need of magical help, as his mortal forces were slowly killed by the Homunculi and Golems. He turned to his teacher, the philosopher and wizard Aristotle. He suggested Alexander seek help from the gods. Joao alone answered Alexander's pleas of help, giving to him four emeralds, which, when activated, would drain and store magic from external objects and beings. In the next battle, Alexander rode into the fray bearing the Emeralds. As Joao had said they would, the Homunculi and Golems were drained of their magic and killed.

"Alexander proceeded onto the magician's themselves and drained them too of their powers. When all of the Pharaoh's magical defenses had been siphoned by the emeralds, he surrendered and Alexander took Egypt for himself."

"Fascinating little yarn," scoffed Rembas with unsuppressed sarcasm, "but why is one of these charmed rocks lying powdered in the Caves of Illothin?"

Tirmal shrugged. "I cannot say. When Alexander died, the stones were stolen by thieves unknown. Over the centuries, only two of the emeralds have been recovered, and both of them now lie in the highest security vaults of the Mountain of Antiquity."

"Then clearly," Varez said brusquely, "another of them has been found."

"But why would they destroy it?" Steel asked, so quietly that he might've been asking himself.

"Well…" Fauna began slowly, rubbing her chin, "perhaps they drained so much magic that the stone could not hold it all."

Tirmal sighed loudly. "Anything is possible, I suppose, but I cannot be sure. I am no expert of Grecian lore, and I have only heard the stories of the Emeralds twice."

"Even if that *is* why the Emerald was destroyed," Eion said in tones of exasperation, shaking his head, "that still leaves us to question why they would drain the caves of their magic."

No one spoke for a moment, taciturn in their pondering.

"Maybe someone wanted to lower any defenses that may be surrounding the shield?" Tyler asked timidly.

More silence followed the question, though this one was of a different nature, one with an apprehensive and angered character.

"By my beard, you may be right," Varez said, stroking his mustache.

"Ozmodion?" Fauna asked fearfully.

"I doubt it," Brunariun said knowingly. "Word of Eion's council could not have reached his ears so quickly, especially since Avria was not present for Vundin's prophecy."

"And Ozmodion would prefer something more subtle, I think," Eion said. "Though this hardly makes matters better. Someone, who has, or had, access to Emeralds of Alexander, has taken the magic of the Caves of Illothin *and* quite possibly the Shield of Gorothar."

"Only one thing to do then, is there not?" Rembas stated in a chipper manner. When they all looked at him blankly, he rolled his eyes and said, "Comb the caves and look for this lost shield."

At this, there was much mumbling and grumbling. Some were objective, some were uncertain, others were angry, and others quiet. A few of them eventually agreed, though this only provoked further outbursts of anger and argument. The debate became so heated, that at one point Bruanriun began to roar and spout flame and Varez unsheathed his war axe. It was only when Eion shifted his vocal cords and shouted, "*ENOUGH!*" in a voice magnified tenfold that the confrontation subsided.

"Enough," Eion repeated hoarsely as he shifted his vocal cords once more. "That is not solving anything. We will put it to a vote then, shall we?"

There were again many mutters and murmurs, but they all generally agreed this was the best thing to do.

"Right," said Eion, clearing his throat, "All for combing the caves, as was *intended*?"

There were more whispers after this, but eventually they all raised their hands, if a little uneasily.

"Good," smiled Eion, as he lowered his own hand, "Now I suppose we should divide into groups."

There was much confusion and arguing as they tried to split up, but ultimately they came to consent to one decision. Brunariun, Tyler, Fauna, and Steel would be one group, as would Beast, Varez, Eion, Anthony, and Flame. The third group would be Gwen, Rembas, Tirmal, and Caitlyn.

As one, the three groups ventured into the one passage leading out of the first chamber. They marched together for a time, until they came to a fork in the tunnel. Eion's group took the right, and the rest went left. A few more yards and they came to another split. This time, Brunariun's group took the left passageway, and Gwen's went right.

The journey in the dark was a quiet one. Tirmal and Caitlyn did not know about Curthlond as Rembas did, and Gwen and the faun were forced into silence. Tirmal, oblivious to their introverted manner, was trying to engage Rembas in conversation.

"So what be your story, my good faun?" he asked as he held his staff aloft, directing beams of light with its ignited tip.

Rembas shrugged. "Oh, you know, the same old tale. A bit of this, a bit of that. Been here, done that."

"Ah," the elf said uncertainly, "No specifics then?"

"Specifics bore, friend. I have tried to keep my life free of specifics. Epics aplenty, but specifics scarce."

"That implies that your life has been an interesting one," Tirmal insisted, apparently desperate for some conversation. Gwen could not

337

blame him. The gloom of the cave was mind numbing and the silence only made it worse.

Amid chuckling from Curthlond, Rembas plunged into an epic in which he single handedly defeated a horde of ogres. Gwen chanced some magic and cast a spell on her eyes, allowing them to penetrate the darkness without Tirmal's staff. The elf and the faun were now in the back of the party, exchanging stories, so Gwen decided to venture a little farther ahead. She turned a corner, careful to stay within the range of the others' voices. Rembas was now educating Tirmal how wood lice could be employed to prevent sea sickness

"The trick," he explained, " is to get them out of your ear before they start nesting."

"Thick-headed moron," Curthlond mumbled lowly as he trotted beside Gwen, dodging her feet instinctively, "He has been in perhaps ten fights in his all life, only two of them were with men, and he lost both of them."

"Mm," Gwen replied distractedly. The hot air of the cave was making her dizzy, and she had to now strain to hear the party's conversations. She rounded another corner, this one turning left. A deathly silence filled the passage now, and the conversations had completely died away. The spell on Gwen's eyes was now wearing off, and she could no longer see through the black veil.

As she stepped into the darkness, her foot snagged against a loose stone. Her head met the wall of the tunnel with a soft *twoop,* and Gwen lost all consciousness.

Chapter 27

The Enslavement

G*roggily,* ***Gwen awakened****,* immediately sensing that something was wrong. Dizzy, and vision fuzzied, she felt weak, drained, tired. She wanted to drift back into unconsciousness, but found that she could not.

She was very warm, wherever she was. Despite her blurred vision, she heard the crackling of a fire nearby, which was responsible for the hazy red hue that filled the...what was she in? She couldn't tell. She knew it could not be the caves; it didn't have the enclosed feeling she had in the caverns. It must've been a room.

She tried to roll over, but was pricked by several straws of dried hay. She noticed that she was overly exposed; her arms and legs were bare and she had no boots on. Puzzled, she tried to rub her wrists which felt uncomfortably pinched. She gasped in fright when she discovered they were clasped in iron manacles. Blindly, her hands followed chains that led from the shackles to a stony wall that was icily cold despite the fire.

Gwen tried to recall a spell to break the chains, but found she couldn't bring any magic to mind. Disturbed, she tried to find the magic inside her, but to her dismay discovered that the haze around her mind quelled that magic as well.

Unsteadily, she tried to stand. It took her several attempts, but eventually she managed it. Her feet felt strangely heavy, and when she reached down to find the source of the weight, she realized her ankles had been clasped in iron as well.

Gwen abruptly sat back in the hay and began to cry. She did not cry because of her imprisonment, but because of her inability to grasp what was happening. Tears flowed from her eyes for many hours, when she unexpectedly heard a door opening on creaking hinges.

"Now, now, none of that," said a chipper voice. Startlingly, Gwen felt the tears subside as soon as the voice's instruction ended.

"Much better, much better," said the voice again. "Jolly good, jolly good. Too much more of that, and you would have surely doused the fire." The voice laughed heartily at its joke.

Gwen heard the scuttling of feet. The owner of the voice was a good ten feet away from her, its shadow silhouetted against the red light from the fire.

"Who are you?" Gwen croaked, her throat sore from crying. "Where am I? Why can't I see?"

At this, there was another hearty laugh. "All in good time, all in good time! I will answer in reverse. You cannot see because you have been given a drug after a little operation. You are in my home, which is in the forest of Ÿalnz Dàr." There was a pause, and then, "And my name is Anaximander, but you will not be calling me that."

Gwen heard more footsteps. The owner of the voice was right in front of her now. "Drink this, drink this. You will feel much better."

Gwen reached out unseeingly and felt a small, very dry, very wrinkled hand holding a cup, filled with some concoction that reeked. Against her will, she felt herself grab the cup, raise it to her lips, and she then drank the contents. She wanted so badly to spit it out—it tasted like river sludge— but found that she could not. As soon as the stuff touched her throat, though, everything was brought back into sharp, firm, clear focus.

She now saw that she was in a small room, perhaps twelve square feet in size, made of stones. The walls were lined with wooden torches and all of them were lit. There were no windows and the only exit was one, lone door directly across from where she sat. She looked up for the source of the voice.

Above her stood an old man who would have barely reached Gwen's elbow had she been standing up. His face was as wrinkled and dry as his hand had felt, though he wore a kind smile. His eyes were the color of seaweed, a greenish-brown. He had a very long, crooked nose that was lined as the rest of his face. His hair was gray and wispy and cut very short, while his chin and upper lip was covered with a small beard. His ears were small but they ended in fine tips.

Gwen frowned when she saw his ears. She knew dwarves did not have ears like that and it was certain that someone of his height and appearance could never be an elf. She decided that he must be a gnome. She knew they appeared in all shapes and sizes. This one was of the short variety.

Gwen then looked down at herself. She wore a brown rag that smelt strongly of onions. The scent brought fresh tears to her eyes. Again she examined the manacles around her wrists, and uttered a small scream when she saw that her right underarm had been disfigured with a long, ropy, pink scar that extended from her palm to her forearm.

She stood up again, this time smoothly, and sprang in to a defensive stance, ready for anything.

"Why am I here?" she asked dangerously, her face contorting in rage.

Anaximander's smile widened, and he said, "Sit".

A strange force rose up inside Gwen, a strong power that urged her to obey what Anaximander had said. Gwen tried with all her might to resist it, but it was too great to stop. She yielded, and felt her muscles relax. She fell to the ground, sitting cross-legged.

"Very good, very good," Anaximander said excitedly. "The ritual has worked. A good thing too, I would have been most upset had it not have when I spent so much. I scrimped, and saved for several years, I will have you know. It is not easy being an alchemist in these parts. Magic users don't always find me, so often times, business is bad."

He stepped away from Gwen and paced back and forth.

"Then there is the trouble of finding the right people once you have saved your money. Took me over five months to find a decent blood-mage who would do it for me. And *then* you need to actually find someone to cast the spells on. And believe me, ever since Ozmodion returned, people avoid this forest like hens do a wolf den. But I found him eventually, blood-mage name of Shravir. Poaching guttersnipe wanted all my money *and* several family jewels. I had to accept his terms sadly; you do not want to fool with blood-mages."

Gwen stared, speechless.

"I was so *frightfully* pleased when Shravir found you in the Caves of Illothin. I never asked him why he was there; he has been frequenting the caves lately. No matter though. Now you are here and now you are *mine*. Oh, I cannot tell you how happy this makes me."

Gwen's stomach clenched uncomfortably when she heard Anaximander put a slight stress on the word "mine". He turned to face her again.

"Sorry about the chains and the drug. When Shravir showed me your Vawn, I thought it best to take every precaution possible in case the ritual failed. Enchantresses are harder to control, I am told. But no fear now! Here you sit, as tame as a house cat!"

He chuckled, and reached into his pocket. He fumbled for a moment then pulled out a key. He used it to unlock the shackles that bound Gwen's wrists and ankles. She cowered into a corner as soon as she was free.

"I don't understand," she whispered fearfully, "What do you mean I'm yours?"

Anaximander again laughed his boisterous laugh. "Dear me, dear me, you really do not know? Gods, I was told that enchantresses were intelligent. You are my blood-slave, dear."

Gwen thoughts leaped back to the Mountain of Antiquity and the servants she had seen there. She remembered their worn expressions, their haunted features, and their resigned movements. She shuddered.

"You lie," she stated defiantly, "I am no one's slave. I am Gweneth Catherine Tal—"

"Silence," Anaximander commanded calmly, his smile stretched even wider, though it now seemed unpleasant. That strange force rose inside Gwen again, that urge to submit to his words. Once more she tried to suppress the feeling, but again she found herself unable to. All will to continue speaking left her, and her mouth clamped firmly shut.

"There, there, now," Anaximander said, the kindness returning to his face, "You must not think me cruel. As I said, these are hard times, and one must fight to live. I promise you, I will be a kind master and treat you very well. Now, I believe you said your name was Gwen? All right dear, let me show you my home and set you about your duties. Up, now."

The urge returned, and this time Gwen made no effort to withstand it. She uncrossed her legs and stood up, as rigid as a tree.

"Follow me," Anaximander instructed, and he turned around, opened the door, and left the room. With a resigned sigh, Gwen slowly followed the old gnome.

☐

"Hellfire!" Eion swore both loudly and angrily. His curse echoed horribly in the main chamber of the Caves of Illothin, magnified tenfold. "That dratted girl's always causing more trouble than she's worth."

Eion now silently chastised himself for these heartless words; he knew he did not mean them. His anger stemmed more from his worry for Gwen rather than his frustration at her knack of finding trouble.

They had combed every nook and cranny of the caves and there was no sign of Gwen. All they had found was her pack being guarded viciously by her cat. It hissed when they had approached and had attempted to scratch out Flame's eyes before he had recognized them.

When asked, all Rembas and Tirmal could remember was Tirmal's staff suddenly extinguishing and a quiet rustling noise. When it had passed them, Tirmal's staff had reignited and they found Gwen missing.

The party had now gathered in the main chamber to discuss matters.

"My, that seems a mite harsh, don't you think?" Rembas asked unworriedly, "I doubt she asked to be spirited away."

"Leave out of it, you mangy animal," Eion said acidly. His mood was indeed sour. On top of Gwen's disappearance, Gorothar's Shield had been found to be missing as well. The faun had delighted in pointing out how he had warned them, but the party's tempers had been stretched so thin that he hadn't pressed the issue.

"Animal, am I?" Rembas asked smoothly, rising from his seat on a boulder and setting his satchel aside. He walked slowly over to where Eion stood. "Such words would cause a lesser being to become violence." He cracked his fingers by clenching his right fist.

Eion would have loved to have drawn *Raz'atr* then, to sheath his sword in Rembas's breast and thereby allowing his tensions to drain. Before he could react on this impulse, Beast stepped in between the two and forced them apart.

"Enough!" he said bad-temperedly, "That solves nothing!"

Fauna trilled with laughter. "Oh, that is rich. You Beast, missing the chance to watch, possibly partake, in a fight? Are you feeling all right?"

Beast's scowl deepened, and he attempted to lunge at Fauna, but Brunariun, sensing trouble, had wrapped her tail around his feet before he could take two steps. Beast fell painfully to the stony floor.

Eion resisted the urge to laugh, with difficulty, and regained his composure. "Peace, friends. Beast is right; we must remain calm."

Beast mumbled something, but, since his face was pressed to the rocky ground, no one heard him. He kicked off Brunariun's scaly tail and got to his feet, dusting himself off angrily. .

"This makes no sense," Tirmal stated, rubbing his chin and smiling slightly. "Nothing could have extinguished my staff without strong magic, and I sensed no enchantments or charms."

"Perhaps you let your spell's magic fade," Varez offered, staring at the ground and twiddling his thumbs.

Tirmal ran his right hand across his face, sighing loudly. "That spell is far too simple to require my attention to it. It should have cast light until I let it die away with a Ceasing Command." He turned his back on the group and muttered lowly, "Dwarves."

"Then whoever had the first Emerald of Alexander returned with a second," Bruanriun said simply.

"But why would they take Gwen?" Tyler asked, shaken at the turn of events. Instinctively, he reached for the hilt of the dagger that was sheathed around his belt.

"Who knows?" Flame said, "Perhaps they sensed her for what she is, perhaps they took her because she was so far ahead. It does not really matter why they took her. We now need to find out who took her and where they hid her."

"Ÿalnz Dàr is immense!" exclaimed Fauna, "We could comb it for decades and we still would not find her. It is foolish to think otherwise."

"We need the full strength of the Resistance," Beast asserted gruffly.

"No," Eion sighed, "We cannot have our armies separate while we are so close to Saurindon. We need to do this stealthily and unseen, and not alert the Ozra anymore to our presence."

"But Eion," protested Steel, "we cannot do this alone. We need help. We cannot risk Gwen being hurt while we search for her furtively. She is practically defenseless."

"Well, that is not *quite* true," said a new voice.

Eion whipped his head around, his eyes darting back and forth madly to find the owner of the voice. He turned around to see Rembas laughing uncontrollably into his hand while Gwen's cat sat on the stony floor about three feet away from the faun. It was smiling.

Eion shifted his bow and nocked an arrow. "Who are you?" he asked dangerously. "A spy? Another one of those blasted shadow-shifters?"

The cat laughed. "No, no. Nothing of the sort. I am a friend, and I have been helping your cause for quite a while now, Eion Shifter, ever since you reached the Silver Ice Sea. I am Curthlond, former enchanter and now tutor to Gwen. I have been teaching her magic for some weeks now."

"It's true Eion," said Rembas, who was now beginning to recover from his fit of laughter, though his voice did break with a giggle occasionally. "I can vouch for him. He has been my friend since childhood, ever since he accidentally lit old man Romis's—"

"Thank you, Rem, do not help me." Curthlond interjected sharply. He looked embarrassed.

Eion fought to restrain another laugh; the sight of an embarrassed cat was so absurdly funny that his entire body shook with suppressed chuckles. He quickly regained his composure and turned to Tirmal. "Place upon him the Constraint of Truth," Eion instructed in elven.

Tirmal nodded, smiling grimly. He turned to face the cat, raised his staff, and uttered *"Bosn ult kief."*

Curthlond began to glow with an eerie green light. His eyes widened, partly in surprise but mostly in anger.

"Ooh, you are a suspicious bunch. Very well, I see that you wish to interrogate me under certain strictures, but know this: I will not tolerate any attempts to take...advantage of me."

Eion chuckled at being threatened by a cat, though he managed to disguise it as deep cough. He then nodded in response to Curthlond, and shifted himself a stool on which to sit.

"Do you bear the Resistance any ill will?" Eion asked.

"None," was Curthlond's reply.

"Do you owe any obedience to Ozmodion, the Ozra, or other enemies of the Resistance?"

"None," again Curthlond answered.

"Will you swear fealty to the Resistance?"

At this, Curthlond hissed. "Fealty? Fealty? You pompous upstart, I will not be enslaved to a war I have no part in. No, I bear you no ill will, but I refuse to lay my life in front of a sword for you."

Eion sighed, rubbing his temples with his forefingers. "Very well, I see we are going to have to trust you. Tirmal, break the constraint."

As the elf prepared to break the magic the bound Curthlond to honesty, Eion retreated into his thoughts. First came anger at Gwen's deception and secrecy, but those thoughts quickly left him and he was instead filled with rational reason for Gwen's desire for magical tutelage; she was an Iltari after all. Thirdly, came relief at the knowing that wherever she was, she would have some weapons at her disposal. Then, fourthly, worry flooded him as he wondered if her newfound magical abilities had anything to do with her disappearance.

"Well, Buttons, ol' chap," Rembas said after Tirmal had severed the magic and Curthlond had returned to his usual color. He covered his mouth with his hand, and then said, "Oh, well I suppose you'll have to be known as Curthlond once more, though, in retrospect, it doesn't roll off the tongue as easily."

Curthlond growled, baring his teeth. Rembas smiled and nodded serenely, and he pulled his pan flute from his satchel and began to play a tune, oblivious to Curthlond's annoyance.

Eion pulled himself away from his thoughts and turned back the hunting party.

"We still have not decided what to do about Gwen," he said pointedly, leaving the thought hang in the air.

Rembas then looked up, taking his flute away from mouth. "You could always get some extra help."

Eion's brow furrowed in irritation. "I have just said we cannot have the whole Resistance—"

"Yes, yes," Rembas interjected as he placed the pan flute once again into his satchel. "The Resistance this and the Resistance that. You forget, Eion Shifter, that there are individuals scattered across the globe who remain neutral. A bag of gold and some clever talking could easily insure their…assistance."

"Such as?" Eion asked, his frustration steadily mounting.

Rembas then pulled his pipe from the bag. He placed some tobacco into it, produced a match, struck in on the boulder, and lit the weed. He took a few puffs before pulling it from his mouth and saying, "There are some in the forest who have special skills in such areas of expertise."

Understanding flooded Eion. "You are talking about bounty hunters and mercenaries." The shifter spat on the ground. "I am not entrusting Gwen's life to some kingless rogue who would slit his own brother's throat so long as the pay was substantial."

Rembas shrugged. "Very well, then. Let's just scamper over to the Five Clearings, then, and tell everyone you have gone and lost an Iltari.

That will tickle them with joy." With that, the faun placed the pipe back in his mouth, smiling in the dark.

Curthlond sauntered toward Eion. "Rembas is, unfortunately, right. I see no other way of safely retrieving Gwen without outside help."

Rembas rolled his eyes. "Thanks for the vote of confidence, Curth," he said, his voice dripping with sarcasm. He turned back to Eion and said, "I knew of one bounty hunter years ago. Curthlond might even remember him. Name of Shravir. Not a bad fellow, as spell casters go. Granted, given his profession, that might not be saying much, but still, you can't be too choosey when you're dealing with blood-mages."

Brunariun shifted uncomfortably at the word, and Varez's eye bulged with shock as he said, "Blood-mage!? See here now, Master Curthlond, I think the less associating with black magic the Resistance does, the better off we will be."

"No no," Curthlond said tiredly, his tail lashing back and forth. "He is not that kind of blood-mage. He only practices blood-enslavement on the side, only when the bounties are scarce."

Tirmal stamped his foot on the ground and threw his hands up in the air, ignoring the clatter his staff made as it fell to the ground. "Oh, not only would we be calling on the aid of a blood-mage, he is also a slaver! What a treat." Elves, Eion remembered, loathed oppressive strictures on life, being creatures of beauty and freedom themselves. They reserved their hate for slave-traders alone.

"If you have any other suggestions, Captain Goldhair," Flame said coolly, "I am sure we would all dearly love to hear them."

Tirmal, of course, did not have any other suggestions, and instead remained silent as he glowered at the red-haired shifter.

As the quiet turmoil grew, Eion weighed the odds. Surely, calling on a blood-mage/bounty hunter was a desperate act. And yet, they had only been allotted five days to find Gorothar's Shield and the Resistance would soon be expecting them. If Eion and the hunting came back without the shield *and* without Gwen…Eion did not care to think of Lord Fairskin's anger.

"Very well, Curthlond," he said, cutting off a now heated argument between Steel and Rembas, "lead us to this Shravir."

Curthlond nodded, and ambled out of the cave.

Eion shouldered his pack, beckoned the rest to come, and bid a silent farewell to the Caves of Illothin.

Chapter 28

The Brunch

*A**naximander was not a cruel gnome*. He treated Gwen very well and apologized many times for her enslavement. It was not uncommon for blood-masters to whip their slaves regardless of the slaves' involuntary obedience, but Anaximander would not hear of this. He gave Gwen full sized meals, set her chores only around the house, and allowed her his guest bedroom which was equipped with a soft bed, a nightstand, and even a window.

Still, Gwen loathed him thoroughly.

Though she ached to escape, the old gnome was like a ball and chain holding her to her prison. Anytime she felt compelled to hurt or kill him, she was met with self-inflicted pain, a clause of the blood enslavement,

Anaximander had told her. She felt herself slowly losing hope, and she resigned herself to her doom.

On the third morning of her enslavement, she awoke early, and stepped outside of the cottage to sweep the patio. It was a pleasant enough looking place, the cottage; standing at two stories tall and dotted with windows. Multiple chimneys protruded from the roof, and many doors led out of the ground floor. The house itself was set in a small clearing in the trees. The overhanging boughs allowed little light in, and faint splashes of sun painted the forest floor, which, like the rest of Ÿalnz Dàr, was carpeted with thick moss.

As Gwen finished sweeping the dust off the patio, Anaximander from the house wearing his best waistcoat.

"There you are, there you are!" He said, sweating profusely, "I have been calling and calling. Drat this house! It is just so big! I have company coming over in…" He paused, and pulled a pocket watch from his pocket. He opened it, look at the time, and let out a squeal of alarm. "A quarter of an hour!! Hurry, hurry! Set the patio table for eight, including myself. Oh dear, oh dear…" and he turned and retreated into the house.

Gwen felt that strange force nudge her to do the gnome's will, but she ignored it, and set about the task by her own volition. She had laid out the plates, forks, spoons, knives, napkins out only just in time, for as soon as the last saucer had been set, Anaximander came scuttling out, squeaking, "They are here! Quick, quick, fetch the cakes! And the tea! And the bread and the butter! Haste, haste!"

Gwen left her master to sweat. She returned to the patio ten minutes later, bearing many cakes and other things her master had asked for, to find that the table was now filled with many people. They were all gnomes, judging by their size and pointed ears, and all of them seemed to be just as wrinkled and aged as Anaximander. They all wore colorful waistcoats, and some donned many variations of decoration. Two wore top hats, and one had placed a monocle in his left eye.

"There you are Gwen!" her master exclaimed from the head of the table. "At last, at last. We're all quite famished."

Gwen nodded. Once she had set all the foods and drinks on the table, Anaximander said, "Thank you, thank you. Now, stay close in case I have more need of you."

Gwen sighed, and dragged a spare chair away from the table to the side of the house. She sat with her legs crossed and remained silent.

Anaximander placed two cubes of sugar in his tea and stirred the liquid with his spoon. "Now, Sophocles, what was that you were saying about Constantine seeing a host of banshees?"

The gnome with the monocle cleared his throat loudly as he spread butter over a seedcake. "Yes, yes, old Constantine said he awoke in the dead of night to hear dozens of wailing voices scream loudly. He jumped from his bed, ran to the window, and saw a large troupe of sallow-skinned women march passed his front gate. Gave him quite a fright, it did; he hasn't been able to step outdoors after nightfall for a week now."

Anaximander chuckled as he reached for a scone. "Pass the butter there, Romulus. Thank you. Hm, sounds to me that poor Constantine's eyes are failing him in his advanced age. There has not been a banshee this far north of the woods for decades."

"Pooh!" exclaimed a gnome with a bright orange waistcoat. "You know very well, Anaximander, that Constantine's eyes are the best out of any of the present company. Advanced age, my foot!" He grumbled lowly and took a sip of his tea.

"That very well may have been true, Archimedes, years ago," Anaximander assured as he finished his third cake. "But I just cannot imagine why the banshees would return to this part of Ÿalnz Dàr. They prefer the Bogs of Zuvé in the south."

The gnome with the purple waistcoat and top hat to match harrumphed loudly as if he had been awakened from a nap. "Well, that is it, is it not? The Bogs are very near the Gap of the Ozra, and we all know that there's a bustle of activity down there, do we not?"

Sophocles chose a chocolate éclair and set it on his plate before saying, "Whatever do you mean, Hippocrates?"

"What, you have not heard? Dear me, Sophocles, behind in the times a little, are we not?"

Sophocles sniffed agitatedly. "Not all of us are incurable gossips like you, Hippocrates. Now, do tell. What goes on at the Ozra's Gap?"

Hippocrates laughed liked a hyena for a few seconds and poured himself a fresh cup of tea. After a few sips, he said, "Well, old Blackheart has got his armies constantly patrolling about there. Cause absolute havoc, they do, too. Cutting trees, setting brush ablaze, and who knows what else. The Resistance is getting mighty close to the Gap, some say, and Ozmodion does not very much like the idea of being caught unawares. Anyway, whatever poor soul that ventures too near the Gap..." Hippocrates paused and slid his right finger across his throat while making a squelching noise. He then winked, and turned back to his tea.

"No banshee would get too ruffled by a few of the Red Sovereign's cronies," the gnome with the blue waistcoat stated flatly. "Their only aversions are to bright light and strong magic."

355

"Oh please, Odysseus," said the gnome with the tassels hanging from his yellow waistcoat—the one they called Romulus, "Please do not be such an insufferable know-it-all. I have not even had my fourth helping yet."

"He's right though, isn't he?" Archimedes chimed. "That knowledge is common enough. I doubt that even Kahn's trolls would dare brave the bogs to perturb the banshees."

"Well, then, I do not see any sense in this, then," so said the gnome in the red coat. "The only spell caster in Saurindon would be old Blackheart himself."

"What, you have not heard the tales, Copernicus?" asked Hippocrates incredulously. "My, I must set myself about finding some friends who are not all complete ignoramuses."

"I certainly would not lament the loss," said Sophocles, buttering another scone.

"What tales do you mean, Hip old boy?" Anaximander queried, his mouth filled with bread.

"Well, just this: my old friend Julius was about the forest one day, when he came across a little pixie who said she had just seen the Gates of Angar Vûn open to produce forth a mad satyr riding a shadow wolf as a steed. She also said that no less then one hundred goblins were seen to follow him and all addressed him as "sir". What is more, with her fairy eyes, she also saw many shadowy apparitions follow him, too. At his command, they brought him bolts of lightning and he clasped them in his hand and said loudly, 'Behold, Axunrult the Terrible. Flee, O fools! Flee before me, lest thou would see your bones turned to fire and your skin to ash!' And he rode away, his goblin lackeys following stupidly behind."

Romulus laughed so wildly that bits of cake sprayed from his mouth. While those who were seated across from him groaned in disgust, he said,

"Oh, good one Hip! A demonically possessed satyr astride a shadow wolf? Even a mortal would not believe such poppycock!"

Hippocrates' eyes narrowed. "It is the truth, I say. His eyes were a wicked red and a black scimitar was fastened at his belt. He, too, wore a cape that billowed around him magnificently as he gave his little speech. That poor little pixie was frightened out of her wits, the dear thing."

"Absolute tripe, methinks," Sophocles said haughtily as he adjusted his monocle.

"No one asked what 'youthinks', you portentous popinjay," Hippocrates muttered quietly.

"Indeed. One more magician surely wouldn't put the banshees into such a fuss. Why, there are more spell casters in one acre of Ÿalnz Dàr then there is in the whole of Saurindon Gorge," Odysseus claimed while he wiped his mouth clean with a napkin.

"Ah, to understand the minds of such monsters would be quite a gift, yes?" Anaximander asked serenely. He helped himself to another cake and dunked it into his teacup.

"Speaking of monsters," said Archimedes suddenly, "I have heard reports of hydra being driven across Gaurya."

"*Really?*" inquired Copernicus interestedly. "My, those Gauryans have always been a little strange."

"Gaurya itself is a little strange," Sophocles said as he reached for the strawberry preserves. "A country of sheer rock and fire pits. I cannot see why anyone would ever want to live there."

"Oh, but some of the most *fantastic* beasts have made their home in Gaurya," said Odysseus, his eyes misty with thought. "The phoenixes, the rocs, even the papillions have been seen roaming that land. Oh, I wish I could go there."

"Mm. I wish you would go too," Sophocles said.

"Please Archimedes," implored Romulus, "Do not keep us in suspense. Why is Gaurya driving away its hydra?"

Archimedes shrugged. "There are varied accounts. Some say the Gauryan king, Acktov, tires of their additions to the death tolls. Others say that Gaurya is trying to make a profit off the hydra and are, hear this, *selling them* to neighboring countries. And still others say that Gaurya remains ignorant about the hydra's forced march, and that the beasts are being moved by foreigners behind Acktov's back."

"Surely, Acktov will not be complaining," said Copernicus, "Hydra are some of the nastiest creatures that plague this realm. I remember how old Greece had such a time eradicating them."

"Yes. Caused their fall it did. The expenses were just so astronomical," agreed Hippocrates.

"All of the Magic Realm is having interesting troubles, now that I think of it," Anaximander said, unbuttoning the lower buttons of his waistcoat to relieve the stress. "Achilles was telling me only a few days ago that the griffins and hippogriffs have resurrected the same old feud; who is better? Horse ends or lion ends? The Grand Griffin and the High Hippogriff have ceased any communication between the two races, and war is to inevitably follow."

"Oh, yes," said Romulus, slapping his belly jovially. "I recall hearing something of the sort. Also, the wyverns are growing restless. The basilisks have been making their way into the wyvern's territories, and the wyverns can do nothing about it."

"Nothing they can do about it?" asked Odysseus. "Whatever do you mean? Surely, the wyverns have the strength and numbers to combat the basilisks?"

Romulus scoffed. "It is rather hard to combat an enemy who can turn you to stone with a mere glance."

"And let us not forget the turmoil that has gathered 'round the Valley of the Weres," chimed in Hippocrates. "The werewolves are rising in numbers, and they are sure to attack the fomariuns that are clustered in that little vale. The weredragons can do almost nothing about it, so abundant are the werewolves. The centaurs, the fauns, the satyrs, and the minotaurs are all forging weapons, preparing themselves for a climactic battle. Only the onocentaurs and the merpeople of the Lake of Mer remain neutral."

"The weredragons' time has passed," said Sophocles. "Their influence is tarnished and their authority waned."

"It's old Blackheart's return," said Archimedes. "People are panicked, they are scared, and unsure. Without fear, Ozmodion would not be half so powerful."

"Ha!" exclaimed Copernicus, "You would not be so bold as to say that to his face, I am sure."

"What is this that I hear about the cricks facing extinction?" asked Odysseus, cutting off Archimedes' retort.

"Who cares?" replied Sophocles, slapping his hand against the table. "I would not mourn those beasts' deaths anymore than I mourned the chimeras'."

"Hear, hear!" cried Hippocrates heartily.

"Gwen, dear," called Anaximander suddenly, "Could you please fetch us some coffee?"

Gwen stood up without even thinking. She had been deep in thought over the content of the gnomes' conversation. The name of the mad satyr, Axunrul, seemed vaguely familiar, as if she had heard it long ago. Gwen could only assume that she knew this person before she had been enslaved.

359

Many of her memories from her days of freedom were beginning to fade. She did not dwell too much on it though. There was no point in remembering a life she could no longer have. She went to the kitchen and obediently poured the coffee.

Chapter 29

The Enlistment

Blaringly, the alarm sounded. Its source was unclear, but still it rang out piercingly inside the hovel. Shravir, lounging on the worn sofa, grumbled crossly. The magical defense nexus that he had set up around the perimeter of his home was very sensitive; a rabbit had probably triggered it. He sat up, clapped his hands five times, and muttered, *"Maëli."* With that, the alarm died away as quickly as it had come.

The blood-mage rubbed his eyes and looked about his abode, which was comprised of a single room. It was messy, to say the least. Empty bottles were strewn across the floor, accompanied by old rags and remnants of meals long passed. All of the furniture was either worn, ripped, stained, or broken. A table in the right corner was covered with crucibles, bowls, sketches, notes, ink pots, and quills.

Shravir nodded in satisfaction; he liked the disorder of the house. "Chaos is the one thing that makes sense in this world," Shravir's father had always said, and the blood-mage had fully taken the adage to heart.

Shravir stood from the sofa and walked to a cracked mirror that rested on the wall to the left. He studied his reflection interestedly.

He was, contrary to what his profession would suggest, very handsome. His eyes were a light-blue tinged with green. He had high cheekbones and angled features, with shaggy, black hair that hung around it all in an impressive manner. His thin lips parted in a smile to reveal his brilliantly white teeth.

This was not what interested him, though. He was intrigued by the furrow of his brow. The lines in his forehead made him look much older than he was. Shravir sighed, fully aware the cause of his aged appearance.

Blood-magery was a stressful branch of magic. Blood fueled his powers, and oftentimes he had to use his own to cast his spells. It was much easier to use blood from others. Small animals like rabbits, though abundant, did not hold much power. He thought unicorn good, when he could get it, though that was quite a rarity now.

He had not wanted to be a blood-mage in his younger days. He still did not, as a matter of fact. Certainly, he had wanted to be a spell caster, but he would have preferred enchanting or even sorcery much more to blood-magery. But his father had insisted on the dark art. "We live in a dark age, son. There is no money in benevolence anymore."

Shravir turned from the mirror and raised his right hand to study the mark born from his father's insistence. The mark of the blood-mage, the Grarn, was etched into his palm with silvery scar tissue. It was a pentacle with a blooming rose in its center. Shravir could never get over the irony of the mark of such an evil art looking so beautiful. *Magic has rules, but no reason,* he silently mused.

His father had been right, though. Blood-magery had been very kind to Shravir. Blood enslavement was quickly growing in popularity in the woods of Ÿalnz Dàr, and he had been commissioned for such a task only a few days ago. An old gnome said he was desperate for some assistance around his house. Shravir smiled at the gnome's foolishness. "Never let 'em know how much you need it," Shravir's father had told the blood-mage in his younger days. "That is what makes a good, and thus shrewd, businessman."

With such necessity established, Shravir was able to pose an excessive sum, and the gnome was forced to pay it. He had little gold, as Shravir expected, but he did have some family gems that would do the job nicely. "My grandmother left them to me, bless her," the gnome had said sadly as he handed two emeralds to Shravir the day of his commission. "The have been in the family for time out of mind, they have. They were supposed to have some magical properties too, it had been rumored."

Whether they did or not, Shravir had not cared at the time. They were both easily as big as the blood-mage's fist, and would fetch a sum large enough to let Shravir turn his back on the dark magic for life. It was only when he had been poking around in the Caves of Illothin that a simple command caused the emeralds to drain the magic from the surrounding area. The first had exploded into powder and Shravir then felt the caves dead of any enchantments. He swore to then be forever careful with the second However, the loss had not been as great as Shravir had expected. He had found a chest in the cave the pulsed with a lividly bright aura. Shravir had taken it back to his home without second thought.

Try as he might, he had not been able to open the chest, and its enigmatic presence had consumed Shravir's mind, and for days he had thought of nothing else, nor even had left his house for want of opening the chest.

Anaximander had then stopped by to see if Shravir had found a suitable blood-slave. Shravir had not even thought of looking yet. He, of course, lied to the old gnome and said that he had found someone who might suit him. Satisfied, the gnome left, and Shravir returned to the chest.

Later that afternoon, Shravir wondered if there might have been a key to the chest in the Caves and that he had left it behind. Excitedly, Shravir quickly made his way back to Illothin, though this time, he was not alone. A hunting party had congregated in the main chamber, and they were all heavily armed.

Unsettling questions plagued the blood-mage's mind. What if they found the key? How would he ever open the chest? He felt himself for weapons, but discovered that he had only the other emerald. If they had magic, he would quickly make sure that they could not use it. He activated the gem, and the party's magical lights had gone out.

Pleased, Shravir went again about wandering the caves. Try as he might, he found no key. Upset, he decided to make way for home, when one of the members of the party turned the corner of the passage he was walking up. Quicker than thought, he had tripped the figure with magic and then knocked it out with another spell. He bound it in blankets, and skirted the rest of the party. He then exited the caves and ran home.

He was not sure why he had kidnapped it; an irrational impulse in the dark, he supposed. This did, however, solve the gnome's want of a blood-slave. He set the bound figure on his sofa and unwrapped the blankets. He was shocked to see that a sleeping girl now rested on his couch.

Though Shravir was not vain about his own good looks, he was a hard judge of beauty. The sleeping girl, however, was undoubtedly the most gorgeous creature he had ever seen. Her hair, her face, and her lips were all magnificent. Her skin seemed spun from moonbeams, and he could have sworn that it was glowing in the dim hovel.

He was just about to wake her with magic, when a loud rap had come from his door. It had been the gnome. "I have tarried and waited long enough. I *need* that slave. If you do not have a specimen ready now, I must ask that you return those gems.

Shravir could not have abided to have had to give the emeralds back, so he fell back on intimidation, which invariably worked in Ÿalnz Dàr.

"Watch yourself, mate," Shravir had said, "You're out of your league here. It would not be wise to insult me. I am a professional; I always get the job done."

With that, he gestured at the girl on the couch.

"Fine sight, is she not?" asked the blood-mage, "Pains me to part with her. Such a face should be painted on canvas, not bound by manacles."

The gnome sniffed. "I care not for beauty, only for function. Begin the ritual!"

Shravir shrugged. "Your money, chum." He unsheathed a dagger from his belt. Before the chest and the emeralds, it had been the only beautiful thing he had owned. One blue sapphire had been laid into the pommel, and the steel shone like silver fire. "Roll up your sleeve, then."

Hesitantly, the gnome pushed his sleeve up his arm. Shravir grabbed hold of the gnome's wrist, and made a horizontal cut down the forearm. The gnome cried loudly in pain. *Serves you right*, Shravir had thought, *If only you could feel half the pain this girl will endure for the rest of her life.* A pang of guilt ran through Shravir suddenly. He had always known his was a dark art, and now he loathed it more than ever. He shook his head to clear his mind. He would soon turn his back on blood-magery, but in the meantime he needed to perform the ritual.

He then produced a phial from somewhere in his cloak. He filled it with the gnome's blood. He then handed the gnome a white cloth to stop him from spilling anymore. He then moved to the girl. He ignored the quiet moan she issued when he slit her arm, and instead filled another phial with her blood. He wrapped her arm in a cloth too, and then carried the two phials to his work table. He set them down and whispered a string of spells over the two containers of blood. One began to issue steam, and the other fogged with cold. Shravir muttered the last syllable. A faint ringing sound could be heard. When it died, he carried the two phials back to the gnome and the girl. First, he clasped the gnome's wrist once more and let the girl's blood trickle down into his cut. He yelped in pain again, as the girl's blood was boiling with heat. Shravir smiled and tilted the glass higher. When it was empty, Shravir healed the gnomes cut with a quick spell, and then went to the girl to repeat the process. It was only when he had healed her that he saw the mark etched into her right palm. A five-point star with a crescent moon embossed in the center. The Vawn. The mark of the enchanter.

Worry grew in Shravir's heart. No spell caster had ever been enslaved, and Shravir did not know if it was even possible. Still, there was no time to find another, so he warned the gnome and told him to drug the girl until he was sure he could control her. Shravir cast a levitation enchantment on the girl, and the gnome had left towing her behind.

Looking back on all of this, Shravir's guilt returned. It had been cruel to enslave the girl, but he had no choice. "Kill or be killed," his father once said. Such were the rules of Ÿalnz Dàr.

Suddenly, the alarm went off once more, waking Shravir from his thoughts. He furrowed his brow deeper and scratched his head. Most animals knew by now to stay clear of the hovel, for the blood-mage would surely kill them for either food or blood. Too tired to chase them of, he clapped his hands and spoke the incantation again. He then returned to the sofa to continue his night's sleep.

As soon as he closed his eyes, the alarm blared to life yet again. Shravir jumped from his couch and unsheathed his dagger; someone unwanted had come to his home, and he would now defend it.

His walls were very thin, so there was no need to open his door as he shouted, "Begone from this place! There is nothing for you here but death! You have trespassed on the property of a terrible sorcerer! If you would see another day, leave!"

His only answer was a loud blast as his wall was blown apart. Shravir jumped and took cover behind his couch. When the dust settled, he peeked over the sofa to look upon his intruder. As he gazed upon the trespasser, he was met with shock.

"What the devil are doing here?" the blood mage demanded, deeply confused.

The faun brushed himself off and shook his satchel free of dust. "Shravir, old friend, what I'm doing here is entirely beside the point."

Shravir shook his head angrily. "What do you mean 'entirely beside the point'? You triggered my alarm thrice and then blew my wall apart. I think what you are doing here is entirely *the point*, you thick man-buck!"

"Thick man-buck?" said a voice that didn't belong to the faun. "How original. And you give me grief for my insults."

The faun turned to the source of the voice. "No, no. I give you grief for your repetition and wit, Curth. If I addressed your originality, I would only make you cry."

"Rembas!" Shravir shouted warningly, "You had better have a damn good story, or I will curse your arms off!"

The faun only scoffed. "Not if you like walking under your own power, you womt. I have come with some particularly strong friends."

As the faun gestured around him, Shravir registered the existence of a host of other figures. Simultaneously, they all stepped into the light. Shravir was not sure to be frightened or if he should just laugh. On Rembas' right, there was a cat who grinned wickedly. Next to the cat were five people, four of which who had no notable auras. The other, a man dressed in dark robes, lit up the room with his inner pulse of energy. Though his face showed little expression, his eyes were narrowed purposefully.

On the other side of Rembas was a dwarf, who was thumbing the blade of his axe slowly. Next to him was an elf that leaned coolly on his staff, placidly smiling. On his left was a gaggle of people who pulsed with a variation of auras. One had flaming red hair, another was laden with many swords, and the other two glared icily at each other. Beside them (here Shravir gasped with surprise) was a dragon, her orange scales flashing brilliantly.

Rembas indeed was traveling with strong friends, and as he took the party in, Shravir restrained his shock and outrage and addressed Rembas again, this time with the utmost politeness.

"Ahem. Well, Rembas, what can I do for you?"

The faun laughed and opened his satchel to extract his pipe and a match. After he lit it and took a few puffs, he said, "Shravir, that's what I like about you. You're a man who can read the odds and accept them. Very seldom seen these days."

He stepped over the threshold and walked around the shack, his hooves clip-clopping loudly.

"Ugh, Shravir I hope you didn't pay too much for this hovel. Look at those holes in the roof! Shoddy workmanship, all of this."

That stung Shravir. "I *built* this."

Rembas nodded his head absently. "Yes."

"Rembas, quit your pleasantries," barked the dwarf. "Get to the point."

"Oh, yes!" said Rembas, as if he had just recalled some thought he had been battling to grasp. "Now Shravir, we have come not for your hospitality"—He paused, looked around the hovel once more, and chuckled quietly—"but for your services. We have lost a member of our party and we were hoping we could persuade you to help."

Shravir stood from his crouched position and dusted himself off. "Anything is possible."

"Tsk tsk," reprimanded the faun, shaking his head. "Always thinking with your wallet. Kings may die and tyrants might rise again from the grave, but one thing always remains the same: bounty-hunters' greed. Well, I am afraid to say that we do not have with us the funds with which to secure the full array of your talents."

Bloody fauns, Shravir thought irritably. *Always beating around the bush.* "Well, I am afraid to say that I do not work until I see my gold."

Rembas again gestured around at his companions, and his point hit home as the man with the swords unsheathed a dagger. "I was expecting that. Shravir, your profession is rather looked down upon within the Resistance, but—"

"The Resistance?!" interjected Shravir, his eyes bulging. "You are working for the *Resistance*?"

Rembas frowned and took out his pipe. "At the moment, yes, but—"

"Rembas," said Shravir, cutting the faun off once more, "surely you, a native of Ÿalnz Dàr, know the risks in aiding the Resistance in these times."

Before Ozmodion fell, Ÿalnz Dàr had been an area where the line between Ozmodion's territory and the Resistances' holdings blurred; a no-man's land where any sort of allegiance was highly dangerous. Any who blatantly displayed their support for the Resistance met many strange and bizarre dooms.

"The Resistance can offer you protection," said the elf, his smile gone as he registered the grim implication.

Shravir spat on the ground. "So can neutrality."

The dragon growled lowly. "This war will allow no neutrality. You will eventually have to choose a side. And, quite frankly, I think you will find us rather persuading." She grinned, revealing her many pointed teeth.

"We are not asking for you to wield your sword and run into battle," said the man with the red hair. "All we want is you to help us find someone."

Shravir stood with his arms crossed, resolutely silent.

"She is a girl," said the elf, "dark hair, light skin. Slender."

Shravir showed no emotion, but inside he grew uneasy. *Probably a coincidence.*

"She bears the mark of the enchanter," said the cat. Though he spoke quietly, the cat's words echoed loud in Shravir's ears. Years of bounty-hunting had taught him not to trust coincidences, especially those as barefaced as this. He sincerely doubted that the Resistance would think kindly of him if they discovered he had recently enslaved the very girl they were looking for. He thought of a lie and he babbled it out.

"No, no. Nobody like that. I would have seen her too, believe you me. I am sorry, but I really cannot help you. I have got commissions pouring in daily, and I am completely swamped. I just do not have the time to give your problem the attention it deserves. Now, if you will be so kind as to fix my wall…"

But he stopped as a new figure arose. His entrance was very subtle; Shravir had not noticed him until he had stepped into the light. He was tall and strong-looking, with a cloak around his shoulders and a sword belt around his waist. His hair was brown, and wavy. He looked young, and he would have been young too if it was not for his eyes, two gray pools that seemed to revolve around his deep, black irises. He took a few steps closer to Shravir, As he did so, he unsheathing his sword. It shone with a pulsing blue light that illuminated the faint light inside the hovel. He raised it, and let the tip rest on the blood-mage's shoulder.

"You lie," was all he said. There was no discernible feeling in his words; it did not sound like a question, and it did not sound like an accusation. It was simply said. His face showed no expression either, his grey eyes gazing into Shravir's green.

Terrified, Shravir weighed the odds. He realized that the person before him would be a very hard man to fool. A few more silent moments passed. Shravir took a deep breath, and plunged into the true story, fully aware of Rembas laughing into his hand.

Chapter 30

The Goddess

On the slopes of the *Mountains of Midnight*, inside Saurindon, was a monumental temple, so dark that it blended seamlessly into the black mountains against it. Its exterior bore no decoration save for one gargoyle guarding the threshold. Its ugly grimace diverted most of the Ozra, who feared the evils spirits who were whispered to lurk near the old temple. Their dread was not wholly unjustified, for when the winds swept by the temple, horrible screams and ominous moans could be heard emanating from the surrounding mountains and foot hills.

Ozmodion had built the temple with the intention of keeping his minions away. The temple belonged to Avria, Goddess of Death, the only being Ozmodion bent a knee to. He alone worshipped her; the Ozra was ignorantly agnostic.

Today he carried a small goat to the temple; Avria demanded blood sacrifices. He looked to the gargoyle above the entrance way. Ozmodion clicked his tongue five times. The gargoyle shuddered to life.

"Yeah?" it said irritably, as though awakened from a nap. It blinked its piggish eyes twice and registered Ozmodion. "Oh, oh!" The gargoyle bolted upright, adopting a manner of submissive obedience. "I am sorry sir, I did not know it was you, I was distracted by—"

"Enough," commanded Ozmodion, too pressed for time for groveling underlings. "Let me pass."

"Of course, right you are sir, right away." The gargoyle hastily clapped his hands. Though nothing obvious happened, Ozmodion knew that the gargoyle had just disabled the curse that would set any intruder's bones on fire. Ozmodion nodded curtly and stepped into the temple.

Despite its colossal appearance outside, the inners of the temple were dwarfed in comparison. It was a circular room, the center of which was filled by a stone altar and a lone torch. Ozmodion chuckled to himself. Of the many reasons he revered Avria, her need of no luxuries was very prominent. Many of her fellow gods demanded all kinds of trophies in their temples. Avria wanted nothing but the necessities.

Ozmodion set the goat on to the altar. He pulled a dagger from the folds of his robes and began the chant of the sacrificial ritual. His voice started low, but grew in tempo and volume as the chant progressed. As he reached the crescendo, he slid his dagger across the goat's neck, letting the blood fall to the rock.

Ozmodion stood and wiped the blade, when he looked up again, he saw that the goat had disappeared and that Avria stood in its place. She wore a simple black gown and had let her black hair fall loose. As she stepped from the altar, she whispered, "Hello, my Ciroth."

Ozmodion bowed lowly as he took her hand and brought it under the shade of his hood. He then straightened and released it. The sorcerer towered over the goddess, though he still felt very small in her presence.

Avria's eyes suddenly narrowed. "You are uneasy my son. Why?"

Ozmodion hissed lowly. "I find myself unworthy to bother you with my troubles."

The goddess trilled and smiled. "You have no secrets from me."

Ozmodion bowed his head respectfully. He snapped his fingers twice and two seats materialized instantly. Avria said her thanks and took one as Ozmodion positioned his to be across from her.

"You have captured Gwalin, I see," said Avria, her black eyes boring through the sorcerer.

"As per you request, your Esteemed," he replied.

"Have you, too, prepared the potion?"

"It will be ready by the new moon. Why, though, would I take it?"

The goddess laughed again. "It is just a safeguard, Ciroth. Surely you want to leave nothing to chance?"

Ozmodion inclined his head to agree, and yet he still felt ill at ease. "Still…please tell me. Am I to be thwarted once more?"

Avria sighed tiredly. "Alas, but the future is not mine to see. My brother Vundin alone among us may see what is to come."

The warlock heard something in her voice that he had never noticed before. It was a concealed emotion. Whether it masked malice, joy, or sorrow, he was not sure, but he knew that she was keeping something from him.

"Avria,' he said, using her true name to get her attention. It produced the desired effect. She locked her eyes on him intensely, her face quite focused. "I must know. Does the Resistance have the means to bring me down? Am I to die once more?"

The goddess weighed the question before answering. "You speak of death with fear. Surely you would not fear the one thing that would bring you home to me?"

Ozmodion sighed. "Yes, yes, prepared I am for death. Still, I would rather it be postponed. I have still much to do in this life before I pass to the next. I must know: am I thwarted?"

Avria rose from her seat. "Your enemies are gathered and are nigh upon you. Whether you shall thrive or fall is up to you. The future is not set; you write it as we speak. Still, whatever is to come, you will need to prepare the Ozra for a mighty war. Have you set out the recruiting satyr?"

"He rides to Arvya now."

"May he be swift. You shall have dire need of spell casters before the end."

She turned and stepped back on to the black altar. She raised her hands to ascend when she said in parting, "Forget not Ciroth; if you die, so too will all the magic of the world."

Black flames began to lick at the hems of her dress and thick, violet plumes of smoke now obstructed her face. The sickly fire rose higher and eventually consumed her wholly. There was a flicker in the center. Soon the flames shrank and dwindled. Once they had died down completely, Ozmodion saw that he was now alone in the temple.

With the goddess gone, his humility quickly drained and his resolute aura of power grew in size. He clapped his hands thrice and a black nexus formed in the temple. A black shape could be seen as the vortex grew.

Finally, Vaeirnïr Bloodshedder stepped forth from the black nexus, seeming shaken, drawn, and frail. He collapsed to the ground and breathed heavily, mumbling incoherently. Once the dragon was clear, Ozmodion clapped his hands and the black portal dissipated into nothingness.

"I trust that I find you a new general?" asked the sorcerer icily.

A groan, and then the black dragon replied weakly, "Completely, my lord."

Ozmodion chuckled, and turned to leave the temple. "Then come. We have a war to prepare for."

Vaeirnïr sighed, and strained every muscle as he rose from the floor. He stretched his long neck and his colossal wings before he limped forlornly after his master.

Chapter 31

The Liberation

S*uperb! Superb!" exclaimed Anaximander.* "This omelet is quite possibly the most wonderful thing e'er I have tasted!"

Gwen scrubbed at the pan in the sink. "I'm glad." She said in frustration. The remnants of egg were clung purposefully to the metal, and, despite her vigorous efforts, they did not yield.

It was a grayish morning, as the gap in the boughs high above revealed. Gwen was sure it was raining, but the lofty branches shielded the cottage from any weather. The chill air of the forest was all that was felt.

A week now Anaximander had been her master. A week now had she been a slave. A week now she had left behind her old life, which was rapidly fading from her memory. The more she tried to retain it, the more it slipped through her fingers. Flashes of days gone by occasionally sprang to mind, but they left her as quickly as they came. She now glanced at the pinkish mark on her palm with confused interest, certain it was a clue to her past, but unable to grasp any recognition.

"Mm! Mm! Gwen, you are a queen at that stove," called Anaximander from the dining room, breaking her meditation. "Blessed I was the day Shravir brought you to me! I have not had food so good since my dear Gram died. Oh, me, such wonderfully blissful memories. Now, her cobbler would bring old Blackheart to his knees. She had a knack for using only the most ripe of her homegrown peaches. How she did it, I will never know. Saints would kill for her recipes I am sure."

"I'm sure," Gwen repeated, listening only half-heartedly, her interest still focused on the mark.

"Yes, yes. Well, would you be a dear and top off this coffee?"

Gwen sighed and went to get the pot, leaving the stubborn pan in the sink. As she reached for the coffee, she noticed some movements in the trees beyond the cottage. Perhaps the window was just dirty; she hadn't been able to get to it yet, as Anaximander's breakfast was always such a time-taxing chore. She shrugged, and carried the pot to the dining room.

Anaximander had not been boasting when he claimed his family was wealthy. If the looks of the dining room were anything to go by, Gwen would have to say that the gnome had been dangerously modest. A crystal chandelier was suspended over the mahogany table, lighting the room with countless candles. There was an impressive display of flowers in the center of the table, placed in an ancient vase, its surfaced lined with thousands of fine lines, splitting from each other like forks in a river. Each of the ten chairs was handcrafted from the finest oak and beautiful designs had been inlaid in all. The plates were all very fine porcelain, and the silver gleamed with value.

Anaximander sat at the head of the table, his wide girth keeping him from pushing his chair in. The white napkin that he had tucked into his shirt's collar was stained with egg and bacon grease, which somehow diminished the overall grandeur of the room. Instead of a regal master of the home, there was only what seemed to be a very old toddler at breakfast. He held up his mug and smiled in a feral way. Gwen inwardly sighed, then walked to him and filled his cup.

"That will do, that will do," he said as the coffee reached the brim of the mug. "Ah, yes, I really should try to cut back to three cups at breakfast, but old habits die hard."

Suddenly, there was a loud clang outside. Gwen started, but the old gnome only chuckled.

"Not a worry, not a worry. It is probably just some squirrel trying to get into the garden, they do love those acorns from that old tree."

Far from convinced, Gwen returned to the kitchen to battle the pan, this time armed with a wire brush. As she began to scrub, a small butterfly alighted on her hand. Its wings were a fiery orange, with two, deep, black spots in the center of each wing. Gwen set down the brush to see where it might've come from. She saw that she had left the door from the garden to the kitchen cracked slightly. She walked, slowly, to the door, and waved the butterfly outside. However, as soon as it took off from her hand, it turned around and flitted back into the house.

Gwen sighed, too busy with her chores to be perturbed. She turned back to face the pan in the sink. As she picked up the wire brush and began scrubbing once more, she noticed that the dried yolk was slowly changing color, browning as though it was still over the stove. Puzzled, Gwen continued cleaning, but found that the dried yolk was spreading, reclaiming the parts of the pan that it had surrendered to the brush.

Gwen now looked over her shoulder with her brow furrowed. She saw the butterfly fluttering right behind her. Gwen's frown deepened, shook her head, and faced the sink again. She gasped. The brown remnants were now beginning to bubble and grow in volume. It hissed, it popped, it squelched, and changed from brown to black to green.

"Gwen," called the haughty master from the dining room, "when you are done with that batch of dishes, I have finished with these out here. I am going upstairs to have a bit of a lie-down; my belly's full and my head is drowsy."

Gwen opened her mouth to say something but was interrupted from a particularly loud crack from the boiling goo in the pan.

The butterfly returned, and now landed on the counter, shaking its head. Gwen blinked, but as she took a second look, she was sure the butterfly was shaking its head back and forth. Then, to her further surprise and frightened shock, she heard a small voice said, "What, Miss Enchantress, you do not recognize shifting anymore? Tsk, that cat cannot have taught you very well. Now, if you would be so kind as to step back? I will need room."

Stunned, Gwen obeyed the butterfly's instruction without thought. She watched as its features quickly blurred and changed. In a moment, the butterfly had become a man with flaming red hair and rich brown eyes. He was smiling, a smile that Gwen found strangely familiar, but, like all her vague memories, she could not hold onto it long enough to place it.

The redheaded man looked about the kitchen, nodding his head in satisfaction. "Not bad, not bad at all. Surely it beats months and months on the road. I could see myself settling in a place like this. I do not know so much about the décor, but, you know, a little paint, some—"

"Flame!" called another tiny voice, this one sounding as though it was just outside the opened window, "Stow your bloody cheek! Is that wrinkled shortling around?"

The redheaded man sighed, his expression souring as he replied. "Not at the moment, no."

"Well let us in then! We do not have all day. That old fool might have some delayed magical defenses."

The redheaded man scoffed, and mumbled under his breath as he went to the door. "Such foresight, Beast. Your vigilance is an example to us all."

He opened the door that led to the garden beyond. As he did, a strong breeze pushed its way passed him. Gwen waited for someone to come in, but the redheaded man closed the door as soon as the gust ceased. Gwen began to question him, but was cut off as five figures suddenly materialized in the kitchen. One was a cat, black save for the occasional white patch. Another was a man with wild brown hair wearing a brown tunic with leggings to match. The third was a tall man, with black hair and striking features. He seemed uneasy, as though he wished to be anywhere else right now. The fourth was a man with horns and what seemed to be the legs of a stag. He hung a satchel over his shoulder and seemed a bit shaken, but not at all as uncomfortable as the dark, handsome man. The last figure was surely the most subtly impressive. He too was tall, with brown hair, and a cloak worn over his tunic. He had a sword strapped around his waist, which alarmed Gwen slightly. She thought perhaps they were a group of bandits.

"Ugh," shuddered the man with stag legs. "That was undoubtedly the worst sensation I have ever felt."

The redheaded man arched an eyebrow. "What, the shifting?"

"Yes," said the cat. Gwen's jaw dropped. "At least with magical transformation, the change is instantaneous. But with shifting? No, got to be slow about it, give an uncertain sense of indefiniteness."

The man with the wild brown hair snorted. "Ah, you are not being fair. It is different when you shift into something definite. Gases are always a bit more chaotic."

"Well, never again," said the stag-man, who quickly regained his composure. He reached into his satchel and extricated a pipe. He then reached again to pull out some tobacco, which he shoved into the pipe. He did not light it, but simply stuck the stem firmly into his mouth as he looked to Gwen with his royally blue eyes. "Hello there, Gwen! Ran off, did you?" He looked over at the cat, and then the man with the wild brown hair, nodding sadly as he said, "Yes, I have been tempted once or twice myself."

"Moron," muttered the cat lowly.

When Gwen showed no recognition of the man with stag legs, the redheaded man asked, "You do not remember?"

Gwen turned to look at him, and slowly shook her head.

"Hmph," grunted the cat. "That will be the blood-enslavement then. You did a real number on her, Shravir, if she is so enchanted she cannot remember *him*."

He jerked his head towards the man with stag legs, who shrugged and reached into his bag to produce a handful of catnip. With a look of indifference, he tossed it out the window. The cat raised his nose in the air, gasped, and made a mad dash onto the counter and out the window after the plant. The man with stag legs smiled smugly.

"All right then, Eion, how do you want to go about this?" asked the redhead.

The man with the brown hair and the sword stepped forth, his eyes cast down. "You and Beast bring down the gnome. We will see if we can persuade him to break the bond."

The redheaded man and the man with the wild brown hair nodded and left the kitchen to, as Gwen assumed, find Anaximander. The urge rose in her, and she obeyed it.

"Um, pardon me, but my master does not like to be disturbed during his naps!" she called to the two men."

Behind her, there was a small laugh. She turned. The man with the brown hair was looking at her now. His eyes were misty blue-grey, and the irises seemed to revolve around his deep pupils.

"Peace, peace," he said softly. Though his words were simple, they impacted Gwen strangely. It was not like an order issued by Anaximander, but still Gwen found herself obeying him. At his words, her anxiety of the last few minutes was quelled.

There was a scratching sound from outside. The man with stag legs smiled wider and walked to the door, his hooves clip-clopping loudly on the kitchen floor. He turned the knob and pulled the door inward enough to allow the cat saunter in quickly, with the catnip dangling from his mouth. The stag-man shook his head and closed the door.

Suddenly, a loud scream sounded from somewhere in the house, and shouts of, "Unhand me, you ruffians! You hooligans, I will have your hides!" quickly ensued. Moments later, the two men returned, each holding on tightly to Anaximander's arms. He was in a nightgown, wool socks, and a night cap. He looked distraught and embarrassed, which Gwen could not fault him for. When the old gnome saw the uncomfortable handsome man, his face became purple and his rage increased tenfold.

"You! What are *you* doing here!" he roared.

The man looked utterly pained as he mumbled, "Hello, Anaximander."

"Hello! *Hello*? I am dragged from my bed to find you and a host of cretins in my home, and all you have to say is *hello?*"

"'Cretins'?" asked the man with the stag legs. He chuckled quietly and shook his head. "Hardly. They barely fit the bill of 'soldiers'."

The man with the sword stepped forth. He motioned for the two men to release the gnome, which they promptly did. "Well met, Anaximander," said he as he extended his hand. Anaximander did no take it. Unfazed, the man continued. "I am Eion Shifter of the Resistance, and we have—"

"The Resistance?!" interrupted Anaximander, thoroughly perplexed now. "What has the Resistance to do with me? I cannot serve you! I am an old man!"

The man called Eion shook his head. "No, no, you do not understand. We have come to take—"

"Surely you cannot think me a supporter of the Blackheart? Because I am not! Such accusations, I have never been more insulted."

Eion sighed. "No, no one was accusing you. I have been trying to—"

"To think I would live to see the day that the Old War would rise once more and I would be thrown into the mix. Oh, woe! My poor heart." Anaximander clutched his chest. "If you vandals do not leave my home right this instant, I will knock your heads in and use you skulls as flower pots!"

Eion seemed to have had enough, for he unsheathed his sword. It glowed pale blue and seemed to drain the color out of everything around it. Eion let the tip rest on the old gnome's shoulder, smiling slightly.

"I am afraid time is of the essence now, and I have not the energy to waste to argue with an arrogant, crooked runt like yourself. We have come for the liberation of Gwen Talbot, the third Iltari."

Gwen wrinkled her brow at the surname and the title "Iltari", but Anaximander's eyes bulged from his sockets, aghast.

"An-an Iltari?" he stuttered weakly. "B-but, I had n-no way of kn-kn-knowing she was an Il-Iltari."

"Unwittingly or not," responded Eion indifferently, "you did. And that demands immediate liberation."

Anaximander was about to nod, when he froze, furrowed his brow, and slowly asked, "Or what?"

Eion smiled dangerously. "Or suffer the displeasure of the Resistance."

Again, the old gnome asserted himself. "Are you threatening me sir?"

"It would appear so, yes."

"No one threatens Anaximander DoVal've! You sad renegades do not frighten me! Begone, or suffer *my* displeasure!"

Eion shook his head and exhaled loudly. He then looked up and said, "Why don't they listen? Why do they never listen? Do they just not hear me?"

He then lowered his sword and walked to the window. He stuck his head through the threshold and whistled three times. He then walked to stand next the stag-man, still shaking his head tiredly.

The whoosh of rushing air was heard outside, followed by a heavy thud. Then, a giant, reptilian head snaked its way through the window. It had orange scales, and pale green eyes. It mouth was filled with many, sharp, ivory white teeth. Smoke wafted through its nostrils. Upon seeing it, Anaximander let out a high-pitched and very prolonged scream.

"Ahhhhh! A dragon! You brought a dragon? Gods help me. Gods help me!"

"Everyone still waiting in the woods, Brunariun?" asked the redheaded man, taking no notice of the yelling.

The dragon nodded, and said, in what sounded to be a female voice, "But we are getting hungry. I myself am half starved." She smiled, revealing her impressive array of teeth.

"Don't eat me! Don't eat me!" cried Anaximander, who seemed to be on the verge of tears now.

The dragon cocked her head. "*This* is the sod that enslaved her?"

"Commissioned me, uh-huh," nodded the tall, handsome man glumly.

The dragon shook her head sympathetically. Then she brightened and said, "Mind you, I am dead hungry. Do you think I *could* eat him once you break the bond?"

Eion shook his head firmly. "No, Brunariun, you will have to make do for a while longer."

Brunariun sighed, releasing a stream of flame from her opened maw. The fire charred the wall opposite of the window. Anaximander screamed once more.

"Drat," said Brunariun. "Sorry about that."

The man with stag legs sniggered, but refrained from saying anything.

Eion sighed and ran his hands against his face. Then he turned to Anaximander. "Now, good sir, we wish to break the blood-bonds now. After the ritual you shall never hear from us again. What say you?"

Anaximander took a deep breath, his screaming had left him wheezing, and said in a more controlled tone, "No, I am afraid not. Gwen is a superb servant and I really do not think I could manage without her."

Eion nodded as though he had expected the reply. He then shrugged, and turned around as if he were going to leave. But before he did, he said, "All right then, Brunariun, I suppose you can eat him now."

Anaximander's eyes bulged and he began to writhe around in the grip of Flame and Beast. Brunariun grinned widely, and then opened her jaws as she turned to face the panicked gnome. Her mouth was inches from his face, when Anaximander screamed once more.

"Mercy! Mercy! I yeald. Take her and be gone!"

Eion turned on his heel, smiling broadly. "You heard the man, Shravir. Set to work."

The handsome man nodded slightly, and unsheathed a jeweled dagger. He then raised his right palm in Gwen's direction. He had a silvery mark etched into his hand, but before Gwen could get a closer look, he quickly pronounced a word that she didn't understand. Then the mark began to glow with a bright light, and the room was lost from Gwen's mind.

☐

When she awoke, she found that she was on the floor, sitting dizzily. Her vision was blurry, but it did not remain so; the world quickly slipped back into focus, and Gwen found that a myriad of now familiar faces surrounded her. There was Flame and there was Beast, both smiling warmly. Brunariun had snaked her head in further and was growling with affection. Curthlond purred loudly beside Rembas' hooves, and eyed her genially.

And there, too, was Eion, who grinned boyishly as he said, "Welcome back, young one."

Gwen returned their smiles and nodded. She tried to stand up, but found that her legs were weak. She did not mind though; her head was now flooding with the memories that she thought she had lost forever.

Eion straightened and then asked, "Almost finished, Shravir?"

A rough voice replied. "Yeah, just a few Master Links to break, and we will be done."

Gwen craned her neck to see the speaker, but Flame was blocking her view. He stepped aside to reveal the handsome man examining a cut on Anaximander's forearm. Anaximander looked very pale; whether it was from his new wound or having come so close to being eaten by a dragon, none could say. He muttered lowly to himself and he started at the smallest sound. Gwen smiled wryly; the regal master was diminished.

The handsome man now nodded in satisfaction, and he muttered a quick incantation. In moments, the cut on Anaximander's arm mended. The man then stood up, clapped his hands, and bowed.

"There," said he, "the ritual is complete. She is absolutely free.

Gwen narrowed her eyes in hate; she now knew that this was the blood-mage who enslaved her. She raised her right palm, called on the magic, and shouted words she now remembered from the book.

Five bolts of lightning erupted from the five points of the Vawn, all traveling directly towards the blood-mage. His eyes widened in fear; he would not have time to react. Seconds before the lightning struck his heart, though, someone else yelled a spell.

As soon as the last syllable escaped the speaker's lips, the bolts dwindled and vanished, leaving the handsome blood-mage unscathed.

Gwen looked from side to side, trying to find the spell caster. Soon, her anger was too great, and she stood up and made a dash towards the blood-mage to strike him, but Flame and Beast quickly restrained her.

"Peace, Gwen! Peace!" said Beast, struggling to hold on to the enraged girl. "You would still be enslaved without him!"

"I don't care!" she cried, trying to fight them off. "I don't *care!*"

The kitchen door opened again, and Tirmal, Varez, Ryan, Lea, Anthony, Caitlyn, and Tyler all entered, eyes wide. Quickly assessing the scenario, Tirmal raised his staff and pointed it at Gwen as he roared an incantation.

Orange light filled the room. When it passed, Gwen stood immobilized, her face frozen with a look of utter loathing.

Only now did the blood-mage dare to take a step closer to her. "Gwen," he said, his rough voice sounding suddenly soft, "I cannot blame you for hating me. I could apologize infinitely, and still you would not forgive me. I traded your life for a couple of emeralds, and trust me when I say I feel naught but shame for it. Times are hard in this forest, and one must fight to survive. I know this doesn't justify it, but now you at least know my reasons. I vow now, though, that I shall forever turn my back on blood-magery; never again shall one be enslaved by my hand."

As he said these words, he raised his right palm. Gwen now recognized the mark upon it as the Grarn. As the mage made his vow, the silvery mark gradually faded, until Gwen could hardly see it. Soon, it had completely disappeared, leaving behind a clean palm. The man then smiled, bowing his head in reverence.

Tirmal spoke a syllable, and Gwen felt herself flex her fingers as the elf's enchantment lifted. Her face softened, and she stared at the man before her. She was not sure what had just happened, but she had a good guess; the man had just forsaken his magic powers to prove himself.

"It was Shravir, wasn't it?" she asked. He raised his head now, towering over her by a good foot, and smiled as he nodded. "You didn't have to do that."

Shravir shrugged. "I have been meaning to for some time. I thank you for giving me a reason."

Gwen wasn't quite sure how to respond to this. All she could do was smile sincerely.

Eion cleared his throat. "It is late. The Resistance will be expecting us. We must begin our return." He turned to face the gnome, who was still crouched on the ground, mumbling and muttering lowly.

"Farewell, Anaximander."

Anaximander did not reply, nor did he even seem aware that there were others in his Kitchen. Eion turned to Flame, and together they laughed. The small party began to file out of the house until Gwen and Eion were the only ones left. Eion appraised her rags, and quickly shifted them into a tunic and a traveling cloak. Gwen said her thanks, and exited the kitchen. Breathing easy for the first time in days, Eion followed.

☐

"I'm really surprised with you, Shravir," Rembas stated frankly as they walked from the cottage. "The bounty-hunter I knew would not have given up his livelihood for a stranger."

"I think it showed good character," said Curthlond grandly, weaving in between Gwen's legs playfully.

"Or idiocy," the faun retorted with a shrug, unconvinced. "The two have many similar attributes."

As they left the clearing behind, entering the green fringe of trees surrounding the cottage, Eion turned to shake Shravir's hand. "Thank you Shravir. I think an apology is in order. We should not have been so cruel earlier. Is there any way we can make it up to you?"

Shravir laughed. "Let me come with you. I have nothing to go home to now; I have turned my back on my career. I have helped the Resistance once. Perhaps I can do it once more in battle."

Eion grinned widely. "We would be honored to fight beside you."

"Wonderful. I wonder, could I return home once more to gather a few things?"

"I will fly you there personally."

Shravir's smile faltered. "What?"

☐

"You are mad! You are completely mad!" screamed the mouse in the talons of the hawk.

The hawk clicked its beak happily. "We cannot waste any time, Shravir. Besides, there is no joy like flying."

"Ha! Then let me be the hawk and you can dangle from my feet!"

They were soaring over the green roof of Ÿalnz Dàr, and Eion could sense that they would be close to Shravir's hovel by now. His hawk eyes suddenly spotted the old shack, and he dove into a vertical fall to Shravir's great discontent.

"Now really Shravir, take a breath," instructed Eion, "You will pass out if you keep screaming like that."

Eion pulled up at the last moment, and in seconds the mouse and hawk were gone. In there place stood a very collected Eion, and a very shaken Shravir. The ex-blood-mage's hair was wildly tangled, and his breathing was deep and ragged.

"You are a sick man, Eion Shifter. Never again will I leave the ground. *Never.*'

The shifter chuckled, looking forward to the return flight.

The two walked to the door and stepped inside the hovel. Eion took a seat on the torn and stained sofa as Shravir laid out a handkerchief and place sundry items upon it, mumbling to himself as he did so.

Eion looked about the hovel with distaste. Certainly he had seen worse in his travel, but he could not imagine calling a place like this home. Out of the corned of his eye, he saw a chest tucked under a worktable littered with blood-magery tools. Eion felt a pulse with in it, a strong magical pulse. Curious, he turned to Shravir.

"What is in that chest, I wonder?"

Without looking up, Shravir replied, "I am not sure. I found it in the Caves of Illothin and I have not been able to open it."

Eion's jaw dropped, the possible quirk of fate stunning him. He rushed to the table, pulled the trunk out from under it, and examined it. Runes had been carved into it, but the wood was so worn and dusty, Eion couldn't make out the lines, but he had a good guess of what they might say.

"*Magicbane*" he said in elvish.

In a matter of moments, the keyhole glowed from the inside, and the wood hissed with steam. Shravir turned from his handkerchief, gasped, and cried out something that Eion did not hear, his attention consumed by the chest. Its hinges cracked loudly, and the lid split jaggedly. Then, all at once, the magic stopped, and the ruined chest sat as quiet as it had been seconds before.

Eion shifted a dagger, and pried the lid off. Gripping the sides of the box, Eion gasped. Inside the chest was a golden shield, wrought with green emeralds shaped like crescent moons, and the crest of Gorothar had been inlaid with silver in the center. With shaking hands, Eion extracted the famed weapon.

"*The Shield of Gorothar*." Shravir whispered.

"The Shield of Gorothar," Eion repeated, nodding.

"So *that is* why you were in the Caves. I did find it peculiar that a band of travelers would just be vacationing in those black caverns. Countless explorers have looked for that shield."

A lull followed. Eion cleared his throat. "Have you everything you need?'

Shravir turned back to his handkerchief and quickly looked it over. He smiled quickly, and tied the bandana shut. "I am ready when you are."

Eion nodded and lashed the shield onto his back. "If you wish it, I can shift your home so no one else will use it in your absence. Turn it into a boulder, perhaps."

Shravir shook his head. "I do not mean to come back to this place ever again. I only hope that someone will raze it to the ground."

Eion smiled, and raised both of his hands above his head. He concentrated hard on the cottage's roof and wall, and slowly he broke the bonds holding the structure together. Cracks stemmed across the interior. The walls groaned and creaked and eventually swayed to and fro. The far wall broke in half, and the ceiling plummeted toward them. Eion quickly focused his energies on the collapsing roof; it quickly lost substance and dissipated into thin air.

The walls fell to powder, and the broken furniture wilted and spilled its contents. The papers on the worktable ignited and shriveled into ash. A loud crash was heard as the cracked mirror fell to the ground and splintered into thousands of tiny shards.

With one final effort, Eion broke everything into dust, leaving the place to absolute ruin. No one would have known that in this place a cottage had once stood.

Shravir blinked, and then a grin quickly split his face. "Thank you, Eion."

Eion nodded. He returned Shravir's grin, and quickly shifted into the great hawk once more. Shravir sighed sadly, and then submitted to being changed into the mouse for a second time. Eion gathered him in his talons, flapped his wings forcefully, and took to the skies.

Chapter 32

The Gathering

*L**ord Fairskin stared in awe*** as Eion presented him the shield. He was always an elf of faith, but to see another of Vundin's prophecies come true astounded him greatly. He had lived to hear the foretelling of twenty, and fifteen of them had now been fulfilled.

Eion handed the shield to the Elf Lord, smiling slightly. Lord Fairskin's joy of seeing the shield was greater than his curiosity as to why the hunting party was late. When they had all returned to the Five Clearings, they were assailed with greetings and wailings and questions and demands. The resistance was surprised to see the arrival of two newcomers, but Rembas and Shravir would be welcomed once Eion explained that they had helped in the retrieval of the Shield of Gorothar. Also, if Shravir was lucky, The Resistance would never need know about Gwen's temporary enslavement, nor that the former blood-mage who performed the ritual now traveled with them as a comrade-in-arms.

"Fascinating," whispered Lord Fairskin, examining the shield with expert scrutiny. "'Twas nigh three thousands years since last this shield saw daylight. Odin of Arconia once bore this, and Gorothar the Great before him."

Eion frowned. There was a strange gleam in the old elf's eye, one that greatly resembled greed. Though as quickly as it had come, it left when Lord Fairskin handed the shield back to Eion, who took it and lashed it to his back.

"Hope is restored with your return, Eion," said the Elf Lord. He put his free hand on Eion shoulder, the other grasping his staff for support. He smiled. "We were beginning to worry."

Eion nodded and attempted to return his smile. He failed, managing only a weak laugh. He knew that the old elf suspected something had gone wrong during the quest, though he was too noble to come out and ask. The shifter avoided Lord Fairskin's gaze as he replied, "There was no need."

A chuckle, and the Lord Fairskin said, "I suppose not."

The guilt was strangling Eion; Lord Fairskin was like a father to him, and he had never kept a secret from him. He changed the subject.

"So what now? We have fulfilled the terms of the prophecy; are we ready to make for the Gap now?"

Lord Fairskin sighed deeply, then, "The decision will be made tonight. We make for the Perished Pool at dusk." Eion stifled a gasp at the mention of the place. "Think not of it now. You are weary, and you will need rest if we are to march."

It was Eion's turn to sigh, but he did not protest. He clasped the Elf Lord's shoulder and set out for his tent.

◻

"*This* is the Resistance?" Rembas asked with slight distaste as he looked upon the camp in the Second Clearing. "I fail to see why Ozmodion's so fussed."

Gwen frowned. They had caught the soldiers in what seemed a bad time. The encampment was in disarray, with weapons, uniforms, and sundry assortments strewn across the ground. A foul reek, presumably from some rotting meat that had been left out, assailed her nose, making her eyes stream with water. The soldiers themselves did not seem like soldiers at all, but rather a party of maids hurrying to clean the mess, with shields instead of dust pans and tritons instead of rakes. Fletch ran by quickly, and Gwen stopped him to ask what had happened.

"We had been preparing to leave, but when your party had not returned, we quickly mobilized to search for you. Unluckily, some orders were crisscrossed, and pandemonium ensued." He gestured around the camp with a cheerless sigh. Then he nodded in parting, and quickly set off again.

"Me old dad used to say 'chaos is the one thing that makes sense'," said Shravir, who seemed not the least bit perturbed by not being greeted by Fletch, though he had mumbled something about manners as the shifter had marched off.

"Humph, chaos indeed," sniffed Curthlond, as he began to bathe himself. "You will have your fill of chaos long before this adventure is up."

"You missed a spot," Rembas said with a wink.

The cat who was not a cat scowled as best as a non-cat can and resumed licking, which was now accompanied with many grumblings.

They had settled in a long while ago. Gwen returned her pack to her tent, taking no heed of the look of astonishment that Kendal had given her. She set down her sword, her quiver, and her bow, not wishing to be burdened with the weapons of war.

An additional tent had been erected for Shravir's and Rembas' use. Only Shravir had any complaints, which the faun had received with his indifferent chuckle. He refused, though, to part with his satchel, and Gwen had begun to expect that it held more than Rembas let on. Gwen did not pester him with questions, though; he wouldn't answer them even if she asked.

Shravir arched his back in a stretch. "So...what now?"

Gwen shrugged as she walked to a tree stump and sat on it. "I'm not sure. I think the leaders are going to decide whether or not we march to the Ozra Gap."

Shravir laughed harshly. "I cannot see an alternative. You are too steeped in blood to turn back."

Curthlond ceased bathing himself and opened his mouth to say something, but was cut short as a shower of water rained down upon him, drenching him to the skin. Stunned, he turned to face Rembas, who was holding an empty bucket. He shrugged, and set it down next to the fire pit where he had found it. "You still didnt get that spot. Right behind your ears. I thought I would save you some time."

Curthlond growled, shivering violently with cold. "*You*...ooh, if I had—"

"Opposable thumbs?" Rembas offered, as he waved his in a cheery fashion. "Yup, I suspect you would be something then."

Curthlond hissed and pounced on Rembas, who sidestepped the assault, sending the bedraggled cat into the soot of the fire pit. Curthlond blinked twice, sneezed, and then pathetically sauntered away. Rembas smiled. "Ashes to ashes—"

"Rembas, I swear, if you want to keep your tongue, you will refrain from finishing that sentence," Curthlond snapped, without turning back. Rembas shrugged, and extracted his pan flute from his satchel. He pressed the instrument to his lips and played a merry tune.

Gwen laughed, as did Shravir. Gwen had never heard the former blood-mage laugh, and the change it brought about in his face was startling. All his worries seemed to have faded away, and he seemed inestimably younger. His eyes burned with a youthful energy that seemed to make his whole face glow.

They were still giggling when Eion approached them both, his head cocked and his mouth turned down in a questioning frown. Suppressing the last of their chuckles, they greeted the shifter. Rembas either hadn't noticed Eion or had chosen to ignore him, as he continued to play his flute without pause.

"We will be meeting with Nimé tonight," Eion said in response to their greeting, as he shifted himself a chair by a nearby boulder. He took a seat and propped his legs up on top on the bucket Rembas had so recently used.

This caught the faun's attention. He hit a very sour note, causing Eion, Gwen, and Shravir to all flinch and cover their ears. Rembas nearly dropped his instrument, but recovered as he stammered, "N-N-Nimé? *The* Nimé?" he quivered as he returned the pan flute to his satchel, and extracted his pipe to presumably steady his nerves. After he had lit the tobacco and had placed the stem in his mouth, he said steadily, "She hasn't shown herself to anyone but the dryads and naiads for two centuries now. Even the Vigilant Sprites have not caught a glimpse of her. It is said that she manifests herself in the shape of a great oak tree in the heart of the forest, and all who look upon it babble nonsense for the next moon cycle. *Why* does she come to your meeting?"

Eion smiled grimly. "She is providing safe passage for us to the Ozra Gap." He left it at that. Gwen knew Eion well enough to know that asking him to elaborate was useless. She opened her mouth to say something, but was cut off by Rembas as he laughed bitterly.

"Nymph's are lovers of peace. Nimé has no interest in this war," the faun stated confidently.

Eion raised an eyebrow. "Rembas, *of course* she has an interest in this war. Dryads are dying as the Ozra burn and cut down the trees of Ÿalnz Dàr that border Saurindon. Shadows are taking hold of the wood, and Nimé would dearly love to be rid of Ozmodion's malignancy. *All* the demi-gods are taking sides; to do otherwise is to face annihilation. Nimé is charged with the protection of this forest, and she knows that she must place her hope in the Resistance. Times are changing, Master Faun. I suggest you embrace it."

"Do not patronize me, *boy*," Rembas hissed, angry now. "I was here when Dairozn marched his Black Force into these woods. I saw Fleni, the previous nymph of Ÿalnz Dàr, die as she battled the deadly necromancer. Her sacrifice is still sung of in the highest courts in the Magic Realm. I watched as the giants rent Dairozn in two out of vengeance and grief. I watched the Black Force flee. I saw the tears shed for the fallen nymph. I saw the burst of light as Nimé was sent from the Divine World to watch over the forest. I listened as she promised to keep this place safe for eternity. I saw her eyes burn with resolution and eternal life. I watched her walk into the wood, parting the darkness as she went. I heard the songs that the satyrs sang, and I watched the centaurs dance in rapture. Do not think to tell me that times change, you cheeky tripe; I have seen more than you know."

Gwen gazed at Rembas, surprised by his sudden change. She had never seen the faun so angry, his wry, mellow exterior seeming to permeate his whole being. Apparently, this was not the case. Rembas' eyes were narrowed in contempt as he fixed his stare on Eion dangerously. He chewed on the stem of his pipe, too upset to notice. Gwen would have warned him about it, but his glare seemed so menacing that she thought it best to remain quiet.

Eion returned the fomariun's stare, though he was no where near matching the intensity. His blue-grey eyes were hard, and yet they betrayed no emotion. Slowly, his blank look changed as his mouth curved into a half smile. He extended his hand to the faun, and said, "I apologize, Rembas. I did not mean to demean anyone. The fault was mine."

Rembas' look softened, and then he took out his pipe and tapped it over the shifter's outstretched hand. Eion's smile faded as he looked at the ashes that now lay in his palm. He blinked, and then looked back up at the faun, who appeared very pleased with himself.

"Of course it was," he replied simply, then returned the pipe to his satchel.

"Do the world a favor and kill him now, Eion," Curthlond pleaded as he made his way back to the small circle. He was now impeccably clean and dry once more. If Rembas was surprised by this, he certainly didn't let it show on his face.

"Harsh," was all he said.

The cat scowled, but before he could retort, Eion cut him off.

"As I was saying, Nimé will be coming tonight. I ask you all to be present." He turned back to Rembas as he stood from his seat, brushing the ashes clean of his hand. "Rembas, I trust you know the way to the Perished Pool?"

Rembas looked up from his satchel, which he now tossed over his shoulder. He pushed the hair out of his eyes and his face split into a very wide grin.

"Getting a little dark now, isn't she?" he asked knowingly.

Eion frowned and didn't reply. He instead repeated his question. "Do you know the way?"

The faun shrugged, replacing his grin with a look of indifference. "All ways lead there, don't they?"

Eion's let out a loud sigh, and his brow furrowed into a scowl. Irritated, he asked one more time, his tone a tone of warning. "Do you know the way?"

Rembas rolled his eyes and made a tut of reproach. "Yeah, yeah, mellow out, Chuckles. This whole moody streak is really starting to get me down." He waved, and turned to set out into the camp.

☐

The sunset that evening seemed innocent enough. There were no clouds in the sky, and the sun simply seemed to have faded, rather than lighting the sky alight with its usual spectacular array of color. Yet something about it felt ominous, foreboding, as though something very solemn was fast approaching.

Incredible insight, Eion, the shifter mused silently. He made his way through the fringe of trees that surrounded the Third Clearing. He was accompanied by a very taciturn Steel, who seemed to be absorbed with his own thoughts. That suited Eion just fine; he too was in deep meditation. The two were going ahead of the others to make sure the way was secure; Eion did not wished to be hindered any longer by any disappearances.

It was long whispered throughout the forest of Ÿalnz Dàr that Nimé was ailing. Nymphs were tied directly to the Nature Goddess Shiia. When the land suffered, so too did Shiia. When Shiia suffered, so too did her nymphs. Nimé felt the suffering more than her sisters scattered across the globe. Rembas was correct in having stated she had not shown herself to anyone for over two hundred years. Disguised as the great oak tree, she lent most control of the forest to the dryads and naiads. True, this was not the first time such a hierarchy had been established, but now that Ozmodion was regaining power, Eion would've thought that Nimé would be taking control of the forest once more. It was common knowledge that Shiia favored Nimé above all the other nymphs of the Magic Realm, all due to her effectiveness to govern and her vast magical powers. Eion had never met the nymph, but had heard her character was iron-willed and unyieldingly resolute. The forest could only be governed by one with such a disposition. Though the dryads were strong with their powers combined, the forest would only respond to the power of the demi-gods.

The Perished Pool, Eion thought as he crossed into the shadows of the trees. He shuddered, imagining the evil place. Nimé was indeed disturbed if she had chosen that dark landmark as a meeting spot. Nymphs were lovers of beauty and life. The Perished Pool was a place of neither.

They walked in silence for a very long time as darkness surrounded them. The sun was almost completely down, as far as they could tell.

When they came to a place where the vines of many willows now hung above the path in such a quantity that the pair of shifters were forced to unsheathe their swords and cut their way through, Eion held up his hand and all movement stopped. He frowned when he realized that they weren't making headway; the vines regenerated as soon as they were hacked away.

"*Weeping* willows," Steel said with a shrug. A trace of a smile crossed his face briefly, but vanished before it had fully formed

Eion nodded grimly; he knew they were close to the pool now.

☐

"The Perished Pool," Curthlond scoffed, weaving in, out, over, and under the roots of trees that had surfaced through the earth. "How tragic. Why must these demi-gods be so melancholy?"

Gwen wasn't really listening; she was focusing carefully on Rembas, deathly afraid of losing him in the dark. The path they walked was littered with rocks and jagged stones, thick moss and stray leaves. The sound of footfalls echoed loudly throughout the dark forest. Shravir walked a few paces behind her, followed by the rest of The Prophesied Ten.

"Well, when endowed with divine power," Shravir replied as he scratched under his chin, "Not too many are going to be willing to criticize your style."

Rembas scoffed from the front of the party. "They only have power *in place* of style. Divinity is only the latest substitution of élan. Now, keep up; you three in the back are lagging behind."

Gwen chanced a look at the ones addressed; Kendal, Lea, and Caitlyn. The rest had taken Rembas in their stride, but the girls hadn't really warmed up to him. Also, the fact Gwen was an enchantress had disturbed them greatly. They regarded her with an awed fear. Gwen wasn't bothered by this; she had grown apart from them since their arrogance shown at the Mountain. She grinned wolfishly and raised her palm so her Vawn could be seen. She whispered, "*Litha destrisa*" and felt the surge of magic course through her arm as a brilliant flame ignited in the center of her palm. She allowed herself a giggle as she watched the three girls gasp in surprise and fright, and then she turned to look ahead once more, raising her hand high above her head to give all the benefit of the light. To her surprise, the fire began dwindle and flicker as she continued to walk.

"Ah," commented Rembas, not bothering to turn around. He hopped over a particularly hulking boulder, his satchel swinging at his side. "That will be the pool, surely. Yup, I reckon we're damn close now. Light is not welcome here. By some poetic coincidence, neither is life."

Gwen frowned and let the fire die, bringing her arm back to her side. She had to let her eyes adjust to the sudden resurgence of darkness. She struggled to hear the sounds of Rembas' hooves, her only guide now that she couldn't see. She laughed quietly when she heard the girls in the back gasp as they were enveloped by night. She realized it was cruel, and more mortal than immortal to feel the wrath she felt, but the conversation at the mountain still rung through, searing her innards with anger. She knew the feelings would come to pass, but for now, she was content to savor their fright.

They came to a copse of willows. Rembas turned sharply to the left to avoid them, leading them passed a thicket of rose bushes. Gwen frowned, but did not protest; she, after all, did not know the way to the Perished Pool. After taking a second glance, she realized she would not want to stumble about in those trees anyway; they loomed over the group like leering monsters with unpleasant looks.

"They always make these places so inaccessible," Rembas observed, as he continued to lead them along the rose bushes. "Vanity, I expect. Gods always insist their temples and places of worship meet one of three descriptions: ominous, remote, or just downright gaudy. Bloody divinity; no wonder the world's such a mess..."

Gwen did not hear anymore of his angry tirade, for she felt a chill in the wind that permeated her very bones. She shivered, and brought her thick cloak tighter around her shoulders, but to no avail; the cold bit through unyieldingly. Beside her, Curthlond was inching closer, searching for warmth. She welcomed the added insulation around her legs, but found that the cat's hair felt like shards of ice. Her teeth chattered, and her limbs shook violently

Though everyone was else was obviously suffering from the frigidity, Rembas seemed to be completely unaware of the cold. His breath was steady and calm, and he seemed to be searching for something on the right. He stopped at a small parting between the rose bushes, which were growing so high that they towered at least three feet above Shravir's head. He was the tallest in the party.

The faun exclaimed excitedly. "Aha! Here it is. Huh, roses. I forgot. I suppose she just enjoys the irony."

Gwen did not understand what Rembas meant by the dry statement, but she noticed that the roses on the bushes were unperturbed by the frost. The blossoms were all a very deep and vibrant red.

With a final snicker, Rembas parted the bushes with his hands and walked into the narrow space. He made no sound, and soon had disappeared deep into the thicket.

Curthlond sniffed, and mumbled something that sounded like "show-off", but before Gwen could be sure, he bound after the faun and disappeared into the bushes as well. Shravir stepped forth, winked at Gwen, and then he too set off into the thicket.

Once he had disappeared, Gwen was awkwardly aware that she was alone with her mortal friends for the first time since they had begun to climb up the Nalarti Mountains. She felt uncomfortable, and she could not bring herself to look at them. She was about to follow the first three when she unexpectedly felt a hand clasp her shoulder. She turned to find Ryan looking down at her, a cape thrown over his shoulders in an impressive manner.

"Here, I'll break the way," he said with a smile, then side-stepping her, he set off into the copse.

Unsure of what had just happened, Gwen faced the rest of her mortal companions. They looked at her, as far as she could tell in the darkness, with looks of uncertainty, as though they were waiting for her to instruct them or make the first move. She scoffed, and finally stepped through the narrow opening between the bushes.

The thorns on the branches were as sharp as daggers; they ripped into her cloak viciously, and she yelped in pain more than once. The scent of the flowers was strangely rancid, and her head swam as the she inhaled the stench. She held her nose and tried to breathe through her mouth, but the air burned her throat as though she had swallowed burning embers. She abruptly closed her mouth and resigned to suffer the foul reek.

The bushes closed in the farther she went along the path. She found it hard to draw any air in, and was slowly be suffocated by the livid red roses. She was beginning to feel herself fade, when the iron thorns withdrew and light sprung up from nowhere, blinding her. She gulped the fresh air down, and she felt rejuvenating warmth envelope her.

"*Well*," said Rembas's voice from somewhere nearby, "this certainly is something."

◻

Eion turned from the great bonfire to see the arrival of Rembas and the others. He stood up from the hard ground to greet them, missing the warmth as soon as he stepped away from the fire.

"How did you get that going?" Rembas asked, ignoring Eion's outstretched hand. The shifter lowered it, unfazed.

"The dryad's got it going," Eion explained. "Lord Fairskin's not accustomed to the cold."

He gestured at a hunched figure by the fire, a heavy shawl draped around his shoulders. Lord Fairskin leaned heavily on his staff, his eyes misty, as though he was in deep meditation. His lips moved, forming words, but no sound escaped them. As each syllable was formed, the fire seemed to grow a little brighter, and a new burst of warmth ensued.

Gwen stepped forth, looking bedraggled and a little out of breath. Eion sympathized; the Path to the Perished always tested the character of the walker. Its magic was an uncertain type. It reached into the deepest part of the heart and soul to find the walker's deepest fears and then forced the walker to realize them. Eion had heard the screams of loved ones when he had first walked down it. The memory made him shiver.

The rest of the Prophesied slowly filtered out from the bushes, eyes wide and breathing heavily. Kendal flinched involuntarily at the sight of the fire, and Anthony's hair was standing up on the back of his neck, goose bumps rising on his arms. The important thing was that they had made it. Eion chose not to envision what horrors they had just endured.

When they had all emerged from the roses, and had shaken off the effects of the magic, they circled the fire that Lord Fairskin was maintaining. As soon as they put out their hands to feel the warmth, the flames rose from the burning logs, offering no more heat. Eion caught sight of all those present by their light. Breeog and Barthol were off to the right, staring at the airborne fire in wonder. Varez, Tirmal, and Brunariun were now standing by the logs, which appeared as though they had never been lit. The Prophesied stood around the logs as well, not half as surprised by the flying flames as they were disappointed by the loss of warmth. Curthlond, who had been an enchanter and still appreciated the wonders of magic, stared at the blaze in wide-eyed wonder. Rembas stifled a yawn.

High above, the flames were now changing shape and color, all the while shrinking in size, until they alighted on the outstretched hand of a woman that had not been there before. Gwen recognized her as a dryad. She was indeed beautiful, and her attire was simple and elegant, a brown tunic with matching leggings, though something about her struck Gwen as odd. She had learned from the book Curthlond had taken from the Mountain that dryads were supposed to be happy, enchanting creatures that lived in joy among the trees. The woman before her looked nothing even close to joyous; indeed, she seemed tired and troubled. Her eyes were green, but had faded. Her mouth was turned down, and she seemed as though she had grown accustomed to the tired look. Her hair hung limp on her head, littered with twigs, leaves, and bits of bark.

"Nimé is come," she said. She closed her open palm and the light of the fire was extinguished.

Chapter 33

The Nymph

W*ith the fire snuffed out*, the pool could be seen. It wasn't as large or as grand as the name might have suggested. It was perfectly and flawlessly round, set into a small moor of black stone. No plants grew by it and no fish swam in it.

It looked oddly normal, but something about it screamed otherwise. The water was chalky white and swirling in circles. Horrible sounds could be heard from it: screams, moans, raspy breaths. It also either emanated the cold or absorbed the warmth. A layer of fog hovered above the surface, unperturbed by the swirling of the water.

Gwen looked at it in horror. She wanted to know what the sounds were and why the water looked so sickly and violent, but couldn't find her voice to ask. She choked back a scream when Rembas stepped by her side and whispered in her ear.

"It is the window to the Necroverse, the land of the dead," he said. There was a trace of fun in his voice, as though he was enjoying himself. Looking around, Gwen saw that there was plenty of fodder to fuel the faun's enjoyment. Ryan stared on the pool with passive eyes, but the rest of the Prophesied was not so composed. Tyler and Colin clutched each other, their eyes wide with fear. Lea was clearly trying to appear as unworried as Ryan, but she was playing with her hair, a compulsion Gwen knew to indicate her fright and anxiety.

"Those screams," she said to Rembas after a particularly blood-curdling shriek. "What are they?"

Rembas shrugged. "The vestiges of the dead. It is in this place and this place only where the dead may be heard by the living, unless, of course, you are a necromancer or you are talking to a ghost. Neither one is very pleasant. The necromancers are always grim, and the ghosts are always gloomy. Really, it's enough to make one gag." He took out his pipe and filled it with tobacco. He then produced a match and struck it against a rock by his left hoof, but it flickered out as soon as it was lit. The faun let out a sad sigh and returned his pipe, throwing the wasted match over his shoulder in a tired way.

Suddenly, there was a low rumble. The entire party gathered around the pool, save Colin and the rest of the mortals who were frightened beyond movement. They all strained to find where the rumble had come from. Gwen had forgotten about the dryad, and was a little bit startled when she saw the creature walk to the far side of the pool. The dryad clapped her hands thrice and, lo and behold, a second dryad appeared from nowhere, identical to the first. They then faced each other and made a sign with their hands simultaneously. There was another rumble, and the black stone beneath the dryads' bare feet cracked.

Something or someone was coming.

☐

Eion sighed, aware of what was happening; Nimé was making an entrance. The shifter knew the demi-gods to have a certain vanity and sense of egotism not found among the higher gods. Still, there was something different about this magical appearance; it was as lighthearted and as whimsical as was common among the nymphs. Whatever Nimé was manifesting herself into, it wasn't anything cheery.

Abruptly, a small, green shoot erupted from the cracks in the stones. With in seconds, it had grown to a sapling, and in another moment it had doubled in size. Within five minutes, a colossal oak tree loomed over the party. Its leaves were easily as big as Gwen's hand, and she knew that not even Breeog could wrap his arms around the enormous trunk. The dryads, standing on either side of the tree, faced the trunk and knelt in a sign of worship.

A soft breeze stirred the leaves, and a faint whisper resounded from the heart of the oak.

"Hither hath thou come, members of the Resistance..." spoke the voice. *"Alas, your arrival brings unrest back among these trees."*

Lord Fairskin stood from the pile of logs. He raised his arms above his head, staff and sword in hand.

"Nimé! I am Fairskin, Lord of the Vra!"

The great oak shuddered in acknowledgement.

"Nimé, I am Barthol, King of the Zanasha Mountains!" called the dwarven king, raising his hand in peace. He too unsheathed his sword and raised it to the tree.

Eion unsheathed *Raz'atr* and held it aloft. "And I am Eion Shifter! Iltari, Master of Shifters, and the Trenal Os'm! I offer my sword!"

Sparks bounced from the blade as the oak sent a shower of giant leaves raining on them in a manner that resembled bemusement.

Breeog did not introduce himself in any spoken language. Nor did he make any signs of worship or otherwise. Instead, he raised his maw to the air and sent forth a burst of orange flame into the sky, roaring ferociously.

"*That is **quite** enough of that*," said the oak, moving some of the branches that Breeog's flame came close too. The dragon stopped hastily, seeming a little put out.

"*I know who you are, where you come from, where you are going; I might even be able to take a guess at your shoe size. Yes, Resistance, I have helped you much already. By dint of my magic, I have kept the borders of the Five Clearings constantly watched and additional sentinels guard the deep of the forest. But now, the time has come for you to leave the sanctuary of these trees. The Ozra are capturing the creatures of the woods. They are then either killed or tortured out of amusement. Ÿalnz Dàr is threatened, and—*"

The oak stopped short as the dryad standing on the right side of her let out a piercing scream. It ceased in an instant as the color drained from the dryad's face. Her eyes rolled into her head. She then collapsed to the ground, writhing in agony, and then stiffened.

Eion watched this is horror, understanding what had happened; somewhere, miles and miles away, the dryad's tree, the tree she had been

413

charged to protect and to which her very life was bonded, had been cut down. The other dryad screamed in anguish and rushed to the side of her fallen sister, tears streaming down her face. Her sobs echoed chillingly in the small heath as she took the dead dryad's hand in her own and held it to her face.

"*The dryads feel the evil of the Ozra as much as the other people of the forest,*" said Nimé, her tone unchanged. "*Perhaps even more. You have come now to the edge of a war from which there is no turning back.*"

"*I have called you here, to the heath of the Perished Pool, to help deliver you to the Gates of Angar Vûn. The Ozra Gap is simply stiff with Ozmodion's minions. They would be on you before you came within a league of the gates. For this reason, I will set you on a path that is less known, one that perhaps even the Red Sovereign is unaware of. The Old Forest Pass has been hidden since the birth of the New Religion.*"

"But why the Pool, O Nimé?" asked King Barthol, his sword long returned to its sheath. "Why do you give such wondrous news at such a wretched spot?"

The oak shuddered once more, sending a shower of leaves upon them again. Those that landed in the pool burst into flame upon touching the hovering fog. A deep rumble could be heard from the tree as well. Eion realized the nymph was laughing.

"*For the wisdom of the dead,*" she replied. At these words, a figure of grey smoke arose from the pool. As it grew, its details became clearer. It was a specter of a man. Upon his head, a crown of golden leaves rested. He wore a robe of what seemed like spun silver as it glowed blindingly bright. His face was fair, but seemed troubled, as though a great burden preyed on his heart. The apparition opened its mouth, but did not move its lips as it said, "The pass is guarded by a fiend unbreakable. It will endure swords, hinder arrows, and penetrate the thickest shield. To see it is to understand it, to defeat it is to temper it." And then the apparition dissolved into vapor and withdrew into the pool.

Eion furrowed his brow trying to decipher any meaning from the cryptic message, but before he could begin to grapple with the warning, another plume of gray smoke-like substance rose from the pool. This one appeared in the form of a young child. It seemed innocent enough, with his tunic and bare legs and feet, but the bloody pentacle smeared on his forehead somehow ruined the affect.

"Death begets death," it said with the voice of a grown man, "and grief shall spawn grief. Loss will bring betrayal. Rain will fall o'er land, once the apprentice changes hands." And he withdrew.

More confused now, Eion made no more sense of this message then he did the first, but he committed both to memory instinctively. He was about to ask Nimé a question when the third apparition appeared. This one seemed more lively than the previous two; it took the shape of skeleton with a powdered wig on its skull. Eion heard Kendal snort with laughter, but she went silent as a blue fire crept into the skeleton's empty eye sockets.

"A war will be lost without aid from the Heart of Fire," it said hoarsely, and then disappeared into the awaiting pool.

The shifter stared at the pool, which looked as angry and turbulent as ever. He smiled wryly and mused silently to himself.

"*And so is the Necroverse's word*," boomed the great oak. "*Take heed of those words, for whatever meaning is hidden in them, they are indeed vital. But, anon, you must be set onto the road that leads to the Pass. Go to the Sleeping Spring and cross the threshold of the Hallow Hollow. May we next meet in happier times. For now, farewell.*"

Another rumble was heard, this one shaking Eion's very bones. Then all at once, the great oak was illuminated with all the brightness of the sun. It features then seemed to droop and blur, until finally the tree lost its shape entirely and rained down to the ground as silvery dust. It lay by the pool in a great heap that rose to Breeog's shoulder. A strong breeze picked up, and the dust was scattered about the heat. When it had cleared entirely, the living dryad pushed the body of the dead one into the pool, and then sank into the shadows, vanishing from sight.

A chilling silence filled the air, as the members of the party brooded separately. The quiet was broken, though, when Rembas scoffed loudly and with disgust.

"The *Hallow Hollow*?" he said, shaking his head. "Gods, how *do* they come up with those names?"

Chapter 34

The Pass

*T**he weary group returned*** to the Five Clearings at dawn, as the first beams of sunlight poured over the sleepy forest, announcing the new day. Rembas shaded his bright eyes as the stepped away from the shade of trees, grumbling about "a night wasted" and "lack of sleep".

Gwen silently agreed about the sleep bit, but of the night wasted she was not so sure. The prophecies disturbed her, particularly the second one. It was cryptic, which annoyed her, and it was dark, which alarmed her. In a way, she was glad she had not had any sleep; she feared the inevitable nightmares of betrayal and loss.

She did not have long to wonder, because the Resistance began to stir reluctantly from the sea of canvas steps. Breakfast was quickly eaten and camp was then swiftly broken.

"Continuity certainly isnot this army's focus," commented Curthlond, as he trotted between her legs and scampered off to their tent. With a giggle, she ran after him, surprised that she was excited to leave the Clearings.

A half hour later, her clothes were tightly compacted in her pack and her book was neatly stowed away. She had used a shrinking spell to free up some more room and to reduce the weight, and yet the bag still bulged. Not wholly satisfied, she stepped out of her tent. She set the pack aside, and began to take the tent down, but stopped short as it dematerialized.

"Do not bother," said a familiar voice, and in a moment Eion was standing beside her with his outstretched hand directed where the tent was. He smiled as he explained, "This is quicker and more efficient."

Gwen frowned. "Thank you, but I could have handled it."

"Right, right, I forgot, Madame Enchantress. My apologies."

Gwen could not be sure, but she thought she saw a hint of smug temper in his smile. She returned his look with a scowl as she stalked off, aware of the shifter chuckling and shaking his head.

"Hm, seems to me that patience is wearing thin, huh?" called Curthlond as he fell into step beside Gwen.

"I suspect so," she replied shortly. She bypassed a gaggle of shifters who were shouldering their packs and buckling their sword belts.

Curthlond meowed inquisitively, and he shook his head with embarrassment when Gwen raised her eyebrow at him.

"Sorry. Force of habit. I forget that the, uh, well, cat's out of the bag." He laughed at his joke. Gwen did not join him. He then cleared his throat and asked, "So what has got you in such a fine mood then, eh?"

She shrugged nonchalantly, hoping that the gesture would end the conversation. To her disappointment, it did not.

"Come now, what is wrong?" persisted the mangy cat. "Or will you blame this to lack of sleep? Anxiety? Concern?"

Gwen inhaled sharply as she stopped and inclined her head to look severely at Curthlond, who looked back at her with a wide, innocent grin.

"*Must* you know everything?" she asked brusquely, her voice like icy daggers. "Why the curiosity?"

"He's a cat, it's in his nature," replied Rembas, who clip-clopped his way to where they stood. His satchel was, as always, slung over his shoulder carelessly, and he wore his customary mischievous grin.

Curthlond turned to face him quickly as he hissed intensely. "I am *not* a cat!"

Rembas scoffed and waved off the objection indifferently. "So you're pretending to be one; the difference has been duly noted."

Curthlond opened his mouth to reply angrily, but before he could get the words past his lips, Rembas had extracted the pan flute and had begun to play.

"Fauns," muttered Curthlond as he went to sulk by a small shrub.

"Enchanters," mumbled Rembas, and then he continued to play.

"Fighting again, girls?" taunted a voice. Gwen turned and saw Shravir approaching with a pack slung over his shoulder. A stray tress of hair hung across his face and he grinned roguishly.

Rembas played a sour note. He then returned the flute to his satchel, replying, "Nice one, Shrav. Question our gender to get a rise. Bold. Original. Progressive. You must have kept all your victims in stitches."

Shravir's grin flickered, but he retained it. "Ah, now see, on any other day, I would curse your tail off. But you look on a new man, Rembas my friend, a new man."

Rembas chortled, but he managed to disguise it in a sneeze. Shravir frowned and made a rude gesture. Gwen raised her hand to her mouth, giggling quietly.

A horn sounded. Curthlond rotated his ears sharply, swiveling his head to and fro in attempt to find the source of the noise. Gwen, too, searched for the sound. She did not have to look hard, for a shifter was sounding the signal to move out atop a dragon in flight. Three times the horn was blown, and afterward, the whole of the Resistance mobilized into their troops and ranks. Gwen and Shravir exchanged looks and shrugs, and made their way to the shifter platoon.

To Gwen's surprised, she saw that Flora and Fauna's troops were present, realizing that the whole Resistance would be fighting this war. It was not until that moment that she understood how much they were risking; they would be attacking with a full force, leaving no reserves behind. If they lost, the Resistance would disappear, and Ozmodion would walk unchecked. Gwen shuddered at the thought as she pictured the Ozra pillaging the world she had now come to love. She touched the pommel of her sword, partly to make sure it was secure, but mostly because she was scared.

Thrice more the horn sounded, and the leaders came to the front of their armies. Lord Fairskin rode a white mare whose mane waved like liquid gold. It nickered, apparently ill at ease. King Barthol road astride a pony, apparently too regal to walk alongside his soldiers. Breeog, at the front of the dragon division, eyed the beast of burden with keen interest. He licked his scaly lips, but made no movement toward the encumbered creature.

Eion, however, strode to the front of the shifters on his own legs. He was unadorned and unarmored, with *Raz'atr* buckled to his belt. A cloak was thrown over his shoulders, clasped by an emerald brooch. His hair, though disheveled, tied the whole look of boy-turned-war leader together.

Eion's seven captains filed beside quietly, all somber as they looked blankly ahead with grim faces. As usual, no uniformity was found among them; Beast's hair hung down loose and wild, Flame sported an orange cape, and Flora and Fauna had traded their dresses for tunics and leggings tucked into tightly laced boots. All seven had baldrics and quivers slung over their shoulders, their sword pommels glistening in the morning sun.

Rembas, Shravir, and Curthlond stood beside Gwen, anticipating the call to march. It did not come. Instead, Eion pointed to the ground beneath his feet. The earth rumbled and groaned, and then Eion was raised on a stone pinnacle, until he towered twenty feet into the air. He then pointed a finger at his throat, addressing them with his magnified voice.

"We have almost come to the end of our journey. We will march to the Old Pass, but after that, we cannot be certain of what is to come. These past months have been long and difficult, and each of you have proved your merit a hundredfold."

Enthusiastic cheers, applause, and whistles punctured Eion's monologue. He smiled genially, and then raised a hand to continue.

"I ask only this: that you prove your merit once more. Regardless of the odds, I ask that you stand firm, fight, and give it your all. Death will meet many of you, and I grieve that I cannot change that. I will not waste time with words of honorable sacrifice and glorious passing. We are all given a chance to prove ourselves in the face of death and evil. I ask that you rise up and meet this danger with dignity and courage. Win, lose, but surrender not! Know that there are things worth dying for. Let it be sung 'cross the land that we rose to the challenge not in vanity or pride, but in conviction! Let it be told that we faced fire and shadow with swords aloft! What say you? Will we cower?"

"NAY!" roared the Resistance so loudly that Gwen clasped her hands to her ears.

"Would you flee?"

"NAY!"

"Will you submit?"

"NAY!"

"Will we meet the Ozra?"

"AYE!"

"Will we risk life and limb?"

"AYE!"

"Will we fight?"

"AYE!"

"Will you ever surrender?"

"NAY!"

"Then come! TO WAR!"

The resulting eruption of cheers was like a colossal thunderstorm. The very ground shook with the tremor of sound. Birds nesting in the boughs of the trees took flight in panic and fear. Dragons sent bursts of flames after them in elated passion, singeing the poor creatures' feathers. Elves, showing more restraint, raised their staffs into the air, launching blasts of colored magic and smoke. Dwarves cried in glee, beginning a song in their rough language. Shifters nocked arrows against the frames of their bows, sending a shower of the fletched missiles over the company. They sailed for hundreds of yards until they embedded themselves into the trunks of the trees bordering the far side of the clearing.

The pinnacle on which Eion stood began to dwindle and withdraw into the earth. He had unsheathed *Raz'atr* and raised it above his head while cheering along with the rest of the warriors. When the rock had fully disappeared, the leading shifter returned to his place in front of the line. He brought his sword down so it pointed to the trees opposite them.

"TO SAURINDON!" he boomed, his voice still magnified tenfold. Another round of thundering ovation sounded, along with chorus of drums. Finally, Eion returned his sword to its sheath, and set off across the clearing. Breeog, Barthol, and Lord Fairskin followed his example, as the Resistance marched behind, cheering all the while.

For some reason, Gwen could not bring herself to join in the gaiety and excitement; thoughts of journey's end sickened her, and the idea of facing Ozmodion filled her with a feeling she had never known before; it felt like her insides had been empty, stomped upon and put back inside her. As she marched beside the elated Resistance, she imagined what Saurindon would hold for her, shuddering at the thought.

☐

The days passed slowly as they wandered through those trees. Ÿalnz Dàr, which had seemed a lively place when Eion had set out with the others to retrieve the shield, was quiet and still, its residents unseen; not even a squirrel crossed their path.

Still, there was plenty to see regardless of the lack of people. The shifter had forgotten how many places of beauty the old forest held; they passed falls that sent streams and rivers into clouds of mist; they saw great oaks with leaves of silver, branches of ruby, and acorns of sapphire; they came across talking rocks and singing ferns; the encountered swamps where eerie lights hovered above the foggy water.

Though the sights charmed him, they did not quell his anticipation. *Saurindon*, he thought. He had not seen the damned valley since the night he had struck Ozmodion down, when the Resistance surged passed the Gates of Angar Vûn and drove the remaining monsters of the Ozra out. He remembered it well, and he knew it would not have changed over the centuries; Ozmodion's curse would see to that.

It was Taronest that concerned him. He had never been inside its walls, and he was well aware that it would be heavily guarded. Desperately hoping that the Prophesied would have the skill to combat the foes that undoubtedly lurked inside the fortress, he knew that Gwen could take care of herself now, and he wasn't worried about Ryan, but the other eight did not seem so competent. He consoled himself with the fact that he would be allotted twenty shifters to help keep the guards at bay. Also, the Prophesied's training regimen had not stopped, save for the brief time that they had lingered in the Mountain Still, he feared for their safety.

Soon, they came to a place in the forest where a thick, white mist hung about in the air, obscuring their vision. The cool vapor refreshed the army, who were hungry for light and fresh air, two things that the forest seemed to be lacking. Some of the soldiers got to their knees and inhaled the fog deeply. Eion was not so soothed.

"Get up!" he shouted to any who had gotten to the forest floor. "It is the Sleeping Spring! Its mist dulls your senses and tires your mind. Do not fall under its spell so easily; if you fall prey to only the mist, then the stream itself will undoubtedly have you!"

And soon they came to spring itself. They exited a copse of aspens to come to a creek cascading down a wall of granite. It was not moving fast or deep; the water actually seemed quite calm. Still, it was sending the great white fog into the air so thickly that, though there were no overhanging boughs above them, no sunlight came to the forest floor, and they were enveloped in the grey gloom.

"Let none touch the water," roared Breeog over his shoulder. There was a great din as the order was echoed throughout the legion so all would hear it. "He who does will not be awake to see the next day or many after it."

Eion nodded grimly, thinking back on the many stories of fallen heroes who had met their doom at this stream. Countless wayward travelers and lost warriors had stopped to drink at the stream, but as soon as the water touched their skin, they fell into a slumber that would only be broken when the twin stars Dieal and Laeid shined next to one another on Midsummer's Eve; an event that only occurred once every three centuries. Eion looked up and down the banks of the streams, and saw the bleached bones of those who had fallen asleep and had died before they awakened.

He shook his head; there would be plenty of time for nightmares once he came to the Pass. For now though, he gathered about him Steel and Fletch, and together the three of them extended their hands towards the stream and shifted a wide bridge from the mist. After they had secured it and made sure that it would hold, Eion signaled for the other leaders and soldiers to follow him. As they great company crossed, many of them swayed with dizziness. As they faltered, Eion turned and called to them.

"Awaken! Don't let the mist have its way with you!"

Breeog was not so composed. He stood to his full height, raised his head to the sky, and roared long, loud, and sonorously, which was enough to shake any dozers on the bridge to their senses and full alertness. Those who had yet to cross actually jumped in fright. Still, it had the desired effect; none fell to the stream.

As always, it took a very long time for the whole of the Resistance to leave the aspens and gather on the other side. A half hour later, they had all collected on the opposite bank, which was free of trees for about three hundred yards. After that, a thicket of gnarled oaks bereft of leaves loomed, their twisted branch reaching into the mist. No green could be seen beyond the coppice, and there was a wide space between two particularly ancient trees.

Eion gulped when he saw it, recognizing it as the gateway to the Hallow Hollow. The hollow itself was nothing impressive, only a small, round clearing in the center in which a small, marble altar had been erected in homage to Nimé. It was the Pass that disturbed him. He did not know much about it, only what the apparition had said; like the rosebushes surrounding the Perished Pool, it played hell with the mind. He was not sure of the particulars, but he was wise enough to be frightened after seeing Lord Fairskin shudder at the mention of it.

There was nothing for it though; if they were to come to the Ozra Gap unscathed, it would be the Pass that delivered them there.

"Shoulder your packs lads!" he called after they had rested a bit on the soft, wet grass. "To the Pass!"

With a great many groans and mumbles, the host of soldiers stood from the ground, tightened their belts, and followed as Eion, Lord Fairskin, Breeog, and King Barthol set off towards the oaks. Before they reached the trees, Gwen rushed up beside Eion.

"Nervous?" she asked, a strange smile played across her face. Apparently, she had forgiven him for his sarcasm at the Clearings.

Eion returned her grin. "Right down to my boots."

She nodded as she gestured for him to lead. He chuckled, and stepped forth, crossing into the barrier of oaks.

He was deathly unaware of the black falcon that was perched on the branch of an aspen on the opposite shore, who was scrutinizing the shifter closely with livid red eyes.

Chapter 35

The Marshalling

*I**t was this falcon that took off from its perch* on the tree after the last of the Resistance had disappeared into the fringe of oaks and soared over the green roof of the forest. There were many great sights to be marveled, but they held no wonder for the falcon; its steely eyes were narrowed on the horizon. For a day and a night, it flew high above the trees of Ÿalnz Dàr, neither stopping to eat or sleep. Then, at dawn of the next day, when the sun should have peeked up from the east, casting its warmth over the land, the falcon found itself in a blackness that would have been reserved for only the darkest midnight. It was uncanny darkness too; one as though the falcon was really swimming in a cauldron of pitch. Still, the bird's sharp eyes penetrated the veil as though it were midday. He saw that he was now soaring high above a great heath that started at the edge of the forest and ended in the slopes of a black mountain range. It clicked its beak in satisfaction; it had come to the Ozra Gap. At the base of the Mountains of Midnight, it spied two, red gates set in between the peaks. It nodded at its destination, and began to spiral down in great, wide circles.

A quarter of an hour later, it had come to the Gates of Angar Vûn, outside of which sat six sentinel trolls gathered around a great fire, toasting meat. The falcon flapped its wings once, and began to change. The process was quick, and a few of the trolls looked on it with lazy interest. When the transformation was complete, a man garbed in black robes and a scarf around his face stood in the place of the bird.

"Oi!" called one of the trolls, splashing the mead in his tankard about. "It's that shadow shifter bloke! Back already, eh?"

The shifter hissed behind his scarf as it stalked towards the fire. "Give me meat; I have not eaten in three days."

"Bah!" said another one of the trolls, who was roasting a fine haunch of lamb, "This stuff be reserved for us and us alone, mate. Go shift yerself some food! Why the Red Sovereign insisted on makin' ya ten the Maurimim or whatever he calls it is beyond me. We haven't forgotten wha' happened in the Nalarties. You won't have any of *my* supper."

The shifter clenched its fist, cracking its knuckles as he did so. Its red eyes narrowed, and it spoke its next words in dangerous whispers.

"I have performed the task that Ozmodion bayed with more stealth and efficiency then a stupid, dim-witted oaf like you could ever hope to achieve. I know the location of the Resistance. I have paid my labor. I *will* have meat, whether you hand it to me in amity, or if I must first litter the ground with your innards."

The trolls rolled with laughter, sending a spray of mead and bits of meat sailing through the air. To the shifter's disgust, much of it landed on its robes.

"The trolls have proven their merit!" roared another of the monsters, taking a great mouthful of mutton from the leg he held in his right fist. "Time now for you shifter scum to pay yer due, says I! The whole ten of ya ain't worth even one of us!"

In one fluid motion, the shifter unsheathed its thin, red sword, leaped into the air, landed behind one of the trolls, and slid the blade across his throat. The beast had been laughing still as he was murdered, and now his limp form toppled to the ground, his quickly paling face frozen between grin and gawk. The rest of the monsters stood up reflexively, dropping their food and drink and unsheathing their own swords in a rage. The shifter stepped over the corpse of the first troll, its sword held in a defensive staff.

"My brethren and I were born of fire and smoke. We are all trained in the greatest arts of assassination by the Red Sovereign himself. I will have all your throats before you take one step towards me. If you value your lives, let down your weapons and give me meat!"

Trolls, as has been established long before this, are not the brightest of creatures, going in for strength rather than wits. Still, they are quick enough to realize skill when they see it, and all five knew that the shifter was not feigning in the least. With several shared uncomfortable looks, they sheathed their blades and sank back to the ground, offering the shifter a haunch of mutton. The shifter took it with the end of his sword, sitting down and holding the meat over the fire. Its eyes glistened with hunger as it watched the meat cook. After a while, when it was satisfied with color of the sheep and sure it was hot enough to eat, it set the haunch beside itself and took off its scarf. A wide, loping mouth rested beneath its nose, and it was filled with many sharp, black teeth. It flicked its forked tongue toward the meat, and then savagely tore into it. It squelched and smacked its lips, and growled ravenously as it devoured the mutton. The trolls, not very well versed in etiquette either, grimaced in disgust as they watched the starved creature eat.

Soon, all the meat had been cleaned off the bone, but the shifter did not stop there. It cracked the white bone open for the marrow, and began to suck loudly and sickly.

Only after it had downed two tankards of mead did it talk. He wiped its mouth clean with its sleeve, and then wrapped its face with the scarf once more so that only its red eyes were showing.

"The Resistance is nigh upon us," it said in its sexless voice that was uniform among the Maurimim. "They are not, as was expected, marching through the southern road. They have turned west, and they crossed the Sleeping Spring only yesterday. I do not know which road they tread, but they will be here in four days, nonetheless."

"Let 'em come!" laughed one of the trolls, returned to their passive vulgarity now that the shifter was calm and fed. They were not at all fussed that one of their fellows was now lying stone dead, just passed the ring of firelight. "We'll crush 'em! Crush 'em like ants!"

"Aye!" concurred another, after taking a swig from his tankard. "That satyr'll be back soon no doubt, with a host of spell casters in tow!"

The shifter shook its head. "No, it will be many years before Axunrult returns to Saurindon; his labors will take long. We fight this battle without magic."

"Then why send for the magicians, eh?" asked another troll, his eyebrow arced. "I's not like ol' Blackheart to give in to folly. We outnumba the Resistance, aye, but shields don't stop magic. The elves'll have their way with us, certain."

The other trolls growled equally gloomy thoughts, but the shifter only sniggered with dark laughter.

"Fools, it is not your place to question the Red Sovereign's strategies; why do you think he sent out spies? We now know that the Resistance is close, and thus, we have the advantage of surprise. The time has come to marshal the Ozra. We march to war."

The trolls exchanged looks again then they chuckled with their deep laughter and nodded and raised their tankards to the air.

"Tonight," said the shifter.

The trolls stop and turned to face it.

"Whaddya say?" they asked confusedly.

"Tonight, says I," pressed the shifter, rising to its feet. "Muster the Ozra! Sound the horns! To war!"

The hulking monsters stared with gaping mouths. One was still roasting the breast of some wild fowl over the fire; the meat quickly blackened and burned, but so dumbfounded was the troll that he didn't notice.

"Are you deaf?" demanded the shifter, unsheathing its sword in impatience. "Sound the horns! *Now*!"

Upon seeing the sword, the trolls were brought to their senses. They scrambled for their packs, which laid a good way's away from the fire, hidden behind a dead scrub. They each dug into their bags, and each pulled out an alarm horn, each seeming to be crafted from the horns of a goblin. To their lip they place the horns, and they blew simultaneously so that one, low note rumbled across the rocky heath. Thrice they sounded, and then they waited.

Atop the high Gates of Angar Vûn, a voice called down to them. "Oi! Who calls down there, eh?" It sounded like a nightshade.

"Sound the alarm!" roared the trolls back at him. "Sound the alarm! The Ozra marches to war! The Resistance is come! Marshal the Ozra! To war!"

The only reply was another blowing of a horn, this one a little higher and sharper. It too was blown thrice, and then it paused, waiting for the answering sound. Another note, this one even lower than the trolls', called. Then another, and then another.

The shifter grinned behind the scarf, and it quickly shifted into its falcon guise. It took flight and alighted on the top of the Gates of Angar Vûn. Beyond the high gateway, Saurindon could be seen. There the sun was already high and hot; the curse of the Eclipse only extended as far as the Gap. With its sharp eyes, it saw the great, black fortress of Taronest. The Standard of Ozmodion had been raised up its highest tower, and the great host of goblins, trolls, nightshades, and shadow wolves could be seen mustering outside the stronghold's battlements.

The black falcon clicked its beak again.

The War had begun.

Chapter 36

The War

*T**he Pass was long and dark*, and many times it wound around itself and doubled back, coiling like a snake, to the point that progress went almost utterly unnoticed. The trees, old and decidedly wicked, had branches jutting out like the claws of monsters so that the Resistance had to walk single-file to avoid the sharp wooden talons. Bitter winds swept by almost constantly, and were made all the icier by the enclosed space. The only creatures that lurked in the Pass were spiders as big as hands. At night, Eion saw their nasty, red eyes leering at them as they passed; if he listened carefully, he could even hear their mandibles clicking in hunger.

But no danger did they see.

Damn spirits, thought Eion angrily. *Always twisting truths.*

The first apparition had indeed warped reality; Eion had taken its cryptic warning to mean that the Pass held the same kind of magic as the rosebushes surrounding the Perished Pool; a spell that called on the shadows of the mind and brought them to the fore. He had been wrong. The only thing to fear on the Pass was the fear *of* the Pass.

Despite the confined space, they had begun to discuss strategy nightly, and soon their plan was set and the tactics were known by every soldier of the Resistance. As plans unfolded, the broke into their assigned troops, platoons, and legions. Eion, who would be leaving the fray to lead The Prophesied Ten into the heart of the Saurindon, had appointed Steel to take up his command. The two shifters had been lifelong friends, and they smiled and clasped each others' shoulder when Eion had given him authority, though neither one voiced their fear of never meeting again, the risk that was always run in battle.

They had time yet, though. They had left the Pass behind, and now they maneuvered through the great trees that would bring them undetected to the Ozra Gap. This, as always, proved difficult for the dragons that on average were about twenty feet tall and often hit their scaly heads on the boughs and branches, roaring and ejecting flame in anger after each occurrence. Breeog himself, the Dragon King and thus by some natural magic the tallest of all, actually got on all fours and was crawling on the forest floor like some immense lizard. His wings were closed tight, hugging his spiny back for fear of scraping them. He was not at all happy, and if anyone tried to engage in conversation with him, they were met with a low growl as warning to back away.

Each night, The Prophesied Ten were placed through their usual regiment to keep them quick and strong. But now, Eion would pull them aside, and he would discuss with them what they would do when they reached the journey's end and confronted Ozmodion. It was a grim thought, made all the harder with its necessity. Soon, Eion had devised a plan that he thought would work, and the ten quickly committed it to their memory.

Then, at noon on the third day, the great army halted their march. Tirmal knelt to the forest floor and picked up a handful of earth. He smelt it, and then, with a grimace, he stood up, brushing it away.

"We are close now," he said to the leaders in a huddle. "The ground is fallow; the Gap is no more than half a day's march. Look. It is only midday, yet the shadows are creeping into the sky. We near the Desolation of the Eclipse."

Lord Fairskin, already somber from the marching and the prospect of the Gap, looked grave. "So be it. We shall divide into our final division. Send forth scouts, Tirmal; the Ozra will not have us unawares."

Tirmal nodded, and set off to the elf division. He selected three elves that were the strongest, wisest, and surest of foot. They nodded when informed of their task, and then sprinted off into the wood.

Night fell early that day, but it was long after it had fallen that one of the elves returned. His face was caked with dried blood and tear stains. One of his arms had been tied in a rough sling; apparently the injured elf had done it himself. He was heaving from the efforts of returning so quickly.

"They slew Vilini and Nàro," he said in grieved whispers as Tirmal sat him down and cleaned his wounds with worry. "They let me live, only to tell the tale. The Ozra is fully marshaled, and the Gates of Angar Vûn are rigid with guards; General Eion and The Prophesied Ten will never get passed it. We circled the Gap so that we were not caught until we came to the western edge, but I fear that they know where we will exit."

There were anxious looks exchanged among the leaders, the Lord Fairskin ordered that the elf be tended to. Tirmal got the wounded soldier to his feet and helped him hobble to the healers. Meanwhile, Eion, Lord Fairskin, King Barthol, and Breeog all discussed matters.

"There is nothing for it, then," said Eion after a while, gripping the pommel of *Raz'atr* mindlessly. "I will have to lead them over the Mountains of Midnight."

"By which road?" asked King Barthol skeptically. He was leaning on a great pine in a manner that somehow did not befit a dwarf of his years; he looked like a young boy in defiance. "The mountains are a veritable labyrinth of canyons and gorges. If one does not take the right road, one will never see the crest of the first knoll, much less the other side."

"Yes, thank you, Your Majesty," replied Eion, snappish, "I am well aware of it. That is why we will break off now and take the Pass of Hamurlas."

"The Demon Peak?" roared Breeog incredulously as he swiveled his head to face Eion. "Shifter, you cannot! That treacherous mountain is half the reason the Midnights are so feared! It has claimed countless lives—"

"And it is the fastest way into the Gorge besides the Gates," finished Eion, satisfied. "I had not counted on using the Gates; they are always guarded, even when there is no battle. Hamurlas is our best chance."

"Eion, you realize that this is desperate…" began Lord Fairskin, who, fueled by his anger at the murder of the elves, seemed stronger and less dependent of his staff.

"As is our plight!" insisted the shifter with passion. His eyes grew wide and intense. He waited for someone to reply. When no one did, he relaxed, knowing he had convinced them, and moved on to the next issue.

"That leaves us to vie with the safe passage of the rest of the Resistance," he said, calm now, for the need for passion passed. "How will you deliver them into the Gap without being slain in the fringe of trees where there will be no room to maneuver?"

"Astride the dragons, says I," stated Breeog as though that settled the manner. "One elf, dwarf, and shifter to each dragon. Batter them with arrows and curses and even stones, if you wish. The chaos that will ensue will dishearten them; they will not expect an aerial assault."

He paused to let the others soak the idea in. Then, one by one, their faces lit up as the brilliance of the plan hit them.

"It can work," said Barthol, stroking his beard in a musing sort of way.

"It *will* work," insisted the dragon king with a sniff. He turned to Eion. "Ready the Prophesied. *I* will handle the rest."

☐

A few hours later, Gwen was saying her goodbyes to Shravir and Rembas; they would not be joining them in their attack on Taronest. They would instead be taking part in this new, daring strategy Breeog had conceived.

"I suppose it cannot be much worse than being carried in Eion's talons," Shravir mused, attempting light-heartedness for Gwen's sake, but the grim mood was permeating them all except Rembas, who was resolutely indifferent as usual.

"What? Flying dragon back?" asked the faun with a sneer. "It'll be a walk. You'll just have to learn to balance between two, flapping, scaly wings hundreds of feet up in the air while hungry legions of monsters cheer for your fall. It's cake."

Curthlond hissed with irritation, standing beside Gwen legs. "Can you not even *attempt* some civility, you flea bitten nag?"

Rembas raise an eyebrow as he crossed his arms. "Who? Me? I'm civility itself."

Gwen laughed, but it was quickly quelled as the thought of the battle sprang back to mind. Suddenly, she was back in Fairskin Manor, waking long before dawn, on the day they had set out. The minstrel's song came eerily back to mind, haunting and disturbing.

"And I suppose you are an expert at airborne archery, then?" asked Curthlond, attempting a arched brow, an expression that cats have never quite managed.

Rembas grinned and pulled a small crossbow out of his satchel. In single motion he had taken aim, pulled the trigger, and released the already loaded arrow. It sailed for fifty yards and then embedded itself into the trunk of an elm with a *fwwt*. Stunned Curthlond turned to face him again; his jaw dropped with astonishment.

Rembas tutted in pity, shaking his head. "Aw, poor Curthy. Fallen prey to the evils of assumption." He stowed the crossbow with a smile and a wink at Gwen.

"Wow," commented Shravir with a cool smile. "The Ozra do not have a chance then, eh?"

Rembas chortled with satisfaction. "Surely. Between the two of us, we'll have 'em yelping back to Blackheart before midday."

The two laughed, and Gwen joined them, her heart lightening in the momentary joy. Yet her grief quickly returned. Here, on the edge of battle, would she part with the two she had become such good friends with? She prayed silently to every god she could think of that she would see them alive and whole after the battle, if she, herself, was to survive.

It was then that Gwen saw the true evil of Ozmodion. It wasn't his will to consume the Magic Realm, nor was it his ambition to dominate and ensnare all life. It was this: it was that he tore loved ones and friends apart. It was that he spread doubt and discord. It was that he ravaged peace and freedom and caused grief in the hearts of all. It was that he suffocated the world until all the happiness was stamped out and sorrow was the only order of the day.

Her face hardened, and she clenched her fist until her knuckles turned as white as bone. Her whole body went rigid with anger, and she felt the magic burn inside her chest. She wanted to scream some spell, some incantation that would cleanse the whole realm and rid the world of Ozmodion's filth. But, somewhere in the back of her mind, a small voice whispered that it couldn't be done. Angrily, she let the magic fade, and she found herself standing in Ÿalnz Dàr beside her friends once more.

"Hmph, enjoy it you two," said Curthlond with a shrug. "I will not envy you, being volleyed with arrows and boulders and Gods only know what else."

Rembas laughed airily. "Nor will I envy you, trekking Hamurlas and Saurindon only to face the blackest sorcerer of this and any age? Have fun Curth; we'll muddle through without you."

Curthlond snorted in an attempt to seem sardonic, but Gwen sensed some bitterness, as though Curthlond would have rather braved the fray. She smiled; despite their constant quarreling and incessant jeers, Curthlond and Rembas were the best of friends. As she looked at Rembas, she noticed a gleam in his eye that she had missed before, a warm, loving gleam. His eyes darted up to meet hers, and when he saw that he was being watched, he shook his head, clasped his hands, and said, "Well, we ought to be off, I suppose."

Shravir nodded and he adjusted the pack and baldric slung over his pack. "Aye. Not a battle to be fought here." He knelt to the ground and scratched Curthlond behind the ears. "See you later Curthlond. Good luck."

"And you Shravir," purred Curthlond, indulged.

Shravir nodded, and he turned to face Gwen. Unsure of what to do, she waited. He then stepped in and wrapped his arms around her in a fond embrace. She returned the gesture, and she felt very cold once she had let go.

"*Bon courage*," said Rembas to Curthlond, suppressing all emotion as usual. "Keep a keen eye, eh?"

"You too, Rem," said Curthlond with a smile. "Give the Ozra hell for me."

The faun laughed again, and with a nod he said, "For certain!" He then turned to Gwen and he too embraced her. He winked again once they broke apart, and then he and Shravir set off to find their place among the rest of the Resistance.

Gwen swallowed hard. "Do you think we will see them again, Curthlond?"

The cat did not answer. Instead, Eion whispered, "When your heart wants lifting, think of pleasant things."

She turned to look at him. She was surprised to see that his pack had been abandoned, entrusted to Steel, no doubt. He was attired in tunic, cloak, and boots. There was no armor protecting him, and his hair hung limp. He was burdened with a baldric and quiver, but nothing else.

When he noticed that she was studying his attire, he smiled. "I suggest you suit yourself likewise; haste will be a first priority when we scale Hamurlas. Ozmodion's death is crucial. If he is not slain, the Resistance will succumb to the Ozra, so great is their numbers. Besides, armor can do nothing against magic."

Gwen sighed again and nodded, taking her pack of her shoulder. When she asked who to give it to, the shifter only said, "Leave it. We cannot afford to burden anyone."

He then walked away, presumably to ready the rest of the Ten. Gwen would've been fine to leave the pack there, except that the spell book Curthlond had given to her still rested in it. She turned to the cat, her eyes plainly asking what to do. He shrugged and said, "Store it."

She raised an eyebrow. "How?"

"What, you mean you have not studied the section on portals yet? They act as magical safes and can store anything until opened with a spell or object."

Gwen flashed back to the day she had arrived in the Magic Realm, when Eion had turned a key in midair to make *Raz'atr* appear. She quickly set her pack on the ground, pulled out the book, and opened it to the chapter concerning portals. The incantation was simple enough, and as she did not want to be burdened with an object, she decided to make the portal open and close with an enchantment. She prepared herself, and recited the line.

"*Alisi vei maerdo.*"

A hum filled the air, and a slight breeze wafted passed Gwen. She didn't let it break her concentration, though. Instead, she returned the book to the bag, picked it up, and spoke the Sealing Word. In a flash, the pack had disappeared, locked in the portal safe and secure.

"A bit sloppy toward the end," observed Curthlond, who was sitting beside the trunk of an ash tree with his tail lashing back and forth. "But that is to be expected of a novice; you will have plenty of time to hone in on your skills later."

Gwen studied her friend. She hoped he was right. That would mean she would live through the battle. After she had tightened her sword belt, Eion stepped out from behind a pine along with the rest of the mortals and a troop of twenty shifters, who were armed and only protected by mail shirts and helms.

"It is time," said Eion sadly, looking long and hard at Gwen. "You will know what to do when the time comes. Trust in that knowledge."

He then broke off into a run, disappearing among the trees. Ryan was the first to set out after him, his black cloak trailing in the wind. The mortals exchanged looks, and then followed. Next to go were the shifters, apparently accustomed to the weight of the mail, for they were able to run at a lightning pace. Gwen turned to Curthlond, took a deep breath and together they set off after them.

☐

"It's darker," said Shravir, who walked beside Rembas along with the Shifter division. "Has night come so soon?" He was speaking in the dialect of Ÿalnz Dàr, which Rembas found a little odd and more than a little redundant. For whatever reason to not speak in the Familiar Speech, Rembas knew that secrecy could not be one. He was certain that the shifters they marched with could understand them, and anyway, the language of the forest was harsh and rough and difficult to pronounce. He answered, instead, in the Familiar Language, which he preferred.

"No." His eyes flitted to and fro. "We are at the Desolation of the Eclipse. It was very near here that Ozmodion uttered the curse that took hold of both Saurindon and the moon. For reasons that even Blackheart can't explain, the outlying lands have been thrown into perpetual night ever since."

Shravir shivered at the mention of the sorcerer's name. It seemed ill-fitting to utter it so close to the Gap. And they were close to the Gap too, for now the armies were halting, and they were preparing to put Breeog's plan into action. Shravir found it as a small comfort that Rembas was there; he liked the faun, despite his dry and sardonic manner. Besides, he was sure to need a friend before the battle was out.

The lieutenant of the platoon had called their names and directed them to a green dragon with two gnarled horns curving around its head. Rembas stepped up first and Shravir afterwards. The ex-blood-mage felt some of the creatures huge, knotted muscles twitch at the added weight, but they quickly adjusted accordingly.

And then they waited, it took a very long time indeed for all the elves, dwarves, and shifters to be assigned to and mount their dragons. Three quarters of an hour later, after all had been taken care of, the Dragon King Breeog, with the Lord Fairskin, King Barthol, and Captain Fletch on his back, roared, "To the skies!"

Shravir gasped in surprise as the green dragon inhaled deeply, rising in height as his lungs expanded. Then, he felt a sense of lift; the dragon was rising into the air, as were all of his fellows. Shravir clutched at his head as the dragon ascended passed the branches of the tree, which clawed and scraped at his face and the cloak he had thrown over his mail. Then, he felt the cold, night air fill his own lungs. He opened his eyes and saw that they were above the green, leafy roof of Ÿalnz Dàr. In the distance, the Mountains of Midnight could be seen silhouetted against the red glow that came from Saurindon. And then, in simultaneous motion, the great flight of dragon flapped their wings, surging ahead with a great burst of speed. Shravir nearly lost his balance and fell to the forest, but he righted himself in the nick of time. Behind him, Rembas laughed and put a comforting hand on Shravir's shoulder.

"No sense in dying just yet," was all he said, bliss emanating from him.

☐

Belzorg gripped his sword hilt in anticipation. *Sarnor is avenged this night*, he thought murderously, imagining Eion Shifter's beheaded corpse. *Or I die.*

Goblins are heartless creatures, and they would just as soon turn on their kindred as they would any enemy. Still, Belzorg had valued his son as a captain, and he, Belzorg, had been left uncomfortably without a suitable replacement. Eventually, he had chosen a lieutenant, Grick, an officer who had been famed as a harsh taskmaster, though from what Belzorg had seen, he was nowhere near the same league as Sarnor.

The goblin growled as he stood at the front of the goblin division in the Ozra Gap. The beasts stood shoulder to shoulder, stretching far and wide across the valley; their black armor, encrusted with the Insignia of the Eclipse, glinted in the silver moonlight. They said nothing, only waited. Their green, iridescent eyes were fixed on the western edge of the Gap, where the final trees of Ÿalnz Dàr grew thin and frail. Belzorg chuckled to himself, recalling how much the Gap had been extended in the recent months. As he looked toward the west and northern edge of the forest, he saw the many hacked stumps and ashes of trees that had been burned away by the ravaging Ozra. He smiled in brutal satisfaction.

Suddenly, a light breeze blew through the goblins, and Belzorg smelt a strange scent hanging on the air. He chuckled again. The Resistance had come.

He waved at Kahn's second-in-command, Grav, who had taken over the troll armies while Kahn was stationed at Nunren, standing in front of the troll division on his left. The troll captain waved in affirmation, and then turned to alert Olarn and Gorez, who were farther to the left.

Then, Belzorg motioned at the first line of the goblins; the pike men. He motioned them forward, and with exchanged looks of glee, they lowered their weapons and sprinted off towards the fringe of trees.

Belzorg was already savoring victory; the Maurimim had done their job well, gaining the information that would allow the Ozra to crush the Resistance in this final battle. They would be trapped in the trees with little room to maneuver and no room to run. They would surrender within the hour. Pleased by the very thought, he motioned for silence and he strained his ears for the sound of battle.

It never came. Confused, Belzorg squinted into the distance. Nothing. The trees were not stirring and all was still, yet still the breeze persisted, stronger now, heavy with the mingled scents of elf, dwarf, shifter, and dragon. The Resistance was definitely close, but still there came no cries of war or attack.

Then, from the top corner of his eye, Belzorg saw movement above the trees. He whipped his head, and nearly choked in shock. There were dragons, Hundreds of them, all burdened with passengers.

Belzorg growled in self reproach; the Resistance had come by air.

"Archers!" he roared, listening as they came to attention and prepared their bows. "Take aim!" The sounds of the strings tightening echoed in the goblins ears. He raised his hand to signal to fire, but as soon as he did, a whistling resounded. In a flash, a silver arrow dove from the sky and embedded itself into the neck of the goblin standing on Belzorg's right. The ill-fated creature gave a yelp of pain, and then collapsed, dead as stone.

Belzorg growled without turning his head, swearing an oath of vengeance in the harsh language of the goblins. As thoughts of Shifter's death again crossed his mind, Belzorg roared for the first volley of arrows.

☐

"*That's* Hamurlas?" asked Kendal incredulously, pulling her cloak tighter around her with wide eyes. "I don't see what all the hype is about."

Eion shook his head as he looked upon the mountain. True, it did not seem worthy of the name Demon Peak, for it was more of a hill than anything else. The surrounding mountains loomed high and black around it, meshing into the black, star-studded night.

"That hill," Curthlond explained, "has claimed enough lives to make a second Necroverse. It is positively riddled with pitfalls and gorges and hidden gullies and razor rocks. If we even see the crest of Hamurlas, I will count us all very lucky."

The shifter guards nodded in grim concurrence. They shifted their weight uncomfortably, waiting for Eion to give the order to ascend. Their loyalty moved Eion, and he inwardly grieved that many of them would come to a bad end. They were, after all was said and done, shields for the Prophesied.

And the Prophesied themselves. As Eion had expected, Ÿalnz Dàr had seen them greatly changed. Looking upon their grave faces, he saw that the haughty words spoken at the Mountain had left their hearts; they had seen the error in their thoughts and he knew they had accepted their charge.

And Gwen.

With a shake of the head, he shook his thoughts away and looked to Hamurlas. Indeed, it was much shorter than the rest of the midnights, but it was incredibly steep for its size. Silently, he agreed with Curthlond; they would be greatly lucky if they reached the crest whole.

"Come, it is time," he called to his companions. He set off at a brisk jog up the mountain, listening to the loud clank of armor and weapons as the mortals and the shifters followed behind.

□

Astride the dragon Brunariun, Tirmal took aim and fired another of his silver arrows into the Ozra's midst. He smiled with satisfaction when he heard the roar of agony that followed after the missile had found its mark. He reached over his shoulder for the next arrow waiting in his quiver. He pulled it out and nocked it against the frame. He pulled back the string, savoring yet another kill, when he heard a loud harrumph from behind him. Tirmal ignored it, and let loose the arrow, watching it sail and embed itself into the naked throat of a nightshade.

"Varez," Tirmal said, not bothering turn around to face the dwarf, "I really expected better from you. You are acting like a child. It is not my fault you lost your bow. Really, lives are at stake, and you are being petty and sour."

"See here, now, elf," cried the dwarf, offended, "Steel is not being any better."

Indeed, as Tirmal turned to look over his shoulder, he saw that behind Varez, the sword burdened shifter sat with a scowl and arms crossed. Tirmal chuckled at the sight, and then he turned to face forward again.

"So long as he sulks in silence, I am satisfied. You, on the other hand, are distracting me. If I miss even one shot, it will be your head."

"Ha!" Varez fired back. "I would love to see you try. Anyway, you will run out of arrows eventually."

"Not true," replied Tirmal as he took aim again. He fired and did not bother to follow the arrow with his eyes, fully confident his aim was true. "You forget that Steel can simply shift more when I need them."

A mirthless laugh broke from the taciturn captain behind them. "Nothing doing, Snow White. I am not adding to your glory. You want more arrows, get them yourself."

Annoyed, Tirmal absently ran a hand across his fair skin and said, "Then what will be your part in this war, eh? He who moped upon a dragon? Hardly a noble legacy."

He waited for the irate response, but it never came. Instead, the elf heard the sound of a cloak billowing in the wind and many swords rattling in there sheaths. The elf turned to look over his shoulder again. There was Varez, humbled, but Steel was not behind him. Alarmed, Tirmal looked over Brunariun's side. There, plummeting towards the Ozra, was the figure of Steel with two swords unsheathed and extended. The awed goblins over which he fell were too stunned to react in time, and before they registered the threat, the two swords had made their home in two of the monsters' breasts. Amazingly, Steel survived the fall, and now he was swinging the swords in great arcs among the crazed beasts as they converged on them.

Brunariun laughed in her roaring voice. "Oho, so I suppose *that* will be his legacy, eh Tirmal?"

Tirmal narrowed his eyes, and with a tut of frustration, he threw himself over the side of the dragon, unsheathing his sword, muttering, "Shifters" all the while he fell.

☐

The dragons, their fiery breaths almost spent, landed, and their passenger sprung from their backs, unsheathing their weapons and mobilizing into their ranks. In moments, they would meet the Ozra on the battleground. Only twenty minutes into the battle, and already the Ozra were losing.

The shadow shifter allowed a chuckle to escape as he recalled when the troll guards had charged him, the Master of the Maurimim, to prove his worth. He would meet their challenge, not in valor, but in spite.

From the peak of Reor, the mightiest of the Midnights, the ten Maurimim stared upon the battlefield in wicked amusement. They grasped the red hilts of their swords as their black garbs were caught in the howling wind. Still, they had been ordered to wait for Vaeirnïr. The dragon general had lingered at Taronest for some final instruction from the Red Sovereign himself, and already he was long expected.

The shadow shifter was unconcerned though; the longer they waited, the greater the Ozra would need them. Already, the two armies were converging; the clang of blade against blade and spear against shield echoed loudly among the shouts and roars of the warriors. The four divisions of the Ozra had broken against the four divisions of the Resistance like waves against the shore. The archers of both armies sent a never-ending volley of arrows cascading towards one another. The nightshades, the most agile and swift of the Ozra, made their way into the rebel lines, cleaving armor and shield with their scythe-like claws. The trolls wielded their colossal swords like clubs, sweeping at the Resistance's defenses like beaters. The elves sent great curses and spells from their staffs, stunning, eviscerating, transforming, and killing with tireless energy while wielding their swords as well. Still, the Ozra did not stop their attack; though they could not avoid the spells, they still outnumbered the Resistance four to one.

The shadow wolves, blending in almost seamlessly into the night, were not able to get past the Resistance's row of pike men; many carcasses now formed a bloody and broken barrier between the two armies. The dwarves, too, stayed back in reserve, while the shifters fought with swords, bows, elements, and transformed into beasts. From his vantage point atop Reor, the shadow shifter saw that Belzorg ordered the goblins to recede, so great was the toll of the pikes and arrows.

The Maurimim rolled their eyes. The shifter closest to the master softly growled in frustration.

"Fool," he whispered in the uniform voice of the Maurimim. "What is that Belzorg doing? Advancing to the rear?"

"Bah!" said another, "let us pray that he loses his head before this night is out."

"Silence," commanded the master, straining his ears. The sound of flapping wings could be heard quiet and low above the roaring wind. The shadow shifter turned to look to the south. Above the red sands of Saurindon soared the dragon Vaeirnïr, black and foreboding. The shifter backed up several paces simultaneously to allow the dragon room to land. The immense creature was nigh upon them when he flapped his great wings twice and alighted on the peak.

The Maurimim all bowed at the waist in reverence. The dragon did not respond. He only locked his two, hard, red eyes on the Gap.

"How goes the battle?" he asked with menacingly quiet.

The master hissed, "As well as can be expected with Belzorg leading the goblins."

The dragon snarled. "I swear, I am going to eat that bumbling incompetent. Come, we fly now.

The Maurimim chuckled, and together, they raised their hands to sky. The wind changed course, and consolidated above the ten shifters. There, ten wyverns appeared, red and ravenous, their green eyes dancing like sunlight on water. They screeched piercingly, sounding their charge.

"TO BATTLE!" roared Vaeirnïr, taking to the sky with massive force from his wings. The Maurimim unsheathed their red blades and jumped onto the backs of the wyverns as they swooped after the black dragon.

☐

Rembas was among the shifters, wielding a pair of daggers in both hands. His satchel still swung from his side, but he did not let it hinder him. With a grace not to be expected from someone with hooves, the faun danced with his daggers, warding off the innumerable swords of the goblins. The blades were not stout enough to cleave the armor of the Ozra, but Rembas still managed to cut the throats of many of the beasts while distracting them with his spinning dance.

Is this all you can offer, Ozmodion? he thought, while battling with a particularly nasty brute. *I see one thousand years of limbo has not seen you improved.*

And then, of course, he saw Vaeirnïr, followed by another ten airborne creatures. He recognized them as wyverns, for they only had four limbs: their hind legs and their wings. Dragons had six: the four legs and the wings. Still, Rembas knew that wyverns were much more swift and spry. As they flew closer, Rembas noticed that they were also burdened with passengers.

He had not been present for the events in the Nalarti Mountains, but he had had the shadow shifters described to him many times around camp fires and while marching in lines. And now he saw them, garbed in black with their red swords held high as they rode astride the wyverns.

Ah, he thought, rather taken aback. *Blackheart still has some tricks up his sleeves.*

A less composed being would have pointed to the sky and shrieked Vaeirnïr's name. But that was outside of Rembas's independent and valiant character. He instead acted with the nobility he had come to place in everything he ever did.

As he ran away from the fray, he tapped a few elf archers on the shoulder and babbled, "Vaeirnïr, wyverns, and shadow shifters. Take care of it, huh? Great, good luck, I'll be seeing you."

Fully aware of the jeers and cries of outrage, Rembas trotted as fast as his stag legs could carry him to the elf division; he knew the shifter would be thanking him for bringing spell casters once those wyverns and their riders began their descent.

☐

Progress was, as expected, painstakingly slow. Hamurlas had many paths that led to roads that were cheats and dead ends, or roads that led to gorges and hidden pits. But Eion had learned the right way from Lord Fairskin, thus he took them to the right trail that led to the right road.

But still, even the right road was marred and riddled with treacherous slopes and ravines that would've claimed them had they been going any faster. Far away in the east, Eion saw the dominating blackness that covered the Ozra Gap. He knew that the Resistance and Ozra would have met by now, and they would be battling even as they climbed. He also knew (a grim thought, this one) that their survival depended on he and the others conquering Hamurlas before slaying Ozmodion.

To make matters worse, the clouds overhead were gathering thick and dark, threatening to let loose a storm upon the mountains. Rolling clashes of thunder could already be heard in the distance.

And hour passed, and then another. Soon, they found themselves only half way up the Demon Peak, and the others were beginning to worry.

"Eion!" called Ryan, who was toward the back of the party helping Kendal and Eric along, "We're running out of time! I don't know how long the Resistance is going to be able to hold out! We have to move faster!"

Though Eion saw the reason in this statement, he found himself angered for some reason. "We will not lead the Resistance to their death, and I am afraid that is the only alternative to a slow pace," he called back.

To his surprise, this calm language seemed to escalate Ryan's temper. "Bother slow pace! We won't help the Resistance by wandering 'round the hills while the Ozra outnumbers them four to one!"

Too tired and too preoccupied to exchange a round of prissy arguments with an adolescent, Eion ignored him, irritated at being needlessly reminded of the overwhelming odds that the Resistance faced. His thoughts flashed to the angry legions of monsters that Ozmodion had ensnared and corrupted to evil: the colossal trolls, the swift nightshades, the savage shadow wolves, and the brutal goblins. He knew all too well what the sourcer was capable of.

Still, he would have greatly preferred battling the Ozra than scaling this labyrinth of rock only to confront the Red Sovereign. It wasn't that he was afraid; it was that he was uncertain. So much rested on him. After all, though the Prophesied were destined to help him, it was Eion's fate to either kill Ozmodion, or be killed.

He was awakened from his thoughts as he saw Ryan run passed him up the mountain. More than a little angry now, Eion called to him, but Ryan feigned deafness and continued on. The shifter scoffed agitatedly as he turned to one of the shifter guards.

"Watch the others," he instructed with more sharpness than the guard deserved as he shifted into his hawk guise. Thrice he flapped his wings, pushing powerful gusts of wind beneath, and he rose to the skies. He then set off after the idiot boy whom he could now see dodging the many rocks and boulders of Hamurlas with difficulty.

"Ryan, you fool," he squawked in English when he was close enough to be heard. "Turn around! Already you are on the wrong path. There is a nice sized ravine up ahead, and if you keep veering to the right, it will embrace you with an open maw."

Between heaving breaths, Ryan managed to reply without looking behind him. "Leave off....you pesky...fowl. I don't need your help...I'll do....it my....self."

Hawks can't scoff, but Eion managed a similar sound. "Oh, will you my lad? Come, come, even I am hard pressed to remember the valley. It will be hard enough finding our way around Saurindon with memory and instruction alone. But here *you*, a young whippet who has *never* seen it before are rushing off like a maddened delinquent to attack a sorcerer who can kill you with a snap of his fingers. Where is your thinking? Have you lost your mind? You will be ashes before you take your third step into Saurindon."

If Eion had learned anything in his brief time in the Mortal Realm, it was that human's failing weakness was their vanity. Certainly, some were able to weave masks of false security, and others lashed out with more force, but each and every one could not stand being doubted. Insult them in any other way, but *never* hurt their pride.

This held true for Ryan. Eion saw from his bird's eye view that Ryan's teeth were gritted and a burning look of fury lit his eyes. But instead of halting and turning back to the right road and the rest of the party, the moronic boy seemed only to be spurred by Eion's jibes and insinuations. He increased in speed.

Eion had enough. He began to change.

A great shadow covered the mountain as the immense roc descended with talons outstretched. He was just about to clasp Ryan's shoulders when the boy unsheathed his sword and flailed it around. He was in a beautiful rage now, one so grand that his skill of the sword seemed to be quelled. Still, it was enough to do considerable damage; the blunt face of the sword rapped Eion's talons. He, in turn, screeched in discomfort.

"Give it up, you upstart!" he roared in English, after crying a vivid curse in Roccish. His feet still smarted and he was sure that there would be a welt. He'd shift it later. For now, he ascended a little higher to avoid a lone pine that grew in his way. Ryan, too skirted this, sharply turning to the left, but not at such an angle that he would be returned to the right road. Now, his pace was slowing from weariness. Eion seized his opportunity and began to descend again. As quick as he was, though, Ryan was quicker. He turned on his heel and sunk into a horse stance with one fluid motion. A look of doubt crept into Eion's eyes, but he did not slow; his talons flexed involuntarily as he extended them.

As he was about to grab the boy, Ryan jumped into the air, landing forcefully on Eion's back. Groaning, he swiveled his neck to see Ryan running between his great wings, and then finally jump right before he reached Eion's tail feather. He somersaulted once in midair before rolling to the ground to absorb the shock. To Eion's further displeasure, the cocky youth turned around to yell his triumph.

And then tripped over a rock and went sailing through the air.

Quickly, Eion wheeled about and dove after him. He watched as Ryan hit the ground painfully and did a few rolls before he disappeared out of sight. Concerned now, Eion shifted back to his usual self and sprinted after Ryan. He stopped short as he saw and immense gorge before him, hidden by the disarming rocks. With trepidation he looked over the edge, and nearly cried with relief as he saw Ryan about twenty feet below him, clinging on to the wall of the gorge like grim death. Eion saw that his grip was faltering, though, and the shifter also saw that the gorge was so deep that the bottom could not be seen, swathed in the blackness of the unknown depths. Regardless, Eion could barely repress the urge to say, "I told you so."

Instead, he shifted his arm into a rope, and continued to extend until he was sure Ryan would be able to reach. But Eion was astonished to see that the dratted wretch batted it away.

"Take it or die," Eion said simply, too frustrated and tired to be consoling.

"Leave me alone!" Ryan called back, determined to dig himself out of his own mess. A crack of thunder, a flash of light, and Ryan tried to make his way up, futilely looking for another hand-hold. Normally, Eion would have been delighted to watch his efforts, but too much time had been wasted already. He swung the rope back towards the boy. Now Ryan unsheathed a dagger and slashed the rope with it. (it was unwise to do otherwise; nerve fiber was a tricky business and even the most masterful shifter could make a mistake) and he screamed when he felt the cold iron slice Ryan's one life line.

"I said leave!" Ryan called again. "I can take care of myself."

Eion shifted his arm back to normal and proceeded to nurse his wound. "So be it!" he answered, petulant. As he repaired the cut, he called, "I just hope you're ready to answer for these injuries when you do get up here...that is, *if you can.*"

Silently, he chastised himself for the childish rousing. Still, he had just been battered many times for trying to save someone, and the lack of gratitude rather stung him.

Again, with his vanity prodded, Ryan's temper came to boil, and he immediately began to climb the wall. Amused, Eion watched now that the injury was mended.

"Almost a meter!" he called down to him. "Good work! Should only take you another hour to reach the top.

Ryan gritted his teeth. Quite unsure of what had so suddenly taken hold of the youth's mind, Eion continued to watch lest his strength failed him and he fell. After another gargantuan effort, Ryan had covered another foot.

"Keep coming. You ought to be out by the time winter comes ag—" but he stopped short as Ryan faltered and he slid down the rock face twelve feet. Quickly, the shifter sprung into action and shifted his arms into chains, sending them down for Ryan to grasp. Again, he slashed at the shifted arms with his dagger, but he then lost his footing and slid another ten feet.

"Stay still! I am coming down!" Eion quickly shifted into a gargantuan spider, but he saw that the stone face would not support his weight. A quick series of possibilities flashed through his mind. Selecting one, he made the change and threw himself over the edge.

The nightshade sailed over the ravine and landed on the opposite wall, embedding its claws into the stone. It swiveled its head to look at Ryan, who was now trying, with little success, to undo his sword belt to alleviate some of the weight. The nightshade clicked its tongue, and then called to him.

"I said stay still! The more you move, the weaker the rocks become! Stay still; I am coming over."

Whether panic was gripping him, or he was simply ignoring him, Ryan didn't respond. Instead, he shifted his weight slightly, and with his free hand, he stabbed his dagger into the rock edifice. Before Eion could cry out his warning, Ryan had shifted his weight again and then, supporting himself by the first dagger, unsheathed his second and stabbed the rock again, this time a little higher.

The effect was immediate. A crack split from the first dagger, creaking as it spread. Then fissures began to split from the second, spider webbing across the whole rock face crystallizing water on a window.

Abandoning all thoughts of jumping to the other side, Eion quickly assessed everything. He reached out and tried to shift the cracks back together, but they were too quick; they now stretched from the cliff and extended down until they could no longer be seen.

Then he heard the groan. It was low and screeching, a harbinger of the inevitable. Eion sighed resignedly. He made the appropriate change, and reached out his now extended arm. Almost begrudgingly, Ryan let go of the lower dagger and attempted to take Eion's hand, but the claws prevented him from doing so. It took Eion a moment too long to unshift them. In that brief pause, the opposite wall of the gorge collapsed. Flailing his arms like a man drowning, Ryan tried to take Eion's hand. Their fingers brushed against each other for such a fleeting second that, years later, when Eion looked back on it, he wondered if they ever did.

"No!" cried the shifter, but it was too late. Ryan fell, swallowed whole by the welcoming darkness far below. It was only then that the clouds overhead let loose the rain.

☐

The tallest tower of Taronest was unique among the other eight. The others housed armories, dungeons, and reserve chambers for whatever use would be required of them. They were each topped with a sentry post, which, normally, was guarded by at least four goblins, night and day.

But the tallest had another use. Directly connected to Ozmodion's chambers, it had no walls, or sentries, or battlements of any kind. The top was flat and constructed of black slate. Inside it wound a lone staircase, bereft of windows or torches. These Ozmodion climbed presently, his hands clasped behind his back.

Most of his incantations, conjurations, and enchantments required little or no preparation, so great was his power. Still, there was one which necessitated special conditions and preparations; the summoning of the Eclipse.

He ascended his staircase and stepped out into the night air outside of the fortress. Looking over the side, he saw the sentries standing watch, their vigilance somehow lessened with the prospect of being left behind in battle. Even from here, Ozmodion heard their low mutterings and grumbles. He ignored it; he had other things on his mind.

Instead, he directed his attention to the center of the flat surface. A snap of his fingers, and then a fiery five point star erupted to life. He walked to it, and stepped over the fire into the Pentagram in the core of the star. Then, he raised arms and head to the sky.

There were no clouds that night, and the heavens were dotted with thousands upon thousands of stars, each twinkling with all the brightness of miniature sun. He looked passed them and directed his attention to the silvery orb that hung full and large among them. Mentally, he ran through the incantation, and then began.

With each syllable, the fiery star blazed hotter, rose higher, though the sorcerer was too enthralled to pay heed to the increased heat and light. On the last word, he made a complex sign with his outstretched hands, closing his hidden eyes as he did so. A surge of magic coursed through him, and he did not need look at the moon to know that it was undergoing its ritual metamorphosis.

Satisfied, Ozmodion clapped his hands, extinguishing the star, and walked back to where the staircase emerged, chuckling as he descended.

He came to his private chambers, but instead of going to sit in his great, red throne, as was his custom, he went to the thick, black cauldron that rested in the center of the room. Beside it, on a small, stone plinth, was a goblet wrought from iron. He grasped it, and dipped it into the pot, filling it with oozing, violet liquid that bubbled inside. When it was full, he lifted the cup to his lips and drank the potion in one gulp. He then returned the chalice to the plinth, awaiting any change. Avria said there would be none, so he did not worry when he felt nothing different. With that, he walked to the great doors that separated the room from the rest of the fortress. They opened with a clap of his hands, and with a swish of his cloak he walked into the hall. He traveled down the corridor until he came across a brigade of goblins that were patrolling the halls with their swords resting over their shoulders. They halted and quickly stood at attention when they saw the red sorcerer. He hissed with distaste—they leered unpleasantly even when they groveled—and then addressed them coldly.

"Make ready my sedan," he whispered authoritatively. "We make for the Gates of Angar Vûn; I wish to be there when the Resistance falls."

☐

As usual, the effect of the Crimson Eclipse was instantaneous. The Ozra gave pause and looked to the sky and roared their joy and emboldened resolve. The Resistance, too, halted, staring at the moon with forlorn trepidation. Steel did not bother to share in their gaze; he had seen the Eclipse far too many times to be shocked by it. Instead, he prepared for what was to happen next. Invariably, once the Eclipse had been summoned, the Ozra redoubled their efforts, a fierce brutality ignited inside of them.

Being of a resourceful type, Steel built an advantage on the Ozra's momentary break and slew three of the nearest nightshades. As he expected, that roused them back to battle-readiness, both the Ozra and the Resistance.

He and his troop were engaged between the lines of the goblin and nightshade division, and, until now, they had been making glorious headway. The goblins, too big to cluster together, were overwhelmed as three shifters would pounced on them, searching for (or sometimes creating) weaknesses in the monsters' armor, and so slaying them quickly and strategically. The nightshades were also engulfed by the shifters' onslaught; though they were the swiftest of the Ozra, the infinite surge of attackers confused them, quelling their ability to defend themselves.

But the Eclipse changed that. Heartened by the knowledge that the Red Sovereign was with them, they found the strength to combat the Resistance. The goblins chuckled their throaty chuckles and began slashing left, right, and every which way, cleaving armor and head with depressing regularity. The nightshades pounced on the backs of the shifters, and with their scythe-like claws they slit exposed throats in systematic unison.

Fury stole over Steel, and he unsheathed another sword. Armed with both hands, he wielded the deadly metal as though they were extensions of his limbs rather than weapons. Soon, the ground was purple and saturated with spilt nightshade blood. The shifter allowed himself a grin, but it quickly disappeared.

The trolls were making their way toward the shifters and nightshades, brandishing huge, wooden clubs the size of tree trunks. Steel's platoon, assessing the danger, backed away, trying to immerse themselves deeper into the nightshade division. Steel could not blame them; they were no match for the trolls. But Steel knew that he had to do something to stop the stinking brutes. Too tired to shift form, he strengthened his armor and ran toward them, swords held aloft.

Three of the closest looked at him and guffawed stupidly. The first grasped his club with both hands and raised it above his head, but he hesitated to bring it down, supposedly because he was debating where to hit. Steel lunged forth, sheathing both of the blades deep into the monster's gut. It groaned and dropped its club. Steel didn't wait for it to collapsed, instead, he pulled his swords from the carcass and arced them towards the next troll, whose exposed neck met the tip of the sword that Steel clenched in his right hand. Emboldened, he turned to the last troll, but was stopped short as its club collided with him. He was sent soaring through the air, landing agonizingly by an upturned boulder.

His head swam, and it took a moment or two for things to come back into focus. When they did, two things were clear. He was in excruciating pain, and now the troll was coming toward him with his club raised. As the shifter braced himself for the death blow, he saw a huge, hulking figure coming from behind the troll. Steel's eyes nearly popped out of his head when he recognized what it was.

An ogre.

The ogre approached swiftly, but the troll, dwarfed in comparison, was oblivious to it. Steel knew that ogres were very territorial, and it was obvious that it thought Steel was his kill.

The shifter's theory was proved when the ogre placed its massive hands on the trolls shoulder, spun it around, picked up over its head, and hurled it into the fray, where it landed on top of five goblins with a deafening crunch.

Now Steel watched as the ogre turned back to him; black drool dripped from its very sharp teeth. With its face inches from Steel's, it slowly opened its mouth. Then...

"Y'okay, Steel?" it said in a familiar voice. The sword-burden shifter started.

"*Beast?*"

The ogre grinned, and then transformed to become the wild-looking shifter. His head was cocked inquisitively.

"Are you ok?" he repeated, now concerned as he saw the odd angle of Steel's limbs. Steel managed a weak smile and attempted to shake his head, but his back pained him too much to do so. Beast frowned.

"Quick, we will get you to the healers." He stretched his hand towards Steel, rendering him as a small sparrow. Then, Beast morphed into a hawk. The bird of prey trotted over to the sparrow, carefully taking him in his talons, and then flapped off as gently as he could towards the hospital tents far behind the front lines.

☐

The pelting rain was coming down in great, grey sheets. The dry earth of the hill absorbed it rapidly; none of the water pooled up or formed streams. It simply disappeared into the ground. Gwen's cloak was long soaked, but she paid no heed to the cold water.

She stared into the abyss, her vision blurred by the welling tears. Mentally, she flicked through every spell she had ever read, but nothing came to her. It did not matter though; she knew that there was no spell to resurrect the dead.

They all stood at the edge of the gorge. Some wept, while others could only stare in stark grief. The shifter guards, who hadn't known Ryan well, stood back respectfully several yards away from the edge, muttering their condolences in low voices.

Eion, however, was standing on the opposite edge, eyes wide with shock and anguish. Gwen could not blame him. She knew that he must've seen this as his own fault. There was part of Gwen that wanted to believe this was true, that wanted to hold him responsible. But she knew she couldn't. She knew it was Ryan who had brought his own fate.

It was Eion who probably contributed most to Gwen's distress. Never had she seen him like this. In all her memories of him, Eion was always either smiling or emanating with calm. He did neither of these now. He just stared into the gorge like many of the others. But his eyes...his eyes were the most disconcerting of all. They showed an emotion that Gwen had never seen in him or any other before; a pain mixed with failure and overwhelming, distraught uncertainty. Then, to her horror, Gwen realized that she shared with him the same feeling.

She could hardly see anything now, so thick were the tears, yet they refused to stream down. She wiped her eyes and sniffled quietly. At her feet, Curthlond rubbed his head against her legs comfortingly. She looked down upon him and tried to smile. Failing that, she managed to murmur some kind of acknowledgement and thanks.

Eion, however, was shaken from his grim angst by a particularly loud wail from Kendal. He blinked, and then he sprung from the ground, leaping to the other side of the gorge. He did not look anyone in the eye. He only said, "Come. We are near the summit. There will be time for mourning, but it is not now."

Lea, more composed then either Kendal or Caitlyn, looked up sharply. "Eion, we can't! It's too dangerous. What if someone else winds up...like..." But her voice broke, and she couldn't go on.

Eion still looked to the peak of Hamurlas and not at the group. "If we do not act quickly, then the Resistance will fall. Ozmodion will rise up and conquer this Magic Realm, and eventually, he will break the barriers of the Reflection and move to dominate the Mortal Realm. Your families, your friends, all will come to know his malice as they are slowly suffocated by his iron fist. The forests will dry and shrivel; the lakes will disappear into dust. Would you have Ryan's sacrifice be wasted? Would you suffer

Ozmodion to slay and corrupt your loved ones? We must go on. There are some things that are *worth* dying for. Come; we will be at the crest at the end of this hour."

And he set off, slower, as though weighted with a great burden. The shifter guards, matching his pace, followed, their steely eyes fixed on the horizon.

Gwen sighed raggedly and took a painful step after them, finally aware she was drenched with rain.

☐

It was a quiet march. No one spoke; they hardly breathed. In single file, with Eion at the lead, they trekked the mighty Hamurlas with only the sound of rain fall to break the silence.

Gwen felt hollow. If the death of Gorbon and the loss of Axunrult only shook her, Ryan's death shattered her. A year ago, they'd have been sitting together in school, happily ignorant of the mystic world separated by the magical barriers of the Reflection. But now Ryan was…

She couldn't bring herself to believe it. The very thought was so alien, so *impossible* that it seemed like it hadn't happened. But the sorrowful faces around her screamed otherwise. Many had tearstains running down their faces from their bloodshot eyes, while the others seemed so void of any feeling that Ryan's death was utterly confirmed.

These thoughts carried her for an hour or so, and she was so deeply pondering that she didn't notice that the rain had stopped. It wasn't until they had reached the crest of the mountain that Gwen was brought back from her troubled thoughts.

Saurindon unfolded before them, and she stared at it in terrified wonder. It was so immense; the descriptions and stories she had heard did not do the valley justice. It was an absolute sea of red sand, stretching to the horizon and out of sight. It was bereft of any trees or lakes or rivers or life of any kind; a fallow wasteland of crimson earth, neatly tucked behind the black Mountains of Midnight, which, like the Emerald Plains, formed a horseshoe around the desert.

And at the center of Saurindon, so far away that it seemed like a model in miniature, stood the infamous Fortress of Ozmodion: Taronest. Unlike Fairskin Manor far in the north, Taronest had been built for wars; it looked able to withstand any attack. It had but one gate, with an iron portcullis that would not yield even to the bitterest sword. Its nine towers were too high for arrows to reach; whatever archers that were posted on top of them would make easy sport of any intruders. Draped over many of the walls was a black banner with a red half circle embossed in the center: the Standard of Ozmodion.

"It's so far..." she started, but she was cut short by Eion.

"Yes, but before we can even set off across the Red Plateau, we must descend to the base of Hamurlas. Fortunately, this side is..." here he paused, and cleared his throat. "considerably less treacherous. Still, we must be wary; though the mountain is less dangerous, Ozmodion will have certainly kept some of the Ozra behind for sentries and reserve. Our goal rests entirely on stealth. If we're seen, we are as good as dead."

He allowed them a short rest now that they had conquered Hamurlas. They sat in silence while taking long draughts from their water skins and nibbling on the dry pieces of bread they had taken with them. Taciturnly, they looked as one to Saurindon.

They had made it this far. They had come far and through many dangers and adventures, and they had made it. The gorge looked up at them tauntingly, reminding them of their final task, of the true purpose of their quest. It was a grim thought.

After a while, Eion urged them to their feet. The guards, unquestionably loyal to their king, jumped up and immediately strapped their shields to their backs and tightened their sword belts. The mortals, tired with woe and overexertion, were inclined to mumble. They too adjusted their belts and chain mail. They stretched and arched their backs, futilely trying to comfort themselves. Eion clapped his hands, and led them down into the gorge. Trailing behind, Gwen hesitated. Curthlond picked up his ears and meowed questioningly.

Gwen smiled sadly and shook her head, taking one last look at Taronest. Then, with forced kind of laugh, she set off to follow the rest of the group, bidding a sad and silent farewell to Hamurlas. And to Ryan.

☐

Nothing escaped Vaeirnïr's eyes. Red and livid, they absorbed everything. Yet they were searching for something in particular, in both the sky and on the land, for Vaeirnïr had a deeper intention that spurred him to battle.

Whatever hindrance he met, he quickly dealt with savage ferocity. Dragons oftentimes flew up to attack him, but they soon learned to avoid the black general after he had sent more than a dozen to their deaths. But he never forgot his greater purpose; though many arrows and elven spells rose up in attempt to quell him, he focused on only one thought: revenge.

A great red light lit up the sky as he belched a stream of red flame from his maw, sending it after a bluish-green dragon that had ventured to near. The impotent creature started and veered sharply away. Vaeirnïr allowed himself a chuckle, and he dipped down a little, combing the battlegrounds for his quarry. He smelt him; it had been centuries since his soul resided in his body, but he still hadn't forgotten the scent. His forked tongue flicked out as he tasted the air. He was close. Very close.

Looking down, he saw that he had flown to the northern edge of the Ozra Gap. With a rumbling growl, he tilted his wings and turned his tail so that he veered to the right. A volley of arrows was fire, aimed directly for his underbelly. He paid them no heed, knowing that they would fall short of their mark by forty feet. Foolish archers, did they not know that he was Vaeirnïr Bloodshedder? The *true* dragon king? It would be this night that he reclaimed his throne and destroy the usurping traitor who had ripped him from body and mind.

He looked about him, and saw the ten Maurimim wreaking havoc upon their wyvern steeds. The dragons presented the most opposition, yet the elves far below would occasionally raise their staff and send curses hurtling towards the shadow shifters and their mounts. Though the dragons were bulkier and of greater strength, the smaller wyverns were better able to maneuver, weaving in and out the surrounding dragons while sending quick jets of fire from their jaws. The shadow shifters themselves were all armed with bows of black yew and arrows with white shafts. They sent swarms of the deadly missiles raining down upon the resistance, taking careful aim to bring down the enemy archers first. They were succeeding.

The wind shifted and swept toward Vaeirnïr. The scent was stronger than ever. He whipped his head around instinctively toward the smell.

There he was. His grandson did not look much like him; his scales were a myriad of red, silver, and black, and his teeth were a shiny gold instead of pale ivory. But he recognized the same look in his eyes; an untamable fierceness.

The two dragons roared their battle cries when their eyes met and they quickly rushed towards each other, preparing to viciously rip each other to shreds.

"Tonight, Breeog," roared Vaeirnïr as he fended of the enemy claws, "you will die."

"Nay, Bloodshedder," his grandson replied with equally cold intensity. "It is you who will finally die."

A roar tore from the black dragon, then, "We shall see! We shall see!" And thus, in a deadly dance far above the ground, the two titanic beasts battled, raining blood upon the Ozra Gap as they slashed.

☐

Between the black, craggy recesses of the foothills of the Mountains of Midnight, they saw the temple. Black and looming, it seemed like a place that would only be fit to worship Avria, the Goddess of Death. It seemed strange in the daylight—the infinite night was limited to only the outlying lands near the Mountains of Midnight—as though it did not belong outside of the hours between sundown and sunrise.

Eion looked at it and weighed the odds. Thus far, he had heard no sounds of sentries, except for the far away activities of those guarding Angar Vûn. He thought for certain that Ozmodion would have guards patrolling the whole of the valley. He had been wrong, apparently

Ozmodion intended to strike the Resistance with full force and leave Saurindon relatively unprotected.

Bold. Admirable, thought Eion begrudgingly. He was loathe to admit that the benefits far outweighed the risk, and Ozmodion was an exceptional strategist to propose such a campaign.

Eion hated him for it. Though he knew that Ryan's death had been no one's fault but Ryan's, Eion credited it to Ozmodion, the latest in a long line of murders and assassinations. Ryan's life was now one more that called for revenge. Eion would answer it, or would succumb to death himself.

He halted suddenly. He heard the sound of clanking armor and swords. He turned to the mortals and the shifter guards, motioning for them to stand to stay still. Then he strained to hear the sound again.

He did not have to wait long. The sound came again, louder, closer. It seemed that the absent sentries had finally come. Quietly, Eion shifted into a plume of smoke. He led the wind carry him up and over the temple. He looked across the red moorland, searching for the source of the noise. He found it. Stricken with fear and shock, he condensed his form and tried to blend in with the wall of Avria's temple.

Twenty goblins marched about half a mile from the doors of the temple, four of which were burdened with a golden red sedan chair. Eion did not need to wonder who it carried; Ozmodion was going to Angar Vûn, supposedly to watch the great battle from a distance. The blatant arrogance angered Eion beyond words, but he kept his temper in check, knowing that any rash action at this critical point would doom the Resistance.

Instead, he drifted back where the rest of the group waited, shifting into his usual form. They socked their heads and furrowed their brows when they saw the look on Eion's face. He didn't keep them in anticipation long, quickly relaying what he saw.

"The Red Sovereign is a few hundred feet away from where we stand. If he makes it to Angar Vûn, he will be too guarded for us to get near. Now is our chance to bring him down. Our only hope is to take down his guards and strike now when he doesn't expect it."

Conviction and passion dripped from his tongue, and he knew that a wild strength would be burning in his eyes, but he saw from their faces that they were more than a little uncertain. The shifter, unwaveringly devoted, betrayed no doubt, but the mortals' expression loudly sounded their qualms. Kendal and Caitlyn exchanged dubious looks, and Colin and Brad shifted their wait from leg to leg. Eric's face was paler than usual. Even Gwen, though wreathed in her aura of power, seemed apprehensive, while Curthlond seemed downright twitchy.

Too pressed to ponder to their fear, Eion unsheathed *Raz'atr*. The sunlight seemed to dim a little with sword held high. It pulsed with anticipation, longing to be sheathed in Ozmodion's breast. He then lowered it, and held it in between them all.

"Who is with me?"

There was a brief and awkward pause, but then Eric stepped forth, unsheathing his sword and holding the steel against *Raz'atr*. And then, one by one, the rest followed suit, all with resigned but determined smiles, until finally Gwen placed her blade in. They all looked at each other in comradeship, and then they lifted their weapons into the air as one.

After they had all returned their blades to their sheaths, Eion gathered them closely, the mortals and the shifters, and quickly devised a plan.

Varez cursed his foolishness. He saw now that the ploy should have been obvious to him, but he was so engaged in the battle he hadn't seen it coming. Now, as the three, hungry shadow wolves closed in about him, Varez saw it could have been so easily avoided.

He had been fighting alongside a legion of dwarves in the shadow wolf division. Because both the wolves and the dwarves fought close to the ground, they had been at a stalemate for a long time. The dwarves had held their axes firmly, and the wolves had countered by forming a large ring around them, snarling and growling menacingly. Still, neither dared attack; if the dwarves were to run first, the wolves would be on them before they could make even one kill, and the wolves could not attack with out meeting the bitter steel of the axes.

Finally, perhaps out of boredom, one of the dwarves had unfastened his crossbow from his belt and, in one fluid motion, raised it to eye level and fired it at the closest wolf. It embedded itself right between the wolf's eyes, and in another the moment, the wolf had collapsed to the ground, dead.

The wolves had reacted with swift rage, and with many a yelp and howl, they converged around the dwarves. Varez groaned and swung the great, two-bladed axe he held in both hands as though it weighed nothing. He cleaved a wolf's skull, and then decapitated another.

Now, with three of their fellows fallen, the wolves' fury was fiercer than ever. They lunged and slashed and ripped and tore until only Varez and five other dwarves were left standing. They all shared looks of concern and unease, but they quickly redoubled their efforts.

After twenty minutes of this, many of the wolves had found that it was not worth losing any more of their numbers, running off to find their next prey. Relieved, the five other dwarves followed the wolves' example, and they set out to aid a group of shifters who were combating a pack of nightshades. Varez was about to join them, but he thought it best that he clean his axe first. After he had wiped it and returned the now soiled kerchief around his neck, he looked to where the five dwarves had run off to, but found that a rabid-looking shadow wolf was standing between him and the others. It growled softly.

Varez had sniffed and made to walk the other way, but saw that a second wolf stood there too. It was bulkier than the other, and it was panting in patient expectancy, as though it were bracing itself for attack.

With a quick flick of his eyes, Varez had looked from the second wolf to the first, to the second, and then finally back to the first. He appraised the logistics, but, finding no immediate solution, he decided to buy some time by slowly, slowly taking several paces back.

The wolves growled simultaneously, and then the first barked something in their strange language to the other. It answered with a long, blood-curdling howl. Varez knew that could not be good. He took a readier grip on his axe.

As he had continued to back up, the wolves continued to slink menacingly slowly after him. Then, a third wolf came trotting up beside them, filling the unguarded space between the first two and falling into step. Now Varez was scared. They were pushing him to the west, towards the edge of Ÿalnz Dàr. He knew that if they forced him into the trees, he would have no room to wield his weapons and they would fully have their way with him.

But, as it seemed, he had no need of such worries. He took one last step backwards, and then collided with something solid. He spun around instinctively, and now saw that the wolves had backed him up against a gigantic boulder of granite. He spun around again to face the wolves, and saw that they were laughing quietly.

He gulped audibly, and awaited the inevitable. If he could only reach his crossbow, he still might have a chance. But he knew he could not grab it quickly enough. The wolves would be playing with his ragged corpse in a matter a moments. And so, with a heavy sigh, he quickly muttered a prayer to Garon under his breath, and closed his eyes, waiting for the wolves to pounce.

They never did. There came three *whoosh*ing sounds in rapid succession, and then the sound of someone landing from a high jump. Varez peeked from under one eye lid, and then gasped as he saw that each of the three wolves were lying still on the ground with an arrow protruding from each of their necks. Eyes wide open now, Varez turn around in search of the archer.

There was Fletch, leaning casually against the granite, examining his nails with interest.

"Trouble, Varez?" he asked coolly, not bothering to look up from his cuticles.

Varez grumbled, but then he laughed his barking chuckle. "None, thanks to you, old friend."

"Mm. Well, if you are done, we have a battle to get back to." He jerked his head toward the fray, where the sounds of battle rang like tolling bells. He then looked up and stood from his leaning position.

Varez nodded gruffly, and strode forward, clasping the shifter on the shoulder as he strode passed. Fletch returned the gesture and the followed after the dwarf. At Varez's request, neither spoke of the incident ever again.

By dint of Gwen's magic, they walked toward the caravan silent and unseen. Eion knew that Ozmodion would have wards on his person that would detect any magic once it got close to him. This was nothing but a diversion; they only needed to get close enough to take out some of the goblin guards before Ozmodion was aware of their presence; once the sorcerer was alerted of danger, he would be able to smite them all with a single curse.

Thus, Eion demanded the utmost stealth possible. He looked over at Gwen, the shrouds of invisibility did not apply to those under the enchantment, to check on her. She looked up at him and smiled, but a strained look crept into her face. It was taxing enough to conceal one's self, but to hide thirty two was clearly exhausting.

"Just a little longer," the shifter sympathized, but he knew that they were very close to the convoy now. He looked ahead, and found that they were only about thirty yards away.

Good, thought Eion. *Within striking distance.*

He motioned them to stop, and then for the shifters to prepare their bows. With grins and chortles, they obeyed, and from their quivers they each pull out one arrow and nocked it against the frame. Then Eion raised his hand and checked the goblins' position one last time. Thirty yards.

He allowed himself a smile, and then he lowered his hand.

The strings were all released with a deafening *twang*, which went, thanks to magic, unheard by the doomed goblins. Eion watched the missiles soar, and found that even he held his breath.

The arrows arched up into the sky and then nosed down toward their targets. They were closing in. fifteen feet, ten, five…

But then they all halted and fell to the ground, leaving the goblins unscathed. The creatures jumped in surprise when they saw them land at their feet, frightened and deeply confused. They looked this way and that trying to search for their attackers, but all in vain; Gwen's invisibility spell was doing its job.

Eion sucked in his breath quickly, trying to think of what to do. Perhaps he should have them fire again. He was about to give the order, but he was cut off as the sedan chair burst into flames. The goblins dropped it with yelps of pain and shock, now worked into a positive nervous wreck.

Eion swore. Many of the mortals jumped. Curthlond hissed.

"I can't hold the spell any longer!" Gwen cried, as the magic faded. Unguarded, the goblins saw them. With many roars and yells, they unsheathed their swords and sprinted after their attackers.

The shifter guards responded in kind. They pulled their weapons from their sheaths and ran to meet the goblins. They converged, and again the sounds of battle filled the air.

Eion ached to join them, and apparently so did Eric and Anthony, who had both put a hand to their swords' scabbard and had taken a step forward. But Eion motioned them to hold back. For now, he was keeping eye on the burning sedan chair. It simply sat there, totally engulfed in crackling fire.

In a grand explosion, it collapsed. But the flames grew; a shape stepped from them.

As the flaming figure emerged, the goblins and shifters battled, knocking sword against shield and armor, or sometimes even grappling with bare fists. They growled and shouted and cursed and roared, oblivious to the greatening flame just several feet behind them.

Then, forty bolts of lightning erupted from it, impaling each goblin and shifter through the heart. It was as though a conductor of puppets had let go of all the strings, and each of them died instantly, crumpling to the red earth.

Eion took a step forward, stopping short as a ring of fire ignited from the great flame. It surrounded the Prophesied and Eion, trapping them in a fiery prison along with the bodies of the fallen shifters and goblins.

Eion turned to the rising flame, but saw that it had been quenched, and in its place stood a figure that Eion had not seen in more than a millennium.

The figure was garbed in a red cloak that shimmered in the firelight. Its face was hidden by the shadow of the hood. Its hands, gray and decrepit, were clasped together and hanging loosely in front of it. It took several steps forward, and then laughed.

"Well met, Eion Shifter," said Ozmodion.

☐

The soldier looked up with eyes full of terror. The chest plate of his armor rose and fell with his heaving breaths, contorting the reflection of the Eclipse high above. An imploring look crept into his eyes; mingled with the fear and mental anguish, it stood out starkly, pleading for life.

Having seen it too many times, Gorez didn't marvel it. Instead, he flexed the claws of his right hand and plunged them into the breast plate, piercing metal and flesh as though they were butter. The soldier tried to scream, but only manage a faint gurgling sound. Then, slowly, he exhaled, and the agony and terror of his face melted away as his features relaxed. Finally, the gentle rise of his armor ceased.

Satisfied, Gorez extracted his claws and held his hand high, examining the red blood staining his purple claws. With a shrug, he flicked his wrist, flinging droplets of blood from the claws to speckle the dead soldier's face with red.

The war was progressing at what seemed a snail's pace to Gorez. He had run into the charge thirsty for blood. But now, as the death tolls mounted higher and higher on both sides, Gorez was beginning to grow bored. Why did the Resistance not surrender? Looking about the Ozra Gap, he saw that the ground was littered with the bodies of fallen elves, dwarves and shifters. Even a dragon carcass or two was to be found among the carnage, thanks to the Maurimim and their wyvern steeds. The nightshade looked into the sky, and saw that the ten dark shadows were still circling, sending volley after volley of arrows while contending with the onslaught of dragons. Above them, two shapes were entangled with each other, breaking apart occasionally only to converge again in a matter of seconds. Gorez allowed himself a chuckle; Vaeirnïr was taking a while with his revenge.

All well and good, but Gorez was beginning to find things rather dull. He looked around lazily, ignoring the commotion and noise of the fray as he searched for a next mark.

Then, to his maddened glee, he saw a notable candidate.

The Lord Fairskin was hobbling about, leaning heavily on his cane. The combatants of both the Ozra and the Resistance ignored him, so enthralled were they in battling each other. The old elf seemed frail, worn too thin. Understandable, since he had marched the hundreds of leagues from his home in the north only to arrive at a war of titanic proportions. Why he was casually strolling through the battle field was beyond him, but he didn't care; all he knew was that Ozmodion would greatly reward the servant that brought him Fairskin's head in a sack.

He stalked towards the old elf, claws extended dangerously. Before he could get close, though, two burly elves stepped in front of them, making an X with their staffs.

"He's mine!" said the first, a tall fellow with shortly cropped hair. His radiant blue eyes bore through him with seething hatred.

"No, this one's mine," the other, shorter elf, with long, dark hair tucked under his helm, challenged.

The nightshade clicked his tongue. "I have no time to posture with a couple elven saplings like yourselves. I will ask this only once: get out of my way if you wish to live."

The two elves moved their staffs to readier positions. A spell formed on their lips, but Gorez lunged before they could speak any syllable. In the blink of an eye, the two elves were lying on the ground, blood pooling from their slit throats, and the nightshade was again creeping closer to the hobbling elf, calm and poised as though nothing had happened.

He made no sound, drew no breath, and was already savoring his victory when a twig broke under his foot.

The elf's head turned toward the nightshade in a blur. Whatever expression Gorez had been expecting, it certainly wasn't the one Lord Fairskin wore. There was no fear like that of the soldier, nor any imploring look of mercy. There was not even a look of steely determination, like the few soldier's Gorez had killed who had died nobly without any sniveling. No, instead there was only look of mild amusement and cheer.

Something was obviously wrong with the demented old elf, if he could look grim death in the eyes and laugh while he himself was using his staff as a crutch.

Fairskin chuckled, shaking his head. "Ah Gorez," he said airily, "must it come to this? Thus far, even the lowest of your underlings have had the sense to steer clear of me. It is not too late; walk away now, and you might yet see tomorrow's dawn."

Gorez chortled and guffawed and snorted, loudly. "Do you really think I will run from a broken-down geriatric like you?"

Fairskin only shrugged, which was difficult while leaning on his staff. "Only if you have any sense."

"Ha! That is rich. My, I absolutely fail to understand why the Vra's kept you around so long."

The elf replied, "I wouldn't expect you to."

A wicked grin split Gorez's, revealing his razor array of teeth. "I am going to enjoy this."

Lord Fairskin's smile became a frown, and he put a hand to his brow in a resigned way. "I am sorry to say that I will not."

"Well then…shall we?"

He nodded, and raised his staff above his head. "As you wish."

The old elf muttered a long incantation. As he did, a bright, red nexus formed around the staff's tip, growing and shrinking with each word. Gorez tried springing forth and attacking, but found that the nexus was so enticing that he could not bring himself to move. Looking at it, he smelt the sweet scents of his old home in the Il'lion Plains. A myriad of old thoughts and memories came flooding back to him, sweeping by and then leaving just as quickly. He remembered roaming across the fields when he had been a pup playing with his brothers and cousins; he remembered learning to hunt from his father and uncles, who showed his how to creep upon unsuspecting deer and other animals; he remembered fighting a rival nightshade during his adolescence. He remembered how he had slashed and slashed so fluidly that the other nightshade had gone off yelping in pain to nurse his wounds; he remembered that he had grown up to be the biggest in the pack, and was thus elected leader; he remembered when Ozmodion's attendant spirit came and cast a spell over their minds.

Emotions of all kinds swirled around him in a frenzied torrent. Rage met joy, and sorrow became anguish. He tried to block the memories, but they played across the nexus long and bright.

Finally, he remembered the task at hand. With a shake of his head, he looked away from the nexus. He clicked his tongue again and stalked toward Fairskin once more.

Then, a bright flash of light erupted from the core of the red nexus. It exploded forth with immeasurable velocity and consumed the entire Gap. It lingered for fifteen seconds, and when it passed, a pile of ashes stood where Gorez had been only seconds before.

And there, left standing was Lord Fairskin, who lowered his staff slowly and placed his weight upon it, shaking his head as if with regret.

☐

For a split second that felt like an eternity, Eion could not bring himself to move or speak. He had imagined this moment for an uncountable number of years, and never once did he expect that it would turn out like this. The guards lay dead on top of the goblins, their eyes glazed and blind, their breathing stopped. The ring of fire burned without fuel; some black magic trickery that no doubt amused Ozmodion.

And there was Ozmodion himself. He seemed exactly as Eion remembered him; tall, broodingly quiet, graceful, menacing. He felt small in the sorcerer's presence, like the little boy that he was when had first met him. He felt the hidden eyes under the hood stare at him, appraising, sizing him up...

The shifter pushed it from his mind. This would be nothing like the last time. Now he was older, stronger, wiser, armed with new weapons, aided by new friends.

"Well met, Ozmodion," he replied stiffly. He bowed mockingly, making his hate clear. The sorcerer only chuckled again.

"So formal. There is no need; we are old friends, are we not? Yes, friends spanning over centuries and, indeed, millennia."

Eion shrugged. "It is good of you to look at it like that." He took a casual step to the right, his hands now clasped behind his back. "I would have thought you would have held some kind of grudge."

"A grudge? Me? Oh, no, of course not. In fact, I ought to be thanking you; those years and years in the void would have driven a lesser man insane. But me, strong and enduring, I was able to put it to use. Yes, I saw the error in my incantations, my spells. I let the energies of the next life fuel and charge me. My eyes have been opened to possibilities I had never prior dreamed of. You look on a changed man...No, I am more than man, greater than mortal. I have gone to the grave and returned. A *mere man* cannot claim as much."

"How lucky for them!" Eion fired back.

Ozmodion looked past him.

"Ah, the Great Prophesied, I presume? At last we meet. I have been waiting for this day for a lifetime now. After all, you can imagine my concern when I read in the Scriptures that it would be ten *mortals* who would bring me down. But hold...I see only nine. Where, then, is the tenth?"

A pain rose in Eion's chest, but he suppressed it and. "He fell."

Ozmodion shook his head with false sympathy. "Pity. I tried to warn you Eion that you would only be forcing these mortals to their deaths. Their blood is on your hands."

"Enough blood has been spilt on your account, Ozmodion. It ends today.'

"Oh, for *sooth*?" the Red Sovereign whispered dangerously, putting small stress on the last word. "I have died once, Eion Shifter; I do not intend to do it again."

Eion smiled, and unsheathed *Raz'atr*. "Then I apologize in advance." He rushed forth with his sword aimed at the sorcerer's heart.

Like thunder cracking after lightning, Ozmodion swiftly unsheathed his red sword and brought it crashing against Eion's. They came together, and then, as one, they pushed each other's blades away with a thrust. They spun, arced their blades, and again the two weapons came together, sending a shower of sparks into the air.

"Attack!" Eion screamed over his shoulder, and then he quickly parried as Ozmodion slashed with *Uthu'rach*. The red blade was a livid red, made all the more intense by the crackling flames. In it, the lives of one thousand forsaken souls were reflected, screaming the vestiges of the past.

Gwen was the first to act. She leapt up beside him, wielding her sword as though nothing else came more natural. Ozmodion took a quick look at her, and then he horizontally slashed his sword at her side. She parried with driving force, and twisted to the left, arched her sword up, and finally brought it down above his head. The sorcerer blocked, but found that Eion was now preparing to thrust his sword at his unprotected chest. Ozmodion growled and barked a syllable.

And invisible force hit Eion head on, sending him back fifteen feet through the air to land painfully on top of the dead body of one of the goblins. By pure fluke, he missed the dead monster's horn. As he righted himself, he saw that both Anthony and Eric had joined Gwen, brandishing swords in their well-choreographed dance into battle.

Ozmodion had no trouble contending; in his hand, *Uthu'rach* seemed like a second entity with a mind of its own. He warded off their attacks almost lazily, not even bothering to use any offensive strategy.

"Is this really all you can summon, Eion Shifter?" he cried over the clamor of the swords. "You disappoint me."

Eion growled and turned to the rest of the Prophesied.

"Come on!" he shouted, and then he turned with *Raz'atr* drawn. There was Ozmodion, his free hand outstretched, and a spell had just escaped his lips. A red bolt flashed from his palm. Eion followed it with his eyes, and when it was in range, he slashed at it with his sword. The blue blade took on the spell's color as it absorbed it, and then flashed white as it sent it hurtling back toward the warlock. He cursed and uttered the cancellation spell, finishing as the betraying curse came within inches of his heart. It dissipated into nothing while *Raz'atr* took back its usual blue sheen.

"Damn that sword," Ozmodion hissed. He swung his at Gwen, who parried it reflexively. "You ought to know by now, Eion Shifter, that the Five Blades are meant only for the worthy."

"How strange then," replied the shifter, thrusting toward the sorcerer, "that you yourself carry one."

Ozmodion chuckled and brought his sword down upon Eion, who quickly shifted size and skirted the blow. *Uthu'rach* was embedded into the red earth. As Ozmodion tried to pull it from the ground, Eion lunged at him, receiving a kick in the chest in return. Ozmodion then extracted it from the ground, and faced his attackers. Now, all the mortals had entered the fight, and together, they surrounded the sorcerer, swords extended.

Ozmodion laughed a crippling sound full of amusement and malice. He sheathed his red sword and addressed them all as the ring of fire closed tighter around them.

"Eion, you surprise me. Do you think you could really best me with only the help of nine novices? Now they will die because of you did not prepare them sufficiently. One can hardly blame you though; no one can resist the might of the Red Sovereign. As you shall now see."

He raised his hands above his hands. Eion knew then it was too late to stop him from casting a spell, but, with luck and Gwen's help, he might be able to make it a less potent one; death curses required concentration and lengthy incantations. He jumped into the air, sword outstretched. Ozmodion took a step back and muttered a spell. Nine rays of blue light flashed from the sorcerer's hands, smiting each of the mortals through the heart.

☐

Rembas tried not to look smug, but it was an expression that came surprisingly easy to him. He wiped his smirk off and tried to adopt the looks of the shifters and elves around him; grim and determined.

The ten Maurimim were still circling above, but now with the prospect of the legion of elves Rembas had brought to the shifter division, they thought twice of attacking; they were in range of the magic staffs.

Thus, Rembas felt compelled to gloat in front of the shifters who had called him coward as he had run from the battle, all of whom were now skulking a little ways away from the rest of the soldiers.

They were all very still; it seemed that the bulk of the Ozra was preoccupied in some other part of the Gap. For now, they were preparing for the attack the shadow shifters would be sure to unleash in moments. No dragons were there, for they too were engaged somewhere else, which was presumably why no soldier of the Ozra was bothering them here.

Rembas whistled lightly, waiting. The silence was long and unwavering, disrupted only by the beating of the wyvern's wings. Then the faun had the sinking suspicion he was being watched. As he looked around, he saw that all eyes were on him.

He shifted uncomfortably. "What? Something on my face? Dirt? Grease? No? Then Gods, what is it!"

An elf stepped forward and bowed respectfully. "We wait for your command, Master—"

"If you finish that sentence, I will eat your face," the faun said severely. "My command? Why? I mean, c'mon, I'm no great soldier, much less a commander."

"You are too modest—" the elf began, a genial smile played across his fair face, but Rembas cut him off again.

"I'll be the judge of that. Come now, what's your reasoning?"

It was the soldiers' turn to shift uncomfortably, but the elf did not budge. "Our captains have fallen, and you have shown your wisdom by weighing the odds and making the appropriate judgment, despite being thought a coward by some of the less insightful." He jerked his head meaningfully toward the group of skulking shifters. Rembas chuckled and shot them a wide grin. Then he turned back to the elf and considered.

"So be it, then," he said after a while. "Um, I guess that you should, I don't know, bring 'em down."

The elf coughed. "Might I suggest we aim for the wyverns and then face the shifters on foot?"

"Your call."

"Actually, sir, it is yours."

"Ah. Yes. Well, sounds good, I say you do it."

"Do what, sir?"

"Bring em down."

"Who might ''em' be, sir?"

Rembas sighed, forgetting that elves always demanded carefully framed orders, questions, and conversations. Therefore, Rembas had never thought much of them; in his mind, anyone who could not read context clues or slang was not worth consorting with.

"Bring the wyverns down. You happy?"

"Delighted, sir," the elf answered as he raised his staff above his head, pointing it at the closest wyvern carefully. "*Veai mordo!*" he roared. A flash of green light erupted from the staff and shot toward the wyvern with incredible speed. It collided with the airborne creature, and engulfed it in a noxious cloud of the same hue. A roar was heard, and when the cloud passed, the wyvern flailed its weakened wings, and tumbled to the ground. Its rider, unharmed, shifted into a falcon and leapt for the doomed beast's back. It circled downward in wide spirals as the wyvern fell to the earth, sending up a huge cloud of dust.

Now, another nine elves raised their staffs, each aiming at a different wyvern and uttering the same incantation. The sky was ignited with the same green light as the nine bolts of magic blasted from the staffs and collided with the wyverns. Each was consumed by the same cloud, and each fell to the ground as their muscles failed them. None of them got back up once they landed. Each of their passengers, however, followed the first's example and shifted into black falcons, spiraling down. They came to a point where they were low enough for the dust from the fallen wyverns to consume, and then they were lost from sight.

So Rembas and the rest waited. After a while, a shadow stepped forth from the dust cloud, followed by a second, and then a third. The dust dissipated; apparently by some group effort of the shifter. When it cleared, Rembas and the soldiers saw that the wyverns were gone, and in their place stood the ten shadow shifters, their long, red swords drawn in uniform fashion. Their red eyes blazed angrily from under the scarves wrapped around their faces.

"We suppose you see that as some kind of victory?" they asked in one, simultaneous, dark whisper. They all took one slow, menacing step forward. "Fools, we are the Maurimim, beings of air and shadow. Slay a thousand of our mounts, and we will only make more."

Rembas scoffed loudly and blatantly. Ten pairs of red eyes turned on him and narrowed questioningly. "Something funny, fomariun?"

Rembas looked over both of his shoulders before he realized they were talking to him. He grinned boyishly. "No. I was just wondering…I mean, after all, you're obviously just flesh and bone, right?"

They hissed. "Yes…"

"Mortal too, yeah?"

"Yes…"

"So, in all honesty, death could meet you just as easily as it could any of us, right?"

The shifters seemed to have had enough. They clenched their gloved hands around the hilts of their swords, and they shuddered with irritation. "Technicalities, all. We are still more than a match for you, riffraff. In addition, with a call of our horns, half the Ozra would be at our sides."

Rembas peered over their shoulders. "Yet they're not here now…hm…interesting odds…"

The first shifter actually laughed at this, if one could call wheezing like the last cry of a dying animal laughing, yet it dripped with amused mirth.

"Take one step," he said, after he had recovered, "and we will spill your intestines on the ground."

Rembas opened his mouth to reply, but then he decided against it. Instead he shrugged and said, "Think fast."

Quicker than thought, he reached into his satchel and pulled out his loaded crossbow. In the same movement, he had taken aim and fired the arrow. It whizzed in a spinning motion, and sped toward the shifter until the shaft had embedded itself between the shifter's eyes. For a brief second, his eyes betrayed a look of astonishment, but it was quickly snuffed out as the shifter died and toppled over.

The other nine shared an equal amount of incredulity. They looked to their fallen comrade, and then to Rembas. The faun was smiling with a look of paramount satisfaction, and he stowed his weapon back in his bag. Then he proceeded to examine his abdomen with mock confusion and interest.

"Strange…intestines are fine. Didn't think you Maurimim blokes would be all bark and no bite."

The remaining shadow shifters took several steps forward with their sword all pointed toward the faun. "You will not live to regale this, fomariun."

Another shrug, and then. "Sadly, neither will you." He turned to the elf beside him. "Captain," he began.

The elf coughed again. "Lieutenant, sir."

Rembas rolled his eyes. "Oh, bleeding hell, *whatever*. Fire at will."

The elf nodded with a grin, and raised his staff. Three elves followed his example, while ten shifters shifted bows, placing two arrows against the frames. The Maurimim looked around, and for the first time, they seemed hesitant. They stopped their advance and some even took several paces back. But at that moment, the elves and the shifters fired their curses and missiles. Rembas turned away, not bothering to watch for he was fully confident all their aims were true. When the lights of the magic and the sounds of the arrows ceased, Rembas saw the elves who had jeered him as he left. He smiled.

"So much for 'coward', huh?"

☐

Breeog was tiring. For time out of mind, he had been the strongest dragon of all; such was one of the requirements of a dragon king. But here he was, high above the battlements of Angar Vûn, exhausted and only getting weaker.

Vaeirnïr must have noticed this, for he abated his slashes and beatings to say, "Weary, O Grandson? Such is unbecoming in the King of the Dragons. Perhaps it is time for the throne to be given away again, eh?"

Breeog's answer was simple: he opened his maw and belched forth a stream of fire. By now, he had lost so much hydrogen in his third lung that he could only manage a weak tongue of flame, but he still drove the point home. Sadly, Vaeirnïr's long neck snaked around it.

"Not today, not ever, O Grandfather," replied Breeog in a faint whisper. "Death will come upon me before I relinquish the throne to you."

Vaeirnïr nodded with false unhappiness. "I fear you are right." He inhaled deeply, preparing for the death blow.

Breeog did not wait for it. He sunk into a steep dive and plummeted past cloud and smoke. A roar behind him told him that the black dragon was now in hot pursuit. He did not care; he knew that he was beyond killing Vaeirnïr now, but he would not allow himself to be forever denied his justice.

He was now above the roof of green that was Ÿalnz Dàr. He judged the distance, and then, with the last of his hydrogen, spewed forth a blast of fire, burning a hole in the leafy roof.

Whoosh! He passed through the thick layer of branches and boughs and limbs. He pulled up sharp, unfurling his wings as far as he dared in the narrow darkness. His speed reduced dramatically, and he was almost at a complete stop by the time his four claws dug into the ground of the forest floor.

Then he slipped deeper into the fringe and kept very still, making no more noise than whisper. Above, a great and terrible roar was heard.

"COWARD!" Vaeirnïr bellowed. "COWARD! DRAGON KING, THEY CALL YOU? I CALL YOU COWARD! HERE YOU SLINK LIKE A DYING RAT AND CRAWL INTO A DARK HOLE WHILE BATTLE IS RAGED! WOULD YOUR SUBJECTS APPROVE? WILL YOU NOT ANSWER? SO BE IT! I WILL DROWN THE RESISTANCE IN ITS OWN BLOOD! AND YOU, I INVITE *YOU* TO SINK INTO UTTER OBSCURITY AND COWARDICE!"

Amid the sound of flapping wings, Vaeirnïr was gone. Breeog thought on his words. *Coward, am I?* True, he was too weak to fly or even breathe fire, but the dragon king knew he was still apt to fight. Slowly, he made his way out of the forest, content with the idea of finishing the rest of the battle by cracking the skulls of Ozra thugs on the ground.

"No!" Eion cried as he watched the bolts hit the nine, but there was nothing he could do in mid leap. He landed, and looked about, terrified of what he might see.

Kendal wore a look that had been caught somewhere between a gawk and a grimace. Brad's mouth was open, as though he had been preparing to scream, but no sound came. All were very, very still...

Eion cocked his head, confused. "Er...what did you do?"

Ozmodion swore when he saw them. "Bah! Froze them; I could not complete the spell. Curse it! And curse *you,* Eion Shifter. You have been a thorn in my side for too long now. Rest assured though, once I kill you, I will duly take care of your *friends.*" He unsheathed his sword and ran at Eion with all the swiftness of the north wind. Eion raised it and prepared himself for the impact. The sorcerer struck with greater force than Eion had ever felt. His shoulder throbbed with a pain that extended all the way down his arm. He shook it off, and prepared to counter the attack, but Ozmodion had already struck again with the same driving force. Now his arm was a veritable fire, and the pain was stretching down the right side of his body.

Tactfully, Eion changed hands, for he was as adept with his left as eh was with his right. Ozmodion now saw the shifter's weakness and quickly he attacked the shifter's weakened right. Eion parried, but it was a feeble block, and Ozmodion found a way through it and slashed his side.

Eion had always known that *Uthu'rach* had had a certain magic that made wounds unbearable and hard to heal. Until now, he had never understood how great that magic was. But as the blood surfaced, he felt a fiery ache in his side that seemed to consume his whole body. He couldn't see; the white hot pain quelled his vision. He heard a piercing scream, and it took him a moment to realize that it was him.

The initial surge of agony subsided, and with it so did his blindness. Ozmodion came swimming into focus, casually leaning on *Uthu'rach* and laughing quietly to himself.

"You have become slower..."he commented in whispers. "One millennium's not seen you improved; you are still the little boy who struck when no one was looking."

Anger fused with pain boiled inside Eion. He did not bother to reply verbally. Instead, he favored a more direct approach.

Ozmodion blocked his attack with a lightning quick motion of his sword. Eion cursed under his breath, and then arched *Raz'atr* at the sorcerer again. Ozmodion parried effortlessly, and then counter attack with a thrust. Eion sidestepped it by a hairsbreadth, and then, during the brief pause that followed, he healed his wound by shifting a new layer of skin on top of it. The pain was still there, but Eion knew that he would no longer be losing anymore blood.

Ozmodion did not seem to have noticed, for now he attacked with a *fleche*, knocking Eion to the ground with the powerful blow.

Breathing heavily, Eion looked up from his back at Ozmodion. The sorcerer wrapped both of his hands around the hilt of *Uthu'rach*, and came to stand right above Eion, the tip of the bladed dangling dangerously close to his exposed throats.

"So, it comes now to this," Ozmodion said almost rhetorically. "It is here, Eion Shifter, at the point of a blade that you meet your end. How noble. It will not be the ravages of old age that will take you, nor disease. You die gallantly on a field of battle. Still, I imagine you find this all frustrating; for more than eleven centuries, you have dreamed of some righteous victory over me, of revenge for your dearly departed family. You honed your skills, and it is only now that you have failed. It seems that the greater Iltari has triumphed. I had once thought to spare you and let you watch the world burn, but I hold no such romantic wishes anymore. Die well." He raised the sword high.

Then, a voice that was neither Ozmodion's nor Eion's roared an incantation. Five rays of crackling electricity soared through the air, came together, and drove into Ozmodion's back. A sound of thunder, and then the red sorcerer screamed in agony.

Eion took the chance and rolled to the right, jumping to his feet in the same motion. Then he whipped his head around, looking for the ally magician. His jaw dropped when he found it.

Gwen had moved from the spot where she had been standing still, her palm outstretched and her Vawn glowing white as the bolts of lightning continued to stem from the five points of the mark. She was smiling, but it was strained from effort.

"H-h-h-h-how..?" Eion stuttered, absolutely dumbstruck.

"I cast a protective shield as the bolt hit. Didn't have time to protect us all; even Curthlond got hit, poor thing."

Eion turned to look over where the rest of the mortals stood frozen. Sure enough, there was Curthlond, his back arched in terror and his mouth opened in a hiss. Eion tore his gaze away and sprung to his feet.

"Well, why did you not help me out sooner?" he demanded. "Where were you when my side was slashed open? I could have been killed!"

Gwen rolled her eyes and retorted with harsh invective. "And as you are whining like a little boy who didn't get his way, I see you *haven't* been killed. You were fine on your own, but I couldn't risk Ozmodion seeing me, until his back was turned. Now, thanks to me, you're free to strike him down. No need for thanks, but do it quick; I can't hold the spell much longer."

Indeed, as Eion looked at the electric beams arcing from her palm, he saw that they were growing thinner and weaker. They were less effectual, as well. Ozmodion, though still bellowing, was regaining some of his mobility. He had lowered *Uthu'rach* and was now trying to turn and face them, assumedly to launch a counter spell.

Seeing the sense in her words, Eion nodded quickly and took a firmer hold on *Raz'atr*, cupping the pommel with his left hand. He inhaled deeply, preparing himself. Then he hesitated. Why, he was never sure, but he hesitated. It was brief and fleeting, but in that short pause, the years passed flashed through his mind with lightning speed.

He watched Sronka murder his father and brothers.
He watched Garon appear and give him the Third Blade.
He watched Ozmodion fall as he slashed him through the heart.
He watched as he wandered the Magic Realm far and wide, honing his skills and growing in body and mind.
He watched as he arrived in the Mortal Realm, setting off for his search for the Great Prophesied.
He watched as he found them.

All this and more passed before his eye for a brief second. They distracted him for a moment too long. Before he could shake the memories away, Gwen lost hold of the spell, freeing Ozmodion from his magical prison.

The sorcerer leapt into the air as soon as he was able. *Uthu'rach* blazed in one hand, and a nexus of black magic flashed to life in the other.

He sailed through the air, not in the direction of Eion, but toward Gwen, who was bent over and breathing heavily from the effort of holding the spell for so long. She would not be able to react in time.

Eion threw *Raz'atr* to the ground and shifted his bow. In the next moment, he had pulled a bow from his quiver, nocked it to the frame, pulled the string back, and released. It flew fast and high, and met its mark in Ozmodion's breast.

The sorcerer faltered in the air. His sword dropped, and the magic in his left palm was snuffed out. Gwen looked up, gasped, and then bounded to the left, just as the red sorcerer crashed to the ground, kicking up a plume of red dust over the flames. It obscured Eion vision and parched his throat with its choking heat. He coughed and raised his hand, shifting the dust into pure, clean air.

When the red haze had passed, Eion saw that Gwen was sprawled out on the ground, breathing raggedly but very much alive and alert. She was looking several feet to the right, where Ozmodion laid face up, unmoving.

◻

They had been backed up against the Mountains of Midnight without any route of escape. Steel pinched the bridge of his nose between his eyes, sighing sadly. They were done for; the Ozra simply outnumbered them too greatly.

And now the Ozra pressed closer, chattering, chittering, chuckling with exultant glee. The goblins, their swords pointing outward, were howling next to the trolls, who fingered their clubs in a longing way, while the nightshades and shadow wolves crept slowly with their claws extended and fangs bared. All were slowly forming a ring around their quarry, stretching from the Gates of Angar Vûn to the western fringe of Ÿalnz Dàr like a host of nightmares realized. Their torches meshed with the light of the Eclipse as though the fires of Avria's hells were being ignited all about them.

A resigned sigh was heard, and Steel looked to the left. There was Rembas, massaging his chin while chewing on the stem of his lit pipe. His free hand was tapping nervously on his opposite forearm, and the hilts of his daggers flashed forlornly from depths of his satchel.

Steel smiled. "Troubled, O friend?"

The faun sighed again. "You know, I could've just walked away from you all, leaving you to find the Caves yourself without a second thought. Wouldn't've done my conscience any harm. But I didn't, and now it's too late to even regret it."

"Regret?" asked Tirmal, leaning tiredly on his staff to Steel's right. A cut stretched from his pointed ear down his jaw bone, caked with blood and in some places still oozing. His armor, like many of the Resistance, had been dented and gashed. The mail covering his arm was missing some links, which had presumably been lost by the hackings and whackings of enemy swords. "Surely, you can have no regret? See here, Master Rembas—" Here Rembas grumbled angrily. "I would have been very sad to know that these past weeks of amity meant nothing to you. You donott really mean that you would have rather been left in loneliness and apathetic boredom in the trees of a sleepy forest? You do not really mean that you find no pride in your valiance and bravery? You have proven your merit and more on the battlefield; you've shown that you are wise and, above all, a great friend. Would you really rather have turned your back on all of that? Do you mean you wish none of this had come to pass?"

Rembas took out his pipe and extinguished the weed. "Yup, I suppose that pretty much sums it up."

Steel forced back a laugh, making a squelching sound that he feared might've been mistaken as a scoff. He needn't have worried though, for Breeog, bloodied and bruised with the membrane of one of his wings torn, boomed with laughter.

"Ho-ho, the faun will never change. I, for one, though, would not have traded this adventure for anything. It grieves me that we all must die, for you have been the greatest of comrades-in-arms and friends that one could ever hoped for."

"Hear hear!" roared Varez, concealed behind the great girth of Brunariun, who was nodding fervently in agreement. Beside her, Fletch, Armor, Beast, Flame, Fauna, and Flora all stood in a semi-circle, speaking their approval and concurrence. Steel watched as Flora nudged her sister encouragingly. Fauna rolled her eyes and then cleared her throat, tapping Beast timidly on the shoulder.

"Uh, Beast?" she asked. The wild-haired shifter whipped around to face her, eyes narrowed with suspicion and steely dislike. "I have something to say. I wish to part on good terms, and I am sorry for our…shared dislike over the years. It makes me sad to think that we were never friends, for, looking back, I see that we would have made possibly the closest of companions, eh?"

A new look spread across Beast's face, a look Steel had never seen on him before. It was disbelieving surprise. Then, to Steel's further amazement, his mouth spread in a warm smile as he placed his hand on fauna's shoulder. "Aye. We would have at that. Perhaps we can right the past wrongs in the next life."

Fauna returned his smile as she nodded, a tear glistening in her eye. "I would like that."

This heartfelt moment was interrupted by a screech from a nightshade somewhere far off. Steel became aware of the pressing hordes of monsters once more. They were dangerously close now, perhaps only five hundred yards away. They would be on the Resistance in moments.

"So now we die?" asked Fletch. There was no lament or fear in his voice. It was simply asked, though it could not be provided with a simple answer. It did not seem as though he were looking one, for he continued in a reflecting, serene manner. "Then we have failed. Ah, pity. Have all our efforts really been all in vain?"

It was the Lord Fairskin who answered him, standing a few feet away and guarded by several elves, all torn and bloodied with many dents on their round shields. "Vain? No, dear Fletch, it was not in vain. Nor have we failed. We halted Ozmodion's progress for a few precious years more. Our legacy will live on in the hearts and minds of all those who dwell in this Magic Realm. With luck, we will have inspired others to resist night and evil as we have. If this holds true, Ozmodion will never win. Yes, we die now, but not the ideals we kept, not the principles we stood for. They will live on. Perhaps our children, and our children's children will know a time without the sufferings caused by the Red Sovereign and his Ozra. That future we have insured. Without us, without our efforts, no possibility would exist."

"Romanticize it all you want," snorted Rembas grumpily, "but still the fact remains: we're about to die."

Steel rolled his eyes testily. "Gods, Rem, you *are* cynical."

Rembas stowed his pipe into his satchel. Without looking up, he replied, "No. Not cynical. Just deathly realistic. That's how I've always lived, and now, seconds from death, I do not intend to change."

"Sounds depressing to me," commented Brunariun with a sniff; Fairskin's speech had greatly moved her.

The faun shrugged with indifference. "To you, it might. To me, it's only clarifying."

"While I cannot agree with your general outlook, faun," said King Barthol, standing regally beside his captain, Varez, "I must consent to your view of our plight at hand. Never have things seemed so bleak. Woe that Eion and his Ten have fallen."

"Yea, but joy that they will not know the black reign that is sure to follow this battle," responded Flame drearily. The Shifter Crest had been marred and scratched on his breastplate to the point where it would be almost completely unrecognizable to the untrained eye.

Steel looked to the approaching army. Three hundred yards. He knew they would not offer them the chance to surrender. They would be firing arrows shortly.

"It will be Ÿalnz Dàr they burn first," observed Fletch, his voice the same serene emptiness that it had been.

The sword-burdened shifter had enough. He unsheathed his sword and yelled, "Enough! I will not have the last moments of my life spoiled by gloom and despair. If we are to die here and now by the swords of shadows and monsters, then let us die with dignity. I will go to the halls of waiting without fear or sorrow. If this is truly it, O friends, then farewell! If we will not see each other in Garon's Heaven, then I will always recall you with the fondest of memories. Die well!"

He was answered by the sound of a series of unsheathing swords. He looked around him, and saw that each of them—except Brunariun and Breeog, of course—held their blades in the same manner as he. He looked over his shoulder and saw the red glint of the light reflected by the thousands of weapons that were held by the Resistance's soldiers.

Steel nodded, and then turned to face his death in the eyes.

The pike men were the closest, but the archers were preparing to take aim only a few feet behind them. Somewhere in the distance, the thunderous roll of war drums sounded low and clear, summoning the last vestiges of Steel's resolution. He tightened his grip on his sword and prepared to feel the fire of the arrows' shafts.

They did not come. Instead, the red light that was cast by the moon flickered. It was short, but it was followed by another flash. Steel looked to the sky, and watched as the Eclipse began to waver. Then, with a screeching and a moan, the red light receded, and the full moon was restored to its size and silver color.

A hideous roar bellowed somewhere in the center of the Ozra. With a flash of fire and smell of brimstone, a black dragon leapt to the skies. It rose in altitude, then, veering to the north, he took flight, traveling swiftly and eventually disappearing passed the horizon.

A red flash of light exploded from behind the Mountains of Midnight. A great rumbling shook the earth, and the drums ceased. There were no more chitterings, there was no more glee. The Ozra's joy became confusion, and then it became fear. They stopped their advance, stepping back from the Resistance with trepidation. Then, all at once, they scattered in all direction, broke ranks, and fled. They screamed and bellowed. They ran every which way and that. Some disappeared into the copse of the forest; some scaled the mountains. The rest ran to the north, up the Ozra Gap and eventually into the trees of Ÿalnz Dàr.

Steel watched them in dumbfounded disbelief. He was not alone, for at that moment, Varez cried into the night air, "What has come over them? Why do they flee?"

Lord Fairskin answered again, chuckling with merriment. "Is it not obvious? Eion has succeeded! He and the Prophesied have not fallen! They have carried out their charge! Ozmodion is undone!"

Lord Fairskin was close to the truth, but he was not entirely correct.

☐

Eion watched Ozmodion closely, waiting for him to make a move. But the sorcerer did not budge, save for the labored breathing. Only the fletching of the arrow protruded from his breast, thumping with the beating of the heart.

Gwen dusted herself off as she stood from the red earth. A stray tress of hair obscured her view; she pushed it behind her ear as she walked to stand beside Eion. The shifter motioned her to follow him. Together, they took a few steps toward Ozmodion, but stopped short as a weak and mirthless peal of laughter tore from the sorcerer.

"Lo! Even in defeat, I am victorious, Iltaris," he whispered faintly. "Ah, yes, Eion and Gwen, you have done naught but buy your pathetic Resistance some time."

Eion rushed to Ozmodion side and kneeled next to him. He took him up by the robes and, pulling him closer, he demanded, "What do you mean?"

Ozmodion laughed again, and then, "Avria had foreseen this, thus she bade me brew a potion that would prevent my death. Yes, you hear me right! You have not killed me again, O Eion Shifter! My spirit will again endure, and I will rise once more!"

"You lie!" Eion shouted into the shadow under the hood. "You lie! I see you here, grappling for life. You will die!"

"If that is so, then it will not be today! No, I will return Eion. When, I cannot say. I have no worries, though; I trust Avria's counsel completely. The Ozra will return here after Vaeirnïr carries out my last instructions. By the time I reemerge, I will have more power than I or even Avria ever dared dream."

Angry tears flooded Eion's eyes. He shook Ozmodion wildly in his grasp. "My parents...Tactics...Gorbon...Ryan."

"All dead," Ozmodion interjected flatly. "And yet you have not avenged them. Let that be your legacy, Eion Shifter. Let it be that you failed to bring justice on your family and friends. Take heart though; when next we meet, I will end your suffering...and your life. Farewell!"

Ozmodion said no more, and then he went limp in Eion's grasp. Eion screamed and shook him wildly, but then Gwen pulled him away.

"Eion..."

"HE IS DEAD! HE IS DEAD, SAYS I! HE LIES! HE HAS PREPARED NO POTION! HE IS DEAD!"

"Shh...come."

She wrapped an arm around his shoulder and pulled him away. Eion buried his face in her shoulder, weeping for reasons he could not describe. The anger was melting into despair and unfathomable grief. He let the tears flow, unafraid of seeming weak in Gwen's presence. He took comfort in her embrace.

After a long time, he sniffled one last time and cleared his eyes. He straightened and looked around. The ring of fire was dwindling as the caster of the spell faded. High above, the moon was full, silver.

He turned to Gwen, who was smiling. Slowly, he returned it.

Then there was an explosion that knocked both of them to the ground. A stunning blast of red light consumed them. Eion threw himself over Gwen, protecting her from the searing heat that he had expected would come with the illumination, but no heat came, nor wind, nor anything else. There was only light and sound. In ten seconds it passed, leaving both of them unharmed.

Eion raised his head and looked around. The mortals were blinking and examining their bodies, the spell upon them broken. Curthlond was standing as rigid as stone, not from magic but by fear. Ozmodion was gone.

Chapter 37

The Beginning

*T**he tent was musty* with the scents of sweat, blood, and fatigue mingled in an overpowering air. It was hot inside too; the thin crack in the door through which Gwen was peering out seemed to mock them with the cold night that lay just beyond. A fire had been ignited somewhere in the distance, though no one stood around it, presumably too occupied with the burying of the dead to rest.

"Slain, but not dead," said a voice. Gwen turned back to the table and saw that it was Lord Fairskin speaking. He was sitting, as usual, at the head of the small committee gathered inside the tent. He was massaging his temples with his forefingers, as had become his habit in the past months. He sighed loudly before finishing with, "Once again, the enemy escapes his death."

No one replied, so grim was the meeting. To Fairskin's right sat Eion, deep in thought and silent. Beside him, his seven captains looked at their laps in some kind of reverent sympathy for their leader, knowing how crushed he was to have been denied his justice again. His disappointment and grief had radiated from him as he had led Gwen and the others to the Gates of Angar Vûn after the explosion. He did not break stride even when they came to the great, red doors. He only shifted an archway large enough for he and the others to walk through. He hadn't bothered closing it.

To Fairskin's left, Tirmal, Varez, and King Barthol sat. Beside them, Breeog and Brunariun snaked their heads through an opening in the tent's roof, flicking their forked tongues in quiet agreement. Curthlond was there too, sitting on top of the table with his tail lashing back and forth rhythmically to a beat of his own. Finally, at the opposite end of the table, was Rembas, his head propped up by his arm tiredly. His satchel was resting by the entrance of the tent, untouched and still full of whatever multitude of things the faun stored in it.

It was a very long time before King Barthol slammed his palm on the table loudly, making everyone start in surprise, and cried, "Bah! He will not elude it again!"

"Be you so sure?" Lord Fairskin inquired lowly. "Twice now, Ozmodion has felt the fires of death, and twice now he has not died. I fear we have greatly underestimated the Red Sovereign. Greatly indeed."

"There is still a chance he might have been bluffing, right?" Flame asked hopefully, his head bandaged and his arm in a sling. His injuries did not seem to get in his way, though; his voice rose and fell with its usual cadence and his eyes were alight as they had always been.

"No, Flame," Eion answered unexpectedly, staring into the wood of the table, "there is not. Ozmodion did not bluff or lie; there was a conviction and a confidence in his voice too genuine to be faked. Also, as I have already said, I believe our scouts have dispelled any hopes of Ozmodion's death."

Gwen cringed at the thought. Five shifters had been dispatched to patrol Saurindon. They returned with reports of a great, black oak tree appearing on top of the tallest tower of Taronest, pulsing with a colossal aura of sorcery. Gwen knew Eion had been right in believing that this was the form Ozmodion's spirit had manifested into.

"And the Ozra," asked Varez, his arms crossed as he reclined in his chair, "what of them?"

Lord Fairskin cleared his throat and took a sip from the goblet of water that rested in front of him. He returned it to the table, and then spoke once more. "The dragons have reported that they are continuing to the northeast, making their way through and out the forest. It is my belief that they will exit towards the slopes of the Weres Mountains and then most likely proceed to make the slow, roundabout journey to the southern countries of Dravina, where Ozmodion's troops still have many holdings, and eventually back into Saurindon by way of the Ashen Cracks."

Rembas whistled. "Awful trip. Gotta pass the Bogs of Zuvé if they are going that way. How splendid; with luck, they might all meet their ends at the end of some banshee's talons."

Lord Fairskin smiled and then chuckled merrily, though he shook his head. "No, I am certain the Ozra will find their way back to Saurindon; they have been well trained in the case of Ozmodion's fall."

"Not too confident, then, were they?" Rembas commented, as though not expecting a reply. He sat back, smug and satisfied.

"What of Vaeirnïr?" Steel asked, looking to Breeog for a reply. The Dragon King growled lowly, flicking his tongue several times before replying.

"North," he said simply. "Far and fast. Where to, I cannot begin to guess. But he is long gone, supposedly carrying out Ozmodion's last order, whatever it may be."

"Are we going to sit, then, like a bunch of ninnies, and let them get away?" King Barthol demanded. "Chase 'em down and pluck 'em off, says I. They will be hard pressed to fight in the forest, and Nimé is, after all, on our side. Let us see how they fare when every creature of Ÿalnz Dàr is hunting for their skins."

"No," said Eion wearily. "No, dear Barthol. As vulnerable as the Ozra might be, the Resistance, too, is weak. A quest like that would be the death of us all."

"Eion is right, I fear," Lord Fairskin said. He had stopped massaging his scalp and now his hands lay folded on top of each other upon the desk, frail and wrinkled, their veins popping out under the dry skin. "If anything, this battle shall have taught us that our numbers a vastly insufficient; if we are to face the Ozra again, we will need to recruit more to fight."

"Like who?" asked Curthlond, stretching his forelegs in a relaxing way, despite the general mood of the council. "Who can you recruit? Ozmodion has already taken the southern countries. In time, he will overtake more. He will conscript whatever soldiers he can fine, and in time, he will enlist the help of some of the races who remain neutral. The banshees, the gargoyles, the ogres, they'll all answer the call of Saurindon. The list of allies is dwindling."

The four leaders of the Resistance sighed in unison. Barthol then grunted, and Breeog hissed. Fairskin nodded tiredly as he waved off

Curthlond's statements. "Yes, Curthlond, we are aware of this. Such problems have long presented themselves. Solutions are what we need, not reminded troubles."

There was another pause. Fletch coughed a few times, probably due to the stuffiness of the tent, but other than that, things were deathly quiet. Gwen wiped away a bead of sweat that had been resting on her brow, cleared her throat, and then finally, unable to stand the awkward silence, broke the lull by asking, "So, what happens now?"

They all turned to face her, their expressions differing as greatly as the months of the year. Rembas seemed bemused, Curthlond concerned, as the rest all wore varying degrees of severity. Eion broke the harsh glares with his trademark half smile.

"The journey home," he said, truly warm for the first time in days. He then looked around at everyone at the table. "Though Ozmodion may not be dead, I think it will take some years for him to return to his old power. We will need all the time we can get. The gods say to ask the help of those we protect. Placate the other races as Ozmodion is sure to do soon. For now, the Resistance needs to rest; it has been eight months since we set out on our crusade, eight months of endless marching, fighting, and dying. Time now for rest. The Ozra will not resurface for some time, and once they do, Ozmodion will still tread carefully until he rises again. Yes, there is time now for grief for the fallen, time now for the tears for the dead. But home calls; I feel we should answer it."

A series of lowed muttering ensued, but they were all murmuring agreement. Gwen saw it in all their eyes; even the steely looks of King Barthol and Varez betrayed the longing of their homes in the far, far north.

Breeog nodded with his normal zeal, smoke wafting through his grin almost deliberately. "Hear, hear! Too long since I have seen the Mirithin

Plateau; too long since I have seen my cave. Ah, my horde is certain to have rusted in my absence! And I am sure I left my library unsorted. Gods, it will be weeks before I can get it in order. Shifter is right; tired are we of this war-waging…for now, at least. Bloodied and bruised, our wounds scream for respite."

Lord Fairskin smiled, but it was a mirthless expression. "Aye. The Red Sovereign again has us at a stalemate I am afraid. So be it; tomorrow, we will begin the long journey home."

Cheers sounded and cups banged on the table. Their grim moods dissipated like smoke on a high wind, and all around her, Gwen saw smiles, heard laughter, and felt joy. For some reason, she could not join them.

☐

That evening, the last of the fallen were cremated, and a joint prayer was said as the bodies burned. Gwen, off to one side with faithful Curthlond at her feet, prayed only for Ryan. The tears she had held since the misadventures of Hamurlas finally fell long and glistening.

☐

The next morning, the immense party broke camp. The many watch fires were extinguished, sending great plumes of white steam into the night air. The tents were shifted or enchanted into nothingness, and soon the great army had gathered into their ranks and platoons. The horns were sounded, and they began to march slowly up the Ozra Gap and into the forest. They did not burden themselves too greatly; without the prospect of the Ozra patrolling the woods, they no longer concerned themselves with the heavy swords and armor. They knew their sheer numbers would protect them from whatever dangers Ÿalnz Dàr had left to offer.

For the days that they wandered the forest, the morale was higher than it had been since the beginning of their long journey. More songs were sung with greater enthusiasm than Gwen had ever heard from the Resistance. It was as though Ozmodion was really dead and gone, which, for all intents and purposes, he was for the moment. But something weighed on Gwen's mind, blocking any happiness she might've felt.

"I'm going to miss you, Rem," Gwen told the faun one day as they were marching between the great trunks of the trees. She was wearing only her tunic and her leggings, with soft leather boots worn from use. She let her hair down, basking in the calm of the woods. She carried no pack; she would leave it locked in the portal until she had need of it.

"Miss me?" he asked, his cocked to one side. As usual, his satchel was swinging loosely from his side. He clasped his hands behind his back and shrugged in his usual way as he said, "I can't see why."

Curthond, trotting between the two, muttered the irritation he reserved solely for the faun. "Do not be thick. You know very well that leaving Ÿalnz Dà⁻ means leaving you. It has been good seeing you again, Rembas, old boy, and I too will miss you."

Rembas scratched his nose, stepping over an upturned tree root as he did. "Curthlond, you're falling prey to assumption again. One would think you'd learn after a while, but, as cats are generally regarded as household pets rather than intelligent logicians, I'll let it slide."

Curthlond cocked his head, too interested to be offended. He bounded a few feet forward and, facing the faun, asked, "What do you mean?"

"As I warned from the beginning, it's not safe to claim any alliance in this forest. Now I have, and because of that, I can't return to my old life." Here he turned to look at Gwen with his disconcertingly deep eyes. "I have outgrown it now, and I will never be satisfied to return to it."

The words hit her hard. Silently, she reflected back on her thoughts by the shores of the Silver Ice Sea. The words Ryan had spoke there were of the same nature, and now they rang loud in her head. She sighed deeply, and let her gloom fill her.

Then the faun shrugged, and he continued with, "Besides, I like being where the action is."

"So...what? Are you saying you are coming with us?" Curthlond pressed, trying very hard to hide his hope.

"Aye. It seems that the lots of the Resistance and I are thrown together for a while longer. Besides, I have not left Ÿalnz Dàr for far too long. It will be grand to see the northern lands again." A misty look crossed the faun's face and he exhaled with content.

The cat cleared his throat and, masking his joy, said, "Ah, that isgood of you Rem."

Rembas looked down at him, and then, drooping his head with sadness, said, "I have only one regret. I now face months of travel with a cat...and I fear I'm allergic."

Curthlond's jaw dropped, and he stumbled over a loose stone. After he collected himself, he said, "Oh, Rem...I am sorry, I did not...I guess then *I* better..."

Rembas then broke into a peal of laughter, actually stopping to lean against a tree. He guffawed for several minutes until he could bring himself to say, "Oh, Curthy, how I *wish* you could have seen your face.

Ah, priceless…thank you, that made my day." He giggled once more and then resumed his slow pace through the forest.

Curthlond's expression only changed a little bit as he watched the faun walk. In it were mingled looks of rage and satisfied expectation. He shook his head, muttering "fauns" as he trotted after Rembas. Gwen wanted so badly to laugh, but thought better of it.

☐

After a week, they had returned to the Five Clearings. Here, Flora and Fauna and their troops would stay, guarding the forest from the impending return of the Red Sovereign and the Ozra.

"Farewell, O Resistance!" said Fauna before they parted. "I pray that we will meet before the next war is come."

"Indeed!" concurred her sister, nodding vigorously. "Do not forget us in this forest. It will not hurt to visit every now and then, eh Eion?"

Eion laughed heartily as he embraced her. "Never, dear Flora, never." He then hugged Fauna and stepped back, allowing the rest of the leaders and captains their goodbyes.

Toward the end, Fauna approached Gwen much in the same manner that she had when they had first met. Her look was still hard, but then she put a hand on Gwen's shoulder and pulled her in close.

"I know your burdens tax you, Gwen Talbot. Keep strong."

The simple words surprised Gwen, and before she could reply, Fauna had released her shoulder and walked away to stand next to her sister. There, the twin captains smiled genially and waved.

"Now, really, goodbye now!" said Flora airily.

"There is no time to delay!" said Fauna.

"Home calls!"

"Nothing left here to keep you!"

"Off with you now!"

"Back to lands well known!"

"Farewell to the cloud-capped towers and fields of blood!"

"Hello to meadows in spring's bloom!"

"But, why waste time chatting?"

"Time for leave to be taken!"

"Farewell!"

"Farewell!"

"Farewell, Flora and Fauna," laughed Eion, taking his place at the head of the army with the other leaders. "May Ÿalnz Dàr always be lucky enough to have sentinels of your kind!"

The twins bowed, and then shifted into nothingness, leaving the First Clearing to the Resistance. Gwen blinked in surprise, both at the twins' sudden disappearance and the stillness of the Clearing. The Resistance was almost completely silent, assumedly thinking of their homes in the north. A look of dreamy eagerness filled the eyes of many of the soldiers; the rest bore smiles of nostalgic thought.

The four kings must have have seen this, for in the next moment, they had signaled the great company to march. Gwen turned around to take one last look at the First Clearing. She would not miss the forest in the slightest. With that in mind, she began the long journey home.

□

The months passed slowly, as times of peace and happiness often do. They crossed the Silver Ice Sea by ship as they had weeks before. Now, though, they did not fret over speed; they let the soft breeze from the south carry them slowly over the water.

When they reached the northern banks, Gwen learned that the dragons would be leaving them, making their way to the Mirithin Plateau to the east.

"I trust you will find your way back from here, eh?" Breeog said in great humor now that he was so close to home. "Ah, I will miss the elvish hospitality at the Esialan River. I may need to call upon your gracious company, Lord Fairskin, after I tire of the roughages of the wild."

Lord Fairskin laughed, leaning on his staff a little less, fueled by sea air. His robes were lighter than usual, as well; spring was here, and the sun pulsed with warmth high above. "Breeog, old friend, I would be honored to offer you whatever courtesy I can. May the winds bear you safely to your caves, and swiftly too; your library will not organize itself!"

The dragon king roared with raucous laughter. "Aye, it will not at that!" He turned to King Barthol and Varez and gave them a smart salute. "And you, Master Dwarves, I would be very happy to see you at the Mirithin Plateau soon; I know that the hordes of dragon hold much of your old treasures. I would recompense you to the best of my ability."

Barthol and Varez exchanged looks of concealed emotion, but then they smiled, and Barthol, turning back to Breeog said, "I want not your gold, O King of Dragons, only your amity. What petty disagreements and wars that dragon and dwarven-folk have shared, I wish to forget; I hold you in higher regard as my friend."

Breeog nodded with his golden grin. "As do I, Barthol King. Your heart is grander than any treasure. Thought I would still wish you come to the Mirithin, if only to share my home for a time."

Barthol stepped forth and extended his hand. "I will at that, Breeog, I will at that."

"Then it is settled," the dragon king pronounced as he wrapped his scaly hand around Barthol's. Then, finally, he turned to Eion. "Shifter...you I hold closest to my heart. I watched you grow from the young boy that you were to the great man you have become. You are more son to me than friend."

Eion smiled and, stepped forth, embracing the dragon. "I will miss you, Breeog. Do not hide too long in your caves."

"Not so long as there are skies to carry me!" answered Breeog as the two parted. He turned to Gwen. "I know what Gorbon meant to you, and I cannot thank you enough for helping him find his final resting place

"I name you Dragon-Friend hereafter. Farewell, Gwen Talbot, and you, too, Great Mortals. The Magic Realm will miss you. Never let the drear of the Old World prevent you from spreading your wings—" here Breeog's unfurled with a snap. "—and soaring to the heavens!" Breeog sprung from the ground, as did the whole of the dragon legion. They ascended higher and higher, until they were only dots in the sky. It was then that Breeog called down to them, "And never forget what have seen here; only then will magic truly be gone in the Mortal Realm!"

And then they took off, veering to the west, roaring and spewing flame in their wake. Many called down their parting words, but most of the majestic beasts were already looking to east with eyes wide and keen. Gwen watched until they had flown over the far eastern peaks of the Nalartis and out of sight. With a regretful sigh, she looked to the great, snow capped mountains that still stood between the Resistance and the end of the journey. Then she looked to Eion, who was already gazing toward her in a wistful manner. He shook his head abruptly when he saw that she was watching him and, turning to the mountains, signaled the shifter division to march once more. Lord Fairskin and King Barthol followed his example, and in a moment, Gwen found herself again amid a sea of clanking boots and trampling soldiers. She looked to her feet to have a word with Curthlond, but saw that he was gone. She looked over to Rembas, and the two old friends were busy reminiscing, and set off toward the mountain range.

☐

They reached the Emerald Plains in another two weeks, and she found them to be much the same as they had been when they trekked it in the opposite direction. It was still lush, and the grass was still green and wet. Birds twittered throughout the wide valley, dispelling any dismal feelings. The mood was light and airy, and Gwen dearly wished she could've stayed and marveled at the wondrous place. But the Resistance was too close now to tarry; they pressed on, trampling the grass in their hurry.

It was while they were trekking the great plain that Gwen found her chance to speak with Curthlond.

"So, what are you going to do now?" she asked him, looking straight ahead though knowing full well that he was trotting, as usual, by her feet.

There was a pause as Curthlond considered the question. Then, with some hesitance, he answered, "I am not sure. Lothilina's curse still holds; I cannot imagine that her madness has abated either. I suppose I will stay with the Resistance. It will not be so bad…Rem will be there. He is good company, if a little obnoxious…and vain…and conceited, and delusional, shameless, ignorant, ridiculously abrasive…" He sighed. "But I will manage. Or I will lose my mind. Whichever comes first."

Gwen giggled, but then looked down at the cat weaving around the high grass that sprung from the earth. "Well, I asked only because I was wondering if you...I mean...it could be a while before I see you again, and I still have a lot to learn about enchanting...so I thought, y'know...maybe you'd like to...come back with me?"

Curthlond halted immediately and arched his head up to look at Gwen. His slit-like irises were narrowed in the bright sun, so dilated that they were only hair-thin lines splitting the cloudy green eyes in half.

"Really?" he asked, his voice quivering with hopeful wonder. He sat back on his hind legs, never one taking his eyes off her. "Do you mean it? You want me to come to the Mortal Realm with you?"

Gwen smiled warmly and nodded. "Nothing would make me happier."

Curthlond's face split in a wide, sharp-toothed grin. He began to purr deeply and he jumped toward Gwen in one, high bound. She caught him in her arms and laughed as he licked her face.

"I take that as a yes?" she said, scratching him behind his ears. He nodded as he closed his eyes and purred louder.

"Hmph," said a familiar voice, accompanied by the sound of hoofs trotting closer. "I suppose that's an exclusive offer. I can't see how I can come; the mortals are undoubtedly going to be put off by these legs, eh?"

Gwen turned to look at Rembas, who had fallen into step beside her and crossed his arms angrily. His eyes, however, betrayed no discontent, radiating their usual tranquility in stark contrast to his body language.

She lowered Curthlond to the ground and then, patting the faun lovingly on the shoulder, shook her head. "I'm sorry, Rembas. There's not much to the Mortal Realm, anyway. You said so yourself that you like being where the action is; I can't imagine there being anything more exciting back home."

The faun glared for a moment, but then, with a scoff, he waved it away. "Bah, no matter. I think I'll have more fun keeping the Resistance in check than making a few mortal women scream. Have fun, you two." Then he trotted forth, whistling some tune with his hands clasped behind him.

Curthlond snickered. "He is jealous; I can tell. He will get over it, and I am sure he will have no trouble filling in the hours. Perhaps I will even have a chance to visit him once and again."

Gwen laughed, and again looked ahead as the long miles lay before the marchers far beyond the horizon.

☐

One day in late April, long after they had left the Emerald Plains, the dwarves broke apart from the Resistance, planning to veer to northeast and make for their home in the Zanasha Mountains. Not prone to warm partings, they left with gruff goodbyes, all save Varez, who hugged Gwen long and strongly. He winked at her when they broke apart and then, shaking hands with his good friend, Tirmal, he set off after the great dwarven force.

Gwen watched them for a long while, holding back tears as she saw Varez shrink in the distance. Eion stood next to her, rubbing her back soothingly.

"Life's naught but a series of meetings and partings," he whispered lowly, his eyes fixed on the dwarves as well. "But take cheer, Gwen. You will see Varez again. Perhaps sooner than you think."

She let her head rest on his shoulder and closed her eyes. *Home.* The faces of her parents came swimming into view, making her eyes well even more. Then her thoughts drifted to Ryan. She knew that her home would never be the same without her fallen friend.

The shifter patted her once more on the shoulder. "Come. We are close now."

☐

He was right. In one week, they had come to the lands outlying the Esialan River. Gwen expected to smell the sweet scents of the grass and to hear the loud rush of water that the river usually issued. She waited to hear the call of the myriad flocks of birds that roamed close to the Vra's territories. She strained even to hear the sounds of laughter in the nearby village.

She was disappointed.

No birds. No sweet scents. There were no happy voices of the villagers, and though she indeed could hear the sound of the river, it seemed unnaturally loud and undisturbed. Unsettled, she turned to look over at Lord Fairskin and Eion, the last of the leaders, both of which were at the front of the lines. Neither seemed at ease.

She made her way over to Eion, but he motioned her, mouthing, "Something is wrong." He slowly made his way to the foot of the knell that still separated the company from the village. Gwen looked to the sky and noticed that the blue skies were obscured by great, billowing, grey clouds. She gulped frightfully, and set out after him.

He began to protest when she arrived at his side, but said nothing more when she climbed the hill. He stopped her about halfway, insisting that he at least lead the way. She smiled and motioned him to go ahead. He nodded, and set off at a quick pace. She watched as he reached the crest, and then furrowed her brow when his shoulders slumped at whatever she saw. Concerned, she set off after him.

"Eion, what's wrong…" she began. She followed his shocked gaze and screamed.

The village had been reduced to ashes. The timbers of the cottages and towers lay destroyed, some still burning, others just standing charred and smoldering. Bodies of men, women, and children lay strewn across the valley, long dead. Swords and knives glistened on the ground, the last vestiges of the town's defenses. Just as Gwen was about to look away in desolate horror, Eion pointed past the small dale to a nearby hill.

Fairskin Manor's tallest tower was alone in tact. Everything else was in ruin. Toppled towers lay upon each other, and broken walls, scorched by flame, surrounded the castle redundantly. Bricks and stones and other rubble had fallen into the moat, blocking the flow and causing the water to spill over. The drawbridge had been shredded and splintered, hanging broken by the chains fastened into the cracked mortar.

And amid all this damage, the tallest tower rose high and whole, marred only by the Standard of Ozmodion billowing down its parapet.

Gwen collapsed onto the ground, the strength of her legs suddenly gone. She stared up into the sky, watching the grey clouds swirling with smoke. The visions of the bodies floated passed her eyes. She couldn't push them away. She felt hollow, and was only vaguely aware of a hobbling figure walking to stand by Eion.

She turned to look and saw it was Lord Fairskin. The old elf gawked, disbelieving what he saw. Gwen's heart seemed to drop as he saw a look of immeasurable grief in his eyes; unable to cry or scream, the elf just stared.

Tirmal, however, acted with a little more blatancy. He too gawked when he crested the hill, but his shock was quickly taken as his face screwed up with anger.

"I smell Vaeirnïr...the devil dragon! I will rent his scaly hide from his bones! I apologize for robbing Breeog his vengeance, but now I will have the first Dragon King's head." He raised his staff and uttered a syllable. The tip ignited with a silver flame that crackled in a way that befitted his rage. He raised his hands and shook his sleeves down to his elbows. He was about to release the spell, when Lord Fairskin motioned him to stop with his free hand.

"Hold, Tirmal, "said a voice that Gwen did not recognize, yet it still came from Fairskin's mouth. It was void of any emotion, of any feeling. The words did not rise, nor did they fall. They were quiet and distant, as though spoken far away. "Vaeirnïr is long gone. I would wager that he is at least halfway back to Saurindon now. Besides, no spell would take him. It will be Breeog and Breeog alone who will claim vengeance on him."

"But, my Lord," objected Tirmal, lowering his staff and quenching the spell, "look around you! Our home...Ozmodion's arm has finally reached the heart of the Vra! Hundreds lay dead in our own front yard, and—" but he was cut off as Lord Fairskin faced him with a glance so severe that Gwen instinctively took a step back. She had seen that look once in Mr. Alez, but, as Mr. Alez was only an art teacher and Fairskin an elf of ancient power, Gwen hadn't been half as frightened as she was now.

"I can see all that, yes," whispered the alien voice. "Old as my eyes may be, I am still unfortunate enough to see this travesty. But no amount of magic spells will amend this. Ozmodion has insured one last blow from beyond the grave. As he is beyond our reach, we are unable to counter."

"But what will we do?" asked Tirmal, his voice faltering with heartache.

Lord Fairskin did not answer him. Instead, he turned to Eion and sighed deeply. Then a forced smile stretched across his face and, placing his hand on the shifter's shoulder, he said quietly, "I fear that I was wrong, Eion Shifter. You were right in telling me to seek the help of the other clans. Pity that it took this to make me see that." He looked sadly about the wasted vestiges of the village. "It is time, then, for me to ask help from my brethren."

Eion tore his gaze from the wreckage of Fairskin Manor to look at the old elf. "Who, then, will you go to?

"My cousin Rianl, I think. The Kji is closest to the Vra, and the Orano Forest is not very far from Arconia. Yes, I think it best that we stop and rest here for a while, and grieve for the fallen. Then, I will allow the Vra leave. You should allow the shifters the same liberty. Then, we will all rendezvous in Orano."

Eion bit his lip. "I think it is best though, if the Prophesied are returned first."

Lord Fairskin raised an eyebrow and the turned to look at Gwen. The many wrinkles of his face seemed to stem from the dimples of his grin.

"Well, what say you Gwen?" he asked kindly. "The home fires will burn for a long time...I know that this war has taxed you greatly...you must yearn for home."

Gwen could hardly hide her enthusiasm as she nodded slowly. "Yes. I am ready for home. These passed months have been the greatest of my life; my eyes are open to a world of possibilities. But, I don't think I can stay without some kind of...resolution back home..."

Lord Fairskin nodded and whispered something to Tirmal. The younger elf shook his head, and then, slowed by the misery, set off down the knoll back to where the elves and shifters of the Resistance still stretched far and wide.

"Well," said Lord Fairskin, "I take it that Curthlond will be going with you?"

The cat nodded sadly by Gwen's feet. "Lord Fairskin...I am so sorry...I can only offer my condolences...but—"

"Worry not, friend," said the elf, both hands grasping his staff. "Enough tears will be shed on Ozmodion's account. I do not wish to see more than I must. Peace, Curthlond." He looked up at Gwen. "I will miss you Gwen. We all will. Stay safe in the Old World, eh?"

"I will, Lord Fairskin." She took a step forth and embraced him. He returned the gesture and patted her on the back in a fatherly way. When they broke apart, he whispered, "May the gods watch over you."

It was then that Tirmal returned, with the other eight mortals, the five shifter captains, Rembas, and Shravir following close behind. They all acted accordingly when they saw the desolation. The five shifters mirrored the look of Eion's reaction, though Beast quickly became enraged, and was only calmed down by Kendal gagging at the sight. Quickly, Tyler, whose eyes seemed ready to pop out in dismay. Eric and Anthony fell to their knees, gasping for air like fish pulled from the sea. Caitlyn seemed on the verge of tears while Lea was already past it, her face absolutely glazed as small steams poured from her eyes. Shravir looked very grim and was shaking his head with regret. Rembas's steely eyes stared blankly, all emotion masked.

While Tirmal quickly relayed to them what had happened and what was going to be done, Fairskin said, "Who will return them, then?"

"My captains and I," Eion answered. "I will leave Armor to tend to the army. Steel and the others can take the other eight; I will take Gwen."

The elf nodded. "So be it. I will prepare the transportation then." He hobbled off to one side and, with his staff planted in the ground, muttered a stream of words under his breath.

Eion chuckled with a note of sadness and then turned to Gwen. "It is time for goodbyes, Gwen." He jerked his head toward the small group gathered to their right. All tears were gone, though their stains still shone on the faces of Lea and Caitlyn. Beast still glowered with anger, and he was not alone. Steel was clutching the hilt of his sword so tightly that his arm quivered with the force of his contracted muscles Fletch was stroking his chin thoughtfully, no doubt weighing the possibilities of hunting down the black dragon, but a look in his eye suggested that he saw this illogical.

Gwen sighed, and walked over to where they stood. Immediately, the five shifters stopped their contemplation and advanced to meet her. They all grinned (except for Armor, whose mouth was wrapped in his scarf as usual), their wounds from the great battle long healed.

"Well...this is it, is it not?" asked Steel, his face tired but kind.

"Back to Mortal-Land, eh?" said Fletch, leaning casually on Beast's shoulder.

"It is a shame, huh gents?" asked Flame. "Things are going to be awfully quiet with her gone."

"Certainly," nodded Beast. "We will have no one to wander away from us."

"Or search for," put in Steel.

"Or rescue," finished Fletch.

Armor nodded vigorously. Gwen suspected that the shifter could not talk as she had never heard him say a word.

Gwen giggled and shook her head affectionately. "I'm going to miss you all terribly."

"And we you," said Steel, taking her in his arms and hugging her for a long time, so long that Fletch eventually lost patience and pushed his way to embrace her as well. Soon, all five were battling to hold her, and she, caught in the middle, tried her best to hold them all.

When they broke apart, they turned to say their goodbyes to the other eight. Smiling sadly, Gwen turned to Shravir and Rembas, each stood with their arms crossed.

"Do not forget us now, m'lady," said Shravir, as he hugged her. "Mortal memories are famed for fading."

Rembas then addressed Gwen with genuine kindness. "Gwen, you've more potential than any enchanter I ever met, including Curthy." The cat was talking to Shravir only a few feet away, but, for the first time in Gwen's memory, he did not contradict Rembas. He instead nodded in agreement, and then turned back to finish saying goodbye to the ex-blood-mage. Rembas cleared his throat and went on. "Don't let the mortals beat that out of you. I know you're going to grow frustrated, and maybe even resentful at being left there, but it is for the best. It is where you need to be right now. Keep that in mind. I know you want to be there now, but, I know you well enough to know that you will grow tired of your old ways. Be patient, that is all I ask." He brought her in closer and embraced her. He then stepped back, and winked. After he said his farewell to Curthlond, squeezing in one final jibe that Gwen did not catch, the faun clasped his hands behind his back and set off down the hill. Shravir chuckled, having apparently heard whatever Rembas had said, and followed him.

Gwen watched them go, and laughed as Curthlond walked past her with wounded dignity. She then looked to her eight friends and walked to stand among them. They all looked at her strangely, as though they had not seen her in a long time. She didn't wonder why; none had talked to her since the vain words Kendal, Lea, and Caitlyn had spoken at the Mountain of Antiquity. She cleared her throat, and addressed them all.

"I know that, in your eyes, I've changed. Yes, I wield magic now. Yes, I am an Ilteri. Yes, I am immortal. I know these things are hard to accept; believe me. I've had my time coming to terms with them. But I want you to know that I hold you all very close to my heart, and I hope we can still be friends."

She was about to turn and walk away, but Lea took her by her arm. "Gwen, we have something to say, too. I know that we spoke badly. We were petty to think that we were better than these people. I think we've all changed too." She broke off, looking to the others for support.

Anthony nodded and stepped forth. "Yeah. When we first came here, I used to think greatness was only found in Fairskin, Breeog, Barthol, and others like them. Y'know, unless you had a crown and throne, you weren't anything special. I know that's wrong, now. A soldier lying in the dirt, wounded and broken, is far greater than any lord or liege. A sword is much grander than a scepter, and it takes much greater courage to run with sword drawn than to stay behind the front lines."

"What we're trying to say, Gwen," said Eric, his head inclined so that he looked at the ground, "is that we were wrong. You and Ryan had the right ideas of nobility all along. It's too late to apologize to Ryan." Here, Caitlyn sniffed, but quickly inhaled to quell any sobs. "But we want to make things right with you. Can you forgive us?"

Gwen grinned. "Of course. Friends?"

The eight of them returned her smile and nodded happily. "Friends," they said simultaneously.

A pause followed, but it was broken as Eion stepped towards them and motion Gwen to come with him, smiling as he said, "It is time."

Gwen followed him, waving at the eight as she did. Eion led her to where Lord Fairskin stood. Apparently, he had finished preparing the spell because he beckoned them closer.

"I will transport you two first," he said, almost to himself. "Prepare yourself; the sensation might be a little intense."

"Goodbye Gwen," said Tirmal, "take care of yourself."

"Bye Tirmal," she replied. "And thank you for everything."

Tirmal nodded, and then stepped back as Lord Fairskin raised his staff. Gwen quickly looked down at her feet, seeing that Curthlond was already there, sitting with his tail lashing back and forth in nervousness. She was about to tell him to relax when she found that she herself was holding her breath.

A familiar nexus formed around Lord Fairskin's staff, expelling a red mist that enveloped the three of them. It was much like it had been before. There was a sweet smell, and the vapor felt cool and light on her skin. And then, just as it had so long ago in that history classroom back at Greystone High, the floor gave way and Gwen fell into whatever lay beyond it.

☐

She did not fall very far, this time. In one moment, her feet hit solid ground and the red mist parted to reveal a suburban street lined with houses on either side. Cars were parked in the driveways, and the sounds of the modern world broke upon her like the rising tide. How loud it all seemed: the roars of traffic; the rumble of planes; the blaring of a stereo somewhere down the road. It all seemed so foreign, and it took her a moment to realize that she was standing in the middle of her old neighborhood.

"Ooh," said Curthlond's voice. "Wow...so this is the Mortal Realm?"

Gwen looked down at him. He was staring intently at the asphalt under his feet, as though he had never seen anything so intriguing.

Eion laughed when he saw him. "Aye, this is the Old World. I was a little surprised too when I first came here. If you think pavement's something, wait 'til you get a glimpse of a television."

"Fascinating," replied the cat, shaking his head in astonishment.

Gwen looked up at the sky. It seemed hazy compared to the radiant blue it was in the Magic Realm. The smog from Sacramento hung suspended thick and low; Gwen coughed as her lungs inhaled.

Eion patted her on the back. "It takes a little acclimating. Mortal technology and machinery really contrast with the other realm. You will soon get used to it."

She nodded, and looked at the street sign that rose several feet behind them; her house was only a few blocks away. They could be there in about ten minutes.

Eion seemed to sense what she was thinking, for he smiled and nodded. "And now it is time for the most dangerous part of any journey: the return to home."

Together, the three of them set off up the street, Curthlond trotting a few yards in front of them, marveling at the many sight and frequently asking questions. Eion walked next to Gwen quietly, allowing her reservation. For that, she was grateful. As she looked upon her old suburb, countless thoughts and memories came flooding back. She recognized the stretch of sidewalk where she had learned to ride a bicycle. She saw the old oak into which she had crashed her father's car when he had taught her to drive.

Suddenly, a thought occurred to her that hadn't before. Alarmed, she took Eion by the arm and, cutting Curthlond off as he was asking about one house's sprinkler system, asked, "Eion, my parents…what do they think happened to me? I just disappeared, and…and I've been gone for almost a year!"

"Over a year actually," Eion corrected softly, patting her on the hand. "You lose track. But, no worries. We took care of it all shortly after the ten of you arrived. Lord Fairskin dispatched a troop of elves, and together, they've been trailing your parents, your teachers, and everyone else who might be keeping track of you. With a quick spell, they make someone oblivious to the fact that you're missing, quickly erasing you from their mind. As far as the Mortal World is concerned, you've been here the whole time. But, today, the elves returned, and, by now, the magic on the mortals' minds will be wearing off; soon they'll be aware that you've been missing."

"And what about Ryan?"

"We'll have to stage a death. Shift a corpse, I suppose."

Gwen bit her lip. "And what do I tell them? My parents, that is."

Eion looked her in the eyes and replied with, "The truth. The truth, Gwen. You cannot hide anything like that." He smiled and flicked his nose. "As I am sure you have found out now."

She laughed in spite of herself, thinking back on how her magical talent had been discovered. But it wasn't her enchanting that worried her. It was the fact that she was an Iltari. It was the fact that she was not her father's daughter. She had dreaded this truth since she had found out, and she would do anything to keep it from her parents.

They turned the corner now, and proceeded down the right side of the street. Cars drove by, and Gwen watched in disgust as they emitted clouds of exhaust. She shook her head and focused on the road ahead. They were only a few yards from her street now. Curthlond was still ahead of them, gawking as the vehicle passed.

Gwen sighed. "So, I guess it is all over?"

"What is?" the shifter asked.

"The adventure. I am going to miss it all very much. It pains me to leave Rembas, Shravir, Steel, Fletch, Tirmal…and you."

Eion smiled, though he had long since looked away from her, his eyes fixed ahead on the upcoming street to their left.

Gwen cleared her throat and went on. "Don't get me wrong; I've really missed my home all this time. But, that's just it. Back there, back in the other realm, I've felt more at home there than anywhere else. It just felt…right." She stopped as they turned right onto her street. Curthlond had kept on going straight, and they had to call after him to get him to pay attention. He started and then, after looking over his shoulder, sprinted after them.

"Did you two catch that statue on that lawn? What was it supposed to be?"

"A flamingo," answered Eion, straining to keep his face straight.

"A flamingo! Wow, imagine that…what's a flamingo?"

"A bird, usually found in wetlands. I don't think you'll run across too many here in California, but, hey, you never know."

Curthlond grinned excitedly. "I *love* this place." Then he bounded in front of them again, this time to examine a lawnmower that had been left in front of a garage.

Eion chuckled, and then he addressed Gwen. "I will miss you too, Gwen. And I can appreciate how much you are going to miss the Magic Realm. But this is where you have to be now."

Gwen nodded. "That's what Rembas said."

"Mm-hm. Rembas is wiser than he lets on." He paused, and looked ahead. Gwen did too. Her house was in view now. It was two stories tall, pale grey with black trim. It seemed to have been recently repainted. She wondered what else had changed in her absence. At first glance, though, everything seemed the same. Her father's BMW stood parked in the driveway beside her mother's Jeep. The trees that sprung from the lawn seemed the same, blossoming with the coming of spring.

"Is that it?" Eion asked, following her gaze. She nodded slowly, and then began to cross the street. Eion followed her, taking the house in. Gwen whistled, and Curthlond came running toward them.

"Oh, that is the house then? Wow! Will you look at that architecture! How do you mortals do it?" He then went on to explore the front yard, bounding over the white fence with unchecked exhilaration.

Gwen led Eion up the front steps, past the cars, and eventually to her front door. It looked exactly as it always had, a worn navy blue with a circular window near its top. A new bench had been placed on the porch, and the lamp had been changed. Everything else was the same. She turned to look at Eion, who was chuckling again.

"Ah, Gwen Talbot, I envy you. You have so much to do now. After all, you still have your youth; live it! Life is not all war. Sometimes the greatest adventure can be found in stepping through your front door, after a long day. Yes Gwen, enjoy your time here, and retell your journey to your family, the journey you feel is over."

Gwen arched an eyebrow, inquisitively. "What do you mean? It is over…isn't it?"

Eion laughed as he began to walk down the drive. She followed him with confused interest. "My dear Gwen, have you learned nothing? Has the past year meant nothing to you? I would think you would understand the rules of magic, and the rules of your own destiny. Ozmodion will rise again, and when he does, I will need you and the other eight to help me bring him down. And remember: you are indeed an Iltari, blessed and cursed with a fate that will always call to you. If you really understood all those things, then you would know that this is not the end of your journey. No, far from it. It is only the beginning!"

He winked, and turned to walk to the end of the drive. She stood there, watching him as he stepped out into the middle of the street. He turned around and faced her one more time, smiling his famous half smile. And then he shifted into the hawk that Gwen had come to know so well. It flapped it wings hard as it ran down the street, taking to the skies with momentum and force. It climbed higher and higher, spiraling ever upwards. Then, when it had flown so high that it was only a black speck silhouetted against the sky, it soared to the south, flapping its wings with lazy effort. She watched until it had merged with the haze.

She stood there for a long time, unmoving, unspeaking. Eventually, her silent meditation was broken by Curthlond, who sauntered up to her with his ecstatic grin.

"Whoo! Am I going to have fun here." He looked about, and his smile quickly became a frown. "Where is Eion?"

"He's gone," she answered, still staring into the blue.

Curthlond scoffed. "Such manners. Not even a goodbye. Shifters. Psh. So, now…are you ready to go home?"

Gwen smiled and looked down at her feet, where the cat sat with his head cocked to one side. She nodded. "Yes, I've stayed away long enough." She bent down and scooped Curthlond up in her arms, then carried him up the drive.

"I'm not going to have to play the pet and be Buttons again, am I?" he asked, his eyes scrunched up with dread.

She giggled and shook her head. "No; I'm going to be fully upfront with them. But, if you're planning on wandering around the neighborhood, you're going to have to pretend to be just a normal cat. Deal?"

He nodded his head and extended a paw. "Deal, so long as I do not have to be called Buttons...*ever* again."

She took his paw with her free hand and nodded. Then she looked up at the front door again. All was still; apparently her family had not heard all the commotion outside.

She stopped before she ascended the steps of her porch. One last time, she thought about her thoughts on the shores of the Silver Ice Sea. She had wondered if she ever wanted to see her home again. Later on, in the Mountain of Antiquity, she had wondered if she even could go back to her home. As she stood several feet from the house she had grown up in, she still wasn't sure of either. In fact, she had not felt so much uncertainty as she did now. In quick secession, the events of the last year ran through her mind, and she looked over her shoulder to look at the haze of smog that Eion had flown into, half-heartedly hoping to see him returning.

But no; the hawk was gone. She sighed, almost sadly, but then smiled as she thought of Eion's parting words. Turning back to face the door, she resolved that she would see the Other World and all her new friends again. The thought brightened her spirits, and made it easier to walk up the steps, open the door, and step back into her old life.

Publisher's Note

Our sincere thanks to all our friends and to you, The Reader, for bringing Shifter to life.

Please look for more of Robby Schlesinger's works and others in our growing family of Long Creek Music & Publishing, LLC.

Visit us at **www.LongCreekPeak.com**.

Printed in the United States
202924BV00003B/1-51/P